KT-435-278

★★

'Mind-bending
Kath, Netgalley

★★★★★

'Wow, what a book! This series just gets better and better'
Tina, Netgalley

★★★★★

'A real page-turner'
Lucille, Netgalley

★★★★★

'Captivating: full of mystery, tension,
moral dilemma . . . outstanding'
Peter, Netgalley

★★★★★

'Keeps you guessing until the very end'
Tessa, Netgalley

★★★★★

'This book and this series is fantastic
and I can't wait for more'
Sarah, Netgalley

★★★★★

'Great characters and a fantastic storyline that will
have you unable to put it down'
Tracy, Netgalley

★★★★★

'Definitely for fans of Lisa Gardner,
Karin Slaughter and the like'
Fiona, Netgalley

★★★★★

ABOUT THE AUTHOR

Cara Hunter is the author of the *Sunday Times* bestselling crime novels *Close to Home*, *In the Dark*, *No Way Out* and *All the Rage*, all featuring DI Adam Fawley and his Oxford-based police team. *Close to Home* was a Richard and Judy Book Club pick and was shortlisted for Crime Book of the Year in the British Book Awards 2019. *No Way Out* was selected by the *Sunday Times* as one of the 100 best crime novels since 1945. Cara's novels have sold more than a million copies worldwide, and the TV rights to the series have now been acquired by the Fremantle group. She lives in Oxford, on a street not unlike those featured in her books.

The Whole Truth

CARA HUNTER

PENGUIN BOOKS

PENGUIN BOOKS

UK | USA | Canada | Ireland | Australia
India | New Zealand | South Africa

Penguin Books is part of the Penguin Random House group of companies
whose addresses can be found at global.penguinrandomhouse.com.

First published 2021
001

Text Design by Couper Street Type Co.

Set in 12.5/14.75 pt Garamond MT Std
Typeset by Jouve (UK), Milton Keynes
Printed and bound in Great Britain by Clays Ltd, Elcograf S.p.A.

The authorized representative in the EEA is Penguin Random House Ireland,
Morrison Chambers, 32 Nassau Street, Dublin D02 YH68

A CIP catalogue record for this book is available from the British Library

ISBN: 978–0–241–98513–7

www.greenpenguin.co.uk

To Judith
A very special lady

Previously . . . in the Fawley files

This is the fifth book in the Fawley series, so if this is the first one you've picked up you might like a quick summary of the key members of the team, so you can hit the ground running. Starting, of course, with the man himself . . .

Name	**DI Adam Fawley**
Age	46
Married?	Yes, to Alex, 44. She's a lawyer working in Oxford.
Children?	The Fawleys' ten-year-old son Jake took his own life two years ago. They were devastated and thought they'd never be able to have another child. But now Alex is pregnant again . . .
Personality	Introspective, observant and intelligent, outwardly resilient, inwardly less so. He doesn't care that Alex earns more than he does, or that she's taller than him in high heels. He's good at lateral thinking and bad at office politics. He's compassionate and fair-minded, but it's not all positives: he can be impatient and he has a short temper. He was brought up in a dreary North London suburb, and he's adopted, though he only discovered that by accident – to this day his parents have never discussed it. He doesn't watch crime on TV (he has enough of it during the day); he listens to Oasis and Bach and Roxy Music (Alex once told him he looks like Bryan Ferry, to which he replied 'I wish'); if he had a pet it would be a cat (but he's never owned one); his favourite wine is Merlot and his favourite food is Spanish (though he eats far too much pizza); and surprise, surprise, his favourite colour is blue.

Name	**DS Chris Gislingham**
	(recently promoted from DC)
Age	42
Married?	Yes, to Janet
Children?	Billy, nearly 2
Personality	Chirpy, good-humoured, hard-working, decent. And a serious Chelsea fan.
	'Always described as "sturdy" and "solid", and not just because he's getting a bit chunky round the middle. Every CID team needs a Gislingham, and if you were drowning, he's the one you'd want on the other end of the rope.'

Name	**DC Gareth Quinn**
	(recently demoted from DS, after getting involved with a suspect)
Age	36
Married?	No chance
Personality	Cocky, ambitious, good-looking. Fawley describes him as 'sharp suit and blunt razor'.
	'Quinn took to DS like a dog to water – zero hesitation, maximum splash.'

Name	**DC Verity Everett**
Age	33
Married?	No. But has a cat (Hector)
Personality	Easy-going personally, ruthless professionally. Lacks the confidence she should have in her own abilities (as Fawley is well aware).
	'She may look like Miss Marple must have done at thirty-five, but she's every bit as relentless. Or as Gis always puts it, Ev was definitely a bloodhound in a previous life.'

Name	**DC Erica Somer**
Age	29
Married?	No. But she's just started seeing a DI in Hampshire Police, Giles Saumarez.
Personality	English graduate and worked as a teacher before joining the police (in the first book she's still a PC). Her surname is an anagram of 'Morse' – my nod to Oxford's greatest detective!
	'I watch men underestimating her because she's attractive and in a uniform, and I watch her registering that fact and using it to her advantage.'

Name	**DC Andrew Baxter**
Age	38
Married?	Yes, but no children
Personality	Stolid but dependable. Good with computers so often gets lumbered with that sort of stuff.
	'A solid man in a suit that's a bit too small for him. The buttons on his shirt gape slightly. Balding, a little out of breath. Halfway to high blood pressure. He looks forty but he's probably at least five years younger.'

Name	**DC Anthony Asante**
Age	32
Married?	No
Personality	A fast-track graduate entrant to the police, he's new to the team, having recently transferred from the Met. His parents are very wealthy, and his father is a former Ghanaian diplomat.
	Fawley describes him as *'Diligent, intelligent, technically excellent. He does what he's asked and he takes the initiative when he should. And yet there's something about him I just can't get a handle on. Every time I think I have him worked out, he manages to wrong-foot me.'*

The other members of the team are **Alan Challow, Nina Mukerjee** and **Clive Conway**, in the CSI team, **Colin Boddie,** the pathologist, and **Bryan Gow,** the profiler.

Prologue

So you know what to do?

Yeah I'm on it

You're absolutely sure you want to do this?

FFS you got a better idea?

Just saying. Coz if this goes wrong...

It won't. Not if you do what I said

OK OK I get it

I wouldn't ask if I didn't have to

People like F – they think they can get away with anything. They don't give a shit about other people

Time someone turned the tables

I thought you agreed?

I do but this is way more than a
dose of their own medicine

WAY more

It's the only way to stop it happening again

You get that, right?

Yeah I get it

You'll get your revenge

I told you before. It's not revenge

It's justice

'More fizz, anyone? Dad – how about you? You're not even driving, so no excuses.'

Stephen Sheldon smiles up at his daughter, hovering behind him with the bottle in her hand. 'Oh, go on then. Only good thing about being as old as the hills is not caring about bloody government drinking guidelines.'

His wife shoots him a dry but benevolent look; they both know he has to be careful about his health but it's his birthday and she's going to cut him some slack.

Nell Heneghan leans across and fills his glass. 'Seventy isn't old, Dad. Not these days.'

'Tell that to my joints,' he says with a quick laugh, as Nell moves on round the table topping people up.

I reach for Alex's hand under the table and I can feel the thin fabric of her dress slipping against her damp thigh. God only knows what it must be like to be thirty-five weeks pregnant in these temperatures. There are dots of perspiration along her upper lip and a thin little frown line between her brows the others probably can't see. I was right: this has been too much for her. I did say we didn't have to do it – that no one would expect her to, especially in this weather, and Nell had offered to step in – but Alex insisted. She said it was our turn, that it wasn't fair on her sister to ask her to do it two years running. But that wasn't the real reason. She knows it; I know it. As her pregnancy advances, Alex's world contracts; she's barely leaving the house now, and as for a twelve-mile drive to Abingdon, forget it. I told Nell it's because

3

she's anxious about the baby, and she'd nodded and said she'd felt like that herself at this stage, and it was only natural for Alex to be apprehensive. And she's right. Or at least she would be, if that's all it was.

Outside in the garden, Nell's kids are playing football with their dog, taking it in turns doing penalty kicks. They're eleven and nine, the kids. Jake would be twelve now. No longer a little boy, but not quite yet anything else. Sometimes, before Alex got pregnant again, I'd catch myself fantasizing about how they'd have been together, him and his cousins. Jake was never much interested in sport, but would he be out there anyway, if he was here now? Part of me hopes he'd have done it to be kind, or to please his mother, or because he liked dogs, but there's another part that would want him as surly and uncooperative as any other twelve-year-old. I've learnt the hard way that it's only too easy to start beatifying a child who's no longer there.

Audrey Sheldon catches my eye now and we exchange a look; kind on her part, slightly self-conscious on mine. Alex's parents understand better than anyone what we went through when we lost Jake, but Audrey's sympathy is like her lemon cheesecake – nice, but there's only so much of it I can take. I get to my feet and start collecting plates. Nell's husband, Gerry, makes a half-hearted attempt to help me but I clap him chummily on the shoulder and push him firmly back down in his seat.

'You brought all the food. My turn now.'

Alex gives me a grateful smile as I collect her dessert plate. Her father's been badgering her gently to 'eat up' for the last ten minutes. Some things about parenthood never die. My mother does the same to me. In twenty years' time I'll be doing it myself. God willing.

Out in the kitchen, Nell is stacking the dishwasher, and though she's doing it all wrong I resist the impulse to intervene as I know it'll just piss her off; Alex says dishwashers are like barbecues — men just can't stop themselves muscling in. Nell smiles when she sees me. I like her, I always have. As bright as her sister, and just as forthright. They have a good life, she and Gerry. House (detached), skiing (Val d'Isère), dog (cockerpoo allegedly, but judging by the size of those paws there's at least a quarter polar bear in there). He's an actuary (Gerry, not the dog) and if I'm honest I find Dino a good deal more interesting, but the only person I've ever said that to is myself.

Nell is looking at me now, and I know exactly what that particular look means. She wants to Have A Word. And being Nell, she pitches straight in. Just like her sister.

'I'm a bit worried about her, Adam. She doesn't look well.'

I take a deep breath. 'I know what you mean, and this bloody heat isn't helping, but she's getting regular check-ups. Far more than most women in her position do.'

But most women in her position haven't been hospitalized for high blood pressure and ordered to take complete bed rest.

Nell leans back against the worktop and reaches for a tea towel, wiping her hands. 'She hardly ate a thing.'

'I'm trying, really —'

'And she looks *completely* exhausted.'

She's frowning at me. Because whatever this is, it has to be my fault, right? Out in the garden Ben scores a goal and starts running around the grass with his T-shirt over his head. Nell glances over at them, then fixes her eyes back on me.

I try again. 'She's not sleeping well – you know what it's like in the last trimester. She can't seem to get comfortable.'

But Nell's still frowning. Nicky is now yelling that the goal was a cheat; Gerry gets up and goes to the window, calling to his sons to play nicely in that sententious parental tone we all swear we'll never use. Something else about having kids that never seems to change.

'Look,' I say, 'it's tough with the job but I'm doing as much around the house as I can, and we've got a cleaner coming in once a week for the rest.'

Nell is watching her boys. 'We were talking earlier,' she says, without looking round. 'She says you've moved into the spare room.'

I nod. 'Just so I don't wake her up. Especially given I'm now getting up at stupid o'clock four days a week for the bloody gym.'

She turns towards me. 'Quitting still a bummer?'

The look that comes with the words is cool but not unkind: Nell's an ex-smoker too. She knows all about nicotine displacement strategies.

I try a wry smile. 'A bastard. But I'm getting there.'

She eyes me up and down. 'And toning up a bit too, I see. Suits you.'

I laugh. 'Well, that's a bloody miracle, considering I'm on a packet of Polo mints an hour.'

There's a pause and then, finally, she smiles. But it's a forlorn one. 'Just look after her, Adam, OK? She's so stressed out – this baby means so much to her. I don't know what she'd do if –' She stops, bites her lip and looks away.

'Look, Nell – I'd never let anything happen to Alex. Not now, not ever. You do know that, don't you?'

She glances up, then nods, and I wait. I know what she wants to say, and why she's having so much trouble doing it.

'It was in the paper,' she says eventually. 'He's out, isn't he? Gavin Parrie.'

'Yes, he's out.' I force her to look at me. 'But he's on licence – there'll be strict conditions. Where he can go, who he can see.'

Her lip quivers a little. 'And he'll have one of those tag things, right? They'll know where he is twenty-four hours a day?'

I shake my head. 'Most of them aren't that techy. Not yet. The tags are linked to the offender's address. If he goes out of a specified range the monitoring service gets an alert.'

'And like Gerry said, if he came anywhere even *remotely* near here, they'd have his arse back in prison so fast he'd leave skid marks. Right?'

I take a deep breath. 'Right.'

'So why would he take such a massive risk?' She's willing me to agree now, willing me to belittle her fears. 'He's not stupid – he has way too much to lose.'

'Right.'

She sighs. 'I'm sorry. You probably think I'm completely overreacting. I just can't stop thinking about those threats he made in court –'

She can't possibly know how hard it is to be the man

she needs me to be. But I try. 'He was just venting, Nell. It happens all the time. And I don't think you're over-reacting. Families always worry when offenders are released. The other victims will be going through exactly the same thing.'

'But at least Alex has you,' she says, giving me a wobbly smile. 'Her own private protection officer.'

I don't trust myself to reply to that, but luckily I don't have to. She touches me gently on the arm and reaches for the pile of plates. 'We'd best get on. They'll be wondering what we're up to in here.'

As I walk back into the dining room I wonder what she'd have said if she knew the truth.

Gavin Parrie isn't stupid, she's right about that. And he'd have a hell of a lot to lose, she's right about that too. But he does have a reason. A reason that might – perhaps – be worth the risk.

Revenge.

Because he wasn't just venting, that day, in court.

He was guilty. He knows that and I know that. But there's something else we both know.

Gavin Parrie was convicted on a lie.

* * *

Daily Mail

21st December 1999

'ROADSIDE RAPIST' GETS LIFE

Judge calls Gavin Parrie 'evil, unrepentant and depraved'

By John Smithson

The predator dubbed the 'Roadside Rapist' was given a life
sentence yesterday, after a nine-week trial at the Old Bailey. Judge
Peter Healey condemned Gavin Parrie as 'evil, unrepentant and
depraved' and recommended he serve a minimum of 15 years.
There was uproar in the court after the sentence was announced,
with abuse directed at both judge and jury from members of
Parrie's family in the public gallery.

Parrie has always insisted that he is innocent of the rape and
attempted rape of seven young women in the Oxford area between
January and December 1998. The case hinged on forensic
evidence found in Parrie's lock-up, linking him to one of the victims,
which he contended was planted there with the collusion of
Thames Valley Police. As he was led away, he was heard issuing
death threats against the officer who had been instrumental in his
apprehension, saying he would 'get him' and he and his family
would 'spend the rest of their lives watching their backs'. The
officer in question, Detective Sergeant Adam Fawley, has received
a commendation from the Chief Constable for his work on the
case.

Speaking after the verdict, Chief Superintendent Michael Oswald
of Thames Valley Police said he was confident that the right man had
been convicted and confirmed that no other credible suspect had
ever been identified in the course of what became a county-wide

investigation. 'I am proud of the work done by my team. They went to enormous lengths to find the perpetrator of these appalling crimes and bring him to justice, and it is absolutely unacceptable that they should be subject to either threats or intimidation. Police officers put their lives on the line on a regular basis to protect the public, and you may rest assured that we take all necessary steps to ensure the continued safety of our officers and their families.'

Jennifer Goddard, mother of one of the victims who committed suicide after her ordeal, spoke to reporters outside the court after the verdict, saying that nothing was ever going to bring her daughter back, but she hoped she could now rest in peace: 'The man who destroyed her life is finally going to get what he deserves and pay the price for what he's done.'

* * *

At St Aldate's, Sergeant Paul Woods is spending the afternoon on reception, and is very far from happy about it. He works the giddy heights of the custody suite these days but the civilian desk officer is on holiday and the PC covering her has food poisoning, and Woods drew the short straw. And along with it, a short fuse. It's far too bloody hot for a start. BBC Oxford said it might hit 30 degrees today. *30 degrees.* It's bloody indecent, that's what that is. He's propped open the main street door but all it's allowing in is fumes. And more people. A good half of them are just looking for some respite from the sun – there's never been so much interest in the leaflet stand, that's for sure. It can go weeks without needing to be refilled, but suddenly they're all out of *How To Protect Your Home From Thieves* and *Things To Look Out For When You Shop Online.*

There's a group milling around it right now – tourists clearly, and mostly Chinese.

Woods glances up at the clock. Another twenty minutes before he can take a break. The tourists around the leaflet stand are talking eagerly among themselves now. One is gesturing towards Woods; she appears to be trying to get up the courage to come and talk to him. He draws himself up to his full authority, and at six foot two and sixteen stone that's a lot of gravitas in every sense. It's not that he's trying to discourage her *as such*, it's just that he knows from dreary experience that these sorts of questions can almost always be answered by any half-decent map. He really has had his fill of unofficial trip-advising over the years.

He's saved, as it turns out, by the bell. Just as the Chinese woman starts to approach the desk, the phone goes. It's the woman on the switchboard – another civilian, Marjorie something. She must have got the short straw too.

'Sergeant Woods – can you take this one, please? I've tried CID but there's no one in. It's Edith Launceleve.'

He picks up his pen, momentarily irritated that he never has known the correct way to write that bloody place. Whose bright idea was it to call a college after someone nobody can spell?

'OK,' he says heavily. 'Put them through.'

He raises his hand grandly to the Chinese tourist as if he has the Chief Constable on the line.

'Is that Sergeant Woods? Jancis Appleby here, Edith Launceleve College.'

It's the sort of voice that makes you sit up straight.

'How can I help you, Miss Appleby?'

'I have Professor Hilary Reynolds on the line.'

She says it as if even a minion like Woods will have heard that name. And actually, he has, but right this minute he can't for the life of him remember when —

'The Principal,' she says briskly. 'In case you may have forgotten. Hold on, please.'

Now that does bring him up short. The bloody *Principal*? What could possibly be so important that the Principal gets on the blower? What is she even doing in the office at the weekend?

The line clicks into life again.

'Sergeant Woods?'

Not the female voice he was expecting and he loses the first few words remembering Hilary can be a bloke's name too.

'I'm sorry, sir, could you say that again?'

'I said I'm afraid I need to report an incident involving a student at the college.'

Woods' eyes narrow; 'incident' can cover a multitude of sins, from the mortal to the extremely mundane.

'What sort of incident would that be, sir?'

An intake of cultured, well-educated but slightly irritated breath. 'A serious incident, Sergeant. I'm afraid that's all I'm prepared to say at this stage. Could you put me through to Detective Inspector Fawley?'

* * *

It's hot in Boars Hill too, but somehow it seems a lot more bearable up here. No doubt some of that comes with the altitude, but the thirty-foot swimming pool and well-stocked poolside bar are definitely helping. Those come with the altitude too, though that's an elevation of a rather different kind. Given the address, you don't need to be a fully paid-up member of CID to make some shrewd deductions about the sort of house this was likely to be, but Gareth Quinn was, all the same, quietly impressed when he saw what lay behind the wrought-iron gates that swung silently open for his Audi A4, newly valeted for the occasion. A good acre of lawns (also valeted for the occasion, though he wasn't to know that), a parterre and orange trees, and a scatter of what estate agents probably call 'useful outbuildings', shunted discreetly out of sight of the chiselled neo-Palladian pile and its uninterrupted prospect of 'That View'. The bristle of construction cranes is unfortunate but in all other respects the spires lie dreaming down there this afternoon in the shimmering heat, just as Matthew Arnold once saw them.

Quinn had no idea how loaded Maisie's parents were when he met her. At first glance, she was just another of those pony-tailed French-nailed girls with their soft smiles and their crisp vowels. Avocados, he calls them: ripe, ready and green. Though not quite so green, in this case, that she was prepared to go to bed with him on the first date, and in the almost unprecedented ten days it took for that to happen he realized she had rather more to her than most of her identikit predecessors. She made him laugh and she listened, but she didn't give him an easy ride, and he found himself having to articulate *why* he believed what he did, some of which surprised even him. He also realized – and this was fairly unprecedented too – that he actually liked her, as much out of bed as in it.

Which is why, even though he's always had an almost ana-phylactic reaction to the idea of meeting his girlfriends' parents, he's not only here but *still* here, long after he'd agreed with Maisie that they would leave. The beef was rare, the wine likewise, and Ted and Irene Ingram are decidedly not what it said on the tin. Yes, they have a lot of money, but they're not shy of showing it, which was never going to be a problem with Quinn. The two men edged around the Brexit bear trap for a good half-hour before Ingram let slip which side he was on, whereupon they fell on each other with all the relief of oppressed fel-low devotees. In Oxford, at least, theirs is most definitely the Leave that dare not speak its name.

So all in all, Quinn has been enjoying himself royally. By the time the phone call comes through there's even an imp in the back of his brain whispering that Maisie is the Ingrams' only child, and if in-laws are inevitable then these two might not be such a bad option. There's a bottle of 1996 Sauternes on the table now, and a box of Havana cigars, and Quinn has slid Maisie his car keys. Which, as the look on her face makes clear, is also pretty much unprecedented. She glances at him now, as his mobile goes: it's the ringtone he uses for calls from work.

As he reaches for the phone, Quinn glances round the table, smiling his contrition. 'I'm really sorry – they wouldn't be calling if it wasn't important.'

Ingram waves the apology away. 'Of course. Maisie explained this might happen. I completely understand. It's an important job, what you do.'

Irene Ingram pushes back her chair tactfully and Mai-sie gets to her feet. They start clearing the plates, and

Quinn walks away down the garden. Perhaps he's doing it to get a better signal, but then again, perhaps he'd rather Maisie's father didn't hear him answering with his current rank.

A few yards further on he finally takes the call.

'DC Quinn.'

'Woods here.' Quinn can hear the traffic in the background; Woods must be at the front desk. He makes a perfunctory apology for ruining Quinn's Saturday but it's clear from his tone that he's not getting a bloody weekend so why the hell should CID.

'Just had the Principal from Edith Launceleve on the blower asking for Fawley.'

Quinn frowns. 'What's wrong with the duty inspector?'

'Tried that. Nothing doing. Sorry.'

'OK, so –'

Woods interrupts him. 'I'd have called Gislingham, *as DS*, but given he's out till Wednesday –'

Quinn ignores the snipe. He's got used to all the not-so-subtle digs about his demotion. He could have got a transfer, but when he decided not to, he knew the price would be sucking it up. And some of the bolder wags have, of course, taken great delight in using exactly that phrase. But he only has himself to blame: he let his dick rule his head and got involved with a suspect. He was lucky he didn't get fired. But he'll show them – he'll get his stripes back. It's just a matter of time. In fact – who knows? – perhaps this call is a golden opportunity. With Gis away, a slam-dunk chance to show his class.

'No worries,' he says airily. 'What is it – what have you got?'

By the time Woods has finished, the opportunity is looking rather less than twenty-four carat, but there's no need for Ted Ingram to know that. As far as he's concerned, this is a mega-important hush-hush murder case requiring the attention of a fast-track officer destined for greater things. The sort of man, whispers the imp, Ingram would positively welcome as a son-in-law. Quinn squares his shoulders, lifts his chin and starts back up the grass towards the pool.

* * *

Adam Fawley
7 July 2018
14.35

A call from Quinn is just about the last thing I was expecting. He's at his girlfriend's parents' today – he made a big thing about how nonchalant he was about it, which rather indicated the opposite to me, but that's Quinn all over. He's been deputizing for Gis while he's away, but we don't have a big case on at the moment – certainly nothing that would merit a call at the weekend. I'd have thought Quinn would relish the chance of flying solo again, even though I did make it abundantly clear it's just unofficial 'standing in' not official 'Acting'.

We're all still in the dining room when he calls. The afternoon is reaching the fuggy stage, though Alex's dad is still chirpy – as garrulous as I've seen him in years. I've always liked Stephen. It's the anomaly of in-laws: the same age as your parents, and you can end up knowing them almost as long, but if you're lucky – as I've been – they have your back but they don't press your buttons. Though that could just be because they don't know where the dangerous buttons are.

Alex flickers an anxious look at me as the phone goes, but says nothing. She has one hand curled round her belly and she's fiddling with her napkin with the other. She's getting tired. I need to start manoeuvring people to leave.

Out on the patio, I take the call.

'Quinn? What is it?'

'Sorry to bother you, boss. I'm meeting Ev at Edith Launceleve. There's been an incident involving a student.'

I frown – I know Quinn's being uber-careful not to balls anything up at the moment, but does he really need to call me about this? But then I remember that most of the students have already gone down for the summer so it's unlikely to be just the usual vomit-and-shouting undergraduate excess.

'What are we looking at?'

'Not sure yet.'

'So why –'

'Apparently the Principal asked for you specifically. His name's Hilary Reynolds. Ring any bells?'

A small one, a long way away – a conference a couple of years ago?

'I googled him,' says Quinn, 'and apparently he's some hot-shot human rights lawyer.'

I was right – it *was* that conference –

'He's just been appointed to that parliamentary advisory panel on whole-life tariffs. You know, the one Bob O'Dwyer is on.'

That's all we need: Robert O'Dwyer is the Chief

Constable. But creds to Quinn for checking, rather than just ploughing straight in like the Lone Ranger.

'OK, I'll need to take my in-laws home first, but I can be there in about an hour.'

*　*　*

Edith Launceleve College – EL to its students – sits on fourteen gardened acres straddling the Banbury and Woodstock Roads. Not very far from town, according to any normal notion of geography, but still the equivalent of Outer Mongolia in the excitable microcosm that is the University of Oxford. It's been mixed for more than thirty years, but it was founded as an institution for the education of young women, by a vigorous Victorian spinster who simply wouldn't take no for an answer, and named after the twelfth-century patroness of the nearby Godstow nunnery, who was by all accounts equally energetic and equally bloody-minded. EL's accumulated an impressive roll call of alumnae in its hundred-plus years, including several generations of women who had – and needed – exactly the same tenacity. Quinn's not to know, but DC Asante's mother was one of them. She now runs a FTSE-100 company, but the number of other women doing the same can be counted on the fingers of one hand. EL's splendid isolation from town and all its temptations was no doubt seen as an advantage by its uncompromising foundress, but it's definitely a downside these days – when the University has open days they have to resort to chalk marks on the pavement to tempt sixth-formers that far north. On the other hand, it does have one Unique Selling Point: there's almost always some-where to park. Maisie finds a space right opposite the lodge and turns off the engine. Quinn sits for a moment, staring across at the gates.

'One of the girls in my year at Burghley Abbey went here,' says Maisie.

Quinn turns. 'Yeah?'

She nods. 'She said it was OK but it didn't really feel like Oxford. I mean, there are blokes there now and everything, but she said it still came off like a girls' boarding school.'

Quinn turns back to look again. There's a group of young people standing chatting by the main door. They're clutching files and the obligatory water bottles, but there are ID cards on lanyards round their necks, so it's a fair bet they're summer school, not permanent. They seem happy enough, either way. Smiling, looking to the future with confidence, perfectly balanced across race and gender. It could be the cover shot for the college brochure.

'Do you want me to wait till your colleague arrives?' asks Maisie.

He turns to her again. 'Nah, no need. Ev only lives ten minutes away – in fact, I'm surprised she's not here already.' He pushes open the door. 'I'll see you back at the flat – if it's going to be a long one I'll give you a bell.'

'OK, see you later.'

She starts the engine and pulls away, turning right at the junction in a screech of rubber. Quinn smiles, despite his precious tyres. That girl has balls; she drives almost as fast as he does.

He crosses the road as Everett's Mini pulls into the space Maisie just left. He assumed she'd walk down from her flat in Summertown, but perhaps she wasn't at home when she got the call. He hardly ever sees her off-duty so the clothes come as a surprise. Whatever she's been doing, it seems it required a skirt.

'Very natty,' she says as she comes towards him, nodding to his chinos and pink shirt. 'I hope they were suitably impressed.'

He could take umbrage but he decides to smile instead. 'Slayed 'em,' he says. 'Eating out of my hand.'

She hitches her bag higher up her shoulder. 'So what's all this about?'

'Some sort of "incident". But not a 999 job so I'm assuming no one's dead. Woods says it was the Principal who called it in. Refused to say anything more, just kept on saying he wanted to speak to Fawley.'

'Serious, then.'

He nods. 'The boss is on his way. But, right now, your guess is as good as mine.'

Ev has a guess all right, but decides, for now, to keep that to herself.

Quinn goes to check in with the lodge, and Ev waits outside; he doesn't need her holding his hand, especially if he's bigging himself up as surrogate DS. The group by the door has dispersed now, and the courtyard is empty. Bits of glitter and confetti are caught in the paving, the last fragments of Finals. She can feel the heat coming off the stone through her thin sandals.

'OK,' says Quinn, coming back towards her again. 'They said Reynolds' office is on the first floor. Turn right down the corridor and up the stairs. The PA will meet us there.'

*

It's surprisingly cool inside, but something about the parquet flooring and the echo of their feet has Ev thinking of disinfectant and imminent hockey sticks. The upstairs corridor is a good deal plusher, and the PA is hovering, looking slightly irritated. She gives the impression she knows to the second how long it should have taken them to cover the distance and they have woefully underperformed.

'Professor Reynolds is just on a call – please take a seat, it won't be long.'

The PA returns to her desk, but the visitor chairs have a distinct waiting-for-detention look about them which is hardly appealing. As for Quinn, he doesn't seem able to keep still. He spends the next five minutes scrutinizing the framed photos of the teaching body, until the PA's intercom beeps and she gets to her feet.

'This way, please.'

The office is certainly impressive, if only in terms of size. Wood panelling, windows over the garden, more framed photographs, this time of the previous heads of the college. They're all women. Unlike the person walking towards them, hand outstretched.

'Hilary Reynolds – you must be Detective Sergeant Quinn?'

Ev sees Quinn open his mouth but Reynolds has already moved on.

'DC Everett? Please – take a seat.'

'So,' says Quinn, after a moment. 'You asked to see us?'

Reynolds frowns. 'You don't think we should wait until DI Fawley arrives?'

Quinn shifts a little. 'He said we should start without him. You know what it's like, weekend traffic, tourists –'

Reynolds sits back, fingertips together. 'This whole situation is *extremely* delicate.'

Quinn nods. 'We do understand, sir, but until we know what it's about –'

Ev glances at him and then at Reynolds. 'If it helps, I have done sexual offences training.'

Reynolds turns to face her. He doesn't say anything but she can see from his face that she's bang on.

He clears his throat. 'Yes, DC Everett, well guessed. This is indeed an issue of that sort.'

Everett takes out her notebook; Quinn may be playing at being one of the grown-ups but someone still has to do the heavy lifting.

'Perhaps I can take some details? I'm assuming no one is in need of immediate medical assistance?'

Reynolds gives a quick, sharp shake of the head. 'No, nothing like that.'

Quinn sits forward a little; he evidently feels the need to reassert the initiative. 'An official complaint has been made to you, as head of the college?'

Reynolds nods. 'The appropriate internal processes will in due course be put in motion as required by University protocols, but I felt the circumstances warranted an immediate referral to the civil authorities.'

Sounds like he cut-and-pasted that from the latest Equality and Diversity policy handbook, thinks Everett, as she makes a note. Leaving no arse uncovered, that's for sure.

'I see,' says Quinn. 'Perhaps you could talk us through the "issue" as you understand it. You told my colleague at St Aldate's that one of your students was involved?'

Reynolds starts fiddling with something on his desk. 'A postgraduate. One of our brightest. Transferred here from Cardiff at the beginning of Michaelmas term.' He glances at Ev and waves a finger at her notes. 'October, in other words.'

Gee, thanks, she thinks. As if a low-life like me could possibly know that.

'And the other person involved?' she says evenly.

Reynolds' expression has darkened. 'I'm afraid the other party is one of the college academic staff.'

It doesn't come as any surprise – certainly not to Ev, and not only because she's done sexual offences training.

'OK,' says Quinn, who's going to lose his patience very quickly if there's much more pussy-footing about. 'Perhaps it would be easier if we talked direct to the parties involved?'

* * *

'Do you want another glass of wine?'

Erica Somer looks up, shielding her eyes against the sun. She's sitting on the terrace of Giles Saumarez's house. Three fishermen's cottages knocked together into a long, low, whitewashed space with polished stone floors and windows overlooking Southampton Water. It's cool and airy inside, but out here the sunlight is blinding. At least a breeze has got up now; out on the estuary, among the tankers hauling towards the refinery, there are four or five small yachts leaning into the wind. Somer has never sailed, never wanted to, but she yearns suddenly to be out there, on the water, on her own. No

23

one to think about, no one to answer to, wholly at the mercy of the current and the bright blue air. It's the impulse of a moment only, and hard on its heels comes a pang of remorse. She should be grateful she's here at all – at this amazing house, with Giles, who's put so much effort into this weekend but doesn't undo it all by telling her so every five minutes, like most blokes would. He's bought the wine he knows she likes, put flowers in their bedroom, fresh towels in the shower. It's been a beautiful day, and they've had a beautiful lunch. Literally. Crumbly white cheese, golden focaccia sprinkled with rosemary and salt, ripe figs, prosciutto, cubes of deep-orange quince jelly – the table was crying out for a #foodporn hashtag.

She shakes her head now: the glass Giles poured for her more than half an hour ago is still almost full.

He pushes up his sunglasses so he can look her in the eye. 'Everything OK?'

She nods quickly, reaching for the glass, making an effort.

'Yes, fine, just felt a bit off earlier, that's all.'

He sits down next to her.

'We don't have to go out tonight if you don't want to. It's just that last time you were here, you said –'

'No,' she says, cutting across him. 'I want to go. Will you please just stop *fussing*.'

She looks away, at the water, the gulls, the wheeling boats. Anything to block out the hurt and bewilderment in his eyes.

*   *   *

Hilary Reynolds isn't the first head of house I've come across in this job. Principals, Provosts, Wardens — the handles may differ but they all grow the same masterly veneer; that grand self-assurance that comes of habitual High Table dining, an entire organogram of domestic staff and a great deal of getting your own way. Reynolds is no different; or at least not at first sight. It takes me a moment to realize quite how much anxiety is running in this room. And who's generating it.

He's in the far corner, leaning against the window seat. He must be twenty-two, twenty-three; pale skin, toffee-coloured hair bleaching to blond at the ends. A dark tattoo on one forearm, something spiky and sinister, like a Venetian mask. He's taller than me, and broader too. The physique of an athlete; I'd go for rugby if you forced my hand.

'Inspector Fawley,' says Reynolds with a small cough, 'I'm grateful you were able to join us. This is Caleb Morgan. He's with the Mathematics faculty, working on compressed linear algebra for large-scale machine learning.'

Condescending *and* inconsequential; I have to hand it to Reynolds — as irrelevant information goes, that was pretty stellar.

Quinn must be sensing my irritation because he steps in quickly. 'There's been an allegation of sexual assault, boss.'

I stare at him. What the fuck is he playing at? This is Policework 101 – get your facts together *before* you go any-where near the perp. And I mean, *all* your facts.

I pull Quinn to one side. 'What's he doing here?' I say quietly. 'You didn't think you ought to speak to the *victim* first?'

He flushes. 'I did,' he says. 'He *is* the victim.'

I turn to look at Morgan. His pale-blue eyes are intent on my face and I feel myself flush. And now I look properly, I can see the livid red mark on his neck. But even though it goes against all the training, against everything they drum into us these days, I just can't stop myself thinking – this lad is six foot two, he's built like a full back, surely he could have defended himself –

'So,' says Reynolds, looking at Quinn and then at me, 'now we've got that straightened out, I imagine you'll want to speak to Professor Fisher?'

Ev glances quickly at me. 'Professor Fisher is Mr Morgan's supervisor –'

Reynolds cuts across her. 'I would, of course, prefer that you did *not* conduct that interview on college premises, especially given that the incident did not take place here. Professor Fisher's address is Monmouth House, St Luke Street,' he says, sitting back in his chair. 'And it being a Saturday afternoon, I would imagine it's more than likely you will find her at home.'

Her?

Morgan's assailant was a *woman*?

* * *

In Risinghurst, Alex Fawley is saying goodbye to her sister. It's taken the best part of half an hour to get both the dog and the boys into the car, and the dog was definitely the easiest of the three. Gerry is in the driving seat now, impatient to be away before one of his sons decides he needs the loo for the third time.

Nell reaches her arms around her sister, holding her close.

'You will tell me if you need anything, won't you?'

'I'm fine, really. Adam's being wonderful.'

Nell pulls away. 'When he isn't rushing back to work when he's supposed to be having a day off, you mean.'

'It's not his fault. Comes with the job.'

Nell makes a face. 'You don't need to tell me – I've known him almost as long as you have.'

There's a sudden bang in the street – a couple of skateboarders, taking advantage of the hill and the speed bump to try out some tricks – but Nell sees her sister flinch, then try at once to disguise it.

'It's only a few lads mucking around – you're just being paranoid. That man – Parrie – he won't be allowed anywhere near you. You do know that, don't you?'

Alex forces herself to smile. 'It's just my nerves – they're all over the place.'

The car door opens and Gerry leans out. 'You coming?'

Nell gives her sister's arm a quick squeeze. 'Remember what I said, OK? If you need anything – and I mean *anything* – I'm only a phone call away.'

Alex nods and Nell gets into the car, but even after they've pulled away, Alex lingers there, her arms wrapped tightly around herself. The two skateboarders are still coasting up and down, flipping and twisting as they come off the slope, but Alex isn't looking at them. She's looking beyond them, through them, at the white van parked a few doors down. There's a man in the driver's seat, with a baseball cap pulled down low over his eyes.

It doesn't matter how many times people tell her that Gavin Parrie will be miles away, that he'll be strictly monitored, under electronic curfew, she still sees him on every corner, in every van, in every shadowed and half-glimpsed face.

Because he knows. And one day – maybe not today, maybe not this week or this month or this year – but one day, he's going to find her, and he's going to make her pay for what she did.

It's 30 degrees but she's shivering suddenly, her hot skin iced with sweat.

*　*　*

PODCASTS > DOCUMENTARIES > TRUE CRIME

**Righting the Wrongs, s3:
The Roadside Rapist Redeemed?**
5 JULY 2018

S3 Ep1: Prologue   / 25:20

Righting the Wrongs: The Roadside Rapist Redeemed? Episode 1. Gavin Parrie served more than 18 years for a series of brutal sex crimes he has always claimed he did not commit. In this podcast, Jocelyn Naismith of The Whole Truth revisits the case and tries to find answers to some of the worrying questions that remain unresolved. Was the original investigation botched? Did one of the victims collude with the police in providing the crucial evidence? Could the real perpetrator still be out there?

[IVY PARRIE]

'Hi, Gav, it's your mum. Just wanted to let you know I got your message about the hearing. We're all rooting for you here, love, and Jocelyn and the team are working really hard on your behalf. See you next week.'

[SOUND OF PHONE CALL ENDING]

[JOCELYN]

My name is Jocelyn Naismith and I'm the person referred to in that clip. The voice you heard was Mrs Ivy Parrie. Ivy is 76, she lives in Coventry, and you just heard her leaving her son a voicemail. She couldn't call him direct because he was in prison. In Wandsworth, to be precise. Serving a life sentence for a crime he has always claimed he did not commit.

The clip was recorded in April 2018, shortly before Gavin Parrie appeared before the parole board. Thanks to the work done by my team, and with the support of Gavin's solicitor, the long battle for justice was finally won, and he regained his freedom in May this year.

This podcast series tells Gavin's story. How he was convicted in the first place, what The Whole Truth organization has discovered about the original investigation, and why we think the real perpetrator is still out there.

I'm Jocelyn Naismith, and I'm co-founder of The Whole Truth, a not-for-profit organization that campaigns to overturn miscarriages of justice. This is Righting the Wrongs, series 3: The Roadside Rapist Redeemed?

Chapter one: Prologue

[THEME SONG – AARON NEVILLE COVER VERSION OF 'I SHALL BE RELEASED' [BOB DYLAN]]

Standing next to me in this lonely crowd
Is a man who swears he's not to blame
All day long I hear him shout so loud
Crying out that he was framed
I see my light come shining
From the west unto the east
Any day now, any day now
I shall be released.

[JOCELYN]

Bob Dylan wrote that song in 1968, the same year Gavin Parrie was born. He was the second of three Parrie boys, sandwiched between the oldest, Neil, and the youngest, Robert (who the family called Bobby). His mother worked part-time as a shelf-stacker in a local supermarket, and his father, Vernon, was employed at what was then the British Leyland car plant in Cowley, on the outskirts of Oxford. The family lived in a small terraced house off the Cowley Road, and all three boys attended the local primary school, and then Temple Green Secondary Modern.

Ken Waring was Gavin's form teacher in his first year at Temple Green.

[KEN WARING]

'He was a bit of a tearaway, there's no getting away from that. Always getting into scrapes. But I never thought he was a bad lad. He struggled with his reading, but looking back with the benefit of hindsight I suspect he may have been dyslexic. But of course, back then, you didn't get assessed for things like that, and you didn't get any extra help either. Kids like him often became disruptive just because they were having trouble keeping up. He was good with his hands, though, I remember that – he always got good marks in Woodwork and Metalwork. I guess I assumed he would follow his father into the car industry. That's what the majority of our lads did.'

[JOCELYN]

By 1984 the family had moved to Manchester. Vernon Parrie had been made redundant from Cowley, but managed to secure another job at a truck assembly plant up north. It came at a bad time for Gavin, who as we've heard, was already finding schoolwork difficult. The transition to a new school proved a challenge too far, and Gavin left the education system that summer with no formal qualifications.

He spent the next two years moving from job to job – some office cleaning, some mini-cabbing, the odd stint labouring alongside his brother Bobby, who was an apprentice plasterer by then. Remember that – it's going to be important later.

It was around this time that Gavin first met the woman who would become his wife. Sandra Powell was 16 and photos of her in the family album show a typical fun-loving 80s teenager. Big shoulder pads, a big smile and big hair. *Really* big hair.

[SANDRA]

'I know, I know, but we all had perms like that back then. My mum used to do mine in the back kitchen.'

[SOUND OF PAGE TURNING]

'I can't even remember the last time I looked at these. And I definitely can't believe I wore all this stuff – look at those legwarmers – what were we even thinking?'

[JOCELYN]

That's Sandra. As you can tell from her voice, there's still some of that bright, sassy teenager left in her, though the intervening years have taken a heavy toll. She lives in Scotland now, and has reverted to using her maiden name (we'll hear why in a later episode), but through it all, she's remained in contact with Gavin and has always been a firm believer in his innocence. But we're getting ahead of ourselves. Back to 1986.

[SANDRA]

[SOUND OF PAGE TURNING]

'Ah, I love that one – that's me and Gav at Blackpool a couple of weeks after we first started going out.'

[JOCELYN]

It's a sweet picture, and not just because they're both clutching candyfloss. Gavin has a shy smile and a mullet haircut that makes him look a bit like David Cassidy. Sandra is acting up for the camera, and even though she's two years younger she looks a lot more worldly, a lot more mature. And according to Sandra, that's a pretty accurate reflection of the early days of their relationship.

[SANDRA]

'It took Gav a long time to adjust to moving to Manchester. He'd left all his mates behind in Cowley, and I think he resented that a bit. He didn't get along that well with his dad either, so I think he was quite lonely. I was definitely his first serious girlfriend, that I do know. He really wasn't that confident back then – it took him so long to ask me out I was beginning to think he wasn't interested.'

[JOCELYN]

But once their relationship started, things moved very fast. Within three months Sandra was pregnant, and by the end of that year they were the parents of a baby girl, Dawn.

[DAWN MACLEAN]

'What's my first memory of Dad? Probably him teaching me to ride my bike when I was about 6.'

[JOCELYN]

That's Dawn. She's a qualified beautician now, married and living in Stirling with two children of her own.

[DAWN]

'I got the bike for my birthday, and I remember it absolutely poured down all day – you know what Manchester's like – but he spent hours outside

with me in the rain while I wobbled up and down. He wasn't always that patient though. I remember he hated anything to do with paperwork or filling in forms – Mum always had to deal with Social Services or the council or our schools. I guess he was always a bit wary of people like that. People in authority. He said they were all out to get you. And let's face it, he wasn't wrong, was he?'

[JOCELYN]

Sandra and Gavin had two further children in the next ten years. Sandra had a job as a hairdresser but Gavin was still stuck with casual labouring jobs, so money was tight, and they couldn't get by without benefits. After a while, the strain began to tell.

[DAWN]

'By the time I was about 11 I knew my dad was struggling. I mean, I wouldn't have used that word, but I knew he wasn't happy. He seemed to be angry all the time, and I think he was drinking, and that just made him even more angry. And sad. I remember finding him in tears one day, upstairs in their bedroom. It was the first time I'd ever seen a man cry and it really scared me. It was after that that everything started to go wrong.'

[JOCELYN]

It was 1997. On May 2nd that year, a 16-year-old girl was attacked in Lockhart Avenue, Manchester. She was dragged into the undergrowth, sexually assaulted and left there, on the side of the road.

Three nights later, Sandra got a phone call.

It was Gavin. He was at Greater Manchester Police HQ, and he'd been arrested.

For rape.

[UNDER BED OF 'I FOUGHT THE LAW AND THE LAW WON' – THE CLASH]

I'm Jocelyn Naismith and this is Righting the Wrongs. You can listen to this and other podcasts from The Whole Truth on Spotify, or wherever you get your podcasts.

[FADE OUT]

* * *

'So if you can come with us now, we'll do the Video-Recorded Interview, and take the samples the CPS will need if the case goes to court.'

It's Ev doing the talking. And no question, doing it bloody well. Perhaps it's the specialist training, but she's managing to be completely unfazed by the killer flip in this case. Unlike me. Even Quinn seems to have got his head round it, though perhaps it's just that he's had longer to get used to the idea. And meanwhile Ev has been calmly taking down the details for the Initial Investigative Report, and talking Morgan through what to expect at the Sexual Assault Referral Centre, and what help he can ask for, and what support he can get. And at the end of it all, when she tells him he can have a male officer as his police point of contact if he prefers, it doesn't surprise me at all that he decides to stick with her.

I've not said much in the last half-hour, and nothing at all to Reynolds, and I was rather hoping to keep it that way, but when we all get up to leave, he clears his throat in that way he has.

'Could you remain behind for a moment, Inspector?'

Ev gives me a questioning look, but I just nod. 'You go ahead. I'll call you later for an update.'

Reynolds must have pressed some sort of button on his desk, because the door opens and the PA appears, tray of tea in hand. Either that or she's been listening to the whole bloody thing on the intercom, which, frankly, wouldn't surprise me.

Quinn looks rather enviously at the tea – we haven't even been offered water thus far – but it's evidently not designed for the likes of him. Silver teapot with a college crest, milk jug, sugar bowl and tongs, plate of lemon slices. And only two cups.

When the door closes behind them, Reynolds turns to me.

'There's a reason I wanted to speak to you, Inspector. Caleb Morgan – it's rather more complicated than it might initially appear.'

More complicated? A *female* professor accused of assaulting a *male* student. Gender politics, university politics. Minefields don't get any murkier than that. What the hell else could there be?

He coughs again. 'He takes his father's surname, but Caleb's mother – she's Petra Newson. I imagine you've heard of her?'

Of course I've bloody heard of her. An extremely combative local MP, with an agenda longer than my service record. If Reynolds hasn't already put in that call to Bob O'Dwyer, odds are Petra bloody Newson has beaten him to it.

I keep my tone even. 'I assume Ms Newson is aware of what's happened?'

Reynolds nods slowly. 'I believe Caleb called her, yes. She's in the US this weekend but is due back in her constituency tomorrow.'

So with luck we may have twenty-four hours' grace. Sufficient unto the day and all that.

I take a deep breath. 'Tell me about Professor Fisher.'

If Reynolds thinks that's a conversational swerve he

gives no sign. He leans forward and starts busying himself with the tea.

'Marina is one of the country's leading authorities on Artificial Intelligence. Not my area, of course,' he says, with one of those apparently-self-deprecating-only-not-really looks academics give you, 'but those in the know tell me her work's been genuinely groundbreaking. And, needless to say, that whole field is extremely media-worthy these days.'

Needless to say, but he still went ahead and bloody said it. I remember now there was a Radio 4 programme about machine learning a few weeks ago, which I vaguely recall having on in the background when I was cooking, but I was distracted and didn't follow it all. Thinking about it now, I reckon it was Marina Fisher who was fronting it; the BBC were bound to want a female voice for something like that.

'Between ourselves,' says Reynolds, proffering me the slices of lemon, 'she's just been approached for this year's Royal Institution Christmas lectures.'

Despite everything – despite the crime she's just been accused of – he still can't quite keep the smugness out of his voice. Which tells me everything I need to know about what sort of asset this woman must be to the college. EL isn't up there with the likes of Balliol or Merton – none of the former women's colleges are. They don't have the prestige, and they don't have the pulling power. But a world expert in something as sexy as AI – that's quite a coup. But the greater the triumph, the vaster the potential elephant trap: I don't need to tell you how 'media-worthy' this story will be.

If it gets out.

'There was a fund-raising dinner last night,' he's saying now, 'for the University's most important Chinese donors. Marina was the keynote speaker. The Faculty is aiming to create the world's leading AI research facility pioneering the use of interdisciplinary methodologies.'

He's beginning to sound like a sponsorship proposal, which perhaps he realizes, because he flushes very slightly and does that cough of his again. It's already starting to get on my tits.

'All this is *highly* confidential, needless to say. Negotiations are at a very delicate stage.'

'Were you there?'

Reynolds gives a quick laugh. 'No, Inspector, I was not. But I hear Marina stole the show. The Vice-Chancellor was relying on Marina to lead from the front and it appears she more than delivered. I'm sure I don't need to tell you that there's a lot riding on this.'

He's going to offer to draw me a diagram next. But I've got the message. Loud and clear. Both the college and the University are going to do their damnedest to prevent this woman going down. And taking them with her.

'Mr Morgan said the incident took place at Professor Fisher's house, last night.'

Reynolds raises an eyebrow. 'Yes – that's what he claims.'

I register the nuance of that 'claims', and wonder in passing if Reynolds' facade of scrupulous objectivity is starting to crack.

'So what was Morgan doing there?'

Reynolds frowns now, and I press my advantage.

'You just told me that Professor Fisher was at a University dinner, so she must have got back quite late. So I'm going to ask again – what was Morgan doing in her house at that time of night?'

Reynolds' frown deepens. 'I'm afraid I don't know. Your officers will have to ask Mr Morgan, but I cannot think of any reason why he should have been there.'

'Is Professor Fisher in the habit of inviting students to her home?'

'I doubt it – indeed, it is explicitly prohibited by college policy, as Professor Fisher will be well aware. We make an exception for occasional social gatherings – Christmas drinks, for example. But Fellows are strictly forbidden from holding one-to-one meetings or tutorials in their private residences. Not least, in these litigious times, for their own protection.'

He's looking unsettled now – as if he's only just realized how disquieting Morgan's story is.

'Who else lives in Professor Fisher's house? Does she have a family?'

He shifts in his seat, making the leather creak.

'I will need to be mindful of privacy issues here, Inspector. Data protection and so on. Someone in your position, you know how it is. But it's common knowledge that Marina lives alone, with her son.'

'How old?'

'Eight, I think. Perhaps nine now?'

I sit back, allow the pause to lengthen a little.

'The address you gave DC Quinn – it's a very desirable part of town.'

That's an understatement. Georgian town houses.

Golden stone, sash windows, wrought-iron balconies; even Pevsner was impressed. A lot are offices now, or flats, but judging from her address, Marina Fisher has the whole three storeys. That's some chunk of real estate.

Reynolds reaches to pour tea. And – apparently – buy time.

'Marina's former husband was a financier,' he says eventually, lifting his cup. 'He returned to Boston after the divorce. I believe Marina got the Oxford house as part of the settlement.' He looks at his watch. 'Now, if you will forgive me, I promised my wife I'd be home over an hour ago.'

There's something he's avoiding here, and it's not just the quagmires of the Data Protection Act. But I'll play the game. For now.

The door opens and the guard-dog PA stands there once again, waiting to show me safely off the premises.

'I trust I can rely on you to keep me in the loop, Inspector?' says Reynolds as I get to my feet. 'This is going to be challenging enough, without being blindsided into the bargain.'

'I'll do my best, sir. But I'm sure you can appreciate that there's only so much I'll be able to tell you.' I allow myself a small smile. 'Data protection and all that. Someone in your position, you know how it is.'

* * *

Thames Valley Police

INITIAL INVESTIGATIVE REPORT

Rape and Sexual Offences

LOCATION AND IDENTITY OF THE PERSON MAKING THE REPORT	Professor Hilary Reynolds, Principal, Edith Launceleve College, Oxford OX2
THE EXACT LOCATION (WHERE POSSIBLE) AND TIME OF THE INCIDENT	Monmouth House, St Luke Street, Oxford OX1 06/07/2018 11.30 p.m.
WHETHER THE PERSON MAKING THE REPORT IS THE VICTIM, THIRD PARTY OR WITNESS, AND THE CAPACITY IN WHICH THEY ARE MAKING THE REPORT	Third party (head of the college, to which report was initially made)
NATURE OF THE INCIDENT	**SEXUAL ASSAULT** Suspect made sexual advances to the victim, which he rejected. The suspect persisted, leading to a minor physical altercation, which resulted in minor scratches being sustained by the victim, and intimate touching in the groin area. It is not yet known if the suspect sustained any injuries. After this altercation occurred, the victim was able to leave the premises.
IDENTITY AND LOCATION OF THE VICTIM (IF KNOWN)	**Caleb Owen Morgan**, DOB 09/11/1995 Address: Flat 34, Graduate Accommodation Block, Edith Launceleve College, OX2
IDENTITY AND LOCATION OF THE SUSPECT (IF KNOWN)	**Marina Imogen Fisher**, DOB 17/01/1976 Address: Monmouth House, St Luke Street, Oxford OX1
WHETHER MEDICAL ASSISTANCE IS REQUIRED AND DETAILS OF ANY INJURIES	N/A Superficial scratches

A FIRST DESCRIPTION OF THE SUSPECT	IC1 Female, 42, 5' 6", approx. 150 lbs
IF THE SUSPECT IS KNOWN TO THE VICTIM, WHETHER THERE IS A HISTORY OF VIOLENCE OR SEXUAL OFFENCES	None
WHETHER STEPS HAVE BEEN TAKEN TO PRESERVE EVIDENCE	Victim advised not to wash and still wearing clothing that he was wearing during incident. Scene is suspect's address and will be secured upon arrest. Suspect outstanding at this time.
WHETHER THERE ARE ANY PARTICULAR CONSIDERATIONS, FOR EXAMPLE, DISABILITY, LANGUAGE AND WHETHER AN INTERPRETER IS REQUIRED	N/A
DETAILS OF THE DEMEANOUR OF THE VICTIM OR REPORTER	Victim was calm, articulate and coherent, and did not appear to be under the influence of drugs or alcohol.
PREFERRED CONTACT POINT IF NOT AT THE SCENE	N/A
IF THE REPORTER WISHES TO REMAIN ANONYMOUS, THE REASON FOR THIS	N/A

ATTENDING OFFICERS	DI A. Fawley DC G. Quinn DC V. Everett	**DATE AND TIME**	07/07/2018 15:45

*   *   *

Taking Morgan to the Sexual Assault Referral Centre by squad car was only going to crank up the rumour mill, so Ev drives down to St Aldate's and picks up a car from the CID pool. It's only a Corsa, and the air con is struggling, which makes the small space even more oppressive. She's uncomfortably aware of Morgan's sheer size, crammed into the back seat behind them, so close she can feel his breath on the back of her neck.

No one says very much. Ev's learnt over the years that it's best to talk as little as possible in these circumstances, even when the Gen Pub in question is in a chatty mood. But Morgan shows no inclination to talk at all. He just stares out of the window, at the tourists and the families and the ice-cream vans; silent, unseeing, sunk in thought. He looks completely desolate.

*   *   *

4.15pm Saturday

It's happened again. Just now. He was out there. I was upstairs and when I looked out of the window there he was, down the road. Too far away to see his face. He always makes damn sure of that. Just sitting there, behind the wheel. _No one_ does that, no one normal anyway. I went straight back downstairs but by the time I got to the door he was gone.

I told myself I'd imagined it. That I'm just being paranoid and overreacting. That there's some perfectly logical explanation — some bloke innocently checking his phone or looking at a map. But I know what I saw.

Jesus — even I think I'm starting to sound crazy now. Writing this stuff down is the only thing stopping me losing it completely. I can't even talk to A, never mind anyone else. People would look sympathetic and say it's understandable, after what happened, but I'll see that look in their eyes. And next time we met that look would still be there.

*　*　*

Adam Fawley
7 July 2018
16.35

I called Tony Asante on my way over to St Luke Street, and though it's barely a ten-minute drive, he's still there before me. His new flat is only about half a mile away; no one else in the team could afford to live this central, but I guess it helps if your mother has the sort of job that gets her on the cover of *Forbes*.

When I park up, Asante's on the other side of the road, leaning against a wall, apparently scrolling through his phone. He's chosen a position out of direct sight of the house, but even if someone was watching they wouldn't pay him particular attention. In his white T-shirt and Ray-Bans he could be anything – tourist, postgrad. CIA.

He's not as absorbed by the phone as he's feigning though: he's at the car before I open the door.

'Afternoon, sir.'

I wonder if he got changed before he came out – it's so bloody hot I can't move without sweating, but Asante looks like he just stepped out of a cold shower. There are still laundry folds in his T-shirt.

He gestures back towards the house. 'I haven't seen anyone go in or out since I got here, but the windows are open, so I assume someone's in.'

'You're up to speed?'

'DC Everett emailed me the IIR. Though there wasn't much by way of detail.'

'She and Quinn are taking Morgan to the SARC now, so we'll know more later.'

He nods. 'So, shall we?'

We ring and wait, and ring again, and the door is opened, eventually, by a small boy. Marina Fisher's son, evidently. If he's eight going on nine he's small for his age. Red shorts and a Winnie-the-Pooh top, and soft blond hair that, personally, I think needs a cut. He stares up at us.

'Who are you?'

I notice, now, that there's a woman in the corridor behind him. She's slender and rather beautiful but she looks tentative, as if she doesn't really belong. Then she moves slightly and I see she has a duster in one hand.

I smile at the boy and show him my warrant card. 'We're from the police. We wanted to have a quick chat with your mummy.'

He shakes his head, over-vigorously, the way small children do.

'She's not here.'

'I see. Do you know where she went?'

He turns to the woman, who taps out something on a mobile phone and holds it out to me. It's a Google translate page. *Faculdade* is evidently Portuguese for 'college'.

I try my best this-is-just-routine smile. 'I assume she

43

won't be very long in that case. Do you mind if we come in and wait – is that OK?'

The woman hesitates, then nods, and we follow the two of them up the stairs to the first floor. There are black-and-white framed pictures all the way. It's like those documentaries about 10 Downing Street, with a full deck of prime ministers going up the stairs. Only here, the pictures are all of the same person. Marina Fisher doesn't just blow her own trumpet, she toots a whole brass section. There are two portraits of her in doctoral robes (I'm assuming one of those must be honorary, but hey, what do I know), one shot of a *Newsnight* panel, one that looks like her doing a TED Talk and another on stage with the Vice-Chancellor and Theresa May. With each picture I pass the stakes inch up. And not just for her.

The sitting room spans the whole depth of the house. Tall front sashes with long muslin curtains shifting gently in the rising heat. Stripped floors, deep ochre velvet sofas and, on one wall, a huge canvas of swirling koi carp that's halfway to abstract – flickering blues and oranges and eddying yellows. You can almost see the water churning. To the rear, the windows look over a small but immaculate courtyard garden, with flowering shrubs elegantly arranged in terracotta pots. The boy must have a playroom somewhere else because there isn't a toy or a mess in sight. The house whispers calm and grace and order. And screams money. Lots and *lots* of money.

Asante, meanwhile, is still staring at the painting.

'Alan Hydes,' he says, gesturing at the signature. 'I know him. Well, not *know*, exactly – my parents have one of his. They met him in Mallorca – he has a studio in the same village.'

He looks embarrassed suddenly and turns away, as if he's said too much. Perhaps it was that 'same' that did it, with its implied second home. He goes over to the table under the window and starts sifting through the pile of magazines. I clocked those myself – given the surroundings, you might have expected *Homes & Gardens* or *House Beautiful*, but these all have navy-blue covers and grown-up titles like *Journal of AI Research* and *Neural Transfer Learning for Natural Language Processing.*

'It's a fascinating area, don't you think?' he says, leafing one of them. 'Apparently IBM think they'll be able to replicate a fully functioning human brain by 2023.'

I glance at him. 'Trust me, there are some things machines will never be able to do.'

He looks up. 'You say that, but this technology is moving so fast – apparently eighty per cent of office jobs could eventually be automated. *Eighty per cent.* Whole armies of employees who'll work 24/7, don't need to be paid, never make a mistake, never complain to HR. And when you add in speech recognition, visual perception, the capacity for decision-making and planning –'

I raise an eyebrow. 'Yeah, right.'

He nods. 'No, really – I mean, I know it sounds like crazy sci-fi, but the sort of machines they're developing now really do have the capacity to *learn* – the more they do something, the better they get at it. It's getting to the point where the machines are actually improving the original spec. And not just in obvious areas like manufacturing, either – AI's going to revolutionize the way pharmaceutical companies develop new drugs. And then there's financial services, healthcare, education –'

It strikes me suddenly that he's trying to give me an *AI for Dummies* briefing without making it too crashingly obvious. I can't work out if I'm grateful or just irritated.

'Not policework, though,' I say, half under my breath. 'I can't see robots running murder inquiries any time soon.'

'Ah,' he says quickly, taking a step towards me, 'that's where you're wrong –'

I flash him a look and he falters. 'Sorry, sir. I didn't mean – it's just that I read this really interesting article about –'

But I never get to find out. Downstairs, in the hall, someone's just come in.

*　*　*

The Sexual Assault Referral Centre is in a quiet street a little way out of town. If you didn't know what it was, you probably wouldn't guess. It doesn't exactly advertise itself – just the obligatory car parking and a bland front sign with a logo of a tree. It could just as easily be a doctor's surgery, a community centre or a primary school. And inside, pretty much the same applies: there's a waiting room with armchairs, a coffee machine and a playpen. And, behind that, a corridor of closed doors. Where the real work happens.

Ev had phoned ahead so the Nurse Practitioner is in the reception area to meet them, but other than her, the

46

place is deserted. Ev knows her vaguely from her training course, but they're both careful not to overdo it on the meet and greet. This is not about them.

'Mr Morgan?' she says, extending a hand. 'My name is Eileen Channon. If it's OK with you, I'll be doing your forensic examination today. I can arrange a male nurse if you prefer, though with it being a weekend there might be a bit of a wait until we can get someone here. But it's totally up to you, if that's what you prefer.'

Morgan shakes his head quickly. 'I don't want to wait.'

'OK, and would you like to speak to an Independent Sexual Violence Adviser at this stage?'

Another no.

'That's fine. I know it's a lot to take in. You can always change your mind later, just let DC Everett know.'

Channon gives him a brief professional smile; enough for human contact, but not so much as to imply that anyone is here to enjoy themselves.

'I have a few forms for you to sign,' she says, handing him a clipboard. 'Sorry about that, but there's no way round it, I'm afraid. It's just some basic questions about your medical history and a consent form for the examination. I'll be back in a few minutes, so take your time.'

Morgan goes to the furthest corner of the waiting room and sits down. There's a box of tissues on the table next to him, and a stack of leaflets on STDs and counselling services. Ev turns away and takes Quinn by the arm, pulling him towards the coffee machine.

'Stop *staring*,' she hisses. 'It's not helping.'

47

Quinn flushes. 'Sorry. It's just that I haven't done this shit before.'

'Neither has Morgan,' she replies in an undertone. 'And if he can cope, so can you.'

* * *

Adam Fawley
7 July 2018
16.56

Her son must have gone down to meet her, because we can hear Marina Fisher talking to him as she comes up the stairs. Perfectly pitched Upper-Middle Mother: slightly overloud, not entirely listening. She sounds decisive, breezy. Unconcerned.

'I want to show you my drawing, Mummy.'

'Lovely, darling, what a clever little boy you are.'

Footsteps, coming closer now, hard heels on the wooden steps.

'I want to show you *now*!' His tone is half pleading, half tantrum. 'It's *important*!'

'Sweetheart – Mummy has some things she needs to do first. Tobin – stop that – I've told you before, you'll hurt me.'

They can hear him stamping now. 'But it's not fair! I want you to talk to *me*! Not them!'

A pause. 'Who, darling? What are you talking about?'

She rounds the corner into the sitting room and her expression changes.

'Who the hell are you?'

* * *

48

'You can leave your clothes behind the screen and DC Everett will bag up what we need afterwards. There's a gown hanging on the back of the door and we have some T-shirts and yoga pants you can change into afterwards.'

Ev wonders how often this place needs that stuff in XXL, but unlike Quinn, she'd never say it out loud.

Morgan's head is down – it has been ever since they came into the room. As if by avoiding eye contact he can pretend to himself that none of this is really happening.

'You want me to take off everything?' he says, a hot blush flaring across his cheeks. 'Underwear and that?'

'I'm afraid so,' says Channon briskly. 'And just to make sure – you're still OK for DC Everett to remain in the room for the medical examination?'

'Yeah, whatever. I just want this over with.'

* * *

Adam Fawley
7 July 2018
16.58

She has quite a presence, even in this large room. She's not especially tall, but she has poise, no question, and she carries herself with confidence – enough confidence to get away with not just the mini-length sundress but a straw fedora and calf-high gladiator sandals, both of which would be getting some serious eye-rolling from Alex if she were here. The look is in stark contrast with the crisp professional images on the stairs, but evidently Fisher's personal style is a good deal less buttoned-up when she's not on public show. There are auburn streaks in the long blonde bob and her make-up is flawless, even in this heat. So much so that, from where I'm sitting, she looks scarcely twenty-five.

There was an edge to her voice, and I suppose it's understandable. Two strangers – male strangers – alone in the house with her eight-year-old child and a cleaner who doesn't speak English. And we're not in uniform.

I get up and walk towards her, holding out my warrant card. 'Detective Inspector Adam Fawley. This is Detective Constable Asante.'

She puts her hand down to touch her son's head; instinctively protective now. The boy is hiding behind her, clinging to her leg, his thumb in his mouth.

'Perhaps the other lady we saw could look after the little boy while we talk? It might be best.'

She stares at me for a moment and then nods.

She bends down. 'Tobin, could you go and find Beatriz and ask her to give you a glass of milk?'

'Don't want milk. Want Fanta.'

'All right, then. Just this once.'

She straightens up and ushers him gently out on to the landing. 'Good boy. I won't be long.'

We all wait until his footsteps fade down the stairs and then she turns to me again. 'So perhaps you could now explain to me what you're doing here?'

'We have some questions. About last night.'

She looks blank, perplexed, the ghost of the smile still hovering on her dark-red lips. As if this has to be some sort of mistake. As if she'll be regaling her friends about it later over rhubarb and tamarind artisan gin. 'Sounds like a bad teen flick.'

But we're not laughing.

* * *

'And as well as not changing your clothes, you also haven't showered since the incident took place, is that right?'

She didn't really need to ask – the air in the small room is stifling now, and it's not just the heat.

Morgan shakes his head. 'I was going to but Freya – my girlfriend – she said I shouldn't.'

Ev's ears prick up: it's the first time he's mentioned talking to anyone other than Reynolds. In cases like these, any sort of corroboration can end up being significant.

Channon is nodding. 'Your girlfriend was absolutely right. But as soon as we're done here there's a shower cubicle next door. That's bound to make you feel a lot more comfortable. Then you can have a cup of tea and DC Everett can take your evidential account. Which is really just a fancy term for a statement.'

'There's no rush,' says Ev quickly. 'Whenever you're ready.'

The room is silent again as Channon goes calmly about her business, quietly explaining what she's doing as she collects and bags forensic swabs from Morgan's body. Face, neck, hands, chest, groin. You'd know he played a contact sport just from the old scars and Channon dutifully notes those too, but what she's looking for are the unhealed. The scratch on his neck, the other, smaller ones high on his chest.

'It's my team,' he says, seeing Everett looking at the tattoo on his forearm. He rubs it self-consciously. 'The Ospreys.'

Channon asks him to stand, and he turns left, turns right, raises his arms, as requested, as biddable as a small child. He's trying to tough this out and everyone is being impeccably sensitive and considerate and discreet, but it's clear, all the same, that he's finding it all horribly intrusive.

He briefly catches Ev's eye and makes a sad wry face. 'And to think I never used to get why so few women report being raped.'

* * *

Adam Fawley
7 July 2018
17.04

'Marina Fisher, I am arresting you on suspicion of sexual assault. You do not have to say anything. But it may harm your defence if you do not mention when questioned something which you later rely on in court. Anything you do say may be given in evidence.'

She's shaking her head, backing away from me. '*Sexual assault?* What are you *talking* about?' Her voice falters, and she feels behind her for the sofa and sits down heavily. When she speaks again, her breath is ragged. 'Who – who said this –'

'I believe you know a student called Caleb Morgan?'

She frowns. '*Caleb?* Caleb says I *raped* him?'

'Professor Fisher, we really need to have this conversation at St Aldate's. Where it can be recorded.'

'St Aldate's – you mean the police station?' Her eyes widen and for the first time she looks genuinely afraid.

I nod. 'It's better that way. Not just for us – for you too.'

She looks down, fighting for self-control, then nods. 'I'll need to call my lawyer.'

'Of course. You can do that when we get there. Can Beatriz stay with the child or is there someone else you want us to call?'

She's silent so long I'm not sure she's heard.

'Professor Fisher?'

She looks up, half startled. 'What? Oh – yes, I'll ask her.'

Asante takes a step towards her. 'And we'll need the clothes you were wearing last night. I assume you've taken a shower today?'

She stares at him. '*Of course I have –*'

Though perhaps she regrets answering so sharply because she bites her lip now. 'Sorry. I didn't mean to be – it's just this whole thing is –' She takes a deep breath. 'Yes, I have showered.'

'We'll need your clothes too. Everything you were wearing last night. Including your underwear.'

Her eyes widen. 'Well, I'm afraid that's already been washed. And my gown is at the dry cleaner's.'

I glance at Asante, who raises an eyebrow, but she forestalls us.

'Look, I know that probably looks *dodgy* or something, but I spilt some wine on it, OK? That's all. And I was going past the cleaner's on my way to college anyway.' She shrugs. 'It was just convenient, all right? If I don't do it now I'll forget, and by the time I drag it out of the wardrobe for the next shindig it'll be too bloody late.'

It might make sense, it might not; but either way it's going to have to wait. I'm not having this conversation here.

'So,' I say, 'could you speak to Beatriz now? And our CSI team will also need access to the premises to conduct a forensic search. DC Asante will stay here until they arrive.'

She holds my gaze for a moment and then nods. 'OK. I'll tell her.'

She seems on the verge of tears.

*   *   *

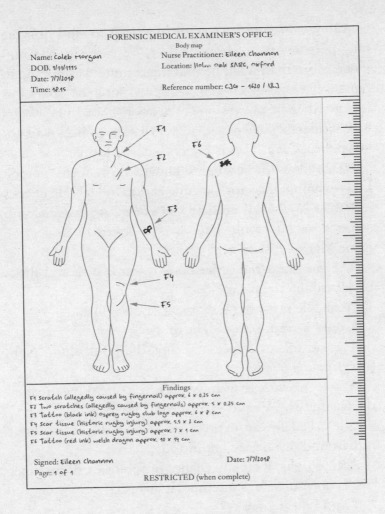

FORENSIC MEDICAL EXAMINER'S OFFICE
Body map

Name: Caleb Morgan
DOB: 1/11/1115
Date: 7/7/2018
Time: 18.15

Nurse Practitioner: Eileen Channon
Location: Holm Oak SARC, Oxford

Reference number: CJG – 1620 / 18.J

Findings

F1 scratch (allegedly caused by fingernail) approx. 6 × 0.25 cm
F2 Two scratches (allegedly caused by fingernails) approx. 5 × 0.25 cm
F3 Tattoo (black ink) osprey rugby club logo approx. 6 × 8 cm
F4 scar tissue (historic rugby injury) approx. 5.5 × 1 cm
F5 scar tissue (historic rugby injury) approx. 7 × 1 cm
F6 Tattoo (red ink) welsh dragon approx. 10 × 14 cm

Signed: Eileen Channon   Date: 7/7/2018

Page: 1 of 1

RESTRICTED (when complete)

* * *

The dry cleaner's is on the Woodstock Road, and it is,
indeed, in a direct line between St Luke Street and Edith
Launceleve. But the affluent of North Oxford clearly have
better things to do on a hot July afternoon than dirty

55

laundry, so Asante isn't at all surprised to find he's the only person in the shop. In fact, he suspects the not-much-more-than-a-lad behind the counter was hoping to bunk off early, given the aggrieved look he shoots at Asante when he pushes open the door. Though he cheers up considerably when he discovers it's the police. And not just police, CID. This is better than the footie.

Asante does his best to rise above it. 'I believe you took in an evening dress for cleaning earlier today?' He checks his tablet. '*Full-length red satin gown with a sequinned bodice and chiffon sleeves*. It would have been booked in under the name Marina Fisher.'

The lad drags the order book towards him and flicks back through the pages.

'Yeah,' he says after a moment. 'Looks like it.'

'Could I see it, please? The dress?'

The lad makes a face and flips the book shut. 'Nah, sorry, mate.'

Asante frowns; they must clean on-site, he can smell the chemicals. 'What do you mean, "no"?'

'She asked for an express job, didn't she – two-hour turnaround. It's been done already.'

Asante sighs. RIP any chance of forensics. Sometimes luck is on your side; sometimes it just isn't.

'Can I take it anyway?'

The lad shakes his head. 'No, sorry, mate. Like I said.'

Asante grits his teeth; frankly, it would be easier pulling them. 'Why not, if you've finished doing it? Look, if it's paperwork you need –'

The lad grins. 'No, it ain't that, mate. It's been *cleaned*, yeah. But it's not *here*. The van picked it up an hour ago.'

'I'm not with you.'

'We *clean* here, but alterations – hems, that sort of stuff – that's done off-site. And according to the docket, this one was a repair job.'

Asante's eyes narrow. 'Exactly what kind of a "repair job" are we talking about?'

* * *

Adam Fawley
7 July 2018
18.43

I'm not in the room when CSI process Marina Fisher, but I am waiting at the coffee machine when Nina Mukerjee comes out. She doesn't look surprised to see me.

'Waiting for an update?' she says, going over to the water cooler. She sticks a paper cup under the dispenser and presses the button. 'We've taken all the usual swabs, but the only thing visible to the naked eye was the slight bruising on her right wrist.'

I frown – I don't remember seeing that. And the sundress was sleeveless –

But then it comes to me. She had a heavy silver cuff bracelet on one wrist. A bracelet big enough to cover any damage. And it was her *right* wrist.

'What did she say about it? The bruising?'

'Claimed it was probably her kid, but couldn't remember exactly how it happened. If you ask me, the marks were too big for a small child, but there's no way to prove it one way or the other.'

'And it couldn't have happened at another time? Earlier that day, say?'

'Impossible to say for sure. It might be worth trying to get hold of any photos taken at the dinner, see if they show anything.'

'Is there likely to be any DNA?'

She raises an eyebrow. 'I wouldn't bet on it. I took fingernail scrapings though I doubt they'll yield much. But you said Morgan hadn't showered, so if there are marks on him and she made them, we've got a pretty good chance of proving it.'

'And how did she seem to you, in general?'

Mukerjee considers. 'Surprisingly composed, actually. She was a bit stressed when she first came in, and the lawyer fidgeting about like a mother hen probably didn't help, but as soon as we got into it she calmed down at once.'

'I guess she's a scientist. Of sorts, anyway.'

'Funnily enough, that's exactly what she said. That she found the environment soothing, because it's what she's used to.'

Mukerjee picks up her water. 'One thing's for sure – she was a lot more composed than most people in her position. The lawyer couldn't wait to get out of there but Fisher made a point of stopping and thanking me. She said that when it came down to it my job was the same as hers: it was all about the facts. And the facts would prove she's telling the truth.'

* * *

When Clive Conway gets to the St Luke Street house it's a uniformed PC who opens the door.

'Afternoon, Puttergill. Some sort of rave round here last night, was there?' he says, scraping his shoes on the mat. 'There's bits of glass all over the step.'

Puttergill looks blank, then ducks his head outside to look. 'Is there? I can't see anything.'

'Curse of CSI,' says Conway with a sigh. 'Every random bit of crap looks like trace evidence.' He unloads his forensic case in the hall and closes the door behind him. 'So you got dumped on too, did you?'

Puttergill grins. 'I was on roster anyway and this place is a hell of a sight nicer than the Cowley Road squad room. Doesn't smell of cabbage for a start.'

Conway smiles drily; Puttergill's only six months out of police training college. He'll learn.

'Anyone else here?'

Puttergill shakes his head. 'There's a cleaner around looking after the kid. Funny little bugger – took one look at me and ran off like a bat out of hell.'

Conway looks sardonic. 'Next time, try not to pull your baby-frightening face.'

Puttergill laughs. 'Just wait till he sees you in your nuclear war gear.'

The other curse of CSI – airtight onesies in a heatwave. Brings a whole new meaning to 'high' summer.

Conway raises an eyebrow. 'Well, unless you've stumbled over a corpse in the conservatory, I think I can wing it with the basics.' He opens his case and pulls out a mask. 'Right, sooner I start, sooner I get a beer.'

* * *

Video-Recorded Interview with Caleb Morgan,
conducted at the Holm Oak Sexual Assault Referral
Centre, Oxford
7 July 2018, 6.15 p.m.
In attendance, DC V. Everett; observing by video
link from adjacent room, DC G. Quinn

VE: OK, as I explained outside, I'm going to try
to get as much detail down now as I can, so we
have as full a statement as possible. We don't
want to ask you to go through this again if we
can avoid it, so please try to tell me
everything you can remember, OK?

CM: OK.

VE: And like I said, we are recording this, and if
there's a court case this tape may be used in
evidence. Do you need me to explain anything
more about that?

CM: No, I understand. And I've got the leaflets and
stuff.

VE: OK, perhaps I could ask you to start by
telling me how you came to be at Professor
Fisher's house yesterday evening.

CM: I was babysitting. She was at that dinner so I
was babysitting Tobin.

VE: Have you done that before?

CM: [*nods*]

Yeah, I do it a lot. The money's useful and
Tobin's a nice kid. I have a brother who's only
a bit older than him. Well, half-brother really,
but I'm used to being around boys his age.

VE: Is it common for dons to use their students as babysitters?

CM: [*shrugs*]

I don't know anyone else who does it. But that's Marina all over – she's not really one for sticking to the rules.

VE: That's what you call her – 'Marina'?

CM: Most of the postgrads call their supervisors by their first names – it's no big deal.

VE: How would you describe your relationship?

CM: [*quickly*]

It's not a *relationship* – not like that, anyway.

VE: I wasn't implying anything. I'm just trying to get a full picture. So you weren't just tutor and student, would that be fair? Given that she trusts you with her child?

CM: I guess. We have a laugh. And she really is phenomenal. Intellectually, I mean. Seriously cutting-edge. What I said about her not sticking to the rules, I meant it in a good way – you can't just do the same old same old, not in our field. You've got to take risks, challenge the status quo.

VE: Sounds like you admire her.

CM: [*shrugs*]

Anyone working in AI would give their eye teeth to be supervised by Marina. I was mega excited when I found out. I never thought it would end like this.

VE: But up until last night there'd never been anything else between you? It had been purely professional?

CM: [nods]

VE: So tell me what happened last night. What time did you arrive at Monmouth House?

CM: 8.00, 8.15. Something like that.

VE: And did you spend any time together then?

CM: She was about to leave, but we had a quick drink before she went – she said she needed a bit of Dutch courage. There was a lot at stake, so I guess she was feeling the pressure a bit.

VE: What did you drink?

CM: I had a beer. She had white wine.

VE: And when did she get back?

CM: Must've been about 11.15, perhaps 11.20.

VE: And you were where, at that point?

CM: In the kitchen. Downstairs, on the lower ground floor.

VE: And how was she – what was her mood like?

CM: Boy, she was *really* flying. Couldn't stop talking – about how well it'd gone, how impressed they'd been. Sounded like she'd completely blown them away.

VE: Did she appear intoxicated?

CM: Well, yeah – I mean, it was a dinner, so she'd had a few. *Quite* a few, if you ask me.

VE: What happened next?

CM: She said she was celebrating and went to the fridge to get a bottle of champagne. She asked me to open it.

VE: And you did that?

CM: I started saying I didn't really want any and I had to get back, but she just laughed at me and said of course I wanted some. I said was she sure she wanted to open champagne when it was already so late – I guess I was really asking if she needed any more, given she'd obviously had quite a lot already.

VE: But you didn't put it in quite so many words?

CM: No, well, she was still my supervisor, wasn't she? Anyway, she said I had to have at least one glass because she couldn't celebrate on her own. Then she said she was hopeless at the corks and would I do it, so I did.

VE: And then what happened?

CM: [*silence*]

VE: Mr Morgan?

* * *

Adam Fawley
7 July 2018
19.24

Fisher's lawyer is a fearsome operator by name of Niamh Kennedy. I've crossed swords with her before. She won't have come cheap, that's for sure, especially on a Saturday night. The premium service obviously includes collecting a complete change of clothes, because Fisher is now in full-blown Cath Kidston mode – floral dress, cotton cardigan, ballerina flats. All of it no doubt carefully selected by Kennedy to make her client look as far removed from a sexual predator as humanly possible. She even has her

63

hair in bunches, no doubt for the same reason. The result is a bizarre *Alice in Wonderland* vibe which is already starting to weird me out. There's nothing childlike about Fisher's face though. She looks hollow-eyed and haunted. Alice woke up and found it was all a dream; that ain't going to be happening here.

I take my seat next to Asante, open my file and go through the requisite procedural box-ticking. And I mean that literally: Kennedy sits there marking off the list of PACE requirements as we go, and makes sure I see her doing it. After all that, finally, we can begin.

I sit back. 'OK, Professor, perhaps you could talk us through your version of last night's events.'

The answer is quick; she was expecting this.

'Caleb had offered to babysit for me while I was at the dinner at Balliol.'

'Offered, or you asked?'

She blinks. 'OK, I asked.'

'And he's done that before – yes?'

She glances away. 'A few times.'

She's not meeting my eye; she knows she's on thin ice here, but I have fatter fish to fry than minor infractions of college procedures.

'What time did you get back after the dinner?'

She shrugs. 'Eleven fifteen? Something like that.'

'And you'd been drinking?'

She looks at me now. There are two spots of colour in her cheeks. 'Of course I'd been drinking. It was an eight-course dinner. *Everyone* was drinking. I admit I had a lot more than I normally would, but I wasn't *drunk*. Absolutely not.'

'So what happened when you got home?'

'I went downstairs to the kitchen. I could hear Caleb down there. He had some music on and he'd been working on his laptop at the kitchen table. We chatted for a bit.'

'About his research?'

'No, not really.'

The colour on her cheeks is deepening. I sense Asante shifting next to me. Kennedy reaches across and touches Fisher lightly on the arm. 'It's OK, you can say.'

'Look,' she says, 'he was flirting with me, all right? He does it a lot. It doesn't *mean* anything.'

'And were you flirting back? I mean, he's an attractive lad —'

She stares at me now. 'A *lot* of men flirt with me, Inspector, and a fair number of women too. Other academics, students, university administrators; chancers in all three of those categories and chancers in general. I don't take *any* of it seriously.'

I nod slowly. 'So then what?'

'He said we should have a drink. To celebrate my so-called "triumph".' There's a bitter note in her voice.

'So-called? I thought you'd secured a big-cheese donor — isn't that worth celebrating? Hilary Reynolds gave me the impression it was a tour de force.'

She gives an acid little sigh. 'Funnily enough, it doesn't feel much like that any more.'

'But it would have done last night, surely? Before all this happened?'

She sits back. '*He* said we should celebrate. *He* got the champagne out of the fridge. *He* opened it. OK?'

'So the two of you had a drink together. Just the one glass?'

She flushes again. 'I think so.'

'You think? You don't remember?'

'I remember I spilt some – on my dress. I remember him filling my glass again.'

She glances at Kennedy, and then at me. Evidently something else they've already discussed.

She takes a deep breath. 'After that, it gets a bit hazy.'

* * *

VE: Mr Morgan?

CM: [fidgeting with his water bottle]

VE: I know this is tough –

CM: She started coming on to me, all right? I was leaning back against the worktop and she came up really close. Like, pressing her body against me. She started asking me if I fancied her.

VE: And do you – did you?

CM: [flushing]

Kind of. I mean, she's a lot older than me but she's pretty hot. All the postgrads think so. And she looked amazing in that dress – anyone would have thought she looked sexy –

VE: It's not a crime to find her attractive, Mr Morgan.

CM: Caleb. You can call me Caleb.

VE: So what happened next?

CM: [takes a deep breath]

Well, she was definitely drunk by then. She'd kicked off the stilettos but she was still

66

swaying, like she couldn't stand up straight. And she was slurring her words. Even if I'd wanted to – there's no way I'd have done anything about it with her in that state.

VE: But you might – under other circumstances? If you thought she knew what she was doing?

CM: [*pause*]
In theory, perhaps. But *only* in theory – it'd have been a complete nightmare in practice. For my research, I mean. And anyway, I've got a girlfriend. It just wouldn't be worth the colossal amount of shit it would've caused.

VE: What happened next?

CM: She started touching me – through my clothes. My shorts. She said, you know, that it proved I did fancy her.

VE: [*softly*]
You had an erection.

CM: [*nods*]
But that didn't mean –

VE: It's just a physical reaction, Caleb. It's not something you can necessarily control. It doesn't mean that any of this is your fault, and it certainly doesn't mean you weren't assaulted.

CM: [*pause*]

VE: Can you go on?

CM: [*looks away, nods*]

* * *

'You're saying you don't remember what happened next?'

Fisher shakes her head.

Kennedy leans forward. 'Look, what *exactly* is this Caleb Morgan alleging?'

'He says Professor Fisher made physical sexual advances, and continued to do so even when he made it clear that he was saying no. Intercourse did not take place, but she did touch him in the groin area.'

Fisher is shaking her head. 'This is some terrible, ghastly misunderstanding. There is *no way* –'

She looks down, puts a hand to her lips, breathes. Then she looks up again. 'Is Caleb OK? I mean, that's the only explanation – he must have had some sort of breakdown –' Her voice falters. 'Look, he's been under a lot of pressure lately. His research –'

'So, to be clear, you're telling us you don't remember *any* physical contact with Mr Morgan?'

'No.'

'And the bruising on your wrist – how did that come about?'

She tugs at her sleeve, then realizes she's doing it and lays her hands flat on the table. 'As I told your technician, it was probably my son. Children are surprisingly strong and don't always know what they're doing.'

If she's aware of the irony in that last remark she gives no sign.

'What about this morning?'

She frowns. 'What about it?'

'When you woke up – were you in your own bed?'

'Of course I was –'

'Fully dressed? Nightclothes, what?'

Fisher raises an eyebrow, derisive. 'I don't bother with what you so quaintly refer to as "nightclothes", Inspector.'

'So you were naked, but you don't remember how you got there?'

She shrugs. 'My gown was on the back of the chair, my shoes in the rack. Everything was as it should be. Apart from the fact that I had a headache and a raging thirst, and a child long overdue his breakfast. Don't tell me that's never happened to you.'

'And it didn't concern you that you couldn't remember much about the end of the evening? Has that ever happened before?'

She sighs heavily. 'Once or twice, if you must know. Usually after champagne. I really should avoid Bollinger last thing at night.'

As fuck-yous go, that was about as deft as it gets.

'That being the case, when we're done here I'm going to ask our CSI officer to take a blood sample. Just so we can all be absolutely clear exactly how much alcohol we're talking about.'

Fisher glances at Kennedy, who nods. 'They're allowed to do that.'

Asante sits forward. 'What about the dress?'

Fisher frowns. 'What about the dress?'

'Why did you rush to get it cleaned?'

'I told you. I spilt wine on it. I didn't want to leave it in the wardrobe in that state. I was worried it might not come out if I didn't have it done quickly.'

'But it wasn't just cleaning, was it? You asked for some repairs to the dress too.'

There's a flicker across Kennedy's face which she's not quite quick enough to hide; this, at least, is news to her.

I open the cardboard file and take out a sheet of paper. It's a scan of the dry cleaner's order book.

Mend ripped neckline and replace sequins (bag of spares supplied by client).

I close the file again and look up. 'What happened, Professor Fisher? How did such an expensive evening dress get damaged at a sedate black-tie bash like that?'

'I don't remember.'

'Or perhaps it wasn't there that it happened? Perhaps it was after that, when you got home?'

She opens her mouth and closes it again.

'I told you,' she says eventually, 'I don't remember.'

*   *   *

VE: So she started to touch you. What happened next?

CM: I managed to pull away a bit and turned round to tip the champagne down the sink. I'd hardly had any of it.

VE: How much had she had?

CM: I think she was on her second glass by then.

VE: So then what?

CM: I was still at the sink, and felt her coming up behind me. She put her arms round me and started putting her hands down the front of

my shorts. You know, inside, trying to grab
my - you know - my penis.

VE: What did you do?

CM: I turned round and pulled her hands away. I
said I didn't want to do this - that *she*
didn't want to do this. She said I was being
ridiculous - we both wanted it. So I said what
about Freya and she just laughed. Said
something about why have prosecco when you
can have the real thing. Then she reached up
and pulled my face down - you know, trying to
kiss me.

VE: And you tried to make her stop?

CM: [*flushing*]
I got hold of her wrist - tried to stop her,
force her away. She still had the glass in her
hand and some of it got spilt. I suppose you
could say there was a bit of a tussle.
[*pause*]
That must have been when she scratched me - I
didn't realize at the time. I don't think she
meant to - she was still pulling at me and her
fingers were in my hair and somehow it must
have just happened.
[*takes a deep breath*]
Look, I'm not proud of this but I did end up
pushing her away.

VE: How hard?

CM: [*flustered*]
Hard enough. I mean, not as hard as I could
have, but I knew I had to be careful - she was

drunk and I'm a lot stronger than she is. But
I didn't know what else to do - she just
wasn't taking no for an answer.

*   *   *

'You're not prepared to answer any further questions, Professor Fisher?'

Kennedy raises an eyebrow. 'My client's position is very clear. These allegations are false, contrived and very possibly malicious. No such incident took place, which means, by definition, that you will find no evidence to substantiate it.'

'How can your client be so sure, when she claims not to remember anything after the opening of the champagne?'

Fisher starts to answer but Kennedy forestalls her. 'Because she is a *professional*. And because conduct of that kind would be entirely out of character, as I'm sure her colleagues will happily confirm. As I said, should you find any actual *evidence* that these events took place, by all means let us know. But take it from me, you won't.'

'What possible motive would Mr Morgan have to make a false accusation? He has everything to lose and nothing whatsoever to gain.'

The lawyer raises an eyebrow. 'You'll have to ask him that, Inspector.'

*   *   *

Oxford Mail online

Wednesday 18 May 2018

Local MP accuses UK universities of failing victims of sexual violence

By Richard Yates

Didcot and Cholsey MP Petra Newson took part in a highly charged debate in the Oxford Union last night.

Speaking in support of the motion *This House Believes That UK Universities are Failing to Protect Students from Sexual Crime*, Ms Newson described the current situation as an 'utter scandal'. 'It's clear to me that universities and colleges are not taking adequate or appropriate action against students accused of rape and sexual assault, and in far too many cases these incidents are not even referred to the police. Even worse, when teaching staff are accused of harassment or assault, some of these institutions are closing ranks and protecting their own. Lecturers – both male *and* female – are *in loco parentis* for the young people in their care, and if this duty of care is abused, they should be prosecuted with all the severity the law allows.'

Royal Wedding celebrations planned across the county
Tomorrow's nuptials at Windsor will be marked by street parties and events across Oxfordshire . . . /more

Man, 23, threatened with knife in mugging
A man has been arrested after an Iffley resident was robbed at knife-point last week . . . /more

Call for new memorial to Romantic poet
Percy Bysshe Shelley was sent down for atheism from University College in 1810, but there's now growing support for a public tribute in Oxford city centre . . . /more

Blue plaque in city centre honours pioneering scientist
A new blue plaque will be erected this week to mark the achievements of Professor Jane Keating . . . /more

Sport: match reports and scores . . . /more

The second speaker, Maria Gleeson, a former student at a Midlands university, attempted to bring an action against her professor two years ago, but ultimately withdrew the charge because the process was so distressing. 'The people who were questioning me obviously had no experience of dealing with this,' she said. 'It was intrusive, and traumatic. I felt like I was on trial, not him.'

Speaking on the other side of the debate, Gareth McFadden of Universities UK, which speaks for 130 of the country's largest institutions, acknowledged that there was growing concern about sexual violence on campuses, and said his organisation had published a detailed report on harassment, violence against women, and hate crime in 2016, which recommended a number of measures to help institutions address this issue and provide better support for victims.

129 comments

* * *

Clive Conway has pretty much wrapped things up at St Luke Street. Not that there was much to do. The two champagne glasses on the draining board had already been rinsed and dried, and without any obvious signs of a struggle he's not sure what else CID could reasonably expect to find. He finishes taking his photos, makes a note to himself to collect the empty champagne bottle from the recycling bin on his way out, and bags up the glasses.

He's packing up to leave when he gets the call.

'Conway? It's Anthony Asante. Marina Fisher's being processed and something's come up.'

'Oh yes?'

'She doesn't have her mobile with her. She thought she did but it isn't in her bag. She thinks it's either in her office at Edith Launceleve or at the house. Can you see if you can find it?'

Conway glances around the kitchen. 'There's nothing down here, but I'll have a look upstairs.'

'Great, thanks. And collect the laptop too, if you can find one – given how sensitive this one's going to be, Fawley wants us to check her phone. Just to be on the safe side.'

'OK, I'll let you know if I find anything.'

He finishes packing up and makes his way up to the sitting room and starts looking round. A few moments later he spots the mobile charging on a coffee table. He bags it and slips it into his case, then straightens up. It's only now he notices that the boy has been in the room the whole time, sitting at a low table under the far window, so intent on whatever he's doing that he doesn't seem to have noticed anyone else is there.

Conway wanders over. The child's working in a large drawing-by-numbers book – a huge, intricate design of what looks like St George and the Dragon. If it'd been one of his own kids the colours would be spilling out of the lines all over the place, but this boy clearly has more patience and better hand–eye coordination than all his three put together.

'That's really good,' he says jovially. 'Must help having so many colours to choose from.'

Conway's kids had Caran d'Ache sets too, but he didn't know you could get them three tiers deep. There must be over a hundred pencils in there. He stands there for a few minutes more, and each time the boy finishes with a colour he watches him put it carefully back exactly where it came from. The table remains tidy, the spectrum in the box perfectly graduated, the only sound the *scratch*, *scratch*, *scratch* against the page.

* * *

The Vowels
online

- Ron Sandford
Well the fisher of men certainly played a blinder last night
15:48 ✓✓

- Vic Gibbins
Blinder's about right if you ask me she was "really" putting it away
15:50

- Ron Sandford
Meow. You were hardly stinting 😺
15:50 ✓✓

- Kate Kesson
Anyone care to enlighten those of us who didn't make the A-list?
15:52

- Kate Kesson
As in did we get the sodding money?
15:52

- Ron Sandford
Safe to say that's affirmative #ker-ching 😊
15:53 ✓✓

- Kate Kesson
Oh God she's going to be even "more" insufferable now #sigh
15:54

- Ron Sandford
We all have our cross to bear 😆
15:55 ✓✓

Type a message

* * *

Conway pulls the front door shut and hears it click behind him. Monmouth House is on a corner so, unlike most of her neighbours, Marina Fisher has side access to her house, and doesn't have to deal with the besetting conundrum facing owners of Georgian terraces from Bath to Bloomsbury: What To Do With The Bloody Bins. Fisher's are just inside the side gate, tucked neatly out of sight in a purpose-built enclosure trailed with clematis. Conway opens the recycling bin to retrieve the champagne bottle, and finds it, as expected, right at the top. He bags it up and is about to close the lid again when he notices for the first time what was immediately underneath. He frowns slightly, hesitates a moment, then reaches into his case for another evidence bag.

* * *

Adam Fawley
7 July 2018
20.15

'OK, I know it's late and it's hot and it's Saturday and you'd all much rather be interrogating a cold beer, but I just want to capture first impressions while they're still fresh.'

I look round at them. Ev, Quinn, Asante. 'So, which one do you believe? And no, it's not a trick question.'

'If you forced me to go one way or the other, I'd go for Morgan,' says Everett. 'He answered all the questions, kept good eye contact. He even admitted he fancied her, which he must have known would complicate matters. But he was asked the question, and he gave an honest answer.'

I turn to Quinn. 'What about you, Quinn?'

He shrugs. 'I can't understand what Morgan's doing here at all. Nothing actually *happened*, so why put yourself through a shitshow like this? *And* risk fucking up your career at the same time? He's not stupid – he must realize there's a sod-all per cent chance of a conviction. Just doesn't add up.'

Ev looks across at him. 'Would you be saying "nothing actually happened" if the genders had been reversed? If it was a male tutor and a female student? No, of course you wouldn't.'

'I know we all know this,' says Asante evenly, looking from the one to the other, 'but sexual assault isn't about sex. It's about power. And Fisher's the one with all the power in this relationship. If she was abusing that power some other way – academically, I mean – then Morgan would have every right to make a complaint. Why is this any different?'

Quinn is shaking his head. 'He's still taking a *massive* risk –'

'What about *her*?' says Ev quickly. 'Coming on to a student like that, knowing he could go straight to the college authorities and report her? That's what *I* call taking a risk.'

'But that's the point,' I say. 'They're *both* risk takers. Morgan said so himself, in interview. He said anyone working in that field has to be prepared to take risks or they'll never get anywhere.'

Ev frowns. 'They're both as bad as each other, is that what you're saying?'

'I'm saying these are both people who might be more prepared than most to play a high-stakes game.'

There's a pause. They're not sure where that gets us and, frankly, neither am I.

'I don't know why CID are even on this,' mutters Quinn. 'Never mind the whole bloody team.'

Classic Quinn, but for once I sympathize. I wouldn't have the entire team on it either, given the choice, but we don't have the excuse of a more pressing case, and – rather more pertinently – I'm anticipating that sooner or later the Chief Constable will be 'taking an interest' or 'just checking in' or whatever apparently-casual-only-clearly-not phrase his PA comes up with. As my first Inspector once put it, 'It's only a suggestion, but let's not forget who's making it.'

'There's something about Fisher,' says Asante eventually. 'I can't put my finger on it but something's definitely off. All that stuff about not being able to remember – it's a bit too convenient, if you ask me.'

'On the other hand,' I say, 'why hasn't Morgan mentioned the rip to the dress? He's been upfront about the fact that there was a physical altercation – why not mention that the dress got ripped in the process?'

Ev shrugs. 'Perhaps he didn't realize? Perhaps he just doesn't remember?'

Quinn gives a dismissive snort and looks away. 'Yeah, right. He can't remember, *she* can't remember. *He said/she said*. It's all bollocks – the whole thing.'

I see Ev about to object and decide to step in.

'OK, we've probably all had enough for one day. But DC Quinn's right about one thing: the CPS will never run with this as it stands. If we get DNA from Morgan's body, it could be a whole different ball game. But meanwhile, whether we like it or not, we can't ignore who his mother is. Not least because I doubt she's going to let us. Remember that debate about sexual violence in the Union a couple of months back? She'd be all over this, even if the victim in question wasn't her son.'

Quinn sighs heavily. 'Just what we need. Being crapped on from a great height by an up-themselves politico.'

'Right,' I say briskly. Because that sort of attitude isn't going to get us – or Quinn – anywhere. 'So let's not give her the satisfaction. Forensics will be at least a couple of days, and that's if we're lucky. So in the meantime, we do our homework. We need to confirm Morgan's story with his girlfriend and talk to Fisher's colleagues, both here and anywhere she's worked in the past. I want to know if there's been even the slightest hint of anything like this before. And check whether any of those people were also guests at the Balliol dinner – let's see if we can find out if there were any signs of damage when she left, either to her or that bloody dress.'

'We'll need to be careful though,' says Asante cautiously. 'This sort of allegation – it would wreck her career. And if it turns out she *didn't* do it –'

'Precisely. So *discretion*, please. I want to eavesdrop on the rumour mill, not start it.'

I stand up; Asante's making a note, Ev is gathering her things, Quinn just looks narked.

'I'll get DC Baxter going on Fisher's phone and I'll also see if we can get Bryan Gow to have a look at Fisher's interview footage. If Asante's right and something really is off here, he's our best chance of nailing it. As for the rest of it, DC Quinn, you're stand-in DS. Over to you.'

Quinn looks up. 'Yes, boss,' he says.

He's perked up already.

* * *

It's dusk, that most deceptive time of the day. The memory of light still in the sky, but the earth dark below. No one's noticed the man parked up by the side of the road, not even the usually nosey old chap who's just gone by with his dog. But why would he? The man hasn't moved for a while – hasn't read a newspaper, turned on the radio, dug a packet of mints out of the glovebox. The vehicle is silent, and so is he. He does nothing. Nothing, that is, but watch.

A few moments later a door opposite opens and a woman comes quickly down the path to the trellis enclosure by the gate. She lifts the lid of one of the bins and drops a black plastic bag inside, before turning and looking up and down the street. She's looking directly at him now and he slides a bit further down in the seat, even though he knows it's too dark, and too far, to see his face.

When the man glances up again two women are coming towards him along the pavement. Yakking away, their toddlers bundled up in buggies. There's an older kid too, a boy with red hair and big glasses, drifting along behind. The man frowns. Mothers are too distracted, too frazzled, to notice pretty much anything, let alone someone just sitting quietly in their vehicle, minding their own business. But kids are different. They don't care. They just stare straight in.

The women are drawing level now, shreds of conversation drifting across.

'I think you just have to tell them –'
'But you know what that place is like –'
'When I spoke to Pippa about it she said the same thing –'

The women pass, but the kid is still dawdling, and the man can now see why. He's stopping at each car, looking at the make and noting something on a small red clipboard. The man's eyes narrow. Just his bloody luck to stumble over the only kid on the planet who wants to be a sodding traffic warden when he grows up.

The boy is closer now, but still too far to read a number plate. Not in this light. He can see the woman, still at her gate, straining forward, trying to see.

The man curses under his breath, reaches for the ignition key and starts the engine.

* * *

When Niamh Kennedy pulls in opposite Monmouth House there are no lights in the tall facade on the other side of the road.

'Beatriz must be in the kitchen,' says Fisher, peering up at the windows. 'Poor woman – I had no idea I would be so long.'

'These things are always interminable,' says Kennedy. 'If you take my advice, you'll have a large glass of wine, a hot bath, and go straight to bed.'

'I will,' says Fisher. 'I just need to spend some time with Tobin first. Heaven only knows what he must be thinking.'

'Kids are more resilient than you think. He'll take his cue from you. As long as you talk to him calmly, he'll be fine.' She reaches across and squeezes Fisher's arm. 'Don't worry, Marina. I know you feel overwhelmed right now, but you're strong. If you were the sort of person who was going to be defeated by this you wouldn't have got this far in the first place.'

Fisher gives a quick nod, then gets out of the car and strides across the road, not looking back. She holds her head high as she struggles to get the key in the door, but as soon as she hears the car pull away her shoulders slump and she half staggers across the threshold into the hallway.

She stands there a moment, adjusting to the gloom. There's a pale shape hunched on the bottom step, which lurches towards her, the eyes huge and ghost-dark in the pale face.

'Where have you been, Mummy? You *promised* you would look at my drawing. I've been waiting for *hours*. Where *were* you?'

* * *

8.15pm Saturday

Just now, when I went out to the bins, he was there. Again. Parked down the road, far enough away that he knew I wouldn't be able to see him — not properly. Then two women went past with pushchairs and I think they must have spooked him because as soon as they got close he drove away.

But it was him. I know it was.

He was <u>there</u>.

* * *

When I get home, the house is in shadow. Inside, there's a single light on in the kitchen, and a note saying there's salad in the fridge if I want it. I pour myself a glass of Merlot and slip upstairs. The door to the baby's room is ajar. It was Jake's, before. A couple of months ago we spent a whole weekend carefully packing all his things away. We didn't discuss it – we didn't need to. We just knew it was time. And now, everything in there is new. Wallpaper, furniture, bedding, curtains; the piles of baby clothes still in their packaging, even the mobile hanging over the cot. The smell of paint lingers. Yellow paint. Everything is white or yellow – not a scrap of blue or pink in the whole place. Alex has known the sex of our child for months but she's never let it slip, not once. Downstairs, the list of names stuck to the fridge is as busy with girls as it is with boys. Added, scratched through, question-marked, ticked. We seem to have finally agreed on Lily Rose for a girl, but we've been brought up short when it comes to boys. Literally: she wants Stephen for her dad, but I hate Steve; I like Gabriel, but she can't stand Gabe. Impasse.

I move softly across the landing, inch open our bedroom door and stand for a moment, listening in the twilight.

Outside, I can hear a distant siren, the murmur of traffic on the ring road, a late last burst of blackbird song.

But here, in the room, my sleeping wife moans softly in her sleep, restless in unquiet dreams.

*   *   *

At just gone 9.00 the following morning Anthony Asante is sitting in the bay window of his apartment, talking to his mother on the phone. He's pulled one of the blinds to screen out the sun but it's already too hot for him to sit there much longer. 'Bay window' probably has you picturing him in a flat in one of those classic Oxford Victorian houses – four storeys, red brick and stone mullions – but you could hardly be more wrong. This bay window is rectangular and juts from the wall like a half-open door, and the flat is a sleek wood-and-white duplex which anyone visiting can hardly believe even exists in this town, especially this close to the centre. But visitors of any kind are largely notional as yet, since Asante has only been here a few weeks. Even if that weren't the case, he's always preferred to keep his private space private. Though he knows he's going to have to make an exception for his parents. He shifts the phone to his other ear, scrolling all the while on his tablet. He's good at multitasking, and in any case, talking to his mother doesn't require too much brain capacity. She's saying something now about taking him for lunch next weekend. Something about a gaudy at her college the night before.

'Don't worry,' she says quickly before he can reply. 'We're going to stay there overnight.'

Asante tries to keep the relief out of his voice. He loves his parents and – rarer – he admires them, but he really doesn't want them staying here. If she'd pushed it, he'd have said he hasn't got round to buying a spare bed (which also happens to be true), but he's grateful, not for the first time, for his mother's ability to work these things out for herself.

'There are plenty of undergraduate rooms available,' she's saying now. 'We may not have had gargoyles or boys, but one thing EL always did have was space.'

'How about The Perch?' he says. 'For lunch? Dad's always liked it there.'

'Perfect,' she says. 'Though we'd better book – it's bound to be packed in this weather. Especially at the weekend.'

'OK, I'll sort that out. Leave it with me.'

'We're so looking forward to seeing your new place, Anthony – are you sure you don't want us to bring anything? We've loads of spare furniture – the loft is practically bursting –'

Asante smiles, but not unkindly. Anything that suits his parents' stucco-fronted Holland Park town house is really not going to fit in here.

'It's fine, Mum, I really don't need anything.'

He finishes the call and wanders through to the kitchen, where the side of the castle mound rises cliff-like only a few feet from the window. His neighbour's black-and-white cat is halfway up the path, prowling for mice. He has one eye and extravagant moustaches, making him look dashingly piratical. The Mound is one of the main reasons Asante bought the place. For some people, the main attraction would have been the bars and coffee shops of the now-chic prison quarter only a few hundred yards away; for others, the five-minute walk from the station. But Asante likes the sheer improbability of the Mound, a thousand-year-old man-made hillock right in the heart of the city. He likes the old brewery and the converted malthouse, and he likes the evocative street names – Paradise Street, Quaking Bridge, Beef Lane. There was a horse hospital round here, in the nineteenth century, and a marmalade factory in the twentieth. The place is not very well known, eclectic and unexpected; rather like Asante himself.

He pours himself a glass of water and pushes the kitchen window open a little further. They do Shakespeare productions in the castle courtyard in the summer, and he can see the edge of the stage and the steps where the audience sit. He's been to a couple of productions now, including a *Henry V* with only four actors that hadn't sounded very promising but turned out to be a wonder. At night, when it's quieter and the trees at the top are flood-lit, he can sit on his balcony and listen to the entire show. It was *Titus Andronicus* last night. Not a play he knew, but the gaggle of schoolkids were clearly lapping it up. Cannibalism, revenge and rape – what's not to like, if you're fifteen.

* * *

Ten miles away as the crow flies, Ev is getting in a quick early visit to her dad. He's only been in the care home for a couple of months and it's taken time to get him used to the place, never mind accept it. She'd been almost as reluctant to agree to it as he was, but after a fall that nearly left him with a broken hip she knew she no longer had a choice. The doctor said so, the manager of the home said so, even Fawley said so. But none of that makes her father's reproachful stare any easier to take, or his simmering self-pity any easier to hear.

She's visited every weekend since, but this is the first time when they haven't had the heating on. Every mobile resident is outside in the garden, which Ev hasn't ventured into before and turns out to be much nicer than she'd expected. Beds of roses, marigolds, petunias – the sort of flowers her father's generation grew up with. But, of course, he still found something to criticize ('the garden-er's one of those greenies, but he won't get rid of blackfly like that with bloody Fairy Liquid'). Still, at least he had a bit of colour in his cheeks when she helped him back into his armchair. And then there was tea and soggy garibaldis, and more daytime TV with its demoralizing adverts for funeral plans and denture fixative and, that euphemism of the decade, 'sensitive bladder'. Ev is uncomfortably aware that the same sort of advertising has started turn-ing up on her Facebook feed – just how old do those people think she is? By half past ten she's had enough, and decides she's earned a decent coffee in the peace and quiet of her own sitting room. She gets to her feet, mumbling something about feeding Hector, only for her father to bark out that his only daughter 'cares more about her bloody cat than she does about me' at foghorn volume. A couple of other visitors turn to stare as she leaves, but one gives her a sympathetic look that says, *Don't worry, I've been there.*

She's picking up speed as she crosses the lobby, the open front door already in sight, when she hears her name.

'Miss Everett?'

She turns. It's Elaine Baylis, the manager. Ev's heart sinks. Another half-hour between her and that coffee. And that's at best.

'I thought it was you – could I have a quick word?' Baylis must have seen the look on Ev's face because her own hardens a little. 'Don't worry, I won't keep you long.'

Baylis can't be much older than Ev, but the combination of a studiously dreary wardrobe and a sanctimonious professional manner gives her the aura of an elderly fifty-five.

She shows Everett into the office and closes the door behind her. Ev takes a seat on one of the uncomfortable plasticky chairs.

'I just wanted to say,' starts Baylis, taking her own seat and tucking her skirt neatly under her – her mother would have been proud – 'we're really pleased your father is settling in.'

Ev wonders if she's speaking on behalf of the whole staff or if it's some sort of Royal We.

'But?'

Baylis frowns. 'I'm sorry?'

'It sounded like there was a "but" coming.' She smiles. 'Or perhaps I've just spent too long interviewing suspects.'

Baylis looks momentarily wrong-footed. Now there's a first, thinks Ev.

'I just meant,' she says, sitting forward now, 'that it's always a relief – for everyone – when a resident starts to feel at home.'

Ev waits. There's something else coming. No question. Like she said, she's been at the interrogation game a very long time.

Baylis sighs. 'I know we talked about this before, before your father became one of us.' She makes it sound like the

Masons. 'But I feel I do need to say it again. Meadowhall is a residential home, not a nursing home. We don't have specialist resources –'

'The Alzheimer's.'

She blinks. 'Yes, the Alzheimer's.'

'The GP says it's still very early stages. He prescribed those drugs –'

'I know, and we're making sure he takes them. But that's about all we're able to do.' She emphasizes the words. 'We don't have full-time medical staff. We wouldn't be able to cope –'

'If it got worse – yes, I know. You told me.'

Baylis gives her a long look, not unkindly. 'It's not a case of *if*, Miss Everett. It's a case of *when*. Alzheimer's always wins in the end.'

Ev's throat is suddenly tight with tears.

'I know,' she says after a moment, her voice betraying her. 'I do know that, I just want – I just want him to be somewhere normal for as long as he can. Somewhere that feels as much as possible like home.'

Baylis nods. 'And that's what we'll provide. But only for as long as *possible*. I just wanted that to be completely clear.'

Everett gets to her feet – if Baylis really was a suspect she'd have exactly the right whip-smart response, the perfect form of words to re-establish the balance of power between them, but something about this office is radio-jamming her brain.

'Sorry,' she mutters, 'I've got to go.'

* * *

The head of the university computer science department was easy enough to track down, but rather harder to persuade to see them at the weekend. When he opens the door of his Abingdon Road house he's rather pointedly dressed in slippers and a purple-and-turquoise dressing gown.

'You're not Moonies, are you?' he says jovially. 'The last bloke who knocked here wearing a suit like that asked me if I wanted to be saved.'

Quinn steps forward, showing his warrant card. 'Acting DS Gareth Quinn. This is DC Asante. Thank you for making the time to see us, Professor Sandford.'

Sandford takes a step back and waves them through. 'I'm in the kitchen. At the back.'

It's a Victorian semi, but unlike most people who live in houses like this, Sandford hasn't knocked through any of the downstairs rooms, so there's a railway carriage feel of doors opening off a passageway that doesn't get enough light. That, combined with the heavily patterned wallpaper and the piles of newspapers and magazines, makes the place feel much smaller than it really is. The kitchen is in a modern extension, but 'modern' is a relative term. Eighties, at a guess. Out the back, what's left of the garden has been slabbed over; there's a white plastic table and chairs on the grubby paving and neglected tomato plants withering in a growbag against the fence. And Sandford clearly isn't much of a domestic goddess within doors either. The kitchen's not that clean under the clutter and the only item less than thirty years old is the large Nespresso machine. The rest is vintage 1985 – the mug tree, the matching tea and coffee jars, and the enamel toaster in the corner that's definitely an original rather than a trendy repro. There's a mug of coffee steaming on the breakfast bar and a plate of newly buttered toast, but Sandford doesn't offer either. He just pulls out a bar stool and gestures for them to do the same.

'Must be serious, to get you chaps dolled up to the nines this early on a Sunday.'

Quinn gets out his tablet. 'We're making enquiries in relation to Professor Fisher.'

Sandford raises an eyebrow. There's a half-smile trying to get out. '*Marina?* Well, well, well. Who'd 'a thought it, eh?'

'It's a confidential matter at present, sir. And it's very important that it remains so. I'm sure you understand.'

Sandford does a zip gesture across his mouth. 'Rest assured, my lips are sealed.' He reaches for a slice of toast and coats it liberally with blackcurrant jam. Asante feels his stomach start to rumble.

'Go on then,' Sandford says, his mouth half full. 'What do you want to know?'

'How does Professor Fisher get on with her students?' asks Quinn.

Sandford nods slowly, chewing all the while. 'She's very popular. Being a media star no doubt helps – sprinkles a bit of fairy dust. Oh yes, she has quite the little following.'

'What about her colleagues?' asks Asante. 'Does she inspire the same admiration there?'

Sandford considers. 'That's rather more *nuanced*, shall we say. No one questions her technical competence, but this is Oxford; excellence merely gets you to first base.'

'What do they think about her public profile?' continues Asante. 'Is that seen as a good thing?'

Sandford gives him a narrow look. 'Well, the "official" line is that having a woman of Marina's standing on the staff can only be a good thing. And if it helps attract girls to the subject, so much the better. Getting the stats up on female applicants is still an unholy grail for every STEM faculty.'

Quinn raises an eyebrow. 'And the "unofficial" line?'

Sandford puts down his toast and wipes his hands on a piece of kitchen paper. 'There are those who think she's too flashy, and her rather – shall we say – *idiosyncratic* style of dress doesn't exactly help. Not that she appears to care, but that's Marina all over.'

'In my experience,' says Asante carefully, 'academic life can be very competitive –'

Sandford is already laughing. 'My God, out of the mouths of babes. The average Oxford department, Detective Constable, is a *very* small pond overstocked with piranhas the size of elks. And the fact that they're so rare only serves to make the female of the species that much deadlier.'

Asante and Quinn exchange a glance.

Sandford gets up and goes over to the coffee machine. 'Safe to say, Marina's most vocal detractors are almost certainly motivated by envy, and almost always other women. One of them famously referred to her as "the sort of marina where the wisest option is a wide berth".'

He gives them a heavy look, turns to the switch and flips it on. The kitchen fills with the thudding gurgle of the machine. Quinn makes a point of staring at the empty mugs, but it cuts no ice with Sandford. He collects his coffee then comes over and joins them again.

Asante takes a deep breath; here comes the point of no

return. They're going to have to trust Sandford to keep his mouth shut from now on, and his demeanour so far has hardly inspired much confidence. 'Have there ever been any allegations against Professor Fisher that you're aware of? In connection with her teaching role?'

Sandford looks intrigued. 'What sort of "allegations"?'

He stares at them, a stare that turns into a gape as the silence lengthens and he finally realizes what they must be getting at. 'Fuck me,' he says. 'You are joking, I take it?'

'Just answer the question, please.'

Sandford sits back a little. 'Well, if you *actually* mean what I *think* you mean, the whole bloody idea is preposterous. Marina has no shortage of male company as far as I can see, and even if she did, she's just not that bloody stupid.'

Asante quietly makes a note, trying to give the impression that this is all perfectly routine, but without any confidence that he's managing to pull it off.

'I believe there was a fundraising dinner on Friday night,' says Quinn. 'At Balliol. Were you present?'

Sandford nods. 'Of course. And if you're going to ask about Marina, she completely aced it. Had the bigwigs eating out of her hand, especially our Chinese friends. They couldn't get enough of her. And that dress – what did they say about Nicole Kidman that time? – "pure theatrical Viagra". At one point during dessert the Vice-Chancellor was heard to mutter that they should have asked for double.'

'That sort of success won't have endeared her much to her female colleagues either, I imagine.'

Sandford smiles drily. 'No doubt. But as it happens, she was the only woman present.'

Asante nods slowly; easy to see what an adrenaline hit that would have been. Fisher must have felt invincible. Invincible enough – and uninhibited enough by all that alcohol – to assume she could ask for anything else she happened to want, and expect to get it?

He clears his throat. 'Professor Fisher has admitted to us that she was drinking at the dinner.'

Sandford raises his eyebrows. 'We were *all* drinking.'

'Were any photographs taken?'

Sandford gives a quick frown. 'Some, I think. I didn't have my phone with me, but a couple were posted on the faculty WhatsApp group yesterday.'

'And you're on that?'

Sandford nods. 'For my sins. I take it you want to see?'

'If you don't mind, sir.'

Sandford fishes about under the scatter of Sunday papers and unearths the phone. 'Here you go. Usual sort of stuff.'

'Your group's called "The Vowels"?' asks Quinn, frowning.

Sandford looks smug. 'Artificial and Experimental Intelligence, Oxford University. AEIOU.'

'Hilarious,' says Quinn.

Sandford's still smirking. 'Thank you, I thought so too.'

Quinn turns back to the phone. There are a couple of formal shots that were probably taken before they went in to eat – a line of men in DJs, monotonously black and white, Fisher queening it in the centre, glittering in her scarlet dress like some sort of tropical insect. She's turned three-quarters to the camera, one shoulder lowered, as if she's done this before. The later shots have people with glasses of port in their hands, and Marina is clearly visible in several, talking to a couple of middle-aged men. Her cheeks are slightly flushed and, judging by their faces, both men are captivated by her, though it's debatable whether it's her cleavage or her conversation that's making the greater impact. Quinn scrolls to another picture, stops, then holds out the phone to Asante with a meaningful look. Marina Fisher, mid-gesture, her right hand raised, her sleeve slipping down. She's not wearing a bracelet and her wrist is completely unmarked.

'Can you send these to me, sir?' asks Asante, sliding a business card across the counter.

Sandford shrugs. 'Sure, knock yourselves out, as our American cousins say.'

Quinn gets to his feet. 'Unless there's anything else you think we should know, I think that's it, thank you. We'll leave you to your breakfast.' *And get some of our own*, he thinks. *Thanks for bloody nothing, tosser.*

Sandford follows them down the hall to the door.

'There was one thing –'

'Oh yes?' says Quinn, turning back to face him.

'Who brought this "allegation" against Marina? I don't think you said.'

'No,' says Quinn. 'We didn't.'

As they walk back up the Abingdon Road towards St Aldate's, Asante turns to Quinn. 'What are the odds this is all over that WhatsApp group before the day is out?'

'Two to one on,' says Quinn grimly.

* * *

97

It'd take a lot more than wild horses to get Clive Conway to work on a Sunday under normal circumstances, but something about the Fisher case isn't sitting right, so as soon as his wife is settled outside in the garden with her brother and his family, he slips upstairs to his office and logs on to the TVP server.

He stares at the screen, then sits back, swinging the swivel desk chair slowly from side to side.

He should be feeling pretty pleased with himself right now, with his hunch amply vindicated. But it's not as simple as that. It rarely is. Because even if *what* he found is clear enough, the *why* and the *how* are going to take a lot more explaining.

His wife is calling up the stairs to him now, wondering where he's got to, reminding him about lighting the barbecue.

He leans forward, grabs the landline phone and starts to dial.

* * *

The porter scans down the list. 'Cornwallis Building. Up the street, turn right. Number six.'

Freya Hughes is at one of the specialist graduate colleges, assembled half a century before from a scatter of Victorian houses and a dining hall purpose-built on one of the back gardens. Everett hasn't been here before, but it seems nice enough. Though she can imagine the more self-important overseas applicants dismissing it as insufficiently 'Oxford'.

Hughes' room is on the top floor of a modern annexe

behind the main buildings. It looks tired, the concrete streaked and stained, and some of the double-glazing clearly blown. Funny, thinks Ev, as she knocks on the door, how none of the university's modern buildings ever quite manage to live up to what was already there. And as for that metal armadillo thing on the Woodstock Road –

'Yes?'

The girl at the door is petite and blonde, with fair skin that must be a sore trial in temperatures like these and eyelashes so pale they're almost invisible. She's holding on to the door, opening it only as far as she has to. She looks not exactly hostile but careful, guarded.

Everett holds out her warrant card. 'DC Verity Everett. I'm here about Caleb Morgan.'

'Oh, yes. Caleb. Of course. Come in.'

She has a nice view. The back of one of the Victorian houses, landscaped into a neat paved area with wooden seating and shrubs and a brick barbecue. The room itself could do with higher ceilings, but it has an en suite and decent carpet. Like the rest of the place, 'nice enough'. Perhaps they should have that as the college motto. In Latin, obviously.

Everett takes the desk chair and Hughes perches on the window seat. There's a mobile phone on the desk, but as soon as she sees Everett glance at it Hughes gets up quickly and moves it further away.

Everett takes out her notebook. 'Caleb is your boy-friend, right?'

Hughes nods.

'How long have you been together?'

'About nine months.'

Ev makes a note. 'And I think he came to see you on Friday night – about what happened?'

Another nod. 'He wasn't going to do anything about it, but I said it was all wrong. That she should never have behaved that way.'

'And "she" would be Professor Fisher?'

'She takes liberties. Not just the babysitting. Other things. She thinks she can get away with it because of who she is. Because she's a woman and gets so much attention.'

'Do you know Professor Fisher? You're doing a different subject, I think? English, was it?'

The girl blinks. 'Yes. And no, I don't know her. I've *seen* her, of course. Around the place. It's hard not to.'

The words alone suggest bitterness, but Hughes' tone is remarkably matter-of-fact and her body betrays no emotion. She's just sitting there, her hands grasped in her lap.

'When you saw Caleb on Friday night, what did he tell you?'

'He said she'd come on to him. That he'd said no, but she took no notice.'

'Do you know if he's spoken to anyone else about this?'

She shifts her position slightly. 'He told his mother.'

Ev makes a note. 'He did that here, when you were with him?'

She nods. 'I pushed him to. And she agreed with me – that he shouldn't just let it drop.'

Ev watches her for a moment. It's hard to see her being

anything other than envious of Fisher – her position, her prominence, her sheer power. Add to that a liberal dose of sexual jealousy and pretty much anything is possible.

But that doesn't mean she's not telling the truth.

*   *   *

There's a point, on the road back from Southampton, when Somer starts to feel she's nearly home. The rise over the Ridgeway, the subtle change in the landscape that marks the sweep down to Oxford. She's done the drive dozens of times since she started seeing Giles, and this moment, like the scenery, has always faced two ways. Backwards, to missing him; and forwards to work and everything she values about her own separate life. Today, for the first time, she's looking only one way. She's not going to think about what she's left behind.

As she passes the turn-off for Compton and East Ilsley she grips the steering wheel a little tighter and puts her foot down.

*   *   *

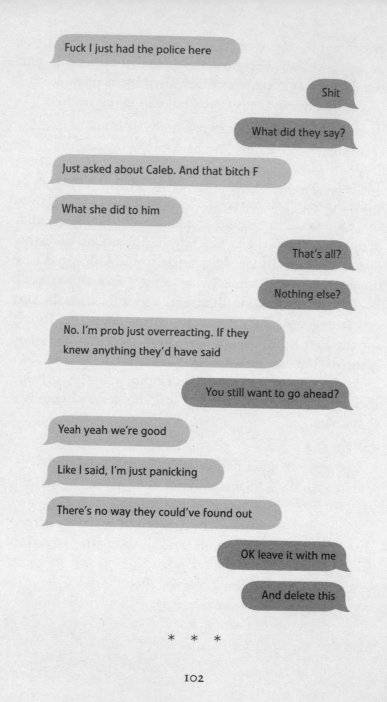

Fuck I just had the police here

Shit

What did they say?

Just asked about Caleb. And that bitch F

What she did to him

That's all?

Nothing else?

No. I'm prob just overreacting. If they knew anything they'd have said

You still want to go ahead?

Yeah yeah we're good

Like I said, I'm just panicking

There's no way they could've found out

OK leave it with me

And delete this

* * *

Alex was still asleep when I left for the gym and I decided not to wake her. She needs rest more than I need to demonstrate my keeper credentials by making her breakfast. But I do pick up two cappuccinos and a couple of almond croissants from her favourite place on my way back from the gym. Though as it turns out, I'm wasting my time.

The first thing I notice when I push open the front door is the smell of coffee; the second is the sound of voices. And it's not the radio. There's someone here.

I drop my keys on the hall table and my bag on the floor, and walk through to the back. Alex is sitting at the kitchen table in one of my old T-shirts, her feet bare, her hair twisted up in a loose knot, and in front of her, yet another bowl of that kids' cereal she can't get enough of at the moment. I tease her about it all the time but she just looks arch and says I should thank my lucky stars it's something so bland (and she has a point – with Jake, it was kippers).

Opposite her, her hands wrapped around my Mr Perfect mug (and yes, that is a joke), is a woman. I've seen her before. Emma something. She was at the same college as Alex years ago, but there isn't really a word for what they are now – not exactly friends but a bit more than acquaintances. She works for the council fostering and adoption service. Last year, when a couple of local builders found a traumatized young woman locked in a basement with her eighteen-month-old son, it was Emma who arranged for Alex and me to foster him for a few weeks. Though lest you should think I really am Mr Perfect I should say at once that it was against my better judgement, and, I suspect, against Emma's too, though we never discussed it. It was my wife's idea, and she is both very persistent and very persuasive. And if you know about that case, and that little boy, and you're wondering what happened to him, Brandon is doing well. He's with long-term foster parents who are hoping to adopt him. It's not my case any more, but I keep in touch. I don't have to, but I do.

'Adam, you remember Emma, don't you?'

We smile at each other, a little awkwardly. I'm uncomfortably aware that I didn't shower at the gym and even my own wife wouldn't want a clincher with me right now. So I just stand there, trying not to look like an oaf.

I raise a hand. 'Hi.'

Emma's smile doesn't quite reach her eyes. She has long strawberry-blonde hair and a pair of silver hoop earrings that she keeps fiddling with. I seem to remember her hair being darker the last time I saw her, but it's been quite a while. I could be wrong.

'Emma just popped by to drop off a present for the baby,' says Alex, levering herself out of her chair. I see now there's a white teddy bear sitting on the worktop beside her. It has a red bow tie and that slightly imploring look soft toys always manage to have.

'We were just having a bit of a catch-up –'

I start to back out of the kitchen. 'Great – absolutely. Totally fine by me.' I gesture towards the stairs. 'I'll just, you know, have a shower. Take your time.'

* * *

'Bloody hell,' says Baxter, sitting back in his chair. He'd had his earphones in but he's pulled them out now and is looking round at the rest of the team. 'I think you lot need to hear this.'

Quinn and Asante have only just got back from seeing Sandford – Quinn's still in the process of hanging up his jacket – but they all know Baxter, and if he says there's something, there's something.

'What you got?' asks Quinn as they start to gather round.

'I had a call a while back from Clive Conway,' says Baxter. 'He's got the results on the prints at Fisher's house. Nothing on the champagne glasses, as expected, but there were prints on the bottle. Both Fisher's *and* Morgan's.'

Quinn frowns. 'But they both said Morgan was the one who opened it, didn't they? So where does that get us?'

Baxter shakes his head. 'It's not just that. Apparently when Conway fished the bottle out of the bin, there was a whole load of broken glass in there too – and it was right at the top, so it couldn't have been in there very long.'

'So?' says Ev, looking increasingly mystified.

'So, it turns out it was another wine bottle – prosecco, Conway said. And there were prints on that too. Two different sets. One lot were Morgan's, but the others are unidentified. But one thing we do know – they're definitely *not* Marina Fisher's.'

Quinn's still frowning. 'And? Am I missing something?'

But Baxter hasn't finished. 'The only reason Conway bagged it up in the first place was because he remembered there were bits of broken glass on the front step when he arrived. Exactly the *same* broken glass. There can't be many ways that got there, can there? Not in that part of town. So barring a clumsy supermarket driver –'

Ev gives him a dry look. 'Oh yeah, fat chance. Trust me, Marina Fisher's Ocado list does *not* include prosecco. I doubt she'd even allow it in the house.'

Baxter raises an eyebrow. 'My thoughts exactly. So I did a bit of digging of my own.'

He leans forward and reaches for his keyboard. 'And as it turns out, a woman called Pat Hart rang 101 at just after nine the night of the dinner. She was on her way to meet a friend at the Playhouse bar.'

He turns up the volume and presses play.

Caller:	Hello? I'm ringing because there's some sort of incident going on at St Luke Street.
Call handler:	What sort of incident, madam?
Caller:	There's a man and a blonde woman arguing in the street. I just went by in a cab and they were really going at it. It looked to me like she'd had quite a lot to drink – she had a bottle in one hand and was waving it about.
Call handler:	Has there been any sort of physical altercation?
Caller:	I couldn't see that much just going past, but I did see him pushing her. Pretty hard, from what I could see – and he's quite a big bloke too.
	[*background noises*]

	Hang on a minute – the cab's dropped me off now and I'm walking back. I think I just heard the sound of breaking glass.
Call handler:	I'm arranging for an officer to attend –
Caller:	No, hold on – they're not there any more.
Call handler:	They've gone into one of the houses?
Caller:	I don't know – not that I can see. They were right there, on the corner, but they're not there now and I can't see where they went. Sorry – I didn't mean to waste your time.
Call handler:	No, that's absolutely fine. It's what we're here for. Could you just hold the line a moment, please, so I can take your details.

Baxter presses pause and there's an audible release of breath. Because even if the caller didn't give the exact address, they all know who she was talking about.

Caleb Morgan and Freya Hughes.

Ev looks around, her eyes wide. 'I was at her place less than an hour ago, asking about that night, and she never said a bloody *word* about this.'

'It's not just that, though, is it,' says Asante quietly. 'What that caller described – the pushing, the fact that Freya was drunk – it's exactly what Morgan said happened with Marina Fisher barely two hours later.'

Quinn is nodding. 'So either he shoved two different women that night –'

'Not impossible,' says Ev. 'Sadly.'

'– or he's manipulating the memory,' finishes Asante. 'Using the detail of a real incident to create a better fake one.' He looks at the others. 'You know what they say — best way to get away with a lie? Wrap it up in a whole lot of truth.'

* * *

'What do you want to eat?'

Emma stayed another two hours in the end. I don't know what they were talking about but it sounded pretty intense from where I was. But then again, that was out in the garden, so I didn't hear it all. Enough, though, to stop me crashing in to get myself some food, and as a result I'm now borderline hypoglycaemic.

'There's some cold chicken,' says Alex, staring into the fridge. 'And those avocados could do with eating too.'

Frankly, right now, I'd give my right arm for pie and chips.

'Everything OK with Emma?' I say it mostly to be polite, but Alex glances at me and gives a heavy sigh.

'She's having a bit of a hard time right now.'

I'm frowning, trying to remember something. 'Hasn't she got a new bloke, or am I making that up?'

Alex takes the mayonnaise out of the fridge and reaches towards the cutlery drawer for a spoon. 'She *had* a new relationship. Past tense. Last time I saw her she was really excited about it, but looks like it's all fallen apart already. She's always had zero luck in that department.'

I make what I hope are the appropriate sympathetic noises.

'And I know she'd like to have kids too.'

She doesn't say any more. She doesn't have to. Emma's the same age as Alex. It's the eleventh hour for her, just as it was for us. Only our miracle happened.

I move across and wrap my arms around my wife. She jumps a little and I assume it's my fault for surprising her, but then she reaches for my hand and places it gently over her belly, smiling up into my face.

'Looks like there are three of us in this hug.'

* * *

'Caleb?'

The line is crackling and breaking up, but he recognizes the voice.

'Hi, Mum.'

'I just wanted to check in – see how you're doing.'

He frowns; there's a delay on the line. An international delay that shouldn't be there. 'I thought you were due back today?'

A sigh. Or perhaps it's just more interference. 'I'm sorry, darling, something's come up here. I can't get to see the senator until Friday. But I've managed to get some other meetings in, and given it's the recess, there's no need to rush back.'

His turn to sigh. Clearly he doesn't qualify as a 'need'.

'Have you spoken to your father?'

He rolls his eyes. 'No. They're still in Sydney. You *know* that.'

'No need to take that tone,' she says crisply. 'At least I'm trying to *do* something. No doubt he's too busy being hipster dad to have time to support his *firstborn*.'

He bites his tongue. His mother is no less absent than his father, it's just a different sort of distance. But he knows from experience there's no point saying so.

'Now,' she says, 'I've spoken to Meredith – talked her through the whole thing – and they're going to call you, OK?'

And now he feels like a shit, because she has, for once, actually done something. 'Thanks, Mum. Appreciate it.'

'Only the best for you, my darling,' she says, with more than a whiff of singed martyr. 'You'll be in good hands – Meredith has a ton of experience in cases like this. So just do whatever she tells you, OK? And don't let yourself be bullied, either. Far too many victims back down because the police and CPS make it too damn ghastly to carry on.'

He smiles quietly. 'Don't worry about me, Mum. I've got it covered.'

* * *

Freya Hughes is hostile even before the door is fully open. 'What's this about? I've already told you everything I know.'

Ev gives a heavy sigh. 'No you haven't, and you know it. So are you going to let me in or would you prefer to do this at St Aldate's? Either's fine by me.'

Hughes' eyes widen for a moment, then she releases her grip on the door.

Ev follows her inside and Hughes turns to face her, folding her arms.

'When I was here earlier, I asked you about Marina Fisher and you said, "*I don't know her.*"'

She frowns.

'But you do, don't you? You certainly know where she lives. You were seen there on Friday night.'

She looks guarded, clearly unsure quite how much Ev knows. 'So?'

'So you never said anything about it. Why not?'

Hughes shrugs. 'It wasn't any of your business. It still isn't.'

'Oh, I think it is, don't you?' says Ev wearily. 'Your boyfriend makes an allegation of assault, and you don't mention that you were round there only two hours before, rowing in the street.'

'It wasn't *rowing* –'

'Well, pick your own word, but whatever it was, it was serious enough for a member of the public to call 101 and report it.'

Hughes turns away. 'I was just annoyed, that's all. We were supposed to go out that night but then Caleb cancelled at the last minute so he could do her bloody babysitting.'

'You were jealous.'

'Yeah, I was jealous,' she says acidly. 'Happy now?'

'So you turned up with a bottle of wine, thinking you could still spend some time together? But I'm guessing he wasn't expecting you.'

She looks sulky. 'It was supposed to be a surprise, wasn't it.'

'But he wouldn't let you in.'

Her expression hardens. 'He said he was working. That he didn't want to be disturbed. Even by me.'

'Especially as you were rather drunk already.'

There's a silence. Then Hughes sits down heavily on the window seat.

'OK,' she says, 'I'd had a few with my mates before I got there. But I wasn't *drunk*.'

'But he still didn't want you in the house.'

She looks away. 'He said I might wake up Tobin. That *Marina* wouldn't like it.' Her sarcasm is venomous.

'And he pushed you away. Quite hard, from what the 101 caller said.'

Her eyes narrow and she's suddenly wary. 'Well, they're wrong. He never touched me.'

'The caller was pretty sure. And she had no reason to lie.'

Even if you do. The unspoken words echo in the room.

'Like I said,' she says. 'It never happened.'

Ev breathes an inward sigh. How many times has she heard women say this? Women who've 'fallen down the stairs', 'walked into a door'.

'You do know that would be common assault, don't you? Pushing someone like that?'

'Oh, *please*.'

'I'm serious. Just because you're clever and educated and well off, doesn't mean you can't be a victim. Domestic violence can happen to anyone. And it often starts just like this – with things that seem trivial, only then there's a next time, and a next –'

'Are you thick or something? There won't be a *next* time, because there wasn't a *first* time.'

Ev makes a note, and takes her time doing it.

'So you smashed the bottle you'd brought and stormed off.'

Hughes' gaze flickers away, but she says nothing. This, at least, she can't deny.

'And then later that same night, he's on *your* doorstep, telling you he's been assaulted. By the same woman you'd been jealous of for months and whose house you weren't even allowed into only a few hours before. How did that feel?'

Hughes flushes. 'It wasn't like that.'

'What was it like then?'

'He needed someone to talk to – he wasn't thinking straight.'

'And you advised him to report her?'

'Of course I did. She tried to *assault* him. He had those scratches – he looked absolutely terrible. Aren't the police always telling people to come forward – that too many abusers get away with it because crimes like this don't get reported? Why should it be different just because it's a bloke?'

Ev nods. 'Yes, you're right, we do say that. But false allegations are just as damaging as failing to make an allegation at all – arguably, more so. So I'm going to ask you straight – did you encourage him to exaggerate what happened or falsify it in *any* way?'

'No.'

'Even though this woman had been monopolizing your boyfriend? Even though you admit how angry you were?'

'No. I didn't. I told him to go to the college and tell them the truth.' She holds Ev's gaze. *Just like I'm doing now.* She slides off the window seat and stands up. 'And I'd like you to leave now, please. I have nothing else to say.'

* * *

When I get to the office the following morning Quinn's already got a whiteboard going. Blown-up pictures of Caleb Morgan and Freya Hughes that look like they come from their student ID cards, four or five snaps from the Balliol dinner, a couple of them a bit unfocused. Not unlike most of the attendees, I imagine, by the end. Quinn's stuck a Post-it with an arrow on it next to one of them. It's pointing at Marina Fisher's wrist.

He comes up behind me as I'm standing there.

'I take it you heard the 101 call?'

I nod; he emailed the recording over yesterday afternoon.

'So, do we talk to Morgan?'

I shake my head. 'I can't see much point – Hughes is refusing to corroborate what the caller said and she's bound to have told him Ev went to see her by now. He's just going to come out with exactly the same story.'

'Makes a difference, though, doesn't it? To the allegation? Assuming we all agree Hughes is talking bullshit and he did actually push her, are we really supposed to believe he did exactly the same thing twice in the same night?'

I shrug. 'We can't prove he didn't. Perhaps he does that sort of thing to women all the time. And even if he did push Hughes, it doesn't mean he wasn't assaulted by Fisher. But you're right about one thing – we can't afford to base this whole case solely on Morgan's word. We couldn't before and we certainly can't now. So – what have we got?'

He makes a resigned face. 'Not much. I managed to speak to a few of Fisher's old colleagues at Imperial last night. The blokes were generally positive – thought she was great at her job, breath of fresh air, just what the department needed, blah blah blah. None of them bought the assault thing – the basic line was Fisher could fuck any bloke she liked so why bother trying to break into Morgan's jockeys. I'm paraphrasing, of course.'

I've lost count of the number of times I've heard that from sexual predators over the years: '*I can have any woman I want – I don't need to rape anybody.*' It never got any of them off the hook and it shouldn't be a get-out-of-jail card for Fisher either. Or am I just being naive? The law is blind, or ought to be, but sexual politics aren't symmetrical. Perhaps that simply isn't possible, however hard we try to rebalance the scales. Remember that old Joe Jackson song? Right or wrong, right *and* wrong, it's different for girls.

'And the women she worked with?'

Quinn makes a face. 'There were only two. One of them said she might have taken Fisher rather more seriously if she hadn't insisted on dressing like a prostitute.'

Yet another comment about her clothes. I can only assume she does it deliberately, to get a reaction. Does she really not care how divisive that reaction is?

'Take it from me,' says Quinn, '"fans of Marina Fisher" is the country's last remaining men-only club.'

I swing round to face the rest of the room. Baxter, Asante, Ev, and now, just coming through the door, Somer. She looks a bit flustered from being almost late, but tanned from a weekend in the sun and the wind. She's caught the sun and it suits her, but she doesn't look rested. She just looks stressed.

'Nice to see you, DC Somer – have you had a chance to get up to speed?'

She nods. 'Yes, sir. DC Everett sent me over some stuff last night.'

My phone pings. Bryan Gow is in reception.

'OK, everyone, while we wait for the DNA let's see if we can make any progress on the digital side.' I look around. 'And at the risk of repeating myself, Caleb Morgan's mother is going to be all over this sooner or later, and my money's on sooner. So do me a favour and keep up to date on the paperwork, all right?'

* * *

JosephAndrews2018 @JosephAndrews2018   9.17
Sending love & solidarity to a friend of mine who's a #sexualabuse victim at #OxfordUni. Abuse BY a professor ON a student. But this time the #abuser was a woman & the #victim was a GUY. This affects everyone, people. WHOEVER you are

#NOmeansNO #MeToo #HeToo

♡ 1   ↻ 7   ♡ 24   ↑

116

Annie Dexter @Adex201918   9.19

Replying to @JosephAndrews2018

This makes me so angry – no-one shd suffer this, men or women. I hope the uni authorities are being supportive & actually *believing* them. There's also loads of support services out there – Samaritans, Nightline, the OU Students Union

#sexualabuseaffectseveryone #MeToo #HeToo

🗨 3   ⇄ 5   ♡ 35   ⬆

Michaela Mitchell @1010101MM   9.22

Replying to @JosephAndrews2018 @Adex201918

12 THOUSAND men suffered sexual abuse in the UK last year, and a significant number of the perpetrators were women. It's not common, but it *does happen*

End #sexualabusebythoseinpower #MeToo AND #HeToo

🗨 1   ⇄ 2   ♡ 2   ⬆

Lorna Bartholomew @9_9_Starfish   9.22

Replying to @JosephAndrews2018

When was this incident? I'm involved in the @OxASV campaign and I've asked around but no one I know has heard anything about it. Are the police involved?

#OxfordAgainstSexualViolence #MeToo #HeToo

🗨 4   ⇄ 6   ♡ 11   ⬆

JosephAndrews2018 @JosephAndrews2018   9.28

Replying to @9_9_Starfish

A few days ago. The police are def on it though whether they're getting anywhere is another matter. Let's just say 'she' is *very* prominent

♡   ⇄   ♡   ⬆

Lorna Bartholomew @9_9_Starfish   9.29

Replying to @JosephAndrews2018

And how is he? Is he getting help?

♡   ⇄   ♡   ⬆

JosephAndrews2018 @JosephAndrews2018   9.29

Replying to @9_9_Starfish

Yeah, doing OK at the moment

♡   ⇄   ♡   ⬆

Oxford Against Sexual Violence @OxASV   9.29

Hearing reports of a serious sexual assault on a male student by a female academic. If you still need proof that #sexualviolenceaffectseveryone this is it. Let's stand strong with the men who've been on the receiving end of this #abuse and get the #HeToo hashtag trending

#VictHIM

♡ 27   ⇄ 65   ♡ 352   ⬆

*   *   *

Back at his desk, Andrew Baxter rolls up his sleeves. In every sense. It's not as hot as it was over the weekend but the office has no air con and the creaky fan in the corner is just circulating hot air. He cracks open a cold Red Bull and picks up Marina Fisher's phone.

* * *

Adam Fawley
9 July 2018
9.34

Bryan Gow is looking irritatingly fresh in a cream jacket and chinos, neither of which I've seen before. He has new glasses too, and — even more startling — a decent haircut. We've worked together for more than five years, but his personal life is still an enigma to me. I've always assumed he had far too many time-consuming geeky bloke hobbies to have room for a relationship, but this new look of his may suggest I'm wrong. Who knows, perhaps there really is a woman out there who put 'Maths-obsessed trainspotting Civil-War re-enactor' under WLTM.

'Interesting,' he says, looking up from the file. 'This one's hardly business as usual, is it?'

I make a face. 'It's a high-wire act over a bloody minefield. Morgan's mother is Petra Newson.'

His eyes widen. 'Ah. I see. Shit.'

I give a grim laugh. 'Yup, all of the above.'

'So you want me to review the interviews?'

I open up my laptop. 'Fisher's, particularly. Asante thinks something is off. Says her body language is all wrong. But there could be all sorts of assumptions at play here. See above under "minefield".'

119

'True, but DC Asante is a bright lad. Let's have a look, shall we?'

* * *

'I don't know, you just look a bit – off, that's all.'

They're in the ladies' loo on the first floor. Somer is leaning back against the basins and Everett's by the window, watching her friend and trying to decide if she should be worried. Somer has seemed so much happier since she started seeing Giles Saumarez. Ev's only met him once, but he seemed almost too good to be true, especially after that ill-advised fling Somer had with the undeniably attractive but calamitously unsuitable Gareth Quinn. Saumarez is in the job as well, so he understands the pressures, but not in the same force, which in Ev's opinion is a far safer idea (not that she's ever tried it). Giles is good-looking, considerate, supportive, funny. What's not to like? The only wisp of a cloud on the horizon was the imminent arrival of his two teenage daughters, coming from Canada for a three-week holiday. Ev knows Somer's been apprehensive about meeting them, and she was definitely much less enthusiastic than usual about going down to Southampton this weekend. Is that what this is all about?

'If it's the girls,' she begins, 'then it's completely understandable –'

Somer shakes her head. 'It's not that.' She takes a deep breath. 'A job's come up. In Hampshire. Giles thinks I should apply.'

Ev's eyes widen. 'What sort of job?'

'In the Domestic Violence Unit. They can't say so publicly but Giles knows they'd really like to appoint a woman and there aren't many obvious candidates in-house. And if I got it, they'd fast-track me through my sergeant's exams.'

'Sounds like you'd be mad not to give it a go. What have you got to lose?'

Somer looks away. 'I don't know. It just seems like a huge upheaval. I'd have to move – find somewhere to live –'

Ev frowns. 'But you'd be living with Giles, surely? Isn't that the whole point?'

Somer shrugs. 'I don't know. He's talked about the job but he hasn't said anything about that.'

'Well, perhaps that's just because he doesn't think he needs to?' Ev takes a step forward. 'Look, you've got a lot on your plate. You haven't been in CID that long, and then there's you and Giles, the girls coming over. You'd be a bit weird if you *weren't* wondering whether upping sticks and relocating your whole life is really that great an idea. But sleep on it for a bit – there's no need to make a decision right away, is there?'

Somer sighs. 'No. There's time.'

'Right, then. Just focus on the girls coming over for now. That's more than enough to be going on with.'

Somer smiles. 'I'm sorry – you're right. It's a great opportunity. I'm probably just overthinking it, as usual. I'm fine. Honestly.'

Ev gives her arm a quick squeeze. 'Well, you know where I am if you want a chat. Whenever, OK?'

After she's gone Somer turns and stares at her reflection

for a long time. The woman in the mirror doesn't look like someone on the threshold of an exciting new chapter. She doesn't look fine, either. She doesn't look 'fine' at all.

* * *

I lean forward and press pause. The video freezes mid-frame. Marina Fisher and her lawyer, and facing them, me. Asante isn't in the shot. Kennedy is saying something; Marina has her hands folded quietly on the table in front of her.

'So, what do you think?'

Gow sits back. 'Fascinating. Fisher's a piece of work, isn't she.'

I raise an eyebrow. 'That's one way of putting it.'

'And the clothes – the little-girl-lost look – is that the sort of thing she normally wears?'

I laugh drily. 'Er, no. One of her former colleagues described her as dressing like a call girl.'

His eyes widen. 'Ow. Or rather me-ow.'

'Quite.'

'I imagine that makes collegiate life a mite abrasive at times.'

'It's not making this case any easier either.'

'And you want to know if she's telling the truth?'

'Well, is she?'

He gives me a narrow look. 'Not entirely, no.'

* * *

Oxford Against Sexual Violence @OxASV   10.02

This latest #Oxford incident is a timely reminder that #sexualviolenceaffectseveryone, men AND women. Pls RT to show support

#HeToo #VictHIM

💬 62   ⟲ 211   ♡ 677   ↑

Ricky Jamieson @Hatrick333   10.02

I was assaulted by my female professor too. It was ten years ago and I never had the courage to #speakout. Standing with the #OxfordVictim today

#HeToo #VictHIM

💬 11   ⟲ 48   ♡ 97   ↑

Darren Jessop @COYSboy4evva   10.04

Replying to @Hatrick333

It happened to #MeToo. Blokes are too embarrassed to speak out because people might think they're weak. And as for the cops – forget it. I never said anything either and it f*cked me up for years. But I'm doing it now

#HeToo #VictHIM

💬 17   ⟲ 35   ♡ 71   ↑

Rupert Deller @DellaFellaxx1313   10.05

Replying to @Hatrick333 @COYSboy4evva @OxASV

Tagging @SurvivorsUK too – they do amazing work supporting sexually abused boys & men & their families

#standupandspeakup #HeToo #VictHIM

💬 27   ⟲ 51   ♡ 75   ↑

Shirley Farrell @3579littlewhiteline   10.06

Replying to @Hatrick333 @COYSboy4evva @OxASV @DellaFellaxx1313

I'm a #rapesurvivor too. My attacker was over 6 feet and 17 stone. There was nothing I could do. It's not the same for men – it just isn't

#womenagainstviolenceagainstwomen

💬 1   🔁   ♡   ⬆

Oxford Against Sexual Violence @OxASV   10.07

Replying to @3579littlewhiteline

Your experience must have been truly horrific. But men really can experience sexual violence too. The nature of it may be different, but it's just as real for the victims. Hope you're getting the support you need

#sexualabuseaffectseveryone

💬   🔁   ♡   ⬆

Kath Beecham @KathyLatte_73065   10.07

Replying to @Hatrick333 @COYSboy4evva @OxASV @DellaFellaxx1313

What worries me is the prospect of this story getting picked up and used by the male violence apologists and woman-haters. It'll be meat and drink to them, sadly

💬 7   🔁 5   ♡ 9   ⬆

Oxford Against Sexual Violence @OxASV   10.08

So moved and proud of the guys speaking up about their experiences of #sexualharassment on campus today

#standupandspeakup #endvictimblaming #sexualabuseaffectseveryone

#HeToo #VictHIM

💬 199   🔁 442   ♡ 1.1k   ⬆️

* * *

Adam Fawley
9 July 2018
11.20

Gow rewinds the tape, then plays it again, slow motion now, the sound on mute. I watch, frame by frame. Fisher keeps eye contact, her hands still calm in front of her. There's no tell-tale fidgeting, no foot tapping. Her body is controlled, her movements minimal.

'And this,' says Gow, 'is where you ask her how the dress got damaged. Watch how she replies.'

On the screen, I see Fisher pause, then mouth 'I don't remember'. That's all. Gow presses stop, rewind and play, slowing it down even more. 'Did you see it that time?'

'What am I looking for?'

'Just before she speaks there's a minute nod of the head – it's almost imperceptible, but it's there. Her words say one thing, but her body says something else. In general, her physical composure is pretty impressive, but a micro-gesture like that, it's beyond the control of the conscious mind. Even if the mind in question does belong to an Oxford professor.'

'So you think she does remember how the dress got damaged, she just doesn't want to say so?'

'That would be my guess, yes.'

'But when she says she can't remember any physical contact with Morgan, that's genuine?'

'Yes,' he says slowly, but he's frowning now, and so am I. There's something here that's not adding up.

Gow hesitates then sits forward. 'Do you by any chance have Morgan's tape?'

* * *

The Vowels
online

- Tim Palmer
Is there something up with Marina, does anyone know? She just pulled out of the BusinessWeek AI conference next month   10:22

- Kate Kesson
Wasn't she the keynote at that?   10:23

- Ron Sandford
Er, I think she may be 'otherwise engaged'....   10:27 ✓✓

- Kate Kesson
What's that supposed to mean?   10:28

- Ron Sandford
My lips are sealed ☹   10:29 ✓✓

- Kate Kesson
FFS Ron, just give will you   10:31

- Ron Sandford
Let's just say I had a visit at the w/e From the 'authorities'....   10:35 ✓✓

- Ron Sandford
🎤   10:35 ✓✓

- Tim Palmer
Holy shit   10:38

Type a message

* * *

127

I load the disk and we watch, and then Gow rewinds it and plays it again, before pressing pause, sitting back and giving me an enquiring look. And now I know what I'm looking for, I can see it myself. Marina Fisher isn't the only one who isn't telling the whole truth. There's something about that night Caleb Morgan doesn't want to admit either. To me, to his girlfriend, perhaps even to himself.

I just have to find out what it is.

There's a knock at the door.

Quinn.

'Sorry to barge in, boss, but there are some people downstairs to see you.'

I frown. 'Can't you deal with it?'

He shakes his head. 'Tried that. They're not having it.'

He hands me a couple of business cards. Thick, textured paper stock, a confident, understated logo. A City law firm so prestigious even I've heard of them. And these people are both partners. I was expecting a top-end Oxford outfit but Petra Newson has gone straight for SWAT.

'OK,' I say, 'show them into the first-floor meeting room, will you?'

He raises an eyebrow. 'You're putting them in the cheap seats?'

I give him a look. 'We don't want them getting too comfortable, do we?'

* * *

'Anything interesting?'

Baxter looks up. Somer's standing behind him, looking over his shoulder.

He gestures at the phone. 'Ev was right about the prosecco. Marina Fisher buys her wine by the case from Berry Brothers & Rudd. She also spends at least a grand a month on clothes and has over ten thousand Twitter followers, how's that for starters?'

Somer nods. 'Doesn't surprise me. Any of it.' She seems distracted, fiddling with the end of her hair.

'Apart from that,' says Baxter, 'I haven't got much. Though as far as I can see there wasn't anything going on between Morgan and Fisher before all this blew up.'

Somer moves round and stands in front of him. 'What difference would that make?'

She's staring at him, her fists clenched, and he blinks; where the hell has this come from? It's not like her. 'It's just that –'

'You think if you're in a relationship with someone you don't get to say no? Is that it?'

Baxter's gone red now; he can sense Asante out of the corner of his eye. He'd been typing but he isn't any more. He's staring at them. The room is gradually falling silent.

'Of course not. But it can make a difference – in court – you *know* that – look what happened with that Met case –'

'I don't believe this,' she says, turning on her heel and walking away. 'I don't *fucking* believe it.'

Baxter stares after her then looks across at Asante. 'Did I miss something?'

Asante shrugs. 'Search me.'

The woman is in a tailored dress, the man in an open-neck white shirt and one of those slim royal-blue suits that seem to be the thing these days. They rise as I enter and we shake hands.

'Meredith Melia,' says the woman as I take my seat, 'and this is my colleague Patrick Dunn. We're representing Caleb Morgan.'

'Thank you for the information, but I'm not sure why you're here. Mr Morgan is the victim of an alleged crime, he doesn't need "representation".'

She smiles. 'I'm sure you can appreciate that Mr Morgan's family are very concerned that he receive the best possible advice and support.'

'He's been offered the assistance of an Independent Sexual Violence Adviser, and he has a dedicated police point of contact. The whole team is working extremely hard on his behalf. I'm not sure what other sort of support Mr Morgan needs that his family can't provide themselves.'

Another smile. 'It's not that simple, though, is it, Inspector? This is a very unusual situation and the issues are both complex and exceptionally sensitive. The family is particularly concerned that Mr Morgan's privacy should be protected.'

'You can rest assured that we will treat Mr Morgan with the same respect and consideration that we give everyone else in his position, male or female, and regardless of who their "family" are.'

The lawyers exchange a glance.

'Perhaps you could take us through the evidence you have assembled thus far?'

'No.'

'You're refusing to do that?'

I sit back. 'I'm under no obligation to. And if, in due course, I reach a point where I do want to have that conversation, I will have it with Mr Morgan. Whether he wants any of you in the room at the time will be entirely up to him.'

The woman frowns. 'We were assured of your cooperation –'

'Really? By whom?'

She opens her mouth to reply but I hear Dunn clear his throat.

'We're all on the same side, Inspector. I appreciate you don't particularly like a bunch of rogue tanks turning up on your lawn but we're not here to trip you up, get under your feet or generally make your life any harder than it already is. But it strikes us – and we hope you agree – that a policy of full and open communication would minimize the possibility of anything untoward appearing in the press, and make a successful outcome a lot more likely.'

I'm tempted to ask whether their client has also been adhering to that 'full and open policy' of theirs, because right now, I wouldn't bet on it.

Dunn looks at the woman. 'I think our best course would be to let Detective Inspector Fawley return to his work. There'll be time enough for a fuller briefing when the DNA results come back.'

I show them back to the front desk and stand there, watching them out through the door and down the street. That comment about the DNA wasn't a throwaway remark or a lucky guess. It was a message, and not a very subtle one: these people have backchannels and they're going to use them. They're giving me a choice: I can do this the hard way or the easy way, but if I know what's good for me I'll shut up and play nice.

They're getting into a car now, a black Merc with tinted windows that's just stopped on the yellow line a few yards up. As it pulls away into the buses and the bikes, I realize suddenly that there's someone else in the street. Someone I recognize.

I hesitate a moment, wondering if it's just a coincidence. But you know by now what I think about coincidences. And as our eyes meet across the traffic, I know I'm right.

We have to wait for a bus to pass, but a few moments later we're standing face to face on the crowded pavement.

'Hello, Adam,' she says.

* * *

Alex Fawley has reached the point in her pregnancy where her baby is a good deal more active than she is. She's always so tired now, and it's not just the heat. When Adam's at work she spends most of the day lying on the bed with the blinds down. She can't even summon the energy to read, just plugs in her headphones or has the TV on in the background, treating it like radio.

She pours herself a glass of iced water and wanders

back into the sitting room. There's no one parked outside. No one unfamiliar, anyway. Just the Hamiltons' SUV and the grey Fiat Uno owned by that woman a bit further down whose name Alex still doesn't know. The white van hasn't been back. Or at least she doesn't think it has. But would he really be stupid enough to use a vehicle he knew she'd be looking for? If it was her, she'd go to a rental place. Get something bland and forgettable. And a different one each time, just to make sure. This man isn't stupid; if he's using a white van it's intentional. Because he *wants* her to know he's there. To scare her – deliberately scare her –

Her heart quickens and the baby turns, uneasy. She sits down slowly, willing her pulse to slow. Adam keeps asking her if everything's OK – if she's seen the van again – and she keeps just smiling and saying no. She doesn't want him worrying – or starting to think she's losing her mind. Because it makes no sense, she knows that: Gavin Parrie is miles from here, tagged, monitored, curfewed. But her fear just won't go away.

She cradles her body now, feeling the baby settle.

'Don't worry, sweet one,' she whispers, the tears gathering in her eyes. 'You're safe. Daddy would never let anyone hurt us. You and I are his whole world.'

* * *

Reynolds can't see me till gone two. The PA tells me he 'has a lunch' so would I 'come to the Lodgings'. No doubt they want to keep the likes of me from contaminating their hallowed turf. Given I have time on my hands, I opt to walk. Up St Aldate's and through Cornmarket. The sun is bringing them all out – Jehovah's Witnesses, a choir of Seventh Day Adventists, the local Islamic centre and a kiosk informing me that '*The Message of the Cross is foolishness to those who are perishing*'. Though parching might be a better word, given the temperature. And all of it jumbled up any-old-how with the payday lenders, a stall selling sunglasses and smiley-face cushions, and that carrot-haired regular who plays the bagpipes. (There's a furious-looking little old lady standing right opposite him with a knotted handkerchief on her head and a placard that says REBUILD HADRIAN'S WALL. That's Oxford for you – never knowingly under-nuttered.) It's six-deep in tourist groups most of the way so progress is slow, though at least most of those are managing to keep their clothes on. Unlike the locals, who are going hell for leather into another round of the Great British Kit-Off. If there was a law against raw bloke moobs in a built-up area I'd need to send for reinforcements.

When I get to the lodgings the flunkey at the door shows me through to the garden. Which is, of course, glorious – a green half-acre of lawns and honeysuckle and rose beds tended to within an inch of their lives. There are a couple of blokes there now, weeding and dead-heading. Needless to say, these chaps are keeping their shirts firmly on. As is Reynolds, who's in a white linen number, sitting under an umbrella with a laptop open in front of him on a mosaic table. He gestures to an adjacent chair.

'Take a seat, Inspector. I won't be a moment. Do help yourself to lemonade. My wife makes it – an old family recipe.'

Forcing me to watch him fiddle about with emails is pretty low-grade stuff as power plays go, but the lemonade isn't bad, so I content myself with the view. Somewhere nearby someone's playing the piano. Mozart. That's not bad, either.

'Right,' says Reynolds a few moments later, taking off his glasses and pushing the laptop slightly to one side. Though he doesn't – I note – close it altogether. 'What can I do for you?'

'We're making headway with the inquiry, sir, but I could do with some more background. A clearer picture of both Morgan and Fisher.'

He reaches for his glass. 'Off the record, you mean.'

'I'm not a journalist – we don't work by those rules. I can't guarantee that anything you tell me won't end up in the public domain, but it won't do so gratuitously. Police officers may be a touch bull-headed on occasion, but we do try to keep out of china shops.'

He smiles, a little uneasily, evidently unsure how to reply. Then the smile subsides. 'So what do you want to know?'

'Let's start with Marina Fisher. I find the situation with her ex-husband a little odd.'

He frowns. 'How so? They got married, they got unmarried, he went back to Boston. It was a lot cleaner than most divorces I've been forced to witness.'

'But that's my point. Joel Johnson went back to the US. How old was Tobin when they separated? A year? Even younger? And yet Johnson was perfectly happy to leave him behind, knowing he'd scarcely ever see him. You don't think that's odd?'

Reynolds gives me a heavy look. 'Not really. Tobin Fisher isn't Joel Johnson's child.'

So that's it.

'In fact, he was the reason for the divorce.'

'Fisher had an affair?'

Reynolds takes a sip of lemonade and puts the glass down. 'I gather "one-night stand" would be a more accurate description.'

'But she's sure the child isn't Johnson's?'

'He was in the US for most of that term. And in any case, Johnson is African American.'

He's looking at me as if this is a tutorial and he's just caught me out for not doing enough prep. And he's right – irritating, but right: I should have known that. I should have looked Johnson up.

'Fisher was at Edith Launceleve at the time?'

He nods. 'It was her second or third year. But I'd known her before that. It was largely down to me that she came here. I was the one who persuaded her to leave Imperial. And it took some doing, I can tell you.'

If I'd come right out with it and asked him what size of dog he has in this fight I couldn't have got a clearer answer. He's up to his neck in it. Mastiff-level.

'I know what you're thinking,' he says. 'And the answer is no.'

'No, what?'

'No, I'm not Tobin's father. I have never had that sort of relationship with Marina.'

I sit back a little. 'Do you know who the father is?'

He shakes his head. 'Like I said, she described it as a one-night stand. It's possible she never even told him Tobin exists.'

'And she went ahead with the pregnancy, even though she must have known it would torpedo the marriage?'

He shrugs. 'She wanted children, Joel didn't. And given her age –'

He spreads his hands as if the rest goes without saying. And it does. Especially to me.

'Has she had relationships since?'

He considers. 'One or two. But before you ask, I can assure you they have all been entirely age-appropriate.'

'So men in their forties.'

'Or older, yes. I have never, in all the years I have known her, seen Marina take any interest in a student or a significantly younger man. This whole episode – it would be totally out of character.'

I note the conditional tense. And move on.

'What about Caleb Morgan? Is this "episode" out of character for him too?'

Reynolds folds his hands on his lap. 'Clearly, I haven't known him as long, given he's been here less than a year. But by all accounts he is an honest, hard-working and – if I dare use such an out-of-favour term – honourable young man.'

'So if I were to tell you, purely theoretically, that he may have had an altercation with his girlfriend on the night of the alleged assault – that he may have pushed her – what would you say?'

His eyes narrow. 'I'd say I find it hard to believe.' He hesitates. 'That wasn't "theoretical" at all, was it?'

I let the silence lengthen, and I see his unease rise.

He reaches for the jug and refills his glass. 'I don't envy you, Inspector, taking this on. We're the other side of the looking glass here; nothing about it makes any sense.'

But then again, this is Oxford. When it comes to through the looking glass, this place wrote the book.

* * *

Chloe Blanchflower @Whitepetal1_99_1   18.22
Anyone else heard about this #Oxford thing with a guy getting assaulted by his female tutor?

#HeToo #VictHIM

💬 4   ⟲ 9   ♡ 9   ↑

Carmel Piper @NosyRosy1998   18.24
Replying to @Whitepetal1_99_1
I've been asking around about that since I saw it on here but no one seems to know anything. Copying @JosephAndrews2018

#HeToo #VictHIM

💬 8   ⟲ 21   ♡ 22   ↑

* * *

Alex Fawley checks her phone again. Still nothing from
Adam. She knows he leaves his mobile in his locker when
he's at the gym, and he did say he might have to go somewhere afterwards, but he's still more than an hour later
than he said he'd be.

She leans over and picks up her tablet, navigates to the
page and presses play. Just as well Adam isn't here because
he'd be furious with her if he knew. When they heard The
Whole Truth organization were going to make a podcast
about the Parrie case he made her promise she wouldn't listen. He said they'd just be out for headlines – that whatever
angle they took, digging about in the past couldn't change it,
so why torture herself going through it all again. It wouldn't
be good for her, and it wouldn't be good for the baby. And
he was right, of course he was right, but she still can't stop
herself. Because she knows what's coming: whatever their
agenda is, whatever 'angle' they come up with, they'll still
have to talk about *her* – about her and about Adam.

And what if they aren't just digging about in the past? What if they've actually found something?

What if they know what she did?

What then?

* * *

Quinn's first in the office on Tuesday. It's almost like old times, back when he was the real DS and not just keeping Gis's seat warm: getting set up for the morning meeting, picking up CID emails. He does another quick check (find a spare marker pen, turn the fan on – much good it'll do), then takes a seat at the front and opens up his tablet. Next arrival is Baxter. Sweating already, and grumbling to himself about parking. He looks around and frowns.

'Ev in yet?'

Quinn shakes his head. 'Haven't seen her. I think Asante's about somewhere. Try the coffee machine.'

'It's too bloody hot for coffee,' mutters Baxter, though that doesn't stop him heading off in the same direction. By the time he gets back, Ev's at her desk, pulling out her notebook. Baxter goes straight over to her.

'Morning,' she says brightly, then frowns slightly. 'You OK?'

Baxter moves a bit closer and seems about to reply but then something changes his mind and he turns away.

Quinn turns to look: that 'something' was Somer, coming in from the corridor. Quinn's eyes narrow. He picked up a bit of an undercurrent on that score yesterday, but no one actually said anything. And Somer does look more preoccupied than usual, no question. She's keeping her head down, staring at her paperwork, avoiding conversation, which isn't like her. He sees Ev go over and say a word or two in a low voice but she gets nothing but a brief shake of the head by way of reply.

They have to wait another quarter of an hour for Fawley, which isn't like him either, and by the time he turns up the silence in the room has started to become uncomfortable. But either he doesn't notice or simply isn't interested in pleasantries this morning. He just pulls out a chair and nods at Quinn.

'Right,' says Quinn, snapping into DS mode. 'We've had Fisher's blood test and tox screen back, and the bloods confirm she'd been drinking —'

Fawley's staring at his phone. 'Which is no great revelation, seeing as she told us that herself.'

Quinn ploughs on. 'Her blood alcohol was easily over the drink-drive limit, but not high enough to cause a blackout on its own. *However*, according to the tox screen she's taking medication for anxiety.' He looks down at his tablet. 'Something called Fluoxetine. Basically the same as Prozac. She's on quite a low dose, but apparently it can cause drowsiness if you drink when you're on it.'

A glance up now. 'But not actual blackouts?'

Quinn shakes his head. 'Not usually, but no doctor's going to get on the stand and rule it out one hundred per cent. At least according to Challow.'

'What about the DNA?'

Quinn swipes his screen. 'Ah, now that's where it gets interesting. Fisher's DNA was definitely present on Morgan's arms and hands. Fisher's lawyer will obviously claim that could have got there just from casual social contact or being in the house, but she's going to find it a hell of a lot harder to explain why it was also on Morgan's face *and* all over his privates.' He looks around with a smirk. 'He didn't get *that* from passing her a glass of chardonnay, now did he?'

Baxter grins, but Fawley is frowning. 'Define "privates".'

Quinn flushes a little. 'Sorry – basically down towards his groin. Definitely under where his shorts would have been so there's no way –'

'But not on his penis?'

Quinn shakes his head. 'No. Just in that general area.'

'And the scratches?'

'Yup,' says Quinn. 'They were down to her too.'

Ev nods. 'All of which tallies exactly with what he told us.'

Fawley glances at her. 'I think we all know where you stand.'

Ev's eyes widen. 'I didn't mean –'

Fawley turns to Quinn. 'And Fisher?'

He shakes his head. 'Nothing on her body or under her fingernails, but given she'd showered we'd pretty much discounted that already.' He stops, makes a face. 'Look, I know the DNA backs up Morgan's version of events as far as it goes, but it's also consistent with a bit of consensual fumble that just petered out. He *says* he told her to stop, but we're never going to prove that. The only people who'll ever know the truth are the two of them.'

'Make that the one of them,' says Baxter, folding his arms. 'Fisher doesn't remember either way. Allegedly.'

Fawley puts down his mobile, takes a breath. 'OK. Just because we don't have sufficient evidence to run with this won't stop people expecting us to. Or assuming that if we don't, it must be down to either bias, incompetence or undue influence.' He stands up now, tucks his phone into his jacket. 'I've arranged to see the CPS specialist rape prosecutor this afternoon. If they say it's worth pursuing, we'll keep pushing; if they don't, we can drop it with a clear conscience and reasonable air cover.'

'If you drop this case it'll be because *I* say so. And not before.'

They swing round. It's Superintendent Harrison, in the doorway.

'And in the meantime, perhaps someone could explain to me how come it's suddenly all over the bloody internet?' Fury is pulsating off him like microwaves.

Silence.

You can almost hear people holding their breath, but Fawley stares him out. 'I wasn't aware that it was –'

'Sharpen up, Inspector,' says Harrison, striding across the room and thrusting a sheet of paper in his face. 'Look at this stuff – Twitter, Facebook – the press office are imploding – I've had Fisher's lawyer on the phone, the ACC wants someone's head on a spike –'

And it's not going to be Harrison's. That much is clear.

'I can assure you, sir,' Fawley begins, 'that no one on my team has been speaking to the press.'

Because it just isn't worth it. Because this is exactly the sort of shit that was bound to follow, and they all know it.

But Harrison isn't listening. 'Don't *assure* me, Fawley. If your lot didn't do this, find out who did. And fast. Otherwise it'll be your sorry arse in front of the ACC explaining why not.' He hurls a glance round the rest of the team. 'And in the meantime, I suggest the rest of you just *do your bloody jobs.*'

He casts another furious stare at Fawley then sweeps out of the room, taking all the remaining oxygen with him.

* * *

Sent: Tues 10/07/2018, 10.35   **Importance: High**
From: InspKarlJacobs@BritishTransport.police.uk
To: CID@ThamesValley.police.uk

Subject: FATAL INCIDENT ALERT: WALTON WELL BRIDGE

At approx 01.25 hours this morning, 10/07/18, a crew of Network Rail engineers working on the line north of Oxford station saw suspicious activity on the above bridge. A freight locomotive was due to pass along the line, but the crew were able to phone through to the driver and halt the train at the last moment. However, the person discovered below the bridge was found to be already deceased. There were no identifying items or documents on the body. The initial assumption was suicide, but examination at the scene identified some injuries that may not be consistent with a death consequent on a fall from height. That being the case, I have fast-tracked the PM.

C. R. Boddie will officiate, and one of my officers will attend. I will keep you informed.

Karl Jacobs
Inspector, British Transport Police, Oxfordshire
Oxford Railway Station, Park End St, Oxford OX1 1HN

* * *

Baxter puts his hand up for tracing the Twitter rumour on the grounds that it would have come his way anyway, and he knows from experience that stepping up is a better look than crapped on.

He has a private bet with himself that Fawley will be chivvying within the hour, but it's barely half that when he looks up from his computer to see the DI standing there. He looks harassed, more harassed than usual, even allowing for the super-charged Super.

'Any progress?'

Baxter sits back. 'Well, I think I may have worked out which account it started from. Fisher's never mentioned by name but if you're part of that whole Oxford thing I bet it'd be pretty bloody obvious who they're referring to.'

Fawley comes round and stands behind him, bending over the screen. 'Show me.'

The phone rings now and Quinn picks up. 'CID.' He listens for a moment, then, 'OK, give me that address again – 62a Shrivenham Close, Headington. Right. We'll send someone over.'

He puts the phone down and gets to his feet, tugging his jacket off the chair. 'Ev? Think I'll need you with me on this one.'

She looks up. 'Problem?'

'Woman's been reported missing. Didn't turn up for work today and hasn't been answering her phone. A colleague's just been over to check and found the front door open but no one inside. That was Uniform on the blower – given no one's seen or spoken to her for over twelve hours they don't want to take any chances. They want one of us to take a look.'

Righting the Wrongs, s3:
The Roadside Rapist Redeemed?
7 JULY 2018

S3 Ep2: Paula   / 23:55

Righting the Wrongs: The Roadside Rapist Redeemed? Episode 2. Gavin Parrie
served more than 18 years for a series of brutal sex crimes he has always claimed he
did not commit. In this podcast, Jocelyn Naismith of The Whole Truth revisits the
case and tries to find answers to some of the worrying questions that remain
unresolved. Was the original investigation botched? Did one of the victims collude
with the police in providing the crucial evidence? Could the real perpetrator still be
out there?

[ARCHIVE OF TONY BLAIR ACCEPTANCE SPEECH, ELECTION NIGHT 1997. FADE
TO 'THINGS CAN ONLY GET BETTER' – D:REAM]

[FADE OUT]

[JOCELYN]

Things may have been about to get better for the country, but for some
people 2nd May 1997 marked the very worst of times.

A young girl called Paula, for one. She spent that night in A&E at
Manchester Royal Infirmary, after being attacked and sexually
assaulted.

And for Gavin Parrie, that night triggered a chain of events that led
eventually to his arrest, conviction and 18 years' imprisonment for the rape
and attempted rape of seven young women in the Oxford area.

So how did an isolated albeit brutal incident in Manchester get linked to a
series of assaults that took place almost a year later, and nearly two
hundred miles away?

I'm Jocelyn Naismith, and I'm the co-founder of The Whole Truth, a
not-for-profit organization that campaigns to overturn miscarriages
of justice. This is Righting the Wrongs, series 3: The Roadside Rapist
Redeemed?

Chapter two: Paula

[THEME SONG – AARON NEVILLE COVER VERSION OF 'I SHALL BE RELEASED']

[JOCELYN]

We're calling this young woman Paula, but that's not her real name. Her case has never come to trial, and her identity has always been protected, but even if we can't divulge her name we've been able to piece together a broad narrative of her life from people who knew her.

Paula had been in the care system since she was 6 years old. Her mother was a drug addict, and she never knew her father. Like Gavin Parrie, she'd dropped out of school early, and by 16 she was earning her living as a sex worker. None of that, of course, excuses what happened to her, but it does explain what she was doing in a known red-light area, in the early hours of the morning.

But Paula wasn't raped by a client, nor by one of the regular cruising punters. She'd never seen her assailant before. But she did *see* him. And in due course she was asked to identify him in a line-up. A line-up that included Gavin Parrie.

But I'm getting ahead of myself. We know why Paula was on Lockhart Avenue that night. But what about Gavin – was he there, and if he was, what was he doing?

The answer, of course, is simple.

Sex.

By early 1997 the relationship between Gavin and his wife, Sandra, was breaking down.

[SANDRA]

'All we seemed to do was argue. About the kids, the house, money. Especially money. His brothers both had proper trades but he was still stuck doing casual work, and going cap in hand to them for the odd labouring job here and there. I think he just found it humiliating, especially with Bobby, him being younger and all that. In the end he spent most of his time sitting about on the couch all day watching TV and drinking cider. And then he'd be out all hours at night and rolling in pissed just when I was trying to get the kids up for school.'

[JOCELYN]

It was hardly the healthiest of lifestyles, and it must have been about this time that Gavin started to develop Type 1 diabetes, though that wouldn't be formally diagnosed for some years yet. And just to flag: that's another one of those apparently insignificant facts that will turn out to be important later.

But back in 1997, it wasn't just Gavin's health that was in trouble.

[SANDRA]

'It got to the point when it was really taking a toll on the kids – they were tiptoeing round him all the time, and Stacey started getting into trouble at school. That's when I knew I'd have to do something. It just wasn't fair on them, never mind me. Though I want it on the record that he never ever hit me. Yeah, he was an angry man, bloody angry, but it was all directed at himself. He thought he'd failed. As a husband, as a dad. As a man.'

[JOCELYN]

Sandra doesn't want to be interviewed about this on air, but it's clear from talking to her that this wasn't the only aspect of the marriage that had gone wrong. The physical side of the relationship had all but disintegrated too, especially after the birth of their third child, Ryan, in 1995. It wasn't long before Gavin was turning to prostitutes for sex.

It was just another example of Gavin's habitual bad luck that he chose May 2nd to make his first foray into the Manchester red-light district. He was driving a white van at the time – another hand-me-down from his younger brother, Bobby. A number of the girls working that stretch remembered seeing it.

This is 'Lexi'. That's not her real name. She's worked Lockhart Avenue for ten years. She knew Paula back then, and remembers what she was like.

['LEXI']

'She was a nice kid. Really small and skinny. Some of the older girls used to mother her a bit. I guess they were worried that she was attracting the perverts, looking so young and that. She wasn't as fragile as she looked, though she was deffo a bit dense sometimes. Naive, you know? Which is the last bloody thing you need in this job. You have to get good at spotting the weirdos. The ones who just want to hurt you. She was crap at that.'

[JOCELYN]

Paula may well have been a little naive, but she didn't become a victim because of it. She didn't go with the wrong punter, because it wasn't a punter who assaulted her. The man who attacked her grabbed her from behind, dragged her into the undergrowth and bound her wrists with cable ties, before attempting to rape her.

And if you think some of that sounds familiar, you're right: all of these came to be hallmarks of the predator the press would later christen the 'Roadside Rapist'.

But all that was months in the future. In 1997, all the police knew was that Paula had been viciously assaulted. And they faced an uphill battle finding who did it because there was no DNA, and no forensics. But they did have one thing on their side.

Paula saw who did it. Only for a moment, as he scrambled to his feet and ran off into the night. But she saw his face.

So all they had to do was find him. Because they knew that as soon as they got him into an ID parade, they'd have their man. Simple, right?

Wrong.

[DESMOND WHITE]

'The first time I saw Gavin was in the custody suite at Northampton Road police station.'

[JOCELYN]

That's Des White. He was Gavin's solicitor back then. Or rather he was the Legal Aid lawyer who happened to be next on the roster the night Gavin was arrested.

It was just after eleven on May 5th, three days after Paula had been attacked. But a lot had happened in those three days.

[DESMOND]

'There was a huge police operation in Lockhart Avenue after the assault. And for the most part the girls were very cooperative. After all, they didn't want a sexual predator on the loose any more than anyone else.'

[JOCELYN]

As it turned out, none of the girls had seen what happened to Paula, though one of them did see a man in a dark hoodie running away about the time the attack took place. But that wasn't much use on its own. The police needed more. And after a couple of days, they got it.

The CCTV trawl yielded footage of a white van accelerating away from the area. It was Gavin's van, still registered at the time to his brother, Bobby. Though it didn't take the police long to trace who'd really been driving it that night.

Armed with the van's number plate, they started to piece together Gavin's movements in the hours leading up to the assault. Soon they could not only place him at the scene, they also had footage of him filling up the van earlier that evening, at a petrol station two miles away.

He was wearing a dark hoodie.

[DESMOND]

'It was all circumstantial, of course. It didn't prove anything. But it was enough for an arrest, and it was enough to get Gavin into an ID parade.'

[JOCELYN]

Gavin was taken to the Northampton Road station and questioned there for several hours, throughout which he steadfastly refused to answer any questions. But the police weren't that concerned. They still thought they had their man. All they needed was Paula to identify him and the case would be closed.

Gavin was Number 3 in the identity parade. He remembers it vividly, because he'd always thought 3 was his lucky number. And perhaps he was right. Because when Paula was asked if she recognized anyone in the line-up, she answered immediately, and without hesitation.

No.

[DESMOND]

'That should have been the end of it. But things don't always go the way they should, especially when it comes to the criminal justice system. The police didn't believe that Paula hadn't recognized him – some of the officers were openly speculating that she'd been intimidated – that Gavin must have got to her somehow and scared her into keeping quiet.

And then the following day the police came up with yet more CCTV, this time showing Gavin in the vicinity of Paula's flat on the morning of the day he was arrested. They said he must have found out where she lived and followed her there, but luckily we could account for him being in the area, because it was only half a mile from the Job Centre. And throughout the whole debacle Paula's story never changed – she hadn't been threatened by anyone, and she didn't recognize anyone in the line-up for the simple reason that they had the wrong man. So in the end the police had no choice. They had to let Gavin go.'

[JOCELYN]
And that really was the end of it. Or, at least, so Gavin thought.

Within a few months he and Sandra had split up, and Gavin had moved back to Cowley. Both his brothers had gravitated back to Oxford by then, so the move made sense, even if it meant he wouldn't see as much of his kids as he'd have liked. He got a flat, started seeing a new girlfriend, tried to make a new start. Life seemed better than it had for a long time.

And then, on January 27th 1998, a 23-year-old woman called Erin Pope was dragged off the street in the outskirts of Oxford, on her way home from work. Her hands were bound with cable ties and a plastic bag pulled over her head. She was found, an hour later, badly beaten, her underwear missing and a clump of her hair ripped out.

The Roadside Rapes had begun.

[UNDER BED OF 'SEX CRIME 1984' – EURYTHMICS]

I'm Jocelyn Naismith and this is Righting the Wrongs. You can listen to this and other podcasts from The Whole Truth on Spotify, or wherever you get your podcasts.

[FADE OUT]

* * *

The uniformed PC is on the doorstep when they arrive. One of the new intake at Cowley Road; Quinn vaguely remembers seeing him once or twice before.

'Acting DS Quinn. What have we got here?'

The PC stands up a little taller. 'I attended the address at 11.06 hours, sir, at the request of Ms Elizabeth Monroe. She was concerned for the occupant's welfare, having been unable to reach her this morning after she failed to turn up at work. I found the door open, no evidence of forced entry, and the premises empty. Sir.'

Quinn smiles drily. 'What's your name?'

He flushes. 'Webster, sir.'

'OK, Webster, there's no need to talk like a Speak Your Weight machine. Ordinary lingo's fine, even in the presence of CID.'

'Yes, sir.'

Quinn heads into the flat and Ev grins at Webster as she passes. 'And no need to call him "sir", either.' She drops her voice to a whisper and winks. 'It just gives him ideas.'

It's a small flat on the ground floor of a converted 1930s semi. Kitchen, sitting room, bedroom, a shower room with no windows. Everything is tidied neatly away as if the owner was expecting people – guests, parents, potential buyers. If this place has been burgled someone's gone to enormous lengths to cover it up. Ev pulls her gloves out of her pocket, then reaches for the handbag lying on the coffee table.

'Purse, wallet and keys,' she says after a moment. 'But no phone.'

Quinn's still working his way round the room. Picking things up, putting them down again.

'Not very, you know, "girly", is it?'

Ev gives him the side-eye. 'I'll pretend I didn't hear that.'

But she knows what he means. There are books and

the odd magazine, sponsor mailings from Barnardo's and Save the Children, a charity envelope for UNICEF, but no trinkets, no ornaments; barely anything personal at all. Not even photographs.

Quinn stops and puts his hands on his hips. 'There's only one toothbrush so odds on she lives alone, but that's about the only thing I get from this place. It's like one of those short-term rentals.'

'There's that,' says Ev, nodding at the copy of *Women's Running* on the table. 'And there are three pairs of trainers in the hall. So we know at least one thing she does in her spare time.'

'Perhaps that's it – something happened while she was out running?'

Ev frowns. 'Having left the front door open when she left?'

'Could have been mugged and had her keys stolen?'

Ev's still frowning. 'And the mugger came back here, decided not to bother nicking anything and put the keys back in her bag? And how did he know where she lived anyway?'

Quinn nods slowly. 'Right. It doesn't really add up.'

'It doesn't add up *at all*.' She puts the handbag down. 'Something's wrong here, Quinn. I know it.'

* * *

Voicemail

DC Andrew Baxter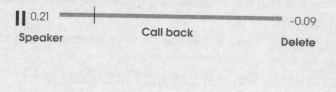

Mobile

Transcription

Sir - it's Baxter. They said you'd just popped out so this is just to say I've done some more work on that Twitter account - the one Marina Fisher was outed in. As far as I can tell whoever set it up knew what they were doing. You'd have to be pretty au fait with IT to cover your tracks that well. But in the circs that probably doesn't narrow it down much. I'll try to do some more digging later.

‖ 0.21 ——————————|———————————— -0.09

Speaker   Call back

                                       Delete

*   *   *

'So you don't know her very well?'

The man shrugs and shakes his head, though Everett's not sure whether that's because he doesn't actually know her or because he hasn't really understood the question. The little girl holding on to his leg is chattering away in what sounds like Polish.

'OK,' she says, handing him her card. 'Do give us a call if you think of anything.'

She goes back down the path and along to the next house. She can see Quinn two doors further on, and when he turns she catches his eye and shrugs. He shakes his head: seems he isn't getting very far either.

This time the door is opened by a woman. Not much more than five feet high, in a bright-yellow sari.

Ev smiles. 'Sorry to bother you. My name is Detective Constable Everett, Thames Valley Police. We're making enquiries about the woman who lives in number 62a. Do you know her at all?'

The woman clasps her hands together. 'Of course. A very nice lady. But I hope she is OK? Nothing bad has happened?'

Ev tries to look reassuring. 'She hasn't been seen since last night. We're just trying to locate her. We've no reason to suspect anything untoward at present.'

The woman looks concerned. 'I see. Oh dear.'

'Did you happen to see her last night? Mrs –?'

'Singh. I am Mrs Singh.'

'So – did you see anything yesterday evening?'

She nods slowly. 'Yes, I did. There was a man. At her door.'

Ev feels her heartrate quicken. She pulls her notebook out of her pocket. 'And when was this?'

'It must have been about nine o'clock. I was cooking and one of those people came to the door. Selling things, you know.'

Nottingham knocker, thinks Ev.

'Could you describe the man – the one at 62a, I mean.'

She looks contrite. 'I am sorry, I was not really concentrating. I was trying to make the salesman go away. My husband does not like those people. I wanted him to go before Rajesh came home.'

Ev doesn't like them much either. It's one of the

unexpected benefits of living in a first-floor flat with an entryphone and no street door.

'The man at 62a – was he tall? Young? White?'

The woman nods. 'White, yes. And dark hair. Quite tall, but everyone looks tall to me.' She smiles, then glances across at Quinn on the next-door step. 'He looked a bit like your friend, perhaps? But I only saw his back. I do not think I would know him again.'

'What was he wearing, do you remember?'

'Oh yes. It was shorts. Shorts and a T-shirt. A white one. And training shoes. Like for running, you know?'

'Do you remember the colour of the shorts?'

Mrs Singh's face crumples a little. 'Oh dear. Not really. Black, perhaps? I am sorry, I am not sure.'

'And the conversation they were having – did that seem friendly to you?'

'Oh yes. I'm sure they knew each other. She let him in, after all.'

'She *let him in*?'

The woman nods. 'Yes, yes. I saw him go inside.'

Ev's making frantic notes now. 'Did you see him leave?'

'No. I was cooking, and then Rajesh came home and it was fuss, fuss, fuss. Husbands – you know how it is.' She gives a conspiratorial smile, which Ev tries to mirror, but never having been married it's a bit of a fake.

'You didn't hear or see anything after that? No arguments, cars leaving suddenly, anything like that?'

Mrs Singh shakes her head. 'No,' she says. 'But there was a car outside I hadn't seen before. When I pulled the front curtains later it had gone.'

'And that would have been around –?'

'The time? Ten thirty. I always go to bed at the same time.'

Ev nods. 'And what sort of car was it? I know this is hard, but if you could remember the make –'

The woman shakes her head with a smile. 'I do not know anything about cars. It was dark. Blue or grey? Something like that. An ordinary car.'

'Ordinary?'

'You know. Not one of these big ones that look like the army.'

'Ah, I see. A saloon. Not an SUV.'

The woman holds up a finger. 'Exactly! Exactly that. That is what I meant.'

When Quinn joins her on the pavement a couple of minutes later Ev's still making notes.

'Looks like you had more luck than me.'

She glances up. 'There was a man at number 62a last night. About nine. Dark, tallish and possibly driving a dark-coloured car.'

Quinn exhales. 'Blimey, that changes things a bit.'

Ev's face is grim. 'It wasn't random, Quinn, and it wasn't while she was out running. She let this predator in.'

* * *

'OK, Baxter, can you get started on her social media, Ev, you're on the parents, and Somer, I want you to go and see her colleagues, especially the one who called it in.'

Back at St Aldate's and Quinn's back in his stride. This is more like it. Real policework. He's not dissing the assault case – well, not as such – but that whole area is a bloody bear trap and whatever you do is wrong. Quinn likes his crime clear-cut. No hidden snares, nothing that'll come back to bite you on the arse. A chance to actually *achieve* something. And if he gets this sewn up before Gis gets back –

But an hour later his initial elation has rather cooled.

'She's not on Facebook? Come on, Baxter, *everyone's* on Facebook.'

'No,' says Baxter stubbornly, 'they're not. And this woman's one of them. There is an Instagram account, but it looks to me like she only set it up to post shots from when she was out running, but after half-a-dozen or so she must have lost interest. She's not on Twitter at all, and the LinkedIn is just professional stuff to do with her work at the council. Whoever that bloke was she let in last night, I don't rate your chances of finding him on there.'

Quinn frowns. 'OK, OK, but keep looking, right? She lives alone so it's a fair bet she's on Match.com or Tinder or something.'

Baxter heaves a loud sigh, but he doesn't argue.

'Right,' says Quinn. 'What about the rest – the mobile? Ev?'

She looks up. 'The last signal was at 9.47 last night at the flat. Nothing since.'

'Did you track down the parents?'

She nods. 'Yes, but they couldn't add much. They weren't aware there was a boyfriend on the scene at the moment and didn't come up with much by way of male friends either. I didn't get the impression they knew much about her personal life.'

'When did they last speak to her?'

Ev flips back through her notes. 'Two and a bit weeks ago. It was her father's birthday. But it was just a call. Not a visit. They live in Bournemouth, so I suppose it would have been a bit of a trek. I for one wouldn't have relished spending two hours on the road in this weather.'

Quinn frowns. 'I thought she didn't have a car?'

'No,' she says, a bit flustered. 'She doesn't. Sorry – it was just a figure of speech.'

'What about Somer?' says Quinn, looking round. 'Wasn't she supposed to be talking to the co-workers? Where is she?'

'Ah,' says Ev quickly. 'I think she just nipped out for a coffee. She won't be long.'

* * *

'Quinn's looking for you. He wants to know why you haven't left yet.'

Somer looks up. She's standing over the sink, leaning in.

'Are you OK?' says Ev, taking a step closer. 'You look like you've been throwing up.'

Somer takes a deep breath. 'Must be something I ate.'

Which is, of course, possible, but Ev isn't buying it. And if she's right, it would explain a lot more than just this. But she's not going to pry; Somer will tell her when she's good and ready.

'Don't worry,' she says, touching her friend lightly on the arm. 'I'll get Asante to go instead. Take your time.'

Somer nods. She doesn't trust herself to speak.

She hears Ev go back to the door, and the sound of it

opening. And then a pause. 'Perhaps it might be an idea to go to the doc's? You know, just to be on the safe side?'

Somer nods again, and after a few moments the door swings shut and she's alone.

She raises her head slowly and stares into the mirror. Her skin looks greenish in the unforgiving light. Ev's right. She's been trying to pretend this isn't happening, but she knows in her heart she can't put it off much longer.

She needs to know.

And then, well, then —

* * *

'Not as bad as it could have been,' says Boddie, snapping on his gloves. 'When I see "railway incident" on the docket I usually assume I'll need a sieve.'

The two CSI technicians exchange a glance. Colin Boddie's mortuary humour is the stuff of legend; they've even set up an 'Overheard in the Morgue' Instagram account (though no one's yet had the courage to tell him that).

'What's the background here?' he says, walking round the head of the table. The woman's body is naked now, the skin waxy, and deep lividity in the back and buttocks. There are scratches, cuts, surface scrapes, dirt encrusted in the long blonde hair, but the damage — at least to the naked eye — is surprisingly slight.

The British Transport Police constable looks up. 'Bunch of engineers found her on the line at Walton Well bridge in the early hours. They thought she'd jumped.'

Boddie glances across. 'They saw her do it?'

The officer nods. 'They saw someone fall. Just as well

they did. There was a thirteen-car Freightliner less than two minutes away that wasn't planning to stop. If that crew hadn't been there –' He shrugs.

Boddie nods. 'Raspberry ripple.'

He bends a little closer, looking at the bloodied nostrils, the wide eyes now starting to cloud.

'OK,' he says thoughtfully. 'Let's see what she's prepared to tell us.'

* * *

The council office is in a Victorian building just off the Iffley Road. The words 'Iffley Parish Institute' are engraved in the stone above the main entrance, but according to the much more assertive modern sign on the edge of the pavement the building is now shared not only by the council fostering and adoption team but a community centre, the Samaritans, a playgroup, and a Silver Threads lunch fellowship.

Asante had the sense to call ahead and make an appointment, but he still spends ten minutes kicking his heels in the waiting area. There's a box of toys in the corner and signs pinned up on the wall behind: *Evacuation in the Event of Fire*, a Public Liability Insurance certificate and a handwritten note from the playgroup organizer: '*Please stack chairs at the end of your meeting so the cleaners can do their job.*'

When someone eventually comes to find him, the room he's shown into looks like what you'd get if you typed 'office' into a Google image search. Cheap furniture, tired pot plant, view over the staff car park. The woman who rises from behind the bland grey desk looks cool in a light-green and purple summer dress. Early thirties, chestnut-brown hair twisted up in a clip and heavy-framed glasses that make her look like a 1950s secretary. It's a reassuring look, he'll give her that. The look of someone who knows what they're doing.

'I'm Beth Monroe. I know a few people at St Aldate's but I don't think we've met?'

Asante smiles, but not too much. 'I haven't been here long. Transferred up from London a few months ago.'

'Really?' she says, gesturing for him to sit down. 'Where?'

'Brixton.'

She nods, more animated now. 'I used to work at the Blue Elephant Theatre. Many moons ago.'

They smile; they have something in common. And then the smile trails away.

'We're all just devastated. It's *awful* – to think something could have happened to her –'

'I gather it was you who went round to the house this morning?'

She folds her hands in front of her. 'It was so unlike her. Not turning up and not calling either. I can't remember when she was last off sick.'

'So the last time you'd have seen her would have been yesterday?'

She nods. 'That's right. She was still here when I left at six.'

'How did she seem to you?'

She considers. 'OK. A bit preoccupied but that was nothing unusual. There are only five of us and we're always swamped. Finding children new families – it's such important work and she takes it so seriously –'

She stops, bites her lip. 'I still can't quite believe this –'

'We think Ms Smith let a man into her flat last night – someone she knew –'

Her eyes widen. 'Oh my God. You think – you think this man may have *abducted* her?'

'We're at a very early stage of the investigation,' says Asante, switching evenly into police-issue platitudinese. 'We just need to talk to him. He was tallish, dark hair. Does anyone spring to mind? A colleague, perhaps?'

Monroe frowns. 'No. The only man on our team is Ed, and he's five foot six and bald as an egg.'

'What about friends, boyfriends? Anyone who might fit that description?'

She shakes her head. 'I don't know much about her private life. She really wasn't one for swapping gossip at the coffee machine.'

'You haven't had any staff events that included partners?'

She smiles ruefully. 'Er, no, all we do is a Christmas party and that's strictly employees only. Even then the budget only stretches to warm cava and Aldi sausage rolls.'

Asante makes a note. 'There's no one else she works with who might know more?'

Monroe shakes her head. 'I don't think so. I was probably the closest she had to a friend in the office. Like I said, she was a very private person. But I can give you their contact details if you want to speak to them.'

Asante shifts forward a little in his seat. 'This is probably an outlier, but is there anyone Ms Smith may have crossed paths with in the course of her job – someone who might have a grudge against her?'

Her eyes widen. 'A client, you mean?'

He shrugs. 'It has to be possible, surely? Like you said, it's life-changing, what you do. And it must be the last chance for some people – the only way they're ever going to have a child.'

'All too many of our clients are in that position,' she says softly. 'It's very sad.'

'Of course. But in situations like that, people can get desperate – they do things they'd never think of doing otherwise.'

'We guarantee our clients complete confidentiality, Constable.'

'I know. And I appreciate why.'

'I want to help – believe me – you've put me in a rather difficult position. Not that you meant to, of course. But I need to talk to a couple of my colleagues so we can decide what's best to do.'

Asante knows a departure signal when he hears one. He gets to his feet and she comes round the desk to shake his hand. Behind the heavy glasses her eyes are a brilliant green, but her face is troubled.

'So you'll get back to me?'

She nods. 'As soon as I can. I appreciate the urgency, I really do.'

Outside, there's a Mums and Toddlers group going on in the main hall, and judging by the smell, Silver Threads had fish for lunch.

He drops a fiver in the Samaritans donations box on his way out.

*　*　*

164

Telephone call with Colin Boddie, pathologist
10 July 2018, 12.50 p.m.
On the call, DC G. Quinn

CB: Ah, Quinn – I gather you're in the hot seat
    while Gislingham's away.

GQ: For my sins. What have you got?

CB: Fatality on the railway line last night. Ring
    any bells?

GQ: Yeah, think I saw the incident alert. Suicide,
    right?

CB: Wrong. Her neck was broken, yes, but that
    didn't kill her, for the simple reason that
    she was already dead –

GQ: OK –

CB: – and had been for at least the previous two
    hours. I would estimate TOD as sometime
    between nine and eleven. The high overnight
    temperatures make it harder to be much more
    specific than that, I'm afraid.

GQ: Hang on, I'm writing this down –

CB: Though whoever did kill her clearly wanted us
    to *think* it was suicide. And he'd probably
    have got away with it too – if those hard
    hatters hadn't spotted her, there wouldn't
    have been anything left to autopsy. I have to
    hand it to him, if you want to obliterate the
    evidence 15,000 tons of freight train are a
    pretty definitive way of doing it.

GQ: So what was the actual cause of death?

CB: Suffocation. There's bruising around the nose, but no fibres in the airway so he probably did it with his bare hands. I've taken some swabs in case there's DNA, but don't hold your breath - it's a fair bet he was wearing gloves.

GQ: You said 'he' –

CB: Almost certainly.

GQ: Just because it usually is –?

CB: No, because there was evidence of sexual assault. No semen present, but extensive bruising in the thigh and genital area, and a pubic hair that I strongly suspect isn't one of hers.

GQ: Shit.

CB: And for the record, no signs of a ligature, either on the wrists or elsewhere.
[*muffled noises in the background*]
Right. I think that's everything. I'll finish the formalities and email everything over. BTP will be handing this one off to you. It's a Thames Valley case now.

* * *

When Everett gets back to the office Quinn comes over to her at once. She only has to look at him to know something's wrong.

'What?' she says, her heart stumbling. 'What is it?'

'Colin Boddie just sent me this.'

He holds out his phone. She doesn't want it to be true but there's no mistaking the picture – the hair, the face –

'It's her, isn't it?'

Everett swallows. 'Yes,' she says, her voice catching. 'It's her.'

* * *

When Quinn puts his head round Fawley's door the DI is standing by the window, looking down at the street. Quinn can't remember the last time he saw him doing that.

He clears his throat. 'Sorry to bother you, but I've just had a call from Colin Boddie. There was a fatality found on the railway line at Walton Well last night. First responders thought it was a suicide but turns out she was suffocated.'

No reply. Fawley's so still Quinn wonders if he even heard him.

'Boss?'

The DI starts a little and turns round. 'Sorry – what did you say?'

'There was a fatality last night, on the railway line. Looked like suicide, but the PM says otherwise.'

Fawley frowns. 'They're sure?'

Quinn nods. 'And there's evidence of prior sexual assault.'

Fawley takes a breath. 'Do we have an ID?'

'That's just it. We were already looking for her. That woman who was reported missing this morning? Boddie sent over a picture. We'll need someone to do a formal identification but it's definitely her.'

'Right,' says Fawley, brisker now. 'What's her name?'

* * *

PC Webster's day is looking up. What started as a routine housesitting job has turned into a full-on crime scene supervision. He's got CSI on-site already, a couple of squad cars out the front and a Sky News van just pulling up a few yards down the street. At this rate he'll be getting on the telly. He drags his phone out of his pocket and surreptitiously texts his mum. No harm in being prepared.

Inside the flat, Clive Conway is working his way through the sitting room. He's bagged up the handbag and taken prints from the door handles and obvious flat surfaces. When Nina Mukerjee appears in the doorway ten minutes later he's on his hands and knees taking carpet samples.

'Any luck?' she says.

'Nothing obvious. I've retrieved a few hairs from the sofa, but they could just as easily be the victim's. Someone's worked pretty hard to make it look like there's nothing to see here.'

'CID say she definitely let a man in last night.'

Conway glances up. 'Doesn't mean this is the crime scene. He could easily have taken her somewhere else. Specially if she knew him.'

'True, but he was in here, though, wasn't he? Even if only for a few minutes. There'll be touch DNA somewhere, however careful he was.'

'Oh, he was careful, all right,' says Conway grimly.

Nina looks around. 'I've finished in the bedroom, so if you need a hand –'

'I'm nearly done here, but you could tackle the hoover bag. Can't see him going to all this trouble and not bothering to run a vac round.'

* * *

168

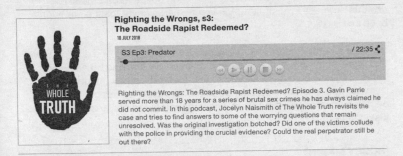

**Righting the Wrongs, s3:
The Roadside Rapist Redeemed?**
10 JULY 2018

S3 Ep3: Predator   / 22:35 📎

Righting the Wrongs: The Roadside Rapist Redeemed? Episode 3. Gavin Parrie
served more than 18 years for a series of brutal sex crimes he has always claimed he
did not commit. In this podcast, Jocelyn Naismith of The Whole Truth revisits the
case and tries to find answers to some of the worrying questions that remain
unresolved. Was the original investigation botched? Did one of the victims collude
with the police in providing the crucial evidence? Could the real perpetrator still be
out there?

[ARCHIVE OF SPEECH BY CHIEF SUPERINTENDENT MICHAEL OSWALD, THAMES
VALLEY POLICE, 7 SEPT 1998]

[JOCELYN]

That's Chief Superintendent Michael Oswald, addressing a press
conference on Monday September 7th 1998. The previous Friday night, the
Roadside Rapist had attacked a third young woman.

The rape of Erin Pope in January that year had been followed, almost exactly
two months later, by an equally savage assault in Botley, to the west of Oxford.

And now, the same predator had struck again.

**I'm Jocelyn Naismith, and I'm the co-founder of The Whole Truth, a
not-for-profit organization that campaigns to overturn miscarriages
of justice. This is Righting the Wrongs, series 3: The Roadside Rapist
Redeemed?**

Chapter three: Predator

[THEME SONG – AARON NEVILLE COVER VERSION OF 'I SHALL BE RELEASED']

[JOCELYN]

The rapist's second victim, 19-year-old biology student Jodie Hewitt, had
been so badly beaten she had to spend ten days in hospital. Jodie was in
her second year at Wykeham College at the time, and in the weeks after
her rape, rumours had begun to circulate that a serial sex assailant was
operating in the city. People started to panic, there were calls for more
police on the streets at night.

But then – nothing. The days started to get longer, the students went down for the long summer vacation, and even if the police hadn't made any obvious progress investigating the first two attacks, at least there hadn't been any more.

Not, that is, until September 4th. It was a Friday, and after a drink in town that night with friends, a 24-year-old trainee solicitor was on her way home. She was on a quiet Oxford side street, only a few hundred yards from her flat, when her attacker struck. She wasn't raped, but only because another man saw what was happening and came to her rescue just in time.

[ROSEY MABIN]

'His name was Gerald Butler, and he was a former soldier, and a bouncer at one of the city's nightclubs.'

[JOCELYN]

That's Rosey Mabin. She reported on the Roadside Rapist for the *Oxford Mail*, and attended Gavin Parrie's trial at the Old Bailey.

[ROSEY]

'Butler told the jury that he spotted the young woman face down at the side of the road. She had a plastic carrier bag over her head, and there was a man straddling her, trying to tie her hands with cable ties. The attacker was thin, about five foot eight, and wearing a dark hoodie.'

[JOCELYN]

There was no social media back then, needless to say, so it took days rather than minutes for the news of the third attack to spread, but Thames Valley Police knew their worst fears had come to pass: their bête noire was back. They called that press conference we heard at the start of this episode because they knew they had to do something to allay local fears.

There was another reason too, of course.

Women needed to be warned.

[ROSEY]

'It was actually me that came up with the Roadside Rapist nickname. A couple of the nationals had been referring to him as the Oxford Ripper, but

after that press conference I wrote a front-pager calling him the Roadside Rapist and it just stuck.'

[JOCELYN]

And you can see why. It's a name that captures all the terror of a predator who targeted his victims out in the open, on streets they walked every day, only yards from other passers-by. Those victims were normal girls, going about their normal business. But it was that very normality that was so terrifying. Because if it happened to them, it could happen to anyone. No wonder people were scared, no wonder young women in Oxford were avoiding going out alone, especially after dark.

As for the investigation, the police were scarcely any further forward. Of course, DNA science wasn't as sophisticated back then as it is now – so-called 'touch DNA' was a long way in the future, for a start. But that didn't matter anyway, because – as the trial would later confirm – the Roadside Rapist never left any DNA at all. No hair, no skin, no semen – there were basically no forensics (a fact which has also hampered subsequent attempts to have the case re-opened, including our own).

The other challenge for the police was that, unlike Paula in Manchester, none of the Oxford victims ever saw their attacker's face. The police speculated – with some justification – that the rapist was using plastic bags for precisely that reason: to make doubly sure he couldn't be identified. There was no CCTV either. In the late 90s, very few buildings had their own cameras, so perhaps it wasn't so surprising that there was never any footage in the area of the crimes. Of course, this could just have been bad luck, or a coincidence, but some of the officers on the case started to wonder whether there might be rather more to it than that.

['MR X']

'As time went on you could definitely see a pattern emerging.'

[JOCELYN]

Those are the words of one of the detectives who worked on the case. We've disguised his voice, to protect his identity.

['MR X']

'It wasn't just the MO that was the same each time. The plastic bag, the cable ties, the hair, the taking of trophies like jewellery or underwear. Over time, we became convinced that this man was also choosing the locations of the attacks very carefully. They all took place on stretches of road that

had no speed cameras or CCTV, where there was dense undergrowth adjacent to the pavement, and no overlooking houses or buildings. That suggested to us that this perpetrator was recce-ing the sites in detail beforehand.'

[JOCELYN]

Thames Valley officers did question people who lived or worked nearby, but it never yielded anything useful. They had no evidence, no leads. But in due course they did have a new theory.

['MR X']

'It was one of the Detective Sergeants on the team who first suggested that the rapist wasn't just casing out the sites of the crimes in advance: he was stalking his victims too.'

[JOCELYN]

The name of that Detective Sergeant was Adam Fawley. And this wasn't the only significant contribution he would make to this investigation. In fact, his work on the case would eventually earn him a commendation from the Chief Constable, and accelerate his rise to Detective Inspector. Because it was Adam Fawley who helped secure the evidence that convicted Gavin Parrie.

So you could say, with some justification, that this case changed Adam Fawley's life. And not just professionally, either.

In September 2000, not quite a year after Gavin Parrie was pronounced guilty and sentenced to life at the Old Bailey, Adam Fawley married a woman called Alexandra Sheldon.

She was a lawyer, and had lived in the Oxford area all her life. She was also the Roadside Rapist's third victim.

[UNDER BED OF 'EMOTIONAL RESCUE' – THE ROLLING STONES]

I'm Jocelyn Naismith and this is Righting the Wrongs. You can listen to this and other podcasts from The Whole Truth on Spotify, or wherever you get your podcasts.

[FADE OUT]

* * *

Alex Fawley presses stop and pushes her tablet away. Her hands are trembling

She knew this would happen – she'd steeled herself against what they'd say, but knowing it and hearing it are not the same thing.

She folds her hands about her belly to still them; the skin that shields her child is warm, but her fingers are freezing.

She needs to talk to Adam.

She'd prayed she wouldn't have to – she didn't want him to know she was listening to this thing. But now – now she has no choice.

* * *

Back at St Aldate's, Somer is feeling the worst kind of sidelined. Because she can't blame anyone else; she's managing to do it all by herself. Ever since the news came in from Boddie, the team has been hectic with adrenaline, but she feels muffled, quarantined. Like those adverts where there's someone sitting in the middle of a busy office, barely moving, while people buzz around them in fast-forward. Those marooned people always have something wrong with them – a cold, a headache, flu – but it's never anything serious. It's always easily fixed. She sighs. It's not that she doesn't care about what happened to the woman on the railway line; she just can't find the energy to do anything about it. She's achieved precisely nothing all morning, and is now rapidly running out of thankless tasks that will stop her thinking and require no thought.

She gets up and wanders over to where Baxter is staring at his screen, the blue light reflected back on his face. There are three empty chocolate wrappers by his mouse pad. As stress indicators go, that's pretty reliable.

'Need a hand with anything?'

He glances up briefly and frowns. 'Fuck me, that's a first. You feeling OK?'

How long have you got? she thinks. 'Hey, don't look a gift horse, and all that.'

He raises an eyebrow. 'Well, if you're sure, you could have a look at that Twitter feed the Super's getting so uptight about. The one that exposed Marina Fisher. I've had a quick look but I haven't gone through all the replies and that.'

'Great,' she says. 'Just send me the details.'

He gives her a dry look then turns to his screen and taps at the keyboard. 'Knock yourself out.'

Somer opens what he's sent her, then sits back. 'This is the one? This is definitely the username?'

Baxter glances up and frowns. 'Yeah. So? Didn't mean anything to me.'

'No,' she says softly, almost to herself. 'But it means something, all the same.'

* * *

It's Ev who picks up the call. 'Asante?' she says, looking up. 'Line three for you.'

He recognizes the voice straight away.

'Ms Monroe, what can I do for you?'

A slight pause. 'What you said before, when you were here –'

Asante reaches for his pen. 'Oh yes?'

'You were asking about any of our clients who might have had a motive – some sort of grudge? I've spoken to my colleagues and even though it goes against all our professional instincts, we've agreed that the circumstances justify making an exception.'

She stops, takes a breath. Asante says nothing. He knows the value of silence.

'There was someone. A couple she was assessing as potential adopters. Unfortunately, they didn't turn out to be suitable.'

'I see.'

'And they were in their forties. It was probably their last chance. The gentleman – he was very angry. Shouting, making threats –'

Asante frowns. '*Physical* threats?'

'Oh no,' she says quickly. 'Nothing like that. He said he had "contacts", that he'd ruin her career, that sort of thing. It was very unpleasant. We were on the point of calling the police.'

Asante gets out his notebook. 'And can you tell me why they were rejected?'

'Not "rejected" – "not considered suitable",' she says quickly. 'And no. I'm pushing it as it is.'

'But that makes it difficult for us to –'

'It was only two or three weeks ago,' she says, cutting across him. 'Couldn't you just say you're speaking to all the clients who'd seen her recently?'

She's shrewd, this woman.

'Fair enough. We can probably get away with that. Can you give me the address?'

He starts to write it down, only to find himself stumbling at the postcode and checking his prejudice. Because it's not Cowley or Blackbird Leys or Littlemore, but sought-after OX2.

'Thanks,' he says. 'I'll do my best not to land you in it.'

She sighs. 'I still feel bad about it. But I'd never be able to forgive myself if it turned out to be him and I hadn't said anything.'

'I'll let you know how it goes.'

'I'd rather you didn't,' she says quickly. And then, after a pause, 'But do pop in if you're passing the Iffley Road.'

When he puts down the phone a few moments later Asante is smiling.

*　*　*

'OK,' says Baxter, leaning back in his chair and looking up at Quinn. 'I've done a sweep of all the CCTV around Walton Well bridge but I've got bugger all to show for it.'

Quinn frowns. 'I don't believe it – there must be *something* –'

Baxter makes a face. 'Nope. The nearest cameras are on Walton Street. He could easily have got to the bridge and out without passing either of 'em.'

Quinn's still frowning. 'You're absolutely sure there are no cameras on the actual bridge?'

Baxter takes a heavy breath. 'I do know what I'm doing, you know.'

'What about Shrivenham Close?'

Baxter shakes his head. 'Nearest footage is from the ring-road roundabout. I gave up counting the number of dark saloons when I got past sixty. Without a make and model we're sunk before we start. And that's assuming he actually went in that direction. There are at least a dozen other ways he could have gone.'

'Yeah, yeah,' mutters Quinn. 'No need to rub it in.'

* * *

'Mr Cleland?'

'Yes, what do you want?'

The man on the step is wearing a pair of white tailored shorts and a bright-pink striped shirt. The shirt is untucked. Behind him, the building looms, florid, immaculately maintained, and rather larger than strictly necessary. If there was ever a contest for Owner Most Like His House, this bloke would walk it.

Asante holds out his warrant card. 'DC Anthony Asante,' he says in his best public-school voice, making sure to pronounce the 'h'. He finds it helps, in OX 2.

The man frowns. 'Oh yes?' He glances quickly down the drive and looks relieved to find the Range Rover is still there. 'What is it?'

'May I come in? It's a little complicated.'

The man hesitates, looking Asante up and down, but evidently decides it's safe to allow him on the premises. It's probably the Burberry tie. That tends to help too.

The sitting room reminds Asante of his parents' house in Holland Park. Expensive furniture, framed antique prints, coffee-table books. But there's an ease about his parents' place, a naturalness, that he doesn't sense here. He looks around, trying to figure out why. Perhaps it's the too-many decanters (Three perhaps, but five? Who needs five?) or the fact that all the prints seem to show people killing things; or perhaps it's just that everything is a little too tidy, a little too arranged. He can't picture a kid in here. Out in the garden, there's a woman sitting under an umbrella on what Cleland no doubt refers to as the 'terrace'.

'Is that your wife?'

Cleland frowns again. 'Yes. Why?'

'Perhaps she could join us? It would save me saying everything twice.'

Cleland's frown deepens but he doesn't say anything, just goes over to the French doors.

'Marianne – come in here for a minute.'

The woman is wearing a turquoise bikini under a white wrap. She has the same prosperous, well-preserved look as her husband, but she's insect-thin, and he senses a dry brittleness under the make-up and the expensively cut-and-coloured hair. Cleland is standing in the centre of the room now, hands in pockets, filling the space.

'So what's this about?' he says.

'I believe you're a client of the council adoption service?'

The woman's eyes widen and she slides a look at her husband.

'That's confidential,' he says. 'And none of your bloody business.'

'I can assure you I know nothing at all about your appli-cation, Mr Cleland, or your circumstances. I just know that you were in their offices recently.'

Marianne Cleland sits forward; everything about her seems tentative. 'If it's about –'

'Let me handle this,' says Cleland. His chin lifts a little. 'Yes, we were there a couple of weeks ago. Whole operation is a bloody shitshow. You'd think they'd be crying out for people like us, wouldn't you?'

Asante keeps his expression neutral. 'What sort of people would that be, sir?'

Cleland flings an arm round. 'Well, look at this place. What kid in his right mind wouldn't want what we've got to offer?'

Asante opts to take out his notebook by way of response. 'I believe you saw Ms Smith, is that right?'

Cleland looks irritated. 'Why bother asking when you clearly know the answer already?'

'I just need to get things straight, sir. It was Ms Smith, yes?'

'She was our case worker,' says the woman. 'She's very nice –'

'Effing incompetent, just like the rest of them,' snaps Cleland. 'Look, has there been some sort of complaint or what?'

Asante shakes his head. 'No, sir. Ms Smith has made no complaint –'

'Well then –'

'Ms Smith has been killed.'

The woman gives a little gasp, but even in that moment, her eyes go first to her husband.

Cleland stares at Asante, his face flushing. 'If you're bloody suggesting –'

'I'm suggesting nothing,' says Asante. 'I'm asking questions. It's what happens in a murder inquiry.'

The word drops like an incendiary.

'Look,' says Cleland, 'I don't know what the hell hap-pened to that woman but we had nothing to do with it. People like us – we don't go around *killing* people. Even when –' He stops, looks away, purses his mouth.

'Even when?' says Asante evenly.

Cleland takes a breath. 'OK, look, you obviously know we had words. It's why you're here, right? Well, yes, we did. I don't have a problem admitting that. She told us we'd been turned down. That we weren't –' he hooks his fingers in the air – '*suitable*. Probably didn't tick enough bleeding-heart liberal boxes, did we. Too rich, too posh, too bloody *white*.' He checks himself, reddens, then runs a hand through his hair. 'I was upset, OK? Annoyed. Any-one would have been, in my position.'

Quite possibly, thinks Asante, but not everyone would have reacted the way you did.

'Did you see or contact Ms Smith after that meeting?' he says.

Cleland's flush deepens. 'I may have sent her an email – in the heat of the moment. You know how it is –'

'So that's a yes?'

Cleland nods.

'Did you go to the office? Try to talk to her in any way?'

'No. Absolutely not.'

'I spoke to a couple of Ms Smith's colleagues earlier, and they said you were seen outside the offices a few days after your last meeting.' He flicks back through his notes. 'Around five p.m. on June 25th, to be precise.'

Cleland blinks a couple of times. 'I was shopping. There's a halfway-decent wine merchant's a few doors further down.'

Asante nods. 'So there'll be a record? At the store?'

'No. I didn't actually buy anything. Not on that occasion.'

Asante makes a note, and takes his time doing it.

'So you weren't hoping to see Ms Smith? Perhaps try to catch her when she left the office at the end of the day?'

'Absolutely not.'

'Or perhaps you thought it would be more discreet to go round to her house? See if you could persuade her to change her mind?'

'Of course not,' he blusters. 'For a start, I've no bloody idea where she lives.'

The woman sits forward. 'And in any case, Hugh would never –'

'I told you,' says Cleland, not looking at her, 'let *me* handle this.'

'Where were you last night, Mr Cleland?'

Cleland opens his mouth, then closes it again. 'Last night?'

Asante nods, pen poised.

Cleland scratches the back of his neck. The eye contact has gone. 'I went for a run.'

'That's right,' says his wife. 'You went out in the car.'

Asante frowns. 'I thought you said you went for a run.'

'I did,' says Cleland. 'I run at Shotover.'

Asante makes a note, his face thoughtful. Shotover must be five or six miles from here, which makes it an odd choice, given Cleland has the University Parks practically on his doorstep and doesn't look like he'd manage much more than a sedate circuit even of that. But proximity might have had nothing to do with it: Shotover Country

Park is no more than ten minutes from Smith's address in Shrivenham Close. An address Cleland claims he doesn't know.

But the man at her door was wearing running gear.

*   *   *

Fawley's door is shut and it takes Quinn a minute to remember that he had the CPS coming in this afternoon. The Fisher case. Though that seems like very old news now.

The CPS lawyer is a woman. Fifties, thick-set. Short grey hair, glasses. She looks like she doesn't take prisoners. Or shit.

'Sorry to bother you – we're about to have a quick meeting about the Smith investigation. The parents have formally ID'd her, and it looks like we may have a suspect too – a bloke she had a row with at work. She turned him and his wife down as potential adopters and let's just say he didn't take it very well. A bit too "entitled", if you catch my drift.'

The CPS lawyer looks up and sighs.

Fawley nods. 'OK, good work.'

Quinn hovers a moment, then gestures back towards the squad room. 'You sure you don't want to –?'

Fawley shakes his head. 'You seem to have it covered. Just keep me posted.'

*   *   *

The Vowels
online

- Tim Palmer
Anyone seen Twitter this morning?
That #VictHIM thing? Seems pretty
clear who they're referring to
13:59

- Ron Sandford
All that stuff about safe 'harbour'
and trawling? LMFAO
14:01 ✓✓

- Kate Kesson
OMG just went and looked! What a
shitstorm! Has anyone heard from her?
14:03

- Tim Palmer
😱 😱 😱
14:05

- Kate Kesson
So who do we think the student is?
The obvious?
14:11

- Vic Gibbins
Don't be too quick with the schardenfreude –
if it happened to her it could happen to
any of us
14:20

- Ron Sandford
I think you'll find that's 'schadenfreude'
14:32 ✓✓

* * *

183

'So we have a definite sighting of Cleland near her office on June 25th, and a man at her door wearing running gear the night she disappeared.'

Quinn is up at the whiteboard, writing furiously. He turns. 'What else?'

'The adoption service don't give out staff numbers or addresses,' says Asante, 'so if Cleland did go round there that night, he must have found out where she lived some other way.'

Quinn considers. 'Electoral roll?'

Baxter looks up, taps briefly on his keyboard, and then makes a face. 'Well, yeah, she's there, but it's only as "E. Smith". There are bloody dozens of 'em.'

Quinn considers. 'He could have followed her home. That sighting – it was near the end of the day, right?'

'Ye-es,' says Asante, clearly unconvinced, 'but Smith's neighbour said she let the man in. Would she really invite Cleland into her home? She knew what he was like – he'd threatened her, sent that shitty email –'

Baxter shrugs. 'Maybe he said he'd come to apologize? Blokes like him, they can turn on the charm –'

'I still don't think she'd have let him in,' says Somer firmly. 'I wouldn't even have opened the bloody door.'

'But it's not *impossible*, is it?' persists Baxter. 'Say he convinced her he came in peace. She offers him a drink, they sit down to talk, but then she says something that pisses him off – tells him she's not prepared to change her decision. He gets angry – he's a big bloke and she's ten stone soaking wet –'

Quinn nods. 'Yeah, I can see that. I can even see him killing her. But the rape? That's a stretch.'

Baxter frowns. But Quinn's right. It doesn't fit.

'On the other hand,' says Quinn, 'I could *definitely* see him panicking afterwards and trying to make it look like suicide.'

He goes back to the board, taps on the map. 'And Walton Well bridge is pretty much in a direct line from Smith's flat to Cleland's pile on Lechlade Road.'

'We can check ANPR,' says Baxter, reaching for his keyboard again. 'At least we know what we're looking for now. That Range Rover is hardly incognito.'

'Check whether the Clelands have a second car,' says Asante, looking across. 'The neighbour said she saw an ordinary dark-coloured saloon, not a big flashy tank.'

Ev gets up and goes over to the board. There's a picture of Cleland taken from his company's website. He's wearing a suit and tie; he looks hefty and confident. She turns. 'Mrs Singh said the bloke at the door looked a bit like Quinn, remember? Well, Cleland doesn't look anything *like* Quinn.'

Quinn gives a wry smile. 'I'll take that as a compliment.'

Somer looks to Asante. 'Cleland's about the same height, though, right?'

Asante nods. 'Near enough. But he's at least a stone heavier.'

Somer frowns. 'Well, it looks to me like Cleland's carrying most of that extra weight in his gut. And Mrs Singh only saw him from behind.'

They stare at the picture. The silence lengthens, but it's Baxter who eventually voices what they're all thinking.

'It could have been him.'

'OK,' says Quinn, with the beginnings of a smile. 'Let's bring him in.'

* * *

Caleb Morgan's bedsit is on the lower ground floor of one of the few North Oxford houses still divided into student lets. A nicer address than Ev was expecting, until she remembers who his mother is. The reception she gets, on the other hand, is pretty much exactly what she expected.

'Oh, just piss off, will you?' he says, making to close the door. 'Freya told me all about you harassing her, making me out to be some sort of bloody domestic abuser. I've got nothing to say to you.'

Everett takes a step forward. 'You're not doing yourself any favours, Caleb. We know it was you.'

'What? What are you accusing me of now?' he says acidly. 'The Rwandan genocide? 9/11? No wait – the grassy knoll – it has to be the grassy knoll.'

She doesn't rise to it. 'It's about that story on Twitter.'

He frowns. 'What story?'

'You know exactly which one. The one about Marina.'

'I have no idea what you're talking about.'

'You're not the only one round here who knows a bit about IT, Caleb. We traced that story all the way back to the original tweet. The account that posted had only been set up earlier that same day. It was in the name "JosephAndrews2018".'

He gives her a studiously blank look. 'Means absolutely bloody nothing to me.'

She raises an eyebrow. 'Yeah, well, that little twist didn't come from you, did it? It came from Freya.'

His eyes flicker and he looks away.

'She does English, right? *Joseph Andrews* – it's an eighteenth-century novel about a sexual predator. Only this time it's the other way round. A *woman* in a position of authority who preys on a much younger man. Just like you and Marina.' She gives him a disdainful look. 'I bet you thought we'd be way too thick to work *that* one out, didn't you? Just your bad luck one of my colleagues did English too.'

He returns her look, contempt for contempt. 'Talk about tenuous. If *that's* what passes for detection at Thames Valley Police –'

'It's not just the name. Whoever set up that account knew what they were doing – they knew how to stay under the radar.' She shrugs. 'Child's play, right? For someone like you?'

He snorts. 'You people – do you *seriously* think I want people knowing what she did to me?'

'No, I don't think you do. But as you well know, there was no mention of your name – not on that post, not on the subsequent tweets – not anywhere. Just all those coded references to a female member of university staff that any-one with half a brain can work out in five minutes.'

'So what are you doing about it? Because if you're look-ing for a leak, someone in CID is a fuck sight more likely, if you ask me –'

Behind him, somewhere in the flat, there's a muffled sound. Not much more than a creak, but enough to sug-gest he's not alone. Freya, thinks Ev. Freya's with him.

He starts to close the door. 'If you've got anything else you want to say to me, talk to my lawyers. And for the avoidance of doubt, if my name does get out, now or at any time in the future, you'll be hearing from *them*.'

*   *   *

'Get your sodding hands off me – how dare you – you'll be hearing from my bloody lawyer –'

Bringing Cleland in was never going to be pretty, but things take an ugly turn when he flatly refuses to come voluntarily and they have to arrest him. There's an unseemly scuffle on his doorstep, witnessed with gleeful disbelief by a cluster of students from the college further along the road, and Asante ends up with an elbow in the face.

'Just as well we came mob-handed,' says Quinn, as Baxter manhandles Cleland down the drive. A couple of the students are taking pictures now and Cleland shouts abuse at them before being shunted indecorously into the car. 'Still, look on the bright side. No probs getting his prints and DNA now.' He holds up a pair of shorts and a grubby white T-shirt, both sealed in evidence bags. 'Or his dirty washing.'

'True,' says Asante, rubbing his jaw. 'On the other hand, I bet that lawyer of his is seriously arsey.'

*   *   *

BREAKING: Fears grow for safety of Headington woman

By Richard Yates

With no reported sightings of her since she left work on Monday, friends and neighbours of a Headington woman are becoming increasingly concerned that something may have happened to her. Residents of Shrivenham Close have reported intensive house-to-house questioning by officers of Thames Valley Police CID, and the arrival of a forensics team, leading to fears that the woman, who has not yet been named, may have come to harm.

This breaking news story is being updated and more details will be published shortly.

Do you live in Shrivenham Close or have information about this story? Email me at richard.yates@ox-mailnews.co.uk

* * *

'Easy does it, sir.'

The petty humiliations of fingerprinting and DNA samples have done little to improve Hugh Cleland's mood. But Sergeant Woods can match him, pound for pound, and he's handled far too many obstreperous drunks to be fazed by a man in magenta trousers. Cleland is still shouting and shoving when Woods clangs the cell door shut and turns to Quinn.

'He'll get bored soon enough,' he says. 'Give me a call when you want him brought up.'

Quinn smiles. 'Oh, I'm in no rush. And his brief is at the sodding opera so he's not going to be popping over any time soon, either.'

More carpet f-bombing from inside the cell.

Quinn's smile broadens. 'And in any case, I reckon our friend could do with cooling down a bit, don't you?'

'I don't know about "cooling down",' says Woods heavily. 'Not in those cells.'

* * *

Adam Fawley
10 July 2018
17.09

I'm just about to have an update with Quinn when the call comes through. Harrison. On my back about the Morgan case again, no doubt. I collect the papers and make my way down to his office. There's been no let-up in the heat all day. The air in this bloody building is solidifying and the carpet smells like it's been scorched.

'Ah, Adam,' he says as I open the door. 'I'm glad I caught you. Take a seat.'

He doesn't look happy. But he never looks happy.

I open the file in front of me and pull out my notes. 'I met the CPS Rape and Serious Sexual Offences specialist this afternoon. We've been through the case and in her view –'

He frowns. 'What?'

'The Caleb Morgan assault, sir. You made it very clear that you wanted it treated as a priority –'

He stares at me. 'We have a dead woman on our hands. I think that's rather more pressing, don't you?'

190

'Enquiries are well underway, sir. DC Quinn has identified a possible suspect, and I'll be getting a briefing from him as soon as this meeting is over –'

He frowns. 'What I want to *know*, DI Fawley, is why you have thus far failed to inform anyone, least of all me, that you had a pre-existing relationship with the victim.'

I stare at him. 'I'm sorry?'

'Don't piss me about, Adam. I'm not in the mood.'

'Honestly, sir. I don't know what you're talking about.'

His eyes narrow. 'According to DC Quinn, the victim was identified at approximately 1.00 p.m. this afternoon, and he passed on that information to you, in person, at 1.15.'

I don't know where this is going, but I don't like it.

'Yes, sir, but I still –'

Harrison leans back in his chair.

'What's the victim's name?'

My turn to frown. 'Emma Smith.'

'And you're still claiming you don't know her?' He looks palpably, mouth-openly incredulous.

'Because I don't. I *don't* know her –'

'In that case, perhaps you could explain to me what you were doing in her flat.'

I stare at him. What the –?

'There are prints,' says Harrison. 'At Smith's flat. *Your* prints.'

And then it hits me. Hard, and too late.

I swallow. 'Unless –'

He raises an eyebrow, sardonic. 'Unless?'

'Unless it's my wife's friend –' I falter, stop.

Christ.

'Seriously, sir. I just didn't make the connection. And I

haven't been into the incident room – I haven't seen her picture so I –'

'She's your wife's *friend*, and you didn't recognize her *name*?'

His scepticism is brutal.

I can feel myself flushing. 'Well, obviously I knew my wife's friend was called Emma, but I'm not sure I ever did know her surname.' I sit forward. 'Sir, I know how it looks, but she was Alex's friend, not mine. They were at university together – they see each other a few times a year. I see her even less than that.'

But he's still not buying it. 'Wasn't it Emma Smith who sorted out that short-term foster placement for you last year – the one I signed off on?'

I swallow. 'Yes, sir, but it was Alex who handled all that – I wasn't really involved. Like I said, sir, Emma Smith and I weren't friends – we were barely even acquaintances.'

'So you keep saying,' he says, 'but you were in her flat all the same.'

I can feel my face reddening. 'Ah, OK. I can explain that.'

'I bloody well hope you can, because right now –'

'I *was* there – at the flat. But it was at *her request*. She came to see me at the station. There was something she wanted to talk to me about.'

He frowns again. 'So why not do it here? Surely that would have been more appropriate –'

'Which is exactly what I said,' I reply quickly. 'And I tried to persuade her to do just that, but she didn't want to make it official.'

'And when was this?'

Shit.

Shit shit shit.

'Yesterday, sir.'

'*Yesterday?* You went to her flat *yesterday?*'

I try to meet his eye but don't quite manage it. 'Yes, sir.'

He takes a breath. Another. 'So you went round to her flat. What time was this?'

'Around nine. She asked me to pop in after work.'

Harrison opens his mouth to say something but I get there first.

'She thought she was being stalked. There'd been someone opposite the house on a couple of occasions, hanging about in the dark for no apparent reason. At least one sighting in a vehicle –'

Harrison sits back, looks at me.

'I went through the usual line of questioning, sir. I asked her about old boyfriends, colleagues, anyone who might have wanted to threaten or scare her. She couldn't think of anyone. I knew – from my wife – that there'd been a recent relationship but she said it was over and she wasn't the one who ended it. So in the end I told her that as things stood there wasn't enough to open an official investigation but she should carry on keeping a diary – if she saw the stalker again she should try to take pictures, and call 999 if she ever felt remotely threatened physically. And then I left.'

I sit forward a little. 'Obviously, with hindsight, I should have done something – and I deeply regret that I didn't, and I know that's going to look bad for the force, but there really wasn't any suggestion that she was in imminent danger –' I'm frantically recalibrating now, trying to *think*. 'But from what DC Quinn said about this man Cleland, surely he's the most obvious candidate –'

But for whatever reason, Harrison isn't with me. I can feel the swell of his irritation and the effort he's making to control it.

'So, the victim found on the railway line is the same age as your wife's friend, she has the same colouring, she has the same first name, and yet for the whole of the last – what is it, *four hours*? – it's never once occurred to you that it might be the same person?'

I swallow. 'Like I said, sir –'

But he's not listening. 'Your *own team* have spent the best part of the day looking for a man Emma Smith let into her flat last night – a man who *fits your description* – and you still never thought this might be more than just a coincidence?'

And I'm the one who doesn't believe in coincidences, as I'm expecting him to remind me right about –

'And how many times have I heard you say –'

I cut across him. 'I'm sorry, sir. DC Quinn has been handling the initial enquiries and, as I said, I spent most of the afternoon with the CPS – I haven't had time to look at the detail. But I can see now that –'

But I don't get to suck up any more shit. Behind me, the door opens. I hadn't been expecting anyone, but Harrison clearly has. He looks up and gives a quick affirmation. I turn round.

Detective Inspector Ruth Gallagher. Of Major Crimes. She gives me a brief nod, her face impassive. 'DI Fawley.'

DI Fawley. Not 'Adam', even though we worked the

Faith Appleford abduction case together barely three months ago. Even though I thought we'd become the nearest thing this job ever gets to friends.

'Ruth.' I can hear the falter in my voice.

Gallagher takes the empty chair. Harrison gestures to her – the floor is evidently hers. My heart is skittering like a nervous horse.

'I just spoke to Ms Smith's parents, sir. They know nothing about any supposed stalker.'

'Supposed'. Fuck.

I try to get her to look at me. 'They must be in their seventies at least – she probably just didn't want to worry them –'

She's staring steadfastly ahead. 'Ms Smith doesn't seem to have had many friends outside work, but I'm in the process of drawing up a list.'

What does she mean, *drawing up a list*? This isn't her case –

'The first name on that list is Mrs Alexandra Fawley. I'm aiming to talk to her first thing.'

Wait a minute – she's going to talk to my *wife* –?

'Perhaps DI Fawley could help you with that, Ruth,' says Harrison, his eyes never leaving my face. 'After all, I'm sure Mrs Fawley must already be fully aware of the situation, given that Ms Smith approached her husband for advice.'

So that's where we are, is it.

I take a deep breath. 'I haven't discussed any of this with my wife.'

He frowns, is about to speak, but I plough on.

'She's only a few weeks away from her due date, and has already been hospitalized once for stress. I wasn't about to risk that happening again by telling her there could be some sort of stalker in the area.'

She's terrified enough already without that. But this I don't say.

'Emma – Ms Smith – didn't want Alex worrying either. That's why she came to the station rather than calling me at home. She said as much – in fact, she used that exact phrase.'

Harrison gives me a look; a look that says, *We only have your word for that.* I should know – I give it to suspects myself often enough.

Gallagher shifts a little in her seat. Embarrassed? Uncomfortable? Who knows. I'd like to think she, at least, would understand about Alex – she has kids herself. But I'm basing that on my experience of her before, when we were on the same side. Right now, it feels like that bet is off.

Harrison is still watching me.

'Where did you go?'

His tone is calm now, almost sympathetic. But I am not deceived.

'Where did I go when?'

'In Smith's flat. Where did you go? The kitchen, the living room, the bedroom?'

I stare him out. 'The *living room*, sir. That's all.'

'And you were there, what, an hour? More?' Gallagher now.

'Less. At most, thirty minutes.'

'But you had a drink, didn't you, in that time.'

It's not a question. Of course – the glasses.

'I had half a glass of wine. I was driving. I didn't even want that, frankly, but I didn't want to upset her. She was in a bit of a state.'

196

Gallagher and Harrison exchange a glance.

'Well, I think that's all for now,' says Harrison. 'Major Crimes will handle the case from now on. Better late than never.'

That was aimed at me: if he'd known I knew Emma he'd never have given it to me in the first place.

He shifts again and his pompous leather chair squeals under his weight.

'For internal purposes, the line will be that the reallocation of the case is a purely procedural matter, not a reflection on DI Fawley's conduct in the last twelve hours.'

'Thank you, sir.'

He frowns. 'You don't get off that easily. Not by a long way. But right now, we have a murder case to solve, and public trust to maintain.'

He sits back and turns, as pointedly as he can, to Gallagher. 'Over to you, Ruth.'

* * *

Interview with Hugh Cleland, conducted at St
Aldate's Police Station, Oxford
10 July 2018, 6.15 p.m.
In attendance, DC G. Quinn, DC A. Asante,
P. Brunswick (solicitor)

GQ: I would remind you, Mr Cleland, that you are
    under arrest. Do you need me to remind you of
    the wording of the caution?

HC: I do watch TV. And I'm not a complete fucking
    imbecile.

GQ: I'll take that as a 'No'. So, last night. Talk us through that again.

HC: [*gesturing at Asante*]

I already told him. I have nothing to add.

GQ: For the benefit of the recording. If it's not too much trouble.

HC: I went for a run, at Shotover.

GQ: You drove six miles, when you could have just nipped down the road to the Parks?

HC: There's no law against driving to take exercise. Not that I'm aware of.

GQ: What did you drive? The Range Rover?

HC: [*pause*]

No.

GQ: Oh? Why was that?

HC: Last time I took it up there some little tyke keyed it.

GQ: Oh dear, how very annoying.

PB: There's no call for sarcasm, Constable.

GQ: So if not the Range Rover, then what?

HC: My wife's car.

AA: And that is?

HC: A Honda Civic.

AA: Colour?

HC: Black.

AA: Registration?

HC: [*pause*]

I don't know. Not offhand. I rarely drive it.

PB: I'm sure we can supply details of the car, if required.

GQ: But you drove it last night?

HC: Like I said –

GQ: Yes, I know what you said.

AA: One of Emma Smith's neighbours saw a dark-coloured saloon parked outside her door at about nine o'clock last night. She doesn't recall seeing the car before.

HC: Well, it certainly wasn't mine.

GQ: You didn't go and see Ms Smith? Perhaps you thought you could get her to change her mind? Let you have a kid after all?

HC: a) I wouldn't have demeaned myself by going cap-in-hand to some council nobody who was only going to say no anyway, and b) even if I *had* wanted to, I didn't know her bloody address. Capeesh?

AA: You could easily have followed her home from work. You were seen on the Iffley Road –

HC: *Buying wine* –

GQ: I thought you said you didn't buy any?

HC: You know what I mean –

GQ: So what time did you leave the house for this run of yours?

HC: About 8.30. There or thereabouts.

AA: And what were you wearing?

HC: What do you think I was wearing? T-shirt, shorts, trainers.

AA: The ones we retrieved from the house? The white T-shirt and black shorts, and the Nike trainers?

HC: I already told you that.

GQ: How long did you run for?

199

HC: I don't know, 20 minutes?

GQ: That's a long round trip for such a short run – half an hour there, half an hour back –

HC: Are you checking my petrol consumption now?

GQ: So by my calculations you'd have got home about ten.

HC: Something like that.

GQ: Your wife will confirm that, will she?

HC: She'd bloody well better.

AA: Did you see anyone while you were running, speak to anyone?

HC: I was *running*. It's not a bloody social club.

Interview interrupted by DS David King and DC Simon Farrow.

DK: Stop the recording, this interview is now suspended.

GQ: What's going on?

DK: Mr Cleland will be returned to the custody suite, pending further investigations, and forensic test results.

HC: What, *overnight*? In the fucking *cells*? You can't do that –

DK: Oh, I think you'll find we can.

GQ: Is someone going to tell me what the fuck's going on?

DK: [*smiling*]
    Afraid that's above your pay grade, *DC* Quinn.

* * *

Sent: Tues 10/07/2018, 19.05   **Importance: High**

From: DIAdamFawley@ThamesValley.police.uk

To: CID@ThamesValley.police.uk, AlanChallowCSI@
ThamesValley.police.uk, Colin.Boddie@ouh.nhs.uk

cc: DIRuthGallagher@ThamesValley.police.uk

Subject: Case no 75983/02 Smith, E

This is to inform you that DI Gallagher's team will be taking on this case with immediate effect.

It has been brought to my attention that Ms Smith was a friend of my wife, so it is not appropriate for me to continue to direct the investigation.

For the record, I knew Ms Smith only as 'Emma'. I met her very infrequently, usually at my own house but also once at her flat. DI Gallagher is fully aware of the circumstances.

I know you will give DI Gallagher's team your full cooperation.

AJF
Adam Fawley
Detective Inspector, CID, Thames Valley Police
St Aldate's Police Station, Oxford OX1 1SZ

*   *   *

Adam Fawley
10 July 2018
20.49

It's nearly nine by the time I get home. I feel like shit, and it's going to get worse before it gets better. Alex is at the door to meet me before I've had time to turn off the engine. Even in the warm light from above the door her face looks wan.

'Thank God you're home,' she breathes as I slide my arm around her shoulders.

'Are you OK? Has something happened? Have you seen that van again?'

'No. Not today.'

She knows it's what I want to hear; that doesn't mean it's true.

She tries to laugh it off. 'And like you said, he's wearing a tag. I'm just imagining things. Overreacting. Blame the hormones.'

'You'd tell me though, wouldn't you? If you'd seen anything? Anyone odd hanging around?'

She frowns, wondering where this is coming from.

'Of course.'

I follow her into the kitchen and sit down heavily at the table. She's fussing about now; it's not like her.

'Actually,' she says, reaching into the fridge, 'there was something I wanted to talk to you about –'

She straightens up, turns, sees my face. 'What's wrong?'

She knows – of course she knows. We've been married a long time.

I take a deep breath. 'Have you seen the local news today?'

She shakes her head with a sad little laugh. 'I never watch that stuff. Every time I see something dreadful I assume you're right in the middle of it.'

I draw her towards me. 'This time I'm afraid it's true.'

I feel her stiffen. 'What do you mean?'

'A body was found on the railway line last night. By Walton Well bridge. I've only just found out who it was.'

'What do you mean, a body – what are you talking about?'

'I'm so sorry, Alex. It was Emma.'

She stares, then sways, and I reach out to steady her.

'Sit down, please. You're as white as a sheet.'

She gropes for a chair, lowers herself into it as if she's in pain.

'*Emma?*' she says, her voice half breath. 'No, no, that can't be right – I only just spoke to her –'

I've seen this so many times. 'But I saw them last week.' Or last month, or last night. They say the cycle of grief starts with denial, but in my experience it's less that than sheer bewildered disbelief.

'I'm sorry,' I say softly. 'Her parents came. It's definitely her.'

She frowns. 'Didn't you just say the railway line? What the hell was she doing there –?'

'Alex –'

'Was it an accident?'

I let the silence lengthen, speak for me. 'No. It wasn't an accident.'

'Oh my God, are you saying she *killed herself*?' There's a gasp but it isn't just the shock. She has her hand to her side.

'Alex – what is it?'

I'm on my feet now but she's pushing me away, rejecting my hand.

'It's just Braxton Hicks – I've been having them all day.'

'Is that what you wanted to talk to me about?'

She shakes her head, trying to smile it off, but her breath is shallow and there's sweat along her upper lip.

'Alex – you're *thirty-five weeks*, for God's sake –'

And now she's clutching her side again and I'm reaching for my car keys. 'That's it – I'm taking you to the JR.'

'No, no.' She grips my arm. 'Please, Adam – you know how much I hate that place. And it's going off now, seriously.'

She breathes, slowly. In, then out; in, then out. A minute passes, and gradually her grasp on my arm softens and she gives me a wobbly smile. 'See? I told you.'

I put the keys down. 'OK, but you need to go to bed right now –'

'In a minute – what about Emma –'

I shake my head. She'll have to know the truth – Ruth Gallagher will be calling, for a start, and I want Alex prepared. But not now. Not tonight.

'We'll talk about it in the morning. Right now what you need is rest. That's the only way I agree not to take you straight to the JR.'

Her head drops and I reach for her hand. Her lips are trembling.

'Oh Lord,' she whispers. 'Poor Em – poor, poor Em.' She raises her eyes to mine, and the tears are brimming. '1992. That's when we first met. *1992*. Twenty-six bloody years. How did that happen?' She puts a hand to her mouth. 'I mean, I knew she'd been unhappy lately, but –'

I could say something. Tell her I know exactly why Emma was unhappy. Tell her I went to see her, to try to help –

But I don't. Perhaps I should. Perhaps you would, if you were me. But you're not, and I don't. I should have told her I went to that flat long before this. Yesterday, as soon as I got back, even though she was exhausted and on her way to bed; or this morning, before I went to work. All I was doing was trying to protect her, cocoon her, keep her and our baby safe, but it's too late now. If I tell her now she'll think I have something to hide. And you wouldn't blame her, would you? Because you're thinking exactly the same. You're wondering why this is the first you've heard of all this – why I never said a thing about it before.

So let me be absolutely clear – just because you didn't see, just because I didn't tell you – at the flat, last night, with Emma? Nothing happened.

Do you hear me?

Nothing. Bloody. Happened.

* * *

This time, Quinn isn't the only one in early. When he pushes open the office door at 7.55 the place is already humming.

'Got the email, I see,' says Everett drily.

Quinn gives a non-committal grunt and goes across to his desk. But Ev's not giving up. She comes over.

'That came out of a blue sky, didn't it – Gallagher taking over? Did Fawley say anything to you – you know, before?'

Quinn shakes his head. He was already smarting at King for showing him up in front of Cleland. And now he's pissed off with Fawley for being the reason.

'It's turning into a bit of a habit,' says Baxter from the other side of the room. He's leaning back in his chair, cradling a Frappuccino.

Ev frowns. 'What is?'

'Gallagher having to tidy up Fawley's mess.'

Somer looks across. 'What's that supposed to mean?'

Baxter shrugs. 'Well, it happened with the Appleford case, didn't it –'

Ev is shaking her head. 'Come on, that was completely different,' she begins.

'No.' Somer, sharper now. 'If he's got a point, let's hear it.'

Baxter holds up his hands. 'Nothing. I was just saying.'

Somer's about to reply but Ev intercepts her with a look. A look that says, *Let it lie.*

Quinn starts unloading his messenger bag. He got it from Jekyll and Hide. It's as close as he could find to the one Asante carries without looking like he's actually copying. Which, of course, he is.

'If you ask *me*,' he says, 'all that stuff about Fawley not knowing who Smith was is a load of bullshit.'

Ev turns to look at him. 'What makes you say that?'

He tugs his tablet out of the bag and puts it down on the desk. 'Well, the thing about not knowing her surname is crap, for a start.'

Somer frowns. 'Why? I bet you don't know the surnames of *any* of your girlfriend's mates.'

'That's different and you know it,' he snaps. 'I've only been seeing her a few weeks – Fawley knew this woman for *years.*'

Somer turns away, her face dark. 'You're just hacked off because it's a big case and they've taken it off you.'

Quinn stands his ground. 'I'm not, actually,' he says

coolly. 'Because it wasn't just that. Not by a long way. This whole thing – it stinks.'

'Oh yeah?' Ev now. 'Care to elaborate on that?'

Quinn squares up to her. 'It was me who took the call when Smith was reported missing.'

'So?'

'*So* I remember repeating back the address.'

But Somer isn't backing down. 'And your point is?'

'My *point* is that Fawley *heard* that. He was right here, at that very moment, in this room.'

He looks to Baxter, who nods. 'He's right. He was.'

Quinn lifts his chin, vindicated. 'So even if you accept the name thing, how do you explain that?'

'I was here too, actually,' says Somer. 'And as far as I remember Fawley was looking at that Joseph Andrews Twitter account when that call came through.' She glances across at Baxter. 'Right?'

Baxter hesitates then nods. This is getting distinctly uncomfortable.

'So it's quite possible,' continues Somer, 'that Fawley didn't even hear what Quinn said. I mean, do *you* remember hearing that address?'

Baxter's eyes widen. 'Me?'

'Yeah, you. Do you remember Quinn saying that address?'

'I'm not sure –'

She flips her hand at him. 'There you are, then.'

'To be fair,' says Asante quietly, 'you'd be far more likely to notice an address if it was one you already knew. It's like someone saying your name. You're more attuned to it.'

'Right,' says Quinn, piling in. 'And he definitely *did* know that address because he'd been there – he said so –'

'But the email doesn't say *when*, does it?' says Somer. 'It could have been weeks before – months –'

Quinn throws up his hands and turns away. 'Whatever. Fuck it. If you're that determined to take his side, go right ahead. But you mark my words – there's something fishy about all this.' He starts fiddling with the papers on his desk, muttering 'time of the month'. Somer's too far away to hear but when he looks up again Ev is glaring at him.

Baxter raises his eyebrows and goes back to the safety of his screen; Asante's clearly regretting ever getting involved.

The room is silent now, but it's the silence of dissent, and the atmosphere isn't much better when the door opens fifteen minutes later and Ruth Gallagher appears. She knows this team – she worked with them only a few months ago – and she can tell at once there's a problem. There are two spots of colour in Somer's cheeks, and Quinn has that defensive-offensive don't-blame-me look she's seen before. Though it's usually on her fifteen-year-old son.

'Morning, everyone,' she says, looking around. 'I'm sure you've seen the email from DI Fawley by now, so you'll be aware that Major Crimes is taking on the Smith murder case.'

No response. They're just staring at her.

She tries again. 'My team are setting up an incident room in the office next door. Assuming we can get the IT to work, of course.'

A flimsy joke, but it's usually a banker ice-breaker. Not

this time, though. Half of them have already gone back to their computers.

The door opens again and Gallagher glances towards it, visibly relieved. 'Ah, there you are. This is DC Farrow, everyone, so if you can hand him what you've got on Hugh Cleland so far that would be great.'

Quinn shuffles his papers into a pile and holds them up, forcing Farrow to walk over and collect them. As one-upmanship manoeuvres go it's pretty unsubtle, but Gallagher isn't about to make a thing of it.

Asante looks up. 'I've already sent you everything from my side.'

'Thank you, DC Asante. Anything else?'

Baxter sits back. 'I was just about to start checking ANPR for Cleland's wife's Honda. I'll email you the reg number.'

Farrow waits in the middle of the room, but it seems that's all he's going to get. Ev sees him hesitate a moment by Somer's desk, but when she doesn't even register his presence he's forced to move on.

* * *

When Nina Mukerjee gets back from the water cooler there's an email waiting for her from the lab. The forensics on the Smith case. That was quick, she thinks, sliding the cup on to her desk and sitting down. She prints out the attachment – when it comes to technical stuff she always prefers paper to pixels – and starts to read.

Ten minutes later she's still sitting there. There's a frown line across her brow. And her water is untouched.

She gets slowly to her feet and makes her way round to Alan Challow's office. He's had the same one for ten years but it still looks like he's hot-desking. No pictures, no desk junk, not even a weary cheese plant. He's tapping at his keyboard, his eyes fixed on his machine.

He glances up at her, but only for a moment, then gestures to the empty chair.

'I got the forensics back on Smith's flat,' she says.

'Oh yes?' He's still absorbed in his screen.

She pushes the sheet of paper across the desk at him. He reads it, looks at her, then reads it again. Then he sits back.

'Shit.'

'So what do we do now?'

He tosses the paper on to the desk.

'There's only one thing we *can* do.'

* * *

Adam Fawley
11 July 2018
9.42

I should have left for work over an hour ago. But I let Alex sleep in, and then the health visitor was running late, and when she did finally arrive it took far longer than I anticipated. Sitting there, hearing the standard advice, collecting the standard leaflets, answering the standard questions; it took all the self-control I could muster not to keep checking my watch. It would have been so easy to tell her that we know all this – that we've done it all before – but it's nowhere near that simple. Not for us. Yes, we had a child, but we don't have one any more. Because our child took his own life, and this woman knows that. So I sit, and I listen, and I find the right words, because I can't risk her thinking I have better, more pressing, more urgent things to do.

But then, finally, she collects up her notes and her handouts and her Etsy bag, and I show her to the door. Where she turns and faces me, square-on.

'Is there something your wife wasn't telling me, Mr Fawley?'

I wasn't expecting her to be so direct. Or, perhaps, so shrewd.

Her eyes narrow a little. 'I'm right, aren't I?'

I hesitate then nod. 'Yes, you are. But it's nothing to do with the baby.'

She gives me a look. 'Right now, Mr Fawley – with your wife's medical history – *everything* is to do with the baby.'

'OK, yes, I get that. It's just that Alex has just had some bad news. A friend of hers has been killed. She's very upset.'

'Oh Lord, how awful. Was it some sort of accident?'

I shake my head. 'No. We thought at first it was a suicide, but I'm afraid we've had to launch a murder inquiry.'

She registers that 'we'. 'Ah yes, I remember now. You're a police officer, aren't you.'

'My colleagues are going to have to speak to Alex today. Which, I know, is very far from ideal, but there's no way round it. Alex was one of the last people to talk to her.'

She nods slowly. 'I see.'

'That's why Alex seemed upset just now – we were talking about it before you arrived. It was after I told her the news last night that she had that scare –'

Another nod. 'I understand. It must be very distressing for her. But thank you – it does help me to have a fuller picture.' She puts her hand briefly on my arm – 'If there's anything I can do to help, just give me a call' – then heads off down the path.

I watch her for a moment, then scan the street, almost automatically. The cars, the people; the men in vehicles, the men on their own. Then I go back into the house to collect my car keys.

It was true, what I said to that woman. Alex knows now how Emma died.

But I still haven't told her I was at her flat.

*　*　*

Simon Farrow hesitates before knocking at Dave King's door. In fact, he pretty much always hesitates before knocking at King's door. He's a good DS, no question – tough, uncompromising. And he gets results, even if he has to be a bit of a shit to do it. One thing's for sure, though – no one could accuse him of being a people person. He can't be arsed to manage down, so his team are forced to manage up, which makes life occasionally explosive and a lot more tiring. Farrow can hear him now, on the other side of the door, talking on the phone. He can't hear what he's saying but King sounds wired, whatever it is.

Farrow takes a breath, knocks, then pushes open the door.

King is on his feet, shunting his mobile into his pocket. 'Sorry to bother you, boss, just checking you wanted me to pick up on the ANPR on the Clelands' car? It matches the description given by Smith's neighbour so it could be the car she saw –'

But King is waving it away. 'Never mind about that crap. I just heard back from forensics. I'm going to see Gallagher. This is fucking *dynamite*.'

*   *   *

When the doorbell goes a second time, I assume it's the postman. But it isn't.

'I thought you said you were going to call first?'

Ruth Gallagher hesitates a moment. 'I was –'

I move on to the step and pull the door closer behind me.

'Look, can it wait? I've not had a chance to talk to Alex yet. Not properly. We had a bit of a scare last night –'

'I'm sorry. Is she OK?'

'Yes, but you'll appreciate why I didn't want to stress her out any more. So can you talk to her later? It's only for background, after all.'

She hesitates. 'Actually –'

I realize now she's not alone. A man with dark sandy hair and a beard has just locked his car and is coming up the path towards us. Even if I didn't already know him, he has to be CID; we're the only idiots wearing jackets in this heat.

I frown. 'You brought King? You really need two of you for this?'

Gallagher flushes, just a little. 'I'm sorry. I think we're

213

at cross purposes. I do need to talk to your wife, but that's not why I'm here.'

King joins us at the step and gives me a supercilious nod; I've never liked him, and the feeling is spectacularly mutual. He was one of my DCs once, years ago. But only once. Let's just say I wasn't too fond of his methods. And when the DS job came up in my team I gave it to Jill Murphy. I don't think he's ever forgiven me.

I turn to Gallagher, cutting King out. 'I don't understand –'

'We're not here for Alex, Adam. We're here for you.'

She's irritating me now. I shunt the door open again and take a step back. 'You want to go through all that crap again? OK then. Come on in. Let's get it over with.'

She shakes her head. 'I'm sorry. We can't do it here.'

'You're taking me in? *Seriously?* Jesus, Ruth –'

I can hear Alex now, calling me from upstairs, asking who it is.

I go to the foot of the stairs. 'It's just the postman – no need to come down.'

I return to Gallagher, drop my voice. 'Look, like I said, we had a scare last night – I thought I was going to have to take her to the JR. Just let me settle her down and I'll come in. Half an hour tops, what difference can that possibly make –'

I see King start to object but Gallagher forestalls him.

'Adam Fawley, I am arresting you on suspicion of the rape and murder of Emma Smith –'

I gape at her. 'No – that's crazy – you don't *seriously think* –'

Gallagher fixes me with her cool grey stare. 'What I *think* isn't the issue. All I know is that faced with the

214

evidence we've now obtained I have no alternative. I *have* to arrest you.'

I can feel the sweat running down my back. I'm trying to make any sort of sense of this – get even the slightest purchase on it – but my brain is in freefall. And on and on in the background, the drone of Gallagher's voice.

'You do not have to say anything, but it may harm your defence if you do not mention when questioned something which you later rely on in court. Anything you do say may be given in evidence.'

The words buckle in my throat. 'I need to talk to my wife.'

* * *

Oxford Mail online

Wednesday 11 July 2018 Last updated at 9:11

BREAKING: Headington woman feared dead

By Richard Yates

A woman reported missing yesterday is feared to have lost her life in an incident on the railway line just outside Oxford station, in the early hours of Tuesday morning. Police were contacted early yesterday after the Headington resident, named locally as Emma Smith, 44, failed to turn up at her place of work. Shortly thereafter the connection was made with a fatality near Walton Well bridge, which is believed to have occurred at around 1.25 a.m.

Commuter anger as railway works continue to cause delays and cancellations
Track improvements and signalling work on the line north of Oxford continue to cause headaches for rail passengers . . . /more

The big Brexit debate – where do local MPs stand?
Didcot and Cholsey MP Petra Newson has been vocal in her support of Theresa May's deal, but other Oxfordshire MPs are more ambivalent . . . /more

Doorstep scammers swindle local pensioner
An elderly Cowley resident was swindled out of over £1,000 by con artists claiming to be 'from the council'. . . /more

Ms Smith was a long-serving employee of the Oxford City Council Adoption and Fostering Service, and had worked at their Iffley Road offices for nearly ten years. Colleagues are said to be 'heartbroken'. 'She was such a lovely person,' said one. 'She was dedicated to her job, and worked tirelessly to find loving new homes and families for children in need. She will be desperately missed.'

No official comment has been made about the circumstances surrounding the incident at Walton Well bridge, but Thames Valley Police have confirmed that a statement will be issued in due course.

Fears for more ancient trees as heatwave takes its toll
After severe damage to a much-loved almond tree outside the University Church, conservationists have warned that others may be at risk . . . /more

'Swan uppers' to sail into Abingdon
The annual pageant of 'swan upping' will be coming to Oxfordshire on July 20th . . . /more

24 comments

Bradybunch1818
How terribly sad – sounds like she gave so much to other people, and yet didn't get the help she needed herself. Happens so often. Please don't forget there are people to help – your GP or organisations like the Samaritans

45641JaneyFitch
Friends of mine used that adoption service and they said all the staff were amazing. Overworked and under-resourced like all these things are these days. Perhaps we should put some of that £350m of EU money into places like that.

Gail_Mallory_Marston
What a dreadful thing to happen – sending #thoughtsandprayers to her family and friends

* * *

'Alex.'

She's lying on our bed, the windows open, the curtains barely moving.

There must be something in my voice because she opens her eyes and starts to sit up. 'What is it? Are you OK?'

I take a step forward. 'Look, this is going to sound insane – it *is* insane – but Ruth Gallagher is downstairs.'

She frowns. 'Ruth? But why –'

'They've arrested me.'

'What do you mean, *arrested*? Arrested for what?'

'For murder.'

Her eyes widen. 'They think you *killed* someone? But –'

'Not "someone". Emma. They think I killed Emma.'

'I don't believe it.'

Her voice is very small and very far away.

There's a noise outside and the door opens. King, in that trendy bloody suit of his, looking as chipper as I've ever seen him. And when he stares at my wife, pregnant, vulnerable, beautiful, there's no mistaking the sneer on his face and I have to work very, very hard not to land my fist right in the middle of it.

I move forward quickly and crouch down beside her. 'You have to believe me – *I did not do this.*'

I can hear King making impatient noises behind me, but I cling on to her hands, force her to look at me. Because this is the moment. The moment she decides. She's a lawyer; she's married to a detective. She knows

217

people don't get arrested on a whim, especially not police officers.

'Look,' I say quickly, dropping my voice. 'I went to see Emma –'

She frowns. 'What? *When?*'

I swallow. 'That night.' She opens her mouth to say something but I don't let her. There isn't time. 'She wanted some advice, that's all. She thought she was being stalked. That must be why they think – there must be DNA at the flat –'

King's hand is on my shoulder now. 'That's enough. Time to go.'

I shake him off. 'There'll be a search team here soon. Don't panic – it's just routine – just let them do what they need to do. But when they've finished, I want you to go to your sister's –'

'No,' she says quickly, 'I want to be here – for you –'

I'm shaking my head. 'It'll make no difference – they won't let you see me. This is going to be shitty enough – I don't want to be worrying about you. I want to know you're safe, OK? *With them.* So will you do that – for me?'

She bites her lip, then nods.

'I'll call as soon as I can and let you know where they've taken me.'

Because it won't be St Aldate's, that I do know.

She nods again. Her eyes are filling with tears. I put my hand gently to her cheek, and then quickly, out of that bastard's line of sight, to her belly. And then I stand up.

'OK, King,' I say.

* * *

The atmosphere in CID had been pretty glacial first thing, and when Ev goes out for a coffee, it takes a certain amount of determination to force herself out of the sunshine and back into an overheated and airless St Aldate's. But it only takes a glance round the office to see that something's changed. When she left, people were staring resolutely at their screens, pretending to be busy, avoiding each other's eyes. But not now. The room is silent, but it's the silence after a meteor hit. The silence of shared catastrophe.

'What is it? What's happened?'

Somer looks up and sees her. Her face is pale.

'Fawley's been arrested.'

'*What?*'

Ev holds her breath, waiting for someone to start laughing, tell her it's just a joke – '*Ha, got you, sucker*' – but all she sees is Asante's bleak stare, Baxter's scowl.

'*Arrested* – for what, for Christ's sake?'

'For murder,' says Somer quietly. 'For murdering Emma Smith.'

Ev looks across at Quinn. Quinn, who said there was something off about the whole case, who said Fawley had something to hide. He meets her eye, shrugs, but says nothing. Seems this time even he doesn't think he needs to rub it in.

'Christ,' breathes Ev. 'But then surely –'

She never gets the chance to finish. Behind her, the door opens and a moment later she finds herself face to face with Gislingham. He has a tan and a big wide holiday smile.

Then he stops in his tracks and stares around.

'Jesus – did somebody die?'

219

It's the Newbury station they opt for. Close enough for convenience; far enough for there to be a reasonable chance no one will recognize me. More than reasonable since, to be honest, I can't even remember the last time I set foot in here. We usually try to process fellow officers with some degree of discretion, but King must have trumpeted our arrival because I can't believe it's usually this crowded on a hot summer afternoon. There's a ripple of 'casual' glances as we parade in, King's hand gripped around my upper arm just so no one's in any doubt who's in charge here, and a low-level buzz starts up as we stand at the desk. But I guess it's no surprise there are rubber-neckers; a DI in detention makes for one hell of a car crash.

The sergeant on duty is playing to the crowd too, labouring over the custody record like it's the first time he's ever seen one of the bloody things.

He glances up. 'I'll be needing your mobile too.'

'Not till after I've called my wife.'

'You won't be doing it from that phone, matey. It's police property.'

'I promised I'd tell her where I am. She's pregnant – this is the last thing she needs –'

He raises an eyebrow. He might as well have said it out loud: *Well, whose bloody fault is that?*

He holds out his hand. I drag the mobile out of my jacket and slide it across the counter.

It's starting to hit home, just how much power I'm losing. Over my life, my movements, even my damn phone. Right now, I can't even take a piss without asking permission. You get used to being in control in this job, and the higher up you go the worse it gets. You lose the knack for subservience too, assuming you ever had it. It strikes me suddenly that I've become a walking cliché. Getting a dose of my own medicine, seeing it from the other side of the fence, going a mile in someone else's shoes. Only trouble is, these shoes are the sort that come with prison fatigues.

When I turn, King is three inches from my face. He's smiling. I can see his teeth.

* * *

'Mrs Fawley?'

The man holds out his warrant card. She doesn't recognize him. Definitely not one of Adam's. He's thin, tentative, slightly embarrassed.

'DC Farrow,' he says, holding the card out a little further. 'Can we come in?'

There's a van parked further down the street.

A white one.

She feels a cold surge of fear. Only this time, it's different.

This time she knows who's inside.

* * *

*Interview with Adam Fawley, conducted at Thames
Valley Police Station, Mill Lane, Newbury
11 July 2018, 12.30 p.m.
In attendance, DI R. Gallagher, DS D. King, Mrs
P. McHugh (solicitor)*

RG: Interview commenced at 12.30. Those present
are DI Ruth Gallagher, DS David King, DI Adam
Fawley. DI Fawley has been cautioned and is
now accompanied by his solicitor, Mrs Penelope
McHugh. Perhaps we could begin by having your
account of the events of Monday night, 9th
July 2018. You have previously admitted that
you went to Emma Smith's flat – what time was
that?

AF: Around 9 p.m.

RG: And I believe that immediately before that you
had been at your gym?

AF: At Headington Health and Leisure, yes. I would
have left at about 8.45. I'm sure you'll be
able to confirm that.

RG: Did you change at the gym before you left?

AF: No, I was running a bit late so I went
straight to Ms Smith's.

RG: So you were wearing –?

AF: A T-shirt and shorts. Trainers.

RG: What colour T-shirt?

AF: A white one.

RG: I see. And you still maintain that you went to
Shrivenham Close at Ms Smith's request?

AF: I don't 'maintain' it – it's what happened. I
saw her in St Aldate's earlier that day and
she asked me to go round.

PM: Given the location, I imagine there will be
CCTV corroborating this.

RG: We will, of course, look into that. And was
this meeting in St Aldate's accidental? She
just happened to be there?

AF: No, she'd made a special trip up from the
Iffley Road in her lunch hour. She wanted my
advice. She said that it wouldn't take very
long, so I offered to drop in on my way back
home.

DK: Did she tell you what she wanted to talk
about?

AF: No. As I explained before, I only saw Ms Smith
for a few moments then. I didn't find out what
the problem was until that night, when I went
to the flat.

RG: So you arrived at about 9.00 p.m. How long did
you stay?

AF: About half an hour.

DK: And what happened during those thirty
minutes?

AF: Again, as I've said before, we talked about
the stalker –

DK: Nothing else?

AF: No –

DK: No small talk *at all*? Not even about your
wife? They were friends, weren't they?

AF: Ms Smith asked after my wife, very briefly, when I arrived. But that wasn't why I was there.

RG: So what course did the conversation take?

AF: She talked me through what had been happening – specific incidents – dates and times –

DK: She'd kept a record?

AF: Informally, yes. But it was more like a diary. It wasn't something she was happy to hand over.

RG: For the record, no such diary has been retrieved from Ms Smith's flat.

AF: Well, it was there that night – it was on the coffee table.

DK: When she went through these dates – did you make notes?

AF: No. When I got out my notebook she got nervous and asked me not to write anything down. She wasn't ready to make an official complaint.

DK: So we only have your word for it.

AF: As I said, she didn't want to escalate things –

DK: So as *I* said, we only have your word for it. Because no one else seems to know anything about this 'alleged' stalker of yours.

AF: I can't speak to that. I only know what she said to me. And as we've since discovered, a man called Hugh Cleland had recently had an altercation with her, and could well have taken it further.

RG: Again, for the record, Hugh Cleland's fingerprints have not been found anywhere in Ms Smith's flat.

PM: What about his DNA?

RG: Samples have been taken from him. We await the results.

PM: Does he have an alibi for the night in question?

RG: Enquiries are ongoing, that's all I can say at this stage.

DK: [*to Fawley*]
So, if Smith thought Cleland might be stalking her, why didn't she tell her boss? Her colleagues?

AF: She told me she'd never seen the man's face. She may have been wary of accusing Cleland until she had proof it was definitely him.

DK: What about her family and friends? She could have talked to them.

AF: My *impression* was that she was a very private person –

DK: Private or not, I find it odd. Very odd. Especially since, according to her parents, Ms Smith had already had a similar experience some years before.

AF: She said nothing about that to me.

DK: Someone who'd had an experience like that, surely they'd be very unlikely to keep it to themselves if they thought it was happening again.

AF: As I've already explained, I'm not in a position to speculate about Ms Smith's behaviour. She was my wife's friend. I barely knew her.

DK: You knew her well enough to have a drink with her.

AF: She offered me a glass of wine. It seemed churlish to refuse.

DK: How much did she drink?

AF: In my presence, just over a glass.

DK: The PM suggested she'd had rather more than that.

PM: There's no way of ascertaining precisely when Ms Smith consumed the alcohol identified at the autopsy. DI Fawley can only comment on what happened in his presence.

DK: So she'd had a bit to drink, she's upset, so, what? You put an arm round her?

AF: No.

DK: Give her some comfort?

AF: No.

DK: After all, she's been through a break-up, she's vulnerable –

AF: *No.*

DK: She's an attractive woman, your wife is pregnant, it's easy to see how one thing could have led to another –

AF: It didn't happen. And I deeply resent your reference to my wife –

DK: Perhaps Smith went along with it to start with – perhaps that's why you thought she was OK with it. Perhaps *she* was the one who initiated it – maybe she'd fancied you for years, who knows. Only then suddenly she's changing her mind – trying to push you off –

AF: [*shaking his head*]

DK: And now she's struggling, starting to scream
the place down –

AF: No. *No no no* –

DK: You get your hand over her mouth – anything
to shut her up –

AF: I did not touch her at any point and she was
alive and well when I left.

DK: You didn't kill her –

AF: No.

DK: You didn't rape her –

AF: No.

DK: You didn't even have consensual sex with her –

AF: No. Absolutely not.

RG: [*slides across a sheet of paper*]
This is a copy of the forensics report which
we received earlier this morning. The lab has
isolated a quantity of male DNA in relation to
the Smith case. And it's not Hugh Cleland's.

PM: But I thought you said you were still waiting
for his DNA results?

RG: We're awaiting *his* results, yes. But this isn't
his. We know that for a fact because it's a
perfect match for someone else. Specifically,
to a sample stored for elimination purposes in
the police national database.

AF: I was at the flat. Of course my DNA is there.

RG: I'm not talking about what they found at the
flat. I'm talking about what they found on the
body.

AF: *What?*

RG: It's very simple. Your DNA was found on Emma
    Smith's body. Perhaps you could explain that
    for us.

AF: It must be a mistake.

    [*pause*]

    The only thing I can think of is that there
    was some sort of accidental contact – perhaps
    our hands touched when she gave me the wine.

RG: You're saying that's what happened?

AF: No, I'm saying that *could* have happened.
    Frankly, I don't remember either way.

RG: Your DNA wasn't just identified in one
    location, DI Fawley, or only on her hands. It
    was all over her body.

AF: No. Absolutely not. *No way* –

DK: Including, and most significantly, in her
    genital area.

RG: In addition, post-mortem examination of that
    area located a single pubic hair. A hair that
    did not originate from the victim. It's a male
    hair. And it came from you.

* * *

Alex Fawley sits in the garden, pretending to read, hearing the search team moving through her home. The low
voices, the footsteps back and forth down the front path.
She won't let herself imagine the ogling neighbours, the
old dears 'just popping out for a pint of milk' to get a better gawp.

The only CSI person she's met is Alan Challow, at one

228

of the St Aldate's Christmas drinks, but there's no sign of him today. He's probably too embarrassed. She knows she would be. The person who seems to be in charge is an Asian woman. She's calm and professional and thorough, but there's something in the dark eyes behind the mask that Alex doesn't want to see. Right now, sympathy is more than she can stand.

The back door opens and the scrawny DC comes down the garden towards her. He could do with a haircut. Every time he flicks it out of his eyes she has to bite her tongue.

'Mrs Fawley?'

She glances up and then back at her book.

'I'm sorry to bother you but could I just ask you a few questions?'

She looks up at him again, shading her eyes against the sun. 'What about?'

'Just some basic factual stuff. What time your husband got back on Monday night – things like that.'

She wants to send him packing, tell him to mind his own bloody business, but she's not stupid. She knows that will only make it worse. And the one thing she really can't face is being taken down to St Aldate's. Sweating in the back of a squad car, stared at, feeling the size of a whale.

'I think,' she says heavily, 'that you should get yourself a chair.'

*   *   *

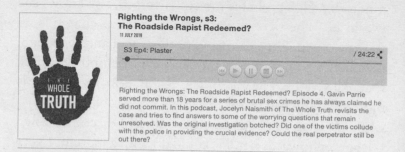

Righting the Wrongs, s3:
The Roadside Rapist Redeemed?
11 JULY 2019

S3 Ep4: Plaster   / 24:22

Righting the Wrongs: The Roadside Rapist Redeemed? Episode 4. Gavin Parrie
served more than 18 years for a series of brutal sex crimes he has always claimed he
did not commit. In this podcast, Jocelyn Naismith of The Whole Truth revisits the
case and tries to find answers to some of the worrying questions that remain
unresolved. Was the original investigation botched? Did one of the victims collude
with the police in providing the crucial evidence? Could the real perpetrator still be
out there?

[THEME SONG – AARON NEVILLE COVER VERSION OF 'I SHALL BE RELEASED']

[JOCELYN]

**I'm Jocelyn Naismith, and I'm the co-founder of The Whole Truth, a
not-for-profit organization that campaigns to overturn miscarriages
of justice. This is Righting the Wrongs, series 3: The Roadside Rapist
Redeemed?**

Chapter four: Plaster

You might be thinking 'Plaster' is an odd title for this episode. But as far as
Gavin Parrie is concerned, it's only too horribly relevant.

Before we go any further I should warn you that this episode includes
details some listeners may find distressing.

We heard in the last episode how the Roadside Rapist's third victim,
Alexandra Sheldon, went on to marry one of the lead detectives in the
case, DS – now DI – Adam Fawley. In our view, this is perhaps the single
most important factor to be considered when assessing Gavin Parrie's
alleged guilt.

But I'm getting ahead of myself again. First of all, we need to retrace our
steps a little.

On the evening of 16th October 1998, Louise Gilchrist was on her way
home from her job at a doctor's surgery in Cutteslowe when she was
dragged into undergrowth and brutally raped. And barely a month later, the
fifth victim, a 19-year-old trainee midwife, was attacked on her way home
from the John Radcliffe hospital in Oxford, sustaining horrendous injuries.

The time between the attacks was getting smaller, and the violence was getting worse. The Roadside Rapist was escalating.

[ALISON DONNELLY]

'I mean, I'd heard about the Roadside Rapist – everyone had. But that was in Oxford. Abingdon was miles away. No one thought it could happen to us.'

[JOCELYN]

That's Alison Donnelly. She's the only one of the surviving victims who's been prepared to talk in public about her ordeal. She was only 21 at the time.

[ALISON]

'I was walking home down Larborough Drive, just a few doors away from my flat. It'd been raining all afternoon so the gutters were overflowing, and when I stopped to cross the road a big truck came past really close and sprayed water all over me. I guess I was distracted for a minute. That's when it happened.'

[JOCELYN]

Alison never heard the man coming up behind her. The man who thrust a plastic bag over her head and dragged her off the street into the undergrowth.

[ALISON]

'I was trying to struggle but I couldn't see – the plastic was sticking to my face. Then I felt him dragging me through the bushes and bundling me into the back of a van. There was plasticky stuff on the floor. I've never been so terrified in my whole life. I thought he was going to kill me.'

[JOCELYN]

We know now that the attacker drove Alison more than ten miles to a car park on the Oxford ring road.

[ALISON]

'He dragged me out of the van and across some asphalt – I could feel it under my feet. Then he threw me down on my back and tore off my underwear and raped me. Then I felt him pull away and stand up and then his footsteps walking away. I just lay there, holding my breath, praying he wouldn't come back.'

[JOCELYN]

But those prayers were not going to be answered.

[ALISON]

'A few minutes later I heard footsteps again, coming closer, and then he was grabbing me and throwing me over on to my face. It was so painful – I'd never had sex that way before. He seemed different now – rougher. Crueller. He must have known how much he was hurting me but he didn't care. I thought he was punishing me for it being over so fast before. He had his hand on the back of my neck, pushing me into the ground, and I couldn't breathe, but when I tried to struggle he started to beat my head against the concrete. And this time, it wasn't over quickly.'

[JOCELYN]

Alison suffered a fractured skull and lost the sight in one eye. Her injuries were horrific.

[ALISON]

'I must have blacked out at some point because when I came to there were flashing lights and police and an ambulance.'

[JOCELYN]

Alison was rushed to the JR hospital, where she underwent emergency surgery. It would be five weeks before she was well enough to go home, and she faced months of rehabilitation. Meanwhile, and for the first time, Thames Valley had a lucky break. There was something embedded in the soles of Alison's shoes, which could only have come from the back of the van.

It was a substance called calcium sulphate. Plaster dust. It was the police's first real clue. And it would prove to be critical.

Nor was that the only development in the case. One of Alison's flatmates remembered seeing a white van parked down their street several times in the days before the attack. It was the first indication that DS Adam Fawley's theory was right: the rapist really could be stalking his victims.

It was important progress, but it didn't come in time to save Lucy Henderson, who was to be his seventh and last victim. On 12th December, she was attacked on her way home from work, bundled into a van and driven to an abandoned industrial site where she was savagely raped. Once again, plaster dust was found on her shoes.

[ALISON]

'After what happened to Lucy the police asked me if I'd do a reconstruction so they could put it on Crimewatch, and I said yes, because I wanted to do everything I could to help. But it was horrible – like reliving the whole thing all over again.'

[JOCELYN]

As the judge in the trial was later to say, Alison showed extraordinary courage and resilience in the face of such a horrendous attack. And now, twenty years later, she's found a new vocation as a counsellor, helping other victims of sexual assault. So something positive did eventually come out of her terrible ordeal.

But, tragically, the same would not be the case for all the Roadside Rapist's victims.

On Christmas Eve 1998, Jennifer Goddard, the mother of his fifth victim, got home to find her daughter had taken an overdose. There was a note by the bed saying that she was sorry, but she just couldn't go on any more. She was only 19.

The Roadside Rapist had claimed his first life.

[UNDER BED OF 'TEARS IN HEAVEN' – ERIC CLAPTON]

I'm Jocelyn Naismith and this is Righting the Wrongs. You can listen to this and other podcasts from The Whole Truth on Spotify, or wherever you get your podcasts.

[FADE OUT]

*   *   *

RG: Interview resumed at 13.10. Those present as previously stated.

DK: Let's get back to those forensics, shall we? Because frankly I'm struggling to come up with any explanation. Apart from the blindingly obvious.

233

AF: There must have been a mistake –

DK: A mistake? *Seriously?* How many times have I heard suspects come out with that exact same crap over the years? *'It wasn't me, I wasn't there.'* That's really the best you can come up with?

AF: Look, if I'd had sex with her you'd have found semen, not just a pubic hair.

DK: You could have used a condom.

AF: *You* may have the sort of marriage where you carry round condoms on the off-chance, King, but I can assure you, I don't.

DK: [*leans forward*]

Explain.

The.

Hair.

AF: [*pause*]

There is no explanation.

DK: [*sits back again*]

Oh, I think there is. Don't you?

* * *

'I still don't bloody believe it,' says Gislingham.

It's gone 2.00 p.m. No one's done any work for hours. Jackets are off, ties are loosened, and the machine in the corridor has run out of cold cans. Someone suggested decamping to the pub a while back, but no one seems to have the willpower to actually get their stuff and go.

'What did Gallagher say again?'

'It wasn't her I got it from,' says Quinn. 'It was that

234

bloke Farrow. According to him, it's the DNA that's the clincher, but when I pushed him he went all need-to-know on me. Though he couldn't resist letting slip that even Fawley won't be able to talk himself out of *this* one.'

'Fuck,' says Gislingham. He still can't believe he came back from the Costa Brava straight into this.

'You want me to talk to Clive Conway?' asks Baxter. 'He owes me one. Or three.'

But Gis is shaking his head. 'Best not. Don't want you landing yourself in the shit. There's enough of that coming down already, by the sounds of it.'

'And in any case,' says Ev hopelessly, 'what difference would it make? There's nothing any of us can do.'

Gis opens his mouth to reply, then closes it again. Because there's someone at the door, his bulk filling the narrow space.

Harrison.

Gis straightens up. 'Afternoon, sir.'

'Ah, DS Gislingham, good to have you back. We could have done with you, the last few days.'

Quinn bristles a little, but takes care it's not quite enough to catch Harrison's notice.

The superintendent moves to the centre of the room. He knows how to command a space.

'I imagine you've all heard the unfortunate news about DI Fawley. Well, clearly I'm not going to discuss the case or go into any detail about the evidence against him. That would be both inappropriate and premature. What I *will* say, is that I am expecting, indeed relying on you, as a team, to demonstrate the highest possible standards of professional integrity. This is *not* your case, and you must under *no circumstances* interfere with the investigation or impede DI Gallagher's personnel in any way.'

He looks around the room, slowly, at each of them in turn.

'And for the avoidance of doubt, this explicitly includes any sort of contact with the press. No "quiet words", no "sources close to the inquiry" – do I make myself clear? There will, needless to say, be no official comment of any kind unless and until DI Fawley is charged.'

Gislingham isn't the only one to wince at that: it's one of Fawley's phrases.

Harrison clears his throat. 'It's bad enough our murder suspect is a Thames Valley Detective Inspector; it'll be ten times bloody worse if that fact gets out.'

He glances around again. Murmurs of 'Yes, sir', 'Of course, sir'.

'There's plenty else for you to be getting on with. The Fisher case for a start – or had that slipped your minds?'

Quinn looks up. 'I thought we were waiting on the CPS –'

Harrison stares at him, and then, pointedly, at Gislingham. 'I'll leave it with you then, *Detective Sergeant*.'

* * *

```
DK:  Let's go back to the stalker.
AF:  I've already explained about that.
DK:  Not to me, you haven't.
AF:  [pause, then slowly]
     I asked her for details of the incidents, and
     then I talked through any likely suspects.
```

Anyone who might have a grudge against her –
colleagues or old boyfriends –

DK: And what did she say?

AF: She was at a loss. She had no idea who it
could be.

DK: So she specifically *didn't* mention this man
Cleland?

AF: [*pause*]
No.

DK: What about the most recent boyfriend – what
did she say about him?

AF: That she hadn't been seeing him long. That it
hadn't been that serious, and in any case he
was the one who ended it. He had no reason to
stalk her.

DK: She actually said that – that this man had
dumped her?

AF: Not 'dumped', no –

DK: But it was his decision to finish it.

AF: Yes. Absolutely.

DK: You see, that's what I'm having trouble with.
This ex-boyfriend.

AF: Why? It's perfectly straightforward.

DK: [*shaking his head*]
I'm afraid it isn't. Not by a long way. Because
there *was* no ex-boyfriend.

AF: I'm not with you.

DK: Emma Smith didn't have a boyfriend. Not then,
not ever. Because Emma Smith was gay.

AF: [*silence*]
No – you must have got that wrong –

DK: Nope. She wasn't exactly out and proud, I'll
     give you that. But she *was* gay. She'd been
     seeing a woman called Amanda Haskell - she
     just came forward after seeing the news
     reports. We've seen emails between them.
     There's no mistake.

     [*sitting back*]

     So everything you just said - it was all a
     lie. All that crap about old boyfriends -

AF: No - absolutely not - that's what she said -

RG: I'm afraid I'm also struggling with this.

AF: Perhaps she meant - look, the only thing I can
     think of is that she referred to a partner and
     I just assumed -

DK: You didn't say that. In fact, you've never
     used the word 'partner'. Not once, at any
     point when you've relayed that conversation.
     I've been keeping a note.

AF: Like I said, I must have just assumed - I
     mean, my wife has never suggested Emma was
     gay - I'd have remembered that -

DK: Speaking of your wife, let's go over again
     exactly what you did after you left Emma
     Smith's flat.

AF: I went straight home. I got back about 9.45.
     My wife was on her way to bed. I made her a
     cup of tea.

DK: And what did you do then?

AF: I had a glass of wine -

DK: *Another* glass of wine -

AF: I watched something on TV.

RG: What?

AF: I don't know. Some American thing.

DK: And you went to bed when?

AF: Probably about 11.00. I don't remember precisely.

DK: And can your wife confirm that?

AF: [*silence*]

RG: It's a simple enough question, DI Fawley.

AF: [*silence*]
No, she can't.

DK: You didn't wake her up when you got into bed? I always do – my wife's always on my case about it.

AF: [*silence*]

DK: Ah, sorry, mate – I forgot. You're in the spare room, aren't you?

AF: How on earth –

DK: What a bummer, all on your lonesome. How long is it now? Three months? Four? Must be bloody frustrating.
If you know what I mean.

AF: The only way you could know about that is if you'd spoken to my wife –

DK: Yeah, well, you know what it's like. No secrets in a murder inquiry, mate.

AF: I'm not your 'mate' –

PM: That was completely uncalled for, Detective Sergeant. DI Fawley is entitled to as much courtesy as any other suspect. Arguably, more.

RG: I apologize for any disrespect that DS King may have –

             [*looking at him*]
             - *inadvertently* displayed.
PM: Thank you -
RG: But the fact remains that there are numerous
      anomalies in your client's version of events.
      Anomalies *and* inconsistencies. As he well
      knows, faced with such anomalies and
      inconsistencies, the police have no choice but
      to investigate vigorously. However
      uncomfortable that may be, on occasion. All
      the same, I think, perhaps, that this might be
      a good time to take a break. Interview
      suspended at 14.15.

                    *   *   *

Nina Mukerjee looks up. There's a man following Alan
Challow's PA through the office; a man she hasn't seen
before.

'Who's that?' she says to Conway.

He glances across and makes a face. 'Dave King. DS in
Major Crimes.'

She frowns; she's been at Thames Valley eighteen
months now and this is definitely the first time she's come
across him. 'Is he new?'

Conway shakes his head. 'Nah – he's been here years.
Just doesn't bother with the likes of us. Usually sends one
of the serfs.'

Nina looks back at King. He's counter cast for 'bruiser
cop', that's for sure. In fact, he'd give Gareth Quinn a run
for his money on the sartorial front. Pink shirt, slim suit,

obligatory beard. He looks like someone in a Saturday-night psychological thriller – the smiley bloke who looks OK on the surface but almost certainly isn't.

Conway makes a face. 'No prizes for guessing he's after the Fawley stuff.'

That figures. Forensics may not normally be worth King's valuable time, but nailing a DI is evidently a very different matter.

Challow's PA is coming towards them now.

'Oh shit,' mutters Conway. 'Down periscope.'

Nina grins despite herself, but the smile fades somewhat when the PA comes to a halt at her desk.

'Alan's asked if you could sit in on this one, if that's OK.'

She doesn't have much choice. Conway grins at her as she collects her papers and follows the PA back to Challow's office. King is already installed: coffee, water bottle, tablet. He and Quinn really were separated at birth. He sits back now, crossing one ankle on the other knee. He's not wearing any socks. Nina's only been in the same room with him for thirty seconds and he's already pissing her off.

'This is DS King,' says Challow. 'He'd like a "heads-up" on anything useful from the Fawley house.'

'The search team has only just got back –'

'Yeah, well,' says King, eyeing her, 'that never stopped any competent CSI I've ever worked with. You must have *something.*'

Nina gives him an eloquent look, then opens her file. 'The clothes DI Fawley was wearing on the night of the murder had already been washed, so we won't be able to

241

retrieve anything useful there. The team did retrieve the training shoes but given the MO involved in the killing, I think it's unlikely they will yield either blood or bodily fluids. Though we will, *of course*, check.' She sits back. 'And there was nothing of any value in the rest of the house. Sorry.'

'No condoms?'

'No.'

'I assume they did check the gym bag?'

A withering look this time. 'Er, yes, funnily enough that did occur to them.'

He frowns. 'What about the Mondeo?'

She takes a breath, counts to ten. 'No, nothing.'

'Did they check the boot?'

Oh for fuck's sake, she thinks. 'Yes. And no – there was nothing visible there either. No fluids, no obvious hair. We've submitted samples for DNA just in case but I very much doubt we'll find anything. And before you ask, the car hasn't been recently cleaned. In short, there's nothing to suggest DI Fawley used that vehicle to transport a body.'

King gives her a sardonic smile. 'Well, I guess if anyone would know to put down sheeting, it'd be a serving police officer.'

'That's assuming,' says Challow quietly, 'there was ever a body in there at all.'

The smile twists into a sour laugh. 'Yeah, right.'

*   *   *

When Freya unlocks her door, Caleb hasn't moved. He's still sitting on the window seat, staring blankly down at the garden, exactly as he was when she left half an hour ago.

'I got tuna and sweetcorn,' she says. 'Your favourite.'

It sounds artificial, and she knows it. She just needs to fill the silence.

She goes over to the window but he doesn't turn, doesn't even seem to realize she's there.

'Caleb?' she says, louder now.

He turns at last and looks up at her.

'Sorry, babe. I was miles away.'

She sits down next to him and puts her arm about his shoulders. 'It'll be OK, babe. Really.'

He nods, but he's not looking at her. His body is rigid against hers.

* * *

Gislingham puts the phone down. 'OK, so that was the CPS lawyer. Apparently she told Fawley there are still some issues she'd like to see bottomed out on the Fisher case before she makes a final decision on whether to pursue it.'

'Fucking waste of fucking time,' mutters Quinn, but the mood in the rest of the team isn't much brighter.

'Come on, guys,' says Gis, trying to inject some energy into his voice. 'Quicker we do it, quicker we get it over with, one way or the other. So – where are we?'

Baxter glances at Quinn, but he's clearly too pissed off to reply.

Baxter takes a deep breath. 'Well, there were deffo some inconsistencies in the statements. Fisher's especially. She claimed not to know how her dress got ripped but

Bryan Gow reckons she's lying, though when she says she can't remember any sort of contact with Morgan, she's telling the truth.' He shrugs. 'Whichever way you look at it, that's odd. What's so special about the dress that it's worth lying about?'

'Good question,' says Gis. 'Let's get her in and ask her, eh?'

* * *

The mood in the Major Crimes office is a good deal more animated than it is next door. Rape and murder, with a DI in the frame; whole careers have been built on less. But Simon Farrow's under no illusions about his own place in the food chain. He hasn't been a DC long – not even a year yet – so he tends to have 'OK to dump on' tattooed on his forehead. Not that he's complaining. He's always wanted to be a detective, ever since he was a little boy and got a Sherlock Holmes set for Christmas. His mother likes to attribute it to growing up with wall-to-wall *Inspector Morse* – 'and we were living in Oxford too' – but at least he's managed to persuade her not to trot that one out in front of his girlfriends. Though it's hard to see John Thaw putting up with the sort of crap Simon's getting lumbered with at the moment. What with the online appeals and the sign posted at Walton Well bridge, they've been inundated with calls, but dealing with them is the arse-end of the task list. They share it round because it purées your brain after a while, and right now it's his turn on the shit shift. Still, as his gran always used to say, they also serve who only stand and wait. Or, in this case, sit and sieve.

He's about to get up for more coffee when one of the other DCs calls across at him.

'Hey, Farrow – must be your lucky day. King just called. He wants you down at Newbury. Pronto.'

* * *

DK: Interview resumed at 16.10. DC Simon Farrow
is now present in place of DI Gallagher. So,
let's cut to the chase, shall we? I've
listened to everything you've said, Fawley,
and some of it makes sense, and no doubt
some of it can even be corroborated. But
there's no getting round the fact that, right
now, everything's pointing to the same
conclusion: some sort of sexual act took
place between you and Emma Smith and she
ended up dead –

AF: No – that's *not* what happened –

DK: You panicked – your career, your marriage,
your whole bloody life would be wrecked if
this came out. So you wrapped the body in
something – plastic or sheeting –

AF: [*shaking his head*]

DK: And shoved it in the back of your car. Your
dark-blue Ford Mondeo.

AF: [*emphatically*]
No.

DK: The car was *seen*. *You* were seen. The
neighbours identified a vehicle matching yours,
and a man wearing exactly what you say you

were wearing, outside Emma Smith's flat on the evening of the 9th July.

AF: How many more times – I *told* you – I was there. Of course they saw me –

DK: And then you went home to your wife as if nothing had happened. She remembers you chatting for a couple of minutes in the kitchen, making her that cup of tea. What she didn't know was that *that whole time* the dead body of one of her oldest friends was in the boot of your car –

AF: This is insane –

DK: You had a glass of wine, watched the telly, and later, when you could be sure there was no one about, you slipped out in the dark and drove to Walton Well bridge. You knew you had to get rid of that body, and you had to do it fast. And where better than on the railway line – a freight train would pretty much do for the evidence, even assuming anyone bothered to investigate. If you were lucky, it would just be filed under suicide and that would be that. But you couldn't risk hanging around, could you, in case you were seen, so you just tipped the body over the parapet and legged it. It wasn't until the following day that you realized what a catastrophic balls-up that was.

PM: For the record, my client categorically denies every single one of these ludicrous allegations.

DK: You dumped the sheeting in a bin somewhere on your way home, and probably did the same with Smith's phone. Though let's not forget, the canal's only a few yards from that bridge –

PM: It's an ingenious story, Detective Sergeant, but speaking purely practically I find it very hard to believe that my client could have driven from Risinghurst to Walton Well bridge – a distance of, what, five or six miles? – without passing a single ANPR device or CCTV camera.

DK: [*passing over a sheet of paper*]
In fact, as you can see, there is a perfectly feasible route. Anyone with Google Maps could do it, never mind a police officer of DI Fawley's rank and experience.

AF: [*swallows*]
What about CCTV at the bridge?

DK: I'm the one asking the questions here. Not you.

* * *

It's the first time Gislingham has encountered Marina Fisher in the flesh, though he's seen the pictures, and had a characteristically measured and objective assessment from Gareth Quinn ('getting on a bit but definitely shaggable'). Though the minute she comes through the door Gis can see what Quinn was getting at. Fisher definitely has something about her, even in these less than ideal circumstances. He's heard all about her extravagant dress sense too, but it comes as no surprise to see she's gone for knee-length and navy today. In fact, if he didn't know any better, he'd be hard-pressed to decide which was the client and which the lawyer.

Quinn closes the door behind them, and they take their seats, women one side, men the other.

'We haven't met, Professor Fisher,' says Gis. 'I'm DS Chris Gislingham, and I'll be running the inquiry for the time being.'

'What about DI Fawley?' says the lawyer quickly. 'I thought this was his case?'

'DI Fawley has been called away to deal with another matter. But rest assured I'm completely up to speed.'

He looks to Quinn, who starts up the recording.

'So,' says Gislingham. 'Before we start, I need to check you've been reminded that you are still under caution. Now, we've asked you back this afternoon to talk to you about the incident with your dress.'

Fisher glances briefly at her lawyer. 'But I've already told you – I don't remember how the gown got ripped.'

'I should tell you we've had a profiler look over our interview with you. An expert in body language. And he's quite sure that you do, in fact, know exactly how the dress got ripped. There's only one explanation we can think of as to why you'd lie about that: because it happened during a sexual assault on Caleb Morgan. An assault you're still saying never took place.'

There's a silence. Fisher shifts in her seat.

'OK,' she says at last. 'You're right. I think I do know how the gown got damaged.'

She takes a breath, reaches for her water.

'I didn't notice the rip when I first got up the following morning – I just wanted a cup of tea and some aspirin. But when I went back up to Tobin's bedroom he was on the floor playing with some sequins – red sequins. He said he wanted them to stick on his drawing.'

'You're saying your son tore your dress – to get the sequins?'

She flushes a little. 'While I was downstairs, yes, I think so.'

'Has he done that sort of thing before?'

Her flush deepens. 'He likes shiny things. And he probably didn't realize how hard it would be to get them off.' She shrugs. 'Like I said before, children don't always know their own strength.'

'Did you ask him about it?'

She looks away, nods.

'And what did he say?'

Her gaze drops. 'He denied it. Said he never touched the gown. That he found the sequins on the kitchen floor.'

'But you didn't believe him.'

She still isn't looking at them. 'There weren't any sequins on the kitchen floor.'

'Have you asked him again – since then?'

She shrugs. 'He's still denying it.' She looks from one officer to the other. 'Oh, come on – he's not the first child to tell a fib because they've done something naughty.'

Gis nods slowly – he's the father of a two-year-old. He knows.

But Quinn's still pushing. 'So why didn't you tell us all this right from the start?'

She glances at him, then looks away. 'It was a family matter.'

Her face is closed; an ice sheet has come down.

* * *

'Thanks for helping with this, Bryan,' says Gallagher. 'I just wanted another pair of eyes. Unofficially.'

Gow looks up at her from the video screen. 'No problem. I was in Kidlington today anyway.'

He looks back at the screen again, then presses pause, a small frown creasing his brow.

'Well?' says Gallagher. Her arms are folded. She looks restless, edgy.

He pushes his glasses up his nose. 'It's a first, certainly. Watching one of these things to decide whether it's a police officer who's lying.'

'He's a suspect. Just like any other.'

Gow gives her a pointed look, then makes a note on his pad.

'Well, is he?' she says, a little impatiently now. 'Lying?'

He glances up at her. 'I could see no sign of it. I'll take the footage back with me and review it again, but there's nothing jumping out right now. He's under acute strain, which is hardly a surprise, but when he denies having committed the crime his words and body language show no divergence. None at all.'

'Dave King would no doubt say that if anyone knew how to do that, it'd be Adam Fawley.'

Gow raises an eyebrow. 'No doubt.'

Gallagher gets the message. 'Look, I know King can

be a bit – unsubtle – but he's a good copper. He has good instincts.'

Gow is writing again. 'If you say so.'

* * *

'So, Professor Fisher, just to be clear, and for the purposes of the recording, you're now modifying your statement to the effect that you do, in fact, know how your dress was damaged.'

Fisher heaves a loud sigh. 'Yes.'

Quinn nods. 'So what about the previous night, with Morgan? Is there anything about *that* you haven't told us?'

'We could do without the sarcasm, Sergeant,' says the lawyer.

'The answer to your question,' says Fisher, 'is no. I remember no more about that than I told you before.'

'Really?' says Quinn, openly sardonic.

She flashes him a look. '*Really.*'

She takes a breath and looks away, and Gis is suddenly aware that she's blinking back tears.

The lawyer looks at her with concern and passes her a glass of water. Then she turns to Gislingham. 'Look, Sergeant, this whole thing is taking the most enormous toll on Marina – she's not sleeping – her son is having nightmares –'

'I'm not sure what you're expecting me to do about that –'

'What I'm asking you to *do* is drop this preposterous case. The whole thing is absurd – it's political correctness gone psychotic.'

Gis opens his mouth to reply, but she's not finished. 'I mean, look at her, for God's sake. Do you seriously think she could possibly have perpetrated a sexual assault on a six-foot rugby player against his will?'

She stares at Gis and then at Quinn. 'Well, do you?'

* * *

You don't often see small children in a police station, so when Somer slips out to buy something for dinner that night it's hard to miss Tobin Fisher, sitting quietly alone on a chair by the main door. She looks around, worried that no one's with him, then notices one of the female PCs is at the drinks machine, collecting a can of Fanta.

Somer hesitates, then makes her way towards him. He has a colour-by-numbers book on his lap, and even though she's now standing in his light, even though there are people passing and noise and phones going, he doesn't look up. She moves round and takes a seat next to him.

'What are you drawing, Tobin?'

* * *

Quinn and Gislingham watch as a uniformed PC shows Fisher and Kennedy out. The lawyer puts an arm around Fisher's shoulders as they reach the lift, and she leans in, almost staggering.

'Was Caleb Morgan that convincing?' asks Gis.

Quinn turns to him. 'Sorry?'

'Just saying. Fisher looked pretty genuine to me. When she picked up that water her hands were shaking.'

'It's in her interests to be convincing. And don't forget all that TV stuff she does. That woman is a performer. She knows *exactly* how to play a crowd.'

* * *

The female PC comes back from the drinks machine and hands the can of Fanta to Tobin. He takes it, but he doesn't look at her or say thank you. Somer's eyes meet the officer's over the boy's head and the woman shrugs, evidently unsurprised. Somer isn't surprised either; in fact, she's beginning to wonder whether Tobin might be on the spectrum somewhere. There's no doubting his intelligence, but he barely functions socially at all. Can someone as well informed as Marina Fisher really not have noticed what's going on with her own child?

The little boy is still colouring in, carefully and deliberately, utterly absorbed in what he's doing. He's filling in one colour range at a time, a rainbow of pencils laid out on the chair next to him, their ends and points neatly aligned.

'Can I see?'

The scratching at the paper stops. He doesn't look up but after a moment he puts the pencil down in the correct place in the line and hands her the book.

Somer looks at the drawing, then takes a breath — realizing suddenly what this is.

* * *

'Something up?' asks Ev.

Somer's a few yards away, by the whiteboard, staring at the pictures from the Morgan case. Marina Fisher's kitchen, the ripped evening gown, the empty bottle of champagne, the photos of Caleb taken at the Sexual Assault Referral Centre.

Ev gets up and goes over, and Somer registers her presence at last.

'Sorry,' she says, glancing across. 'I didn't realize you were there.'

'Penny for them?' says Ev.

Somer turns back to the board. 'I saw Tobin Fisher just now. He was waiting downstairs while his mother was being interviewed. He had a colouring book with him – one of those "educational" things mothers like Fisher get for their kids. Illustrations from Shakespeare, the Greek myths, that sort of thing.'

'O-kay,' says Ev slowly, wondering where this is going. 'And your point is?'

'My point is that up till now he's just been working his way through the drawings one at a time. But the one he's doing now – it's right near the end. There are loads of blank pages in between. He must have deliberately *chosen* to do it.'

'So –?'

'That's just it. What he's doing now is George and the Dragon. The colour-by-numbers thing says to do the dragon in different shades of green, but Tobin's completely ignored it. He's never done that with *any* of the pictures before. I checked.'

Ev frowns. 'So what colour is he doing the dragon?'

'Red,' says Somer. 'All the same shade of red.' She makes a face. 'And that was when I remembered this.'

She points at one of the photos on the board. A shot of Morgan taken from behind. His head and his back and his neck, and the tattoo on his left shoulder.

It's a red dragon.

* * *

The custody sergeant pushes the door open with a clang, then he stands back to let the lawyer through.

'Let me know when you've finished.'

Penelope McHugh nods. 'Thank you.' Then she waits until the sergeant has lumbered back down the corridor and out of sight before stepping forward into the cell.

Her client is sitting on the narrow bed, his head in his hands, the toast and cereal untouched on a tray. There are huge dank stains under his armpits. It shouldn't surprise her; she's been doing this job a long time and she's had suspected murderers for clients before. But never, thus far at least, a serving Detective Inspector.

She's breathing as shallowly as she can. The hot stagnant air is riddled with sweat and piss and despair.

'We could have done this in a consultation room, you know.'

He looks up. 'I could do without another perp walk of shame upstairs.'

It's horrifying, how quickly a human being can fall apart. She knows this man – she's known him for years – but seeing him now, he's a wraith of his former self. All that quiet authority, that sense of latent power held in check – it's all gone. He looks hollowed out, scourged, paranoia ground like dirt into the lines around his eyes –

'I need to talk to you.'

Even his voice has diminished.

McHugh takes a step closer. 'OK. Shoot.'

'I've been thinking – this whole thing – the DNA, the car, the lack of semen – it makes no bloody sense.'

She gives an acid smile. 'You're telling me.'

'So much so that there's only one explanation. Only one way I can even begin to make it all add up.'

She frowns. He's talking too fast, his eyes are too wide. If she didn't know any better she'd think he was deranged. Or high.

'The evidence – it was planted. *I'm being framed.*'

It drops like lead. The guilty ones – they all say that. And she really didn't want this man to be one of them.

He must have seen something in her face because he gets up and comes closer. She has to force herself to stand her ground.

'Look, I know how this must sound – I've heard cons come out with shit like that for twenty years. You think I'm either guilty or crazy, right? Or most likely both. I'm supposed to be a fucking police officer and here I am, babbling like a bloody maniac.'

She starts to demur but he ploughs on.

'Just hear me out – please? – I've gone over it again and again and it's just too coherent – too, I don't know, *pat* –' He looks at her, as anxious as a small child. 'Do you see what I'm getting at?'

She frowns. 'I think so. You're saying that it all hangs together too well to be just a coincidence?'

His eyes light up. '*Exactly*. Because it all *fits*, it all *works*. The evidence is so perfectly put together, all it needs is gift wrap. But crime just isn't like that – not real crime, *unpremeditated* crime. It's messy and random and the perpetrator always fucks at least one thing up. For it to be this perfect someone had to *make* it so.' He stops, takes a breath. 'This whole thing was planned. That's the only theory that makes sense.'

Penelope McHugh isn't so sure about that. There's at least one other possible explanation. He just said as much himself. This man has two decades of experience in the art and science of killing. If anyone could get away with murder, it's him.

'And the person who did it,' he says, the words coming in a rush now as if he doesn't have much time, 'they're clever. *Very* clever. They know about police procedures and they have such a fucking enormous grudge against me they're prepared to kill to get revenge.'

He stares at her as though it's so obvious now that she must have got there already.

'I know who did this. And so do you.'

* * *

Ten miles away, in Abingdon, Alex Fawley is propped up against the pillows in her sister's spare bedroom. It's hard to be invisible if you're eight months pregnant, but she's doing her best. Not to take up too much space in the already-too-crowded sitting room. Not to make every meal about her and how worried she is about Adam. Not to hog the bathroom when Gerry's trying to get ready for work. So even though Nell's in the garden now, with the kids, both off school for yet another Inset day, Alex said she was tired and was going to have a nap. It's cooler upstairs, with the curtains drawn, but still too hot to get comfortable in her state. She can hear their voices drifting up to her from the patio below. Not too loud, because they think she's sleeping. Just the usual minor skirmishes between the boys, the dog barking, Nell trying to keep the peace. Ordinary, happy family noise. Right now – knowing where Adam is and why – it's enough to break her heart.

She checks her watch and it is – finally – nearly time. Her pulse quickens a little as she pulls her tablet towards her and hooks in her earphones.

* * *

PODCASTS › DOCUMENTARIES › TRUE CRIME

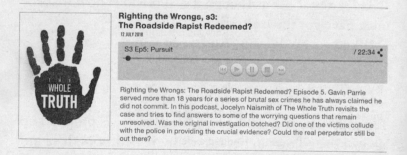

**Righting the Wrongs, s3:
The Roadside Rapist Redeemed?**
12 JULY 2018

S3 Ep5: Pursuit   / 22:34

Righting the Wrongs: The Roadside Rapist Redeemed? Episode 5. Gavin Parrie served more than 18 years for a series of brutal sex crimes he has always claimed he did not commit. In this podcast, Jocelyn Naismith of The Whole Truth revisits the case and tries to find answers to some of the worrying questions that remain unresolved. Was the original investigation botched? Did one of the victims collude with the police in providing the crucial evidence? Could the real perpetrator still be out there?

[THEME SONG – AARON NEVILLE COVER VERSION OF 'I SHALL BE RELEASED']

[JOCELYN]

As we heard in the last episode, on 12th December 1998 Lucy Henderson was attacked on her way home from work. She was thrown into a van, driven to an abandoned industrial site and brutally raped. Once again, plaster dust was found on her shoes, and once again her attacker left no DNA. Lucy was 23, and a graduate student at Marchmain College. She was also the Roadside Rapist's last known victim.

Not that anyone knew that at the time. After the best part of a year and no apparent progress in tracking this assailant down, public panic was at fever pitch. Questions were being asked in Parliament, and the Thames Valley Chief Constable was under pressure to resign.

And then, at last, the breakthrough everyone had been waiting for. On January 3rd 1999 the police made an arrest.

They had their man.

I'm Jocelyn Naismith, and I'm the co-founder of The Whole Truth, a not-for-profit organization that campaigns to overturn miscarriages of justice. This is Righting the Wrongs, series 3: The Roadside Rapist Redeemed?

Chapter five: Pursuit

['VICTIM OF CIRCUMSTANCE' – JOAN JETT]

[JOCELYN]
The story of how Gavin Parrie came to be arrested is perhaps the strangest and most worrying aspect of this whole case. That morning, Alexandra Sheldon, the Roadside Rapist's third victim, filled up her car with petrol at a garage on the Oxford ring road. She was queuing up to pay when she noticed something – something that gave her a violent and terrifying reaction. It wasn't something she saw or heard, it was something she *smelt*.

It was a distinctive, unmistakable odour – an odour she later described in court as 'sweet, like overripe fruit'. She'd only ever encountered it once before. On September 4th 1998. The night she was attacked.

Dr Anisur Malik is an acknowledged expert in this field, and assessed the evidence in the Parrie investigation as part of The Whole Truth case review.

[DR ANISUR MALIK]
'Olfactory stimuli are particularly powerful because they bypass the thalamus and connect directly to the forebrain. Hence their increased capacity to trigger recall.'

[JOCELYN]

In other words, smells don't get processed by the thinking part of your mind – that's why their impact is so strong and immediate. But that's also why we need to be very careful indeed when considering whether this sort of memory is reliable 'evidence'.

So where had this distinctive smell come from? Do you remember back in Episode 2 we talked about how Gavin Parrie had developed Type 1 diabetes? Not many people know this, but if this kind of diabetes isn't managed properly it can lead to a noticeable smell on the breath. A smell like overripe fruit . . .

By the time of that encounter in the petrol station, Gavin's promising new start back in Cowley was crashing and burning. His new girlfriend had left him and he was struggling to get work. He was behind on his rent and hardly ever seeing his kids, who were still with their mother in Manchester. With all that going on, it comes as no surprise to find he was neglecting his health.

So no one's disputing that Gavin was in that petrol station that morning, queuing up to pay behind Alexandra Sheldon. And no one's disputing that she did indeed smell what she says she did. What we *are* disputing is whether the man in the queue was the same man as the one who'd attacked her.

[DR ANISUR MALIK]

'What concerns me in this case was the severity of the reaction. It was only four months after Ms Sheldon had been assaulted, and she may well have been suffering from PTSD. Twenty years ago, the medical profession wasn't as well informed on this issue as it is now.

Smelling such an evocative odour for the first time since the incident could easily have triggered a terrifying flashback. The body would go into fight-or-flight mode – the heart would be racing and the brain would no longer be functioning normally.

As a consequence, law enforcement professionals need to exercise particular caution when dealing with the testimony provided by victims in circumstances like these.'

[JOCELYN]

And all the more so because the next thing Alexandra Sheldon saw was Gavin Parrie coming back out to the forecourt and getting into a white van. Even though the police never spoke publicly about the plaster dust found on the last two victims, the fact that the Roadside Rapist had started to use a van *had* been reported, and extensively.

Alexandra Sheldon reacted immediately – she didn't think once, never mind twice. She got straight into her own car and followed that van. Ten minutes later the driver pulled up in front of a set of lock-up garages off the Botley Road, parked and got out.

['MR X']

'She watched him reach up above the garage door and retrieve a key, go inside for a few minutes, and then come back out and walk round the corner out of sight.'

[JOCELYN]

That's the former police officer we heard from in Episode 3, who worked on the Parrie case.

['MR X']

'Ms Sheldon called DS Fawley at once and he advised her to proceed as quickly as possible to a public place and wait there for the police to arrive. She said she would go to the nearby Co-op store, which was only a few minutes away. A police response team was immediately dispatched, and shortly after 12 noon Mr Parrie was arrested in the Fox & Geese pub.'

[JOCELYN]

Adam Fawley arrived at the scene at approximately 12.25, by which time a full CSI search was underway in the lock-up, and Gavin was on his way to St Aldate's police station in the back of a squad car. Alexandra Sheldon had been at the Co-op all that time.

Or had she? The Co-op didn't have CCTV, and no one there could remember the exact time she arrived.

As for Gavin, he's always contended that – far from going straight to that Co-op, as instructed – Alexandra Sheldon broke into his lock-up, using the key she'd just seen him put back above the garage door. And once she got in, she planted some strands of her own hair on the floor, knowing the police would find them.

You're probably shaking your head right now, aren't you? You're saying to yourself, 'She was an intelligent woman, a lawyer, an ethical person – would she really go so far as to manufacture evidence?'

But think about it for a moment. Alexandra Sheldon was absolutely convinced Gavin Parrie was the man who'd attempted to rape her. She was also desperate to ensure this man was caught – only a few days earlier, the fifth victim had committed suicide at the tragically young age of 19. Alexandra knew that. She also knew the police had no leads, and even if the man she'd followed to Botley really was the rapist, there was no guarantee there'd be any evidence in the lock-up that would prove it. He could walk away scot-free, and be able to assault even more women, ruin even more lives.

So who can blame her if she concluded – in the heightened state of anxiety and fear brought on by the flashback she was experiencing – that she simply had to <u>do</u> something? She had to make sure this man was stopped, once and for all.

And it was in her power to do it.

['MR X']

'Whatever Gavin Parrie may believe, there was never any evidence whatsoever that Ms Sheldon planted evidence to incriminate him. Neither her fingerprints nor DNA were discovered, either on the garage key or inside the lock-up. It's also important to note that the strands of hair recovered were over 10 inches long. Ms Sheldon had had long hair at the time she was attacked but she'd had it cut very short immediately thereafter. In effect, even if she'd wanted to frame Gavin Parrie, she no longer had the "evidence" she'd have needed to do that.'

[JOCELYN]

No one's disputing the length of Alexandra Sheldon's hair that day, or when she'd had it cut. But as every woman knows, we sometimes have items in our handbags, like combs and brushes, that have hair caught in them – hair that could have been there for weeks or even months.

And one thing we do definitely know: it was the hair found in that search that clinched Gavin's conviction. That and that alone.

Because everything else was circumstantial. It could all be explained as mere coincidence. The diabetes, the fact that Gavin's brother Bobby was a plasterer and Gavin had been known to borrow Bobby's van when his own was off the road (it's worth stressing at this point that Bobby always flatly denied having lent Gavin his van on the dates of the attacks, though it was impossible to prove it one way or the other).

There was one further piece of evidence the police had, which they believed was compelling, but the law as it stood at the time prevented them using it in court. This was the fact that Gavin had been questioned about the attack on Paula, the 16-year-old girl we talked about in Episode 2, who'd been assaulted in Manchester before the Roadside Rapes began.

But even if that fact couldn't be brought up in court, it was still hugely significant in Gavin's case. Why? Because as soon as Thames Valley found out about Paula, they basically stopped looking for anyone else. As far as they were concerned, Gavin committed <u>eight</u> attacks: one in Manchester and seven in Oxford.

In their minds, it all fitted: the identical MOs, the fact that Gavin had been living in both cities at the relevant times, even the Oxford rapist's use of a plastic bag – the police theory was that having narrowly escaped being identified by Paula, Gavin started putting plastic bags over his victims' faces, to make sure it didn't happen again.

But we at The Whole Truth believe they were wrong. More than that, we believe they failed. They failed Gavin Parrie and his family, especially his children, who've grown up without their dad. They failed the public; and <u>most</u> importantly they failed the victims. Like all the country's police forces, Thames Valley CID have a duty to investigate serious and violent crimes 'effectively, independently and promptly', as confirmed by the UK Supreme Court earlier this year, in relation to the infamous John Worboys 'black cab rapist' case. And, in our opinion, Thames Valley simply did not do that in Gavin's case.

Back in 1999, Gavin Parrie was convinced that the crucial evidence against him had been planted, and he'd been framed. He told anyone who would listen that he was telling the truth, but no one believed him.

They do now.

And in the next episode we'll tell you why.

[UNDER BED OF 'TIME FOR TRUTH' – THE JAM]

I'm Jocelyn Naismith and this is Righting the Wrongs. You can listen to this and other podcasts from The Whole Truth on Spotify, or wherever you get your podcasts.

[FADE OUT]

* * *

Alex's heart is pounding, drumming so hard against her ribcage she feels bruised from the inside. Even in her overactive middle-of-the-night paranoia, she'd never thought it could be as bad as this. She gets up and starts pacing the small room, feeling a surge of hatred for Jocelyn Naismith – this woman who thinks she has the *answer*, who wants the *truth*, who just tramples about in other people's lives, other people's pain, not knowing or caring what wreckage she might leave behind. The baby bumps and shifts fretfully against her; she feels like she's pumping poisonous adrenaline into her own child.

She sits back heavily on the bed, and reaches for her tablet to check when the next episode is due. Three days – three *days*? – she can't wait that long, can't *not know* that long. And why did it have to be now, of all times? When she can't talk to Adam, can't ask him what to do –

She puts a hand to her mouth, pushing down a sudden panic. How often has she heard her husband say there's no such thing as coincidence – not in policework. What if the timing isn't random at all?

* * *

'Say that again?'

The team are gathered round the whiteboard. Not just Ev now, but Gis, Quinn, Baxter, Asante.

'I was looking through Tobin Fisher's colouring book,' says Somer. 'He's doing a picture of St George and the Dragon. And he's not doing the dragon in green, like he's supposed to. He's doing it in red.' She points at the photo on the board. 'Exactly like *that*.'

'Coincidence?' offers Asante.

'No such thing,' says Ev. 'That's what the boss always says.'

There's the smallest of pauses, an ebb of time in which they all think the same thing, see the same face, then deal with it and move on.

'So the question,' says Gis thoughtfully, 'is how Tobin could have known about Caleb Morgan's tattoo.'

Baxter shrugs. 'Perhaps Morgan took him swimming? I mean, he babysat him a lot, didn't he. It's not impossible.'

'Or perhaps he mowed the lawn,' says Quinn. 'Easy to see him getting his top off in this weather –'

'Marina Fisher doesn't have a lawn,' says Asante quietly. 'The garden is paved.'

Quinn folds his arms and frowns. He hates being corrected, especially by Asante.

'We can check the swimming thing easily enough,' says Everett.

'But what if it's not that?' asks Somer, looking round at the others. 'What if Morgan never went near a swimming pool with Tobin? Because if that's the case –'

There's a silence; it doesn't need spelling out.

'But it doesn't tally, does it?' says Baxter eventually. 'Morgan never said anything about them getting their kit off that night – in fact, he said quite explicitly that they *didn't*.'

'So,' begins Gis, 'either the boy saw the tattoo some other time –'

'And recently,' says Somer quickly. 'He's only halfway through that picture – it has to be within the last week.'

'– or Caleb Morgan is lying about what happened

during the alleged assault. After also conveniently failing to tell us about the incident with Freya on the doorstep –'

He doesn't finish the sentence. He doesn't need to.

Ev turns to him. 'But that was a lie by *o*mission not *co*mmission. It's not the same. He'd have every reason not to mention he'd pushed Freya, but why lie about the sexual assault? What's in it for him?'

Gis looks blank. 'Search me.'

'It's on the Welsh flag, though, isn't it? The red dragon?' says Asante. 'Presumably that's why Morgan got the tattoo in the first place. Maybe Tobin picked it up from that. Maybe it's nothing to do with the tattoo.'

Quinn considers. 'Well, I guess it's possible, but the only time I ever see Welsh flags is rugby or football, and this kid doesn't seem to be interested in sport at all.'

'And Wales weren't in the World Cup either,' adds Baxter, team footie wonk.

'So he wouldn't even have seen the flag on TV,' finishes Quinn. 'Not lately, anyway.'

Baxter clears his throat. 'Maybe we're all overthinking this – what's wrong with the bleeding obvious? Fisher and Morgan were having an affair – they were going at it in the kitchen that night and the kid caught them doing it.'

Gis looks round at him. 'But if that's the case, why didn't Fisher just come out and tell us that right from the start? Why let things get so out of hand?'

'Perhaps she was scared of losing her job,' says Ev. 'If she admitted having an affair with a student she'd probably be sacked.'

'She'll be sacked pretty damn fast if she's convicted of

266

'assault,' says Quinn darkly. 'Those stilettos of hers won't touch the bloody ground.'

'Yeah,' says Ev quickly, 'but that's just it. If she's *convicted* – not if she's just *accused*. Perhaps she decided her best bet was to keep on saying she can't remember and banking on there not being enough evidence for the CPS to pursue the case.'

'OK,' says Gis, 'so being devil's advocate – why did Morgan make the allegation in the first place if they've been banging on the quiet this whole time?'

Ev shrugs. 'Who knows why people do anything? Could be a power play, revenge –'

'Or to get him off the hook with Freya,' says Asante. 'We know how jealous she was – I can see her losing it big time if she discovered Morgan really was having an affair.'

'So – what?' says Somer. 'Freya finds out something happened between Morgan and Fisher that night, and Morgan tries to dodge the bullet by claiming she assaulted him?'

'*Lipstick on his collar,*' says Baxter, '*told a tale to Hughes?*'

'It was the scratches,' says Ev quietly. 'She told me as much.'

Quinn gives her a dry look. 'Yeah, well, you don't get those playing bloody Scrabble, now do you?'

Baxter nods. 'And Morgan wouldn't be the first person to allege sexual assault to get themselves off the hook with their partner.'

The implication hangs in the air: it might well be one of the oldest tricks in the book, but the people who play it are almost always women. Not tough, athletic young men.

'There was one thing,' says Asante slowly. 'At the end

of the interview, Fisher's lawyer said the kid's been having nightmares. Perhaps the dragon thing is connected with that?'

He looks round but they're not joining the dots – not yet.

'What I mean,' he continues, 'is that if Fisher really did have sex with Morgan that night and the kid saw them, maybe that explains why he's so disturbed? Sex probably looks pretty scary if you don't know what's going on and you're only eight.'

Ev is nodding again. 'I buy that. Especially a kid like him. From what I've heard he sounds pretty fragile.'

Gis takes a deep breath. 'OK,' he says. 'It doesn't look like we have much choice. We need to ask Marina Fisher if she'll let us question her son.'

* * *

The lunch they brought me is congealing on its plastic tray. Hardly surprising, given it's been there over an hour. The lad who brought it didn't have the courage to look me in the eye, just dumped it and did one. I might as well have 'pariah' chalked on the door. So when the keys clatter in the lock again I wasn't exactly expecting a social call. I hadn't even remembered Gis was back in the office. It's a measure of how fast I've fallen that I don't find the contrast between me and his post-holiday self humiliating. Though he clearly does. He hesitates in the doorway, then comes in and pulls the door to behind him.

'All right?'

Hard to see how I could be any less 'all right', but what else is the poor bastard going to say?

He shrugs. 'Just wanted to see how you're doing.' He looks round. 'I don't think I've even been to this station before.'

'I'm surprised they let you in.'

He gives a dry smile. 'Turns out the custody sergeant is an old mate from Training College.'

I shake my head. 'All the same. You shouldn't be here. It really isn't a good idea.'

He glances at me and then away again, takes a deep breath. 'Just in case you're wondering – me and the team – none of us think that you – well, you know –'

They don't think I raped and killed an innocent woman and threw her body in front of a train. Well, I guess it's something.

I lean back against the clammy wall. 'Thanks, Gis.'

'So what have they got?'

I shake my head. 'Trust me, you don't want to know.'

'If I didn't want to know, I wouldn't ask.'

I look at him. Is it fair to drag him into this? He has a family, a career. Just because I seem to be throwing mine away, can I really ask him to risk doing the same? But there's another voice in my head – a louder voice – which is telling me he could be my only chance of getting out of this. I need help. Not from Penny McHugh, however sharp she is, but from someone who knows how police investigations work. Someone on the inside.

'Look,' he says now, sensing I'm misgiving. 'I wouldn't

be a DS at all if it wasn't for you. I *owe you*. So if I can help, just let me do it, OK?'

'I don't want to land you in the shit.'

'That's down to me. If there's shit, I'll deal with it. And if I find something, well –'

I've said it before and I'll say it again: if you were drowning, it's Gis you'd want on the end of the rope. And right now, the water is over my head.

I take a deep breath. 'I think I'm being framed. No, I *know* I'm being framed.'

He frowns. He won't want to hear that, any more than Penny did.

'How's that then?'

'The DNA evidence – it must have been faked. Yes, I was in the flat – I've said that right from the start – but I never had sex with her. I never even *touched* her.'

Gis's frown deepens. It's not just that forensics don't lie; he thinks I'm asking him to believe the entire CSI team are lying too.

'But you and Challow are old mates, aren't you? Why on earth –?'

'No,' I say quickly. 'I don't think he has anything to do with it – I don't think any of them do. They just processed the evidence they were given. But that's the point – they were *given* it. Someone staged that scene.'

Someone put my hair there. I don't know *how*, but I know why.

The hair – it's a message.

Because when Alex testified in court that she never planted those strands of hair in Gavin Parrie's lock-up, I knew it was a lie. I'd known for months. Not right at the

270

start – not until it was far too late. But I knew. And I said nothing. I didn't stop her, because it was the only way to stop *him*. He was guilty and we had nothing else. But it was still a lie. And now Gavin Parrie is making me pay.

Gis is staring at me and I drag myself back. 'They're saying I tried to make it look like suicide so the police wouldn't go looking for DNA.'

Gis makes a face; he knows that makes sense. As far as it goes.

'But then I fucked up by not hanging around long enough to realize the engineering team were there and would stop the train.'

'OK, so –'

'But he'd have *wanted* someone to stop the train, wouldn't he? He put that DNA on her body and he needed them to find it, so they'd make the connection – so they'd come after me.'

He frowns again; he's not following me. 'Hang on a mo. *He?* Who are we talking about here?'

'Gavin Parrie.'

His eyes widen. '*Parrie?* You think *Parrie*'s behind this?'

I hold his gaze. 'Who else could it be?'

'But he must be tagged –'

I nod. 'He is. But all the same.'

He hesitates, then nods.

'So what do you want me to do?'

'Find that engineer – the one who called it in. I need to know if he saw anyone else on the bridge just before it happened. Because if it *was* Parrie, he couldn't just throw her over the side and flee the scene. He had to wait – wait until those engineers were close enough that they would definitely see the body fall and have enough time to stop the train.'

Gis jots down a few lines, then he closes his notebook and looks up.

'OK, boss. I'll see what I can do.'

* * *

Marina Fisher pauses at the French doors. Her son is on his hands and knees looking at a stag beetle edging carefully across the flagstones.

'Tobin, darling, I need to talk to you.'

But he doesn't seem to have heard her; he's completely absorbed, completely focused.

The beetle lifts first one leg, then another; its mandibles prod the air as if feeling the way.

'Tobin?'

She steps closer. 'Tobin, I'm talking to you.'

Still nothing.

'Leave that alone, sweetheart,' she says, in the sort of patient tone that has a very limited shelf life. 'I need to talk to you for a minute.'

Again, nothing. She steps out into the blinding sunlight, reaches down for her son's hand and pulls him to his feet. The beetle must sense a change in the air current, because it scuttles away now and disappears behind one of the tall terracotta urns.

'I was looking at him!' wails Tobin. 'And now you've made him run away!'

'I'm sorry, darling, but this is important. Mummy needs to talk to you.'

He pouts and refuses to look at her as she leads him back inside and lifts him on to a kitchen chair. He starts swinging his feet, banging his shoes against the chair legs.

'Tobin, darling, Mummy just had a phone call from her friend Niamh. You remember Niamh, don't you?'

He doesn't answer.

'Well, she's had a phone call from the policemen who came to the house, and they'd like to ask you some questions.'

He looks up, suspicious but intrigued. 'What 'bout?'

She flushes slightly. 'About the last time Caleb was here. Do you remember that night?'

He looks down, starts kicking the chair again. It's getting on her nerves.

'Well, Niamh says it might help Mummy if you could talk to them. It won't be scary or anything. No one will hurt you, they'll just ask you questions. And Mummy will be in the next room.'

Bang bang bang

She reaches out and grasps one of his legs, holding it firmly. 'Don't do that, darling.'

He's still kicking the other leg. And he's still not looking at her. She reaches to his forehead and pushes back the curls. His skin is hot to her touch; he's been out in the sun too long.

'So can you help Mummy, Tobin? Can you be my special, helpful, clever boy?'

The kicking stops. He looks up, almost shyly. 'Is it a game, Mummy, like last time? I liked that game.'

* * *

It's gone six when Erica Somer gets home. She pushes open the main door and climbs listlessly up to her own flat; she can't remember the last time she felt so damn tired. As she rounds the corner from the stairs she can see a bouquet propped against her front door. White roses, a dozen or more, dotted with stems of blue agapanthus. She feels tears coming into her eyes. Giles knows how much she loves those.

She unlocks the door and shoulders it open, drops her bags in the hall and takes the flowers through to the kitchen.

But she doesn't run the tap or look for a vase. What she reaches for is the laptop on the counter.

* * *

Ev doesn't get home to flowers. The only thing waiting at her flat is a vocal and rather disgruntled cat with some issues about the quality of service in this establishment. Ev feeds him, then sticks the kettle on. She's trying to ignore the light winking at her from the landline: there's only one person who'd phone her on that.

'Miss Everett? It's Elaine Baylis at Meadowhall. Nothing for you to worry about – your father's perfectly fine. But I do need to talk to you. Perhaps you could call me first thing in the morning?'

* * *

Gislingham is still in the office – in fact, the only one still in the office. His wife has already phoned twice. Once, to remind him that he promised to be home in time to read

Billy a story. And the second time, an hour later and a little more waspish, to say she's put his salad in the fridge. She didn't need to call to say that – she'll be in, and still up, when he gets home. It's just her way of putting a marker down. She'll cut him some slack for a while, especially after the holiday, but there are limits and they are not elastic.

What he can't tell her, even if he wanted to, is that he isn't even working. He's been faking it pretty well, for a man famously dreadful at lying, but what he's really been doing all this time is waiting for the last member of Gallagher's team to piss off home.

Simon Farrow clearly doesn't have a wife – or a life – since it's gone eight when he finally gets up and pulls his jacket off the back of his chair. Gis leaves it another twenty minutes, the 'Oh shit, I forgot something' moment being the most dangerous part of this whole enterprise. He's made his decision: it's the right thing and he's doing it, but he can't afford to get fired in the process; he only has to imagine Janet's face to start coming out in hives. The twenty minutes crawl by, then he gets up and wanders, with deliberate nonchalance, into the Major Crimes office.

They operate a clear-desk policy in this place. At least, in theory. But people get lazy, they make assumptions. What's there to worry about, after all, when you can't even get on to this floor without a Thames Valley key card?

Farrow's turned his computer off, but Gis doesn't care – that's not what he's after. He takes one more quick look round, then reaches for what he came for.

* * *

They interview Tobin the following morning at the Vulnerable Witness Suite in Kidlington. The room they use for the victims of child abuse. Pale-blue walls, dark-blue carpet; toys, cushions, a playpen; the box of special dolls they use to get kids to talk about body parts and what people in their own family have been doing to them. It makes Ev shudder just looking at it. She's in the adjoining room with the rest of the team, watching the video screen.

Tobin Fisher is huddled on the sofa as far from the door as he can get. His knees are drawn up to his chest and he's looking out at the specially trained female officer from under his fringe. The officer has been chatting away for about fifteen minutes now. Ev has come across her before, and always been impressed. She looks caring and comfortable, but she's not so gushing that the kids get wary and clam up. Though Tobin Fisher may well be her toughest challenge yet. She's talked *Toy Story* and Fortnite and what subjects he likes best at school, but most of the time she's been talking at him, not with. Even when he does answer, he thinks so hard first that you wonder if he's just going to stay silent. As if he's looking for the trap in even the most innocuous question – as if he's been warned (and Ev, for one, wouldn't put it past his mother) that everywhere here there be dragons. Speaking of which –

'Your drawings are really good, Tobin,' says the officer, opening the colouring book on her lap and turning the pages. 'I specially like the dragon.'

He blinks, shifts a little.

'You must have seen pictures of dragons before, to be able to colour them so well.'

He shrugs and says something half mumbled about *The Hobbit*.

She turns the book round and shows him the page.

'The other lady you spoke to – Erica – she said you've been doing this in the last few days, is that right?'

A slow nod.

'The red is fantastic. Really scary. Why did you choose that colour?'

No response.

'Have you seen one like it before somewhere?'

Another nod this time. But he's still not looking at her.

'When was that, Tobin?' she asks softly.

'Caleb has one. On his back.'

'I see. Do you remember when you saw it?'

The boy puts his forehead against his knees. His hair falls forward and she has to edge closer to hear.

'It was in the kitchen.'

'The other night? When he was babysitting?'

He nods. 'I came down to get a drink.'

'I see. And what did you see – in the kitchen?'

There's no answer. She reaches a tentative hand but he shakes her away.

In the room next door, they're holding their breath. It's 50/50 whether she decides she can't push him any further, even though he's on the brink –

When he does speak it's barely more than a whisper, and they can see, even on the video screen, that he's started to cry.

'I don't like Caleb any more. He hurt my mummy. I'm going to kill him. I'm going to kill him with a big sword like George and the dragon.'

* * *

'So what've you got?'

Dave King is hovering behind Farrow, staring over his shoulder at the screen. He's shifting from one foot to the other, fizzy with nervous energy.

Farrow glances back. 'We've verified what time DI Fawley left the Headington gym from the cameras in their car park. It was 8.43. And he was definitely wearing a white T-shirt and dark shorts, just like the witness in Shrivenham Close saw.'

'Yeah,' says King, 'but he's admitting he went over there, so that's no sodding use. His brief'll crap all over that. What else?'

'We've also checked out the route from the gym to Smith's house, but it's all residential – no ANPR, no CCTV, nothing.'

'For fuck's sake –' begins King.

'DC Jenkins also went up and drove it, and it took twelve minutes, which means the timings Fawley gave us tally. So that's something.'

'No it fucking isn't,' says King. 'All *that* is is three steps forward, two steps back.'

'I'm also checking on ANPR for the Clelands' Honda –'

King straightens up. 'I thought I told you to drop that shit.'

Farrow flushes. 'But surely we still need to eliminate him –'

'*No*,' says King, his own colour rising now, 'we *don't*. There is no forensic evidence *whatsoever* linking that tosser to this crime, and there's a whole truckload putting Fawley right in the middle of it.' He stares at Farrow. 'If you're having problems coming to terms with that, I'd be happy to look into a transfer –'

'No,' says Farrow quickly. 'No. No need for that, boss. I'm onside. Totally onside.'

* * *

'And where were they – your mummy and Caleb – when he was hurting her?'

The little boy sits up. He sniffs and wipes his hand across his eyes. It's hard to know what's suddenly changed, but something has.

'By the sink. Mummy was at the sink and Caleb was behind her, pushing her. She looked funny.'

'Really? What sort of funny?'

He shrugs. 'I dunno. Floppy. Like she was sleepy.'

'And Caleb had his shirt completely off?'

He stares at her, then shakes his head.

'So it had just slipped down? That's how you saw the tattoo?'

He nods.

'What about your mummy? Did she have her clothes on?'

He looks away. 'Her dress was pulled up. Like when she goes to the toilet.'

'Did your mummy see you, Tobin?' asks the officer gently. 'Did either she or Caleb know you were there?'

* * *

'Jesus,' says Quinn, staring at the screen. 'As if this wasn't complicated enough already.'

Ev looks dismayed. 'I can't see how an eight-year-old could come up with a story like that unless he'd really seen it.'

'Yeah, OK,' says Baxter, 'so they had sex. But how do we know it wasn't just consensual –'

'Seriously?' says Somer. 'How clear does it have to be?' She looks pale – so pale Ev is surprised she bothered coming in today at all.

Gis looks round at the rest of the team. 'Somer's right. Looks like a crime *was* committed that night. But the victim wasn't Morgan. It was Fisher.'

* * *

'They didn't see me,' says the little boy sulkily. 'I ran away.'

'Back up to your room?'

He nods.

'And that's on the top floor, isn't it?'

Another nod.

The officer checks something in her file. 'But Mummy's room is somewhere else, I think. On the floor below?'

No response this time.

'So you probably didn't hear her go to bed, then?'

He looks away and mumbles something. She asks him gently to say it again and eventually he does.

'I was under my bed.'

'What were you doing there, Tobin?'

He looks down; his lip is trembling. 'I was hiding.'

* * *

280

'But if Morgan raped her, why isn't she saying so?' says Quinn. 'Why doesn't *she* accuse *him*? In fact, why didn't she do that right from the start?'

'Because she can't remember,' says Ev quietly. 'Because Morgan slipped her something.'

Asante nods. 'Classic date-rape MO: she's a bit tipsy already, he makes sure he pours the drinks. And sparkling wine is the predator's best friend. The bubbles disguise the drug.'

'The lab didn't find anything –' begins Baxter.

'They wouldn't,' says Asante. 'If it was GHB, it would have metabolized too quickly to register, even in a full tox screen. That's why those bastards choose it in the first place.'

There's a silence.

'Might be worth noting,' says Quinn eventually, 'that Morgan made sure to rinse those champagne glasses afterwards. Either he had something to hide or he's going to make someone a lovely wife one of these days.'

Somer shoots him a fierce look, but he just ignores her.

Baxter turns towards Everett. 'You've done the sexual offences training, Ev. Wouldn't Fisher have realized the following morning if she'd been raped?'

Ev takes a deep breath. 'Not necessarily – a lot of victims don't. Not if the rapist uses a condom and is careful not to leave any marks. And if nothing looks wrong the following morning.'

'Like Fisher's dress being hung up and her shoes tidied away,' says Asante grimly.

'Right. Exactly.'

'Tobin was frightened, though,' says Somer quietly. 'Frightened enough to hide.'

Baxter folds his arms. 'But even if you're right, where does that leave us? Are we seriously planning to rock up to the CPS and say, "Actually, guys, we've changed our minds. We now think *he* might have raped *her* but all we have to go on is the word of a slightly weird eight-year-old kid backed up by absolutely no hard evidence at all"? Hands up anyone who thinks they're going to buy that.'

No one moves.

He shrugs. 'There you are then. They'd laugh us out of the bloody building.'

Asante frowns. 'It's worse than that. Not only do we have no evidence that he raped her, what we *do* have points in exactly the opposite direction: *her* assaulting *him*.'

'Fisher had already showered,' begins Ev, 'so that was always going to cause a problem with the forensics –'

'No,' he says quickly. 'I'm not talking about that, I'm talking about Morgan. He had her DNA in his groin area, but nothing on his penis. Even if he used a condom there'd be more there than we found.'

'Right,' says Quinn. 'If he really did rape her, he'd have had her all over him.'

'Yeah, OK,' says Ev, 'but it wouldn't have been beyond the wit of bloke to find a flannel, now would it? Even rugby players wash.'

Quinn looks sceptical. 'While keeping her DNA intact on his hands? That's not so easy.'

Ev shrugs. 'Rubber gloves?'

But Quinn's still not convinced. 'So he rapes her, goes to a hell of a lot of trouble to make sure she won't remember it, but *then* goes out of his way to draw attention to himself – and cause himself no end of shit – by reporting her for attempted assault? What's all that about?'

'I think you're right,' says Gislingham. 'There's something else going on here – something we're not seeing.'

Somer looks up, a frown darkening her face. 'Maybe we just haven't been asking the right questions.'

'OK,' says Gis slowly, 'well, now's our chance. Marina Fisher's in the room down the hall.'

* * *

Interview with Marina Fisher, conducted at Kidlington Witness Suite, Oxford
13 July 2018, 12.15 p.m.
In attendance, DS C. Gislingham, DC V. Everett, Ms N. Kennedy (solicitor)

CG: Interview commenced at 12.15, Friday 13th July. This is the third interview in connection with the sexual assault allegations made by Caleb Morgan. I should remind you that you are still under caution. For the purposes of the recording, Professor Fisher's son, Tobin, has just been interviewed by a specialist Thames Valley officer. During this interview, Tobin was asked about the night of July 6th. He says he saw you in the kitchen, Professor Fisher. With Caleb Morgan.

MF: What do you mean he 'saw' us?

CG: The description is consistent with the two of you having sex.

283

MF: But I told you –

CG: That you couldn't remember, I know. Well,
    there might be a reason for that. The way
    Tobin described it, Morgan may have given you
    some sort of date-rape drug. That would
    account for your lack of recall.

MF: [*gasps and turns away*]

CG: Tobin also said he thought Morgan was hurting
    you. Though that may just have been down to
    him not understanding what he was seeing –

MF: [*begins to sob*]
    But I'd have known – the following morning,
    I'd have *known* –

NK: [*quietly, to her client*]
    Not necessarily. Not if he used protection.

CG: So on that basis –

NK: [*interrupting*]
    Can't you just give her a moment, for heaven's
    sake?
    [*silence*]

VE: Professor Fisher, we do understand how hard
    this must be, but what Tobin said – it could
    change everything.

MF: [*struggling for composure*]
    OK.
    [*pause*]
    OK.

NK: Are you sure? You don't have to do this right
    now –

MF: No – I want to. I want to get this over with
    and take my son home.

NK: [*turning to the officers*]
OK, so what *exactly* did Tobin say?

VE: He said Professor Fisher looked 'floppy' and
'sleepy'. That's why we believe she could have
been administered with some sort of date-rape
drug, possibly in the champagne.
[*to Fisher*]
Do you remember if you were watching when Mr
Morgan poured it?

MF: No, he had his back to me. I didn't think
anything of it at the time.

CG: I see. We've already checked the bottle and
glasses, but there was no trace of such a
substance in either. Nor was anything detected
in your toxicology screen, which, as you no
doubt realize, is going to make it almost
impossible to prove.

NK: Why am I not surprised –

CG: Having heard what your son said, is there
anything else you can recall about that night?
Perhaps something that may not have seemed
relevant before?

MF: No. I'm sorry. I've already told you everything
I can remember.

VE: If Morgan hadn't used such a substance
before he might not have realized how long
it would take to take effect, especially as
you'd had a heavy meal. That could account
for the scratches – he might have started to
assault you before you were fully sedated,
and you attempted to defend yourself. Are

you sure you don't remember anything like
that?

MF: [*hangs her head*]
No.

CG: If you *were* given such a drug, it would of
course throw a very different light on the
subsequent accusation made against you. Do you
know why Mr Morgan would have made such an
allegation, that being the case?

NK: Isn't it obvious? He wanted to cover up his
own criminal behaviour by turning the tables
on my client.

CG: That's one explanation. But there may be
others. Revenge, perhaps? Is there any motive
at all that you can think of?

MF: [*despairing*]
No, absolutely nothing. I always thought we
got on very well. I've gone out of my way to
support him –

NK: Are you proposing to charge Morgan?

CG: Clearly we have yet to interview him about this –

NK: You were quick enough to arrest Marina. No
wonder Tobin's been having nightmares – he saw
his mother *being raped* –

*   *   *

'Blimey, he doesn't do things by halves, does he? Must be
nice having parents who can afford to call in a whole
platoon.'

Gislingham and Quinn are back at St Aldate's, watching

as Caleb Morgan and his lawyers are shown into Interview One. Meredith Melia is in a mint-green trouser suit and Patrick Dunn in his trademark white open-necked shirt; he must buy them by the hundredweight. They've brought a bag-carrier too, an earnest-looking young woman in glasses, laden with two pilot cases and a stack of files.

'They're probably full of bricks, just to intimidate us,' says Quinn, nodding towards the bags.

Gislingham gives a grim smile. 'Well, it's working.' He draws himself up a little, then turns to Quinn. 'Find Ev, would you? Let's rustle up a little posse of our own.'

Quinn grins. 'I'll see if I can find you a nice big sheriff badge too.'

* * *

Unlike his lawyers, Caleb Morgan hasn't bothered dressing for the occasion. In fact, Ev wouldn't be at all surprised if they'd told him exactly what to wear: the slightly grubby T-shirt and cargo shorts might as well be a big flashing sign saying, 'Our client is completely relaxed about this whole process.'

By the time everyone has a seat and a glass of water, the room is already fugging up, and Ev's starting to envy that T-shirt. She can feel the sweat prickling under her arms.

Gislingham looks round the table and it's not until the room is absolutely silent that he begins to speak.

'Caleb Owen Morgan, I am arresting you on suspicion of sexual assault on 6th July 2018. You do not have to say anything, but it may harm your defence if you do not mention when questioned something which you later rely on in court. Anything you do say may be given in evidence.'

Morgan is gaping. 'What the *fuck* –'

'Let us handle this, Caleb,' says Melia, turning to Gislingham. 'What the hell's going on? Our client is the *victim* here – oh, but I forgot, men can't *possibly* be victims, can they. This is unbelievable –'

'What *I* would like to know,' says Dunn, cutting across her, 'is what *evidence* you have for this absurd allegation.'

Gislingham matches him stare for stare. 'Contrary to what we previously believed, there was, in fact, a witness to what happened that night.'

Morgan looks incredulous. '*What?*'

Meredith Melia looks up. 'A *witness?*'

Gislingham relishes the pause. 'Tobin Fisher.'

Morgan shakes his head. 'No. No way. He was asleep. I checked on him only a few minutes before Marina got back.'

'That's as may be, but he told us he came down to get a drink.'

Morgan sits back. 'Well, I never saw him.'

'No. That's what he said too.'

A frown flickers across Morgan's brows. 'So what did he say?'

'He said he saw you having sex with his mother.'

The room detonates with silence.

'Never happened,' says Morgan tersely. 'Never. Bloody. Happened.'

'Well, his description was pretty damn detailed,' observes Quinn.

'So what?'

Quinn raises an eyebrow. 'So how does an eight-year-old describe the mechanics of sex unless he's actually seen it? He said you took her from behind, by the way, is that how you like it?'

Morgan shoots him a savage look, then turns to Gislingham. 'Who knows how many lovers Marina's had? He could have seen her with any one of them.'

Dunn sits forward. 'My client makes an extremely valid point, officer. And for the record, I find your colleague's last comment exceptionally offensive.'

'Likewise,' says Melia. 'And in any case, the child is only eight. I doubt anything he says can be considered reliable.'

'True,' says Gislingham, 'he is very young. But we do have specially trained officers with extensive experience in questioning children of his age. Should it come to it, I'm sure the CPS would consider it fully admissible. So, to confirm, Mr Morgan's position –'

Quinn stifles a snort. Melia glares at him.

'Mr Morgan's position is that no such sex act took place between him and Professor Fisher?'

'No,' says Morgan. 'It did not.'

'According to Tobin, you were hurting his mother –'

Morgan starts shaking his head.

'– not only that, he said she looked "floppy" and "sleepy". A description that leads us to believe that some sort of date-rape drug may have been involved.'

Morgan's been struggling to keep his anger down, but this is too much. 'You've got to be fucking *kidding* me – I've never heard so much bullshit in my whole fucking life –'

'Caleb,' begins Melia but he shakes her hand off, his eyes still on Gislingham.

'You're actually *believing* that shit?'

Gislingham shrugs. 'Why would he make it up?'

Morgan leans forward, elbows on the table. 'He's just a *kid*. A pretty vulnerable kid too, frankly. I'm not the only one who thought he might have some sort of a problem. So if you think you can rely on a single word he's saying, I'll have some of whatever you're smoking.'

Quinn and Gislingham exchange a glance. Gislingham turns a page in the file.

'There was also the question of the tattoo.'

Morgan frowns. 'The tattoo?'

'The one on your shoulder. The red dragon?'

'What about it? You knew about that already.'

'Tobin knows about it too,' says Quinn. 'In fact, he's been doing a version of it in his colouring book.'

Morgan looks baffled. 'I really don't see –'

'I suspect your lawyers do,' says Gis drily, glancing across at them.

'Caleb,' says Melia, turning to him, 'can you think of any occasion when Tobin might have seen that tattoo?'

'Oh, right, OK.' He looks away, pulls a hand through his hair. 'Well, yeah, there was definitely one time – I was babysitting and Tobin threw one of his wobblers and spilt his juice all down me. I'm pretty sure I took my T-shirt off and ran it under the tap. I guess he must have seen it that way.'

'There you are,' says Melia quickly, with a gesture at Gislingham. 'Happy now?'

'And in any case,' says Morgan, 'if I'd raped Marina there'd have been evidence. DNA – all of that –'

'Not necessarily,' says Gis, 'as I'm sure your lawyers are aware –'

But Melia hasn't finished. 'And as for Tobin Fisher – I say again, children that age are *extremely* suggestible. No court will ever take that so-called "evidence" seriously.'

'I rather think that's for a jury to decide,' says Gislingham evenly. 'Should it come to that.'

* * *

'So what do you think?' says Quinn, glancing at Gis as he presses the button on the coffee machine. Morgan is on his way downstairs to be processed.

Gis frowns. 'Interesting what he said about Tobin.' There's a pause, then, 'And was it just me or did he react a bit weirdly when we asked him about the tattoo?'

Quinn kicks the machine and it starts to gurgle. 'Nope. It wasn't just you.'

Gis is looking thoughtful now. 'Get me a copy of that interview footage. I'm going to talk to Bryan Gow.'

* * *

'So what did you want to talk to me about?'

Penelope McHugh takes a seat and opens her file, keeping her tone brisk. Her client seems a little more measured today, a little more in control. The fanaticism in his eyes has gone, and he's agreed to come upstairs to a meeting room. The tiny room is as stifling as the cell, but at least all it smells of is far too much plug-in air freshener. Every room McHugh finds herself in seems to have one of those bloody things. It's an occupational hazard in criminal defence.

'Emma Smith's clothes,' he says quickly. 'What she was wearing when she was found.'

McHugh picks up her pen. 'OK.'

'When I left, she was wearing some sort of leggings. Blue. And a T-shirt.'

'What colour?'

He thinks. 'Pale yellow? With some sort of logo on the front? To be honest, I really wasn't looking. Half the time I couldn't even tell you what my wife –'

He stops. Checks himself. Takes a breath.

McHugh pretends not to notice. She flicks back through the file. 'According to this, the victim was wearing a white cotton sundress when she was found. You're sure that couldn't have been what you saw?'

He's shaking his head. 'No. Absolutely not.'

'So she must have changed her clothes after you left and before the killer arrived – that's your position?' She sits back. 'Because I have to tell you, a jury's going to have trouble understanding why anyone would bother getting changed at that time of night –'

He leans towards her, his eyes intent. 'But that's exactly it – she didn't. *He* did. Gavin Parrie. He assaulted her and killed her, and then he changed her clothes. He had to make absolutely sure the only DNA they'd find was mine.'

So we're back to that, she thinks, her heart sinking. The Roadside Rapist's Revenge.

But her client doesn't appear to notice the sudden chill in the air.

'You do know, don't you,' she begins slowly, 'that this

292

case would be a whole lot easier to defend if you *had* had sex with her.' He looks up and she continues quickly. 'I mean, we'd still have trouble explaining the massive coincidence of her killer arriving on exactly the same night, but at least the forensics –'

'It didn't happen,' he says quietly, holding her gaze. 'I love my wife.'

And he does. She's never seen emotion expressed so painfully in a man's face. He might want to lie, but he won't. He can't.

'OK,' she says, picking up her pen, brisker now. 'Anything else?'

He swallows. 'Can you see if you can get access to the PM?'

She starts shaking her head.

'I know – I know – it's a long shot, but it's worth a try.'

'OK,' she says, after a moment. 'I can speak to Gallagher. What do you want to know?'

He sits forward a little. 'See if there was anything missing on the body – jewellery, earrings – Parrie has a thing about earrings. And if any of Smith's hair had been cut or pulled out.'

She frowns. 'No one's mentioned anything like that –'

'It'll be there,' he says doggedly. 'It has to be. Parrie won't have been able to stop himself.'

She takes a deep breath. 'If there's one thing I've learnt in all these years, it's that juries hate conspiracy theories. Lead balloons are buoyancy aids by comparison. You must know that.'

He gives her a despairing look. Perhaps so, but it's all he has.

'OK,' she says, suppressing a sigh. 'Talk me through how it would have worked – as a police officer.'

His eyes flicker with something like hope, and she realizes suddenly that he must have thought she didn't believe him. All this time, he's been assuming that even his own lawyer thought he was lying.

'Parrie knows all about DNA,' he says. 'He was always incredibly careful never to leave biological trace. And he had way more time to clear up with Smith than he did with any of the previous victims. He didn't dump her body at Walton Well until nearly 1.30 – he could have been in that flat for more than *three hours*. Plenty long enough to clean up the scene, wash the body, change her clothes.' He shrugs. 'That's what I'd have done, if –'

If you'd killed her.

The words hang in the air like nerve agent, paralysing her brain.

She pulls herself together. 'What about the electronic tag – how did he get round that? You're suggesting he managed to disable it somehow?'

'Well, did he?' he says quickly. 'Those things do malfunction. Not often, but it does happen. Have you checked?'

'No, I haven't. I will, of course, look into it. But it's a risk – what if all it does is confirm he was miles away at the time and couldn't possibly have done it? We could just be gifting him a gold-plated alibi.'

'Yes,' he says quietly. 'I do know that.'

'And what about the forensics?' she says. 'I get it that he'd have made sure not to leave his own DNA. What I don't get is how he came by yours.'

He's clearly had a lot of time to think about this. He sits forward, eager now. 'The fact that they found my DNA on her body is the best proof we have that I didn't kill her.'

She stares at him. 'Sorry – what?'

He holds her gaze. 'Everything I just said about Parrie also applies to me – only more so. *I* know about forensics, *I* know how murder scenes are processed. Why on earth would I have been so stupid as to leave my DNA all over that flat? All over *her*? I don't know how he did it – I don't know where he got it – but it was Gavin Parrie who put my DNA there.'

She leaves a pause, lets him sweat. And he is. There's a sheen of perspiration beading his forehead.

'That's not quite true, though, is it, Adam? That the same reasoning that applies to Parrie also applies to you?'

He frowns, the zeal curdling in his face. 'What do you mean?'

'You're saying that as an experienced police officer, you'd have cleaned up the scene, changed her clothes, washed the body, right? But you said yourself, all that takes time. And you're right, if it was Gavin Parrie, he had plenty of it. But *you* didn't, did you? You couldn't stay there all night – you had to get home, see your wife, establish an alibi. You'd have had an hour in that flat at the most. Nowhere near long enough.'

He's still frowning.

'I'm sorry,' she says, gentler now. 'I'm just being devil's advocate. But I am worried that if we use that argument, all they'll do is turn it against you. They'll say you knew you couldn't clean up properly in the time so you didn't

bother – you focused instead on finding a way of dispos-
ing of the body that would bypass the DNA altogether.
Hence the freight train.'

He sighs, runs his hands through his hair.

'DS King said as much in the last interview. It would
make the death look like suicide and cause so much damage to the body there'd be practically nothing left to
autopsy. The police probably wouldn't even have bothered to search her flat, far less process it as a crime scene.
In which case, it wouldn't matter how much of your DNA
you left behind, because no one was ever going to find it.'
She sits back. 'You used everything you've learnt from
decades of working homicide cases to commit as near as
dammit a perfect murder. And without that gang of engineers, that's exactly what it would've been. But like you said
before, even professionals make mistakes. That was
yours.'

His breath is ragged now. He's struggling to stay composed. 'So I can't win – is that what you're telling me?
Whatever I say, I can't win?'

'No, I'm not saying that. I'm just trying to be realistic.
But I will check with Inspector Gallagher – find out
whether there were any clothes in the flat that look like
the leggings and T-shirt you saw.'

'Fat chance,' he says grimly. 'Parrie wouldn't be stupid
enough to leave them there.'

She nods. 'I suspect you're right, but we won't know
until we ask. And even if there's nothing in the flat, the
neighbour may remember what Emma had on when she
came to the door that night. And failing that, there could
be other ways to prove she owned clothes like that.

Although it'll mean tracking down either witnesses or photos. It's not impossible, but we don't have Thames Valley's resources. Or their ability to buttonhole Joe Public at will.'

He makes a face and looks away. 'The more I see of the view from this side of the tracks, the less I like it.'

'On the other hand,' she says, trying to sound more positive, 'we can certainly make a very solid case for Gavin Parrie having a motive. And, if we're lucky, there'll be evidence out there somewhere that will either alibi you out or incriminate someone else.'

'What about Cleland?'

'Not as promising as he initially appeared, from what I hear. I believe they've yet to rule him out formally, but without forensic evidence on his clothes or in Smith's flat, I can't see King taking it any further.'

Fawley wouldn't either, she can see that from his face.

She picks up her pen again. 'But if there's footage of his car at Walton Well, that situation could change. I need to chase up on whether they have CCTV on the bridge.'

He makes a rueful face. 'I wouldn't hold my breath. If I know Parrie, he'll have checked out that location long before he used it.'

She frowns. 'How, exactly?'

He shrugs. 'Google Earth? Though I wouldn't put it past him casing it out in person. After all, we know he's worked out how to get round his tag, and we know he has transport – he must do, to get here from wherever he is, transport the body, get away. Worth checking what sort of vehicle he has access to, because there absolutely must be one.'

'Presumably not a white van this time,' she says drily. 'That would be too easy.'

He shrugs. 'Who knows. My wife thought she saw one near the house once or twice lately.'

'Really? Do you have a reg number?'

He shakes his head dully. 'Nope. If I did, I'd have checked out the bloody thing myself.'

* * *

'Freya? It's me.'

His voice is muffled, like he's behind glass.

She grips the phone. 'Jesus, Caleb – I've been trying to get through to you for hours. What's happened – is there something wrong with your phone? This isn't your number –'

'I got a pay-as-you-go. The police took mine.'

Her eyes widen, and she sits down slowly. 'The *police*? Why?'

She can hear noise in the background now, traffic – as if he's out on the street.

'They fucking arrested me, didn't they. They're saying Tobin saw me *raping* her – that I gave her GHB or some shit like that so she wouldn't remember.'

'Oh my God –'

'Yeah, right – how fucked up is that?'

Her heart rate is brutal. 'But, babe, this is really bad – they must be taking it seriously or they wouldn't have arrested you –'

He laughs bitterly. 'Yeah, well, I've been "Released Under Investigation" while they dig about for dirt.'

She swallows. 'What did your lawyers say?'

'That they won't be able to prove it – that there's no forensics and they'll just be relying on Tobin's word for it. And we all know what a lying little fucker he is.'

'Yeah,' she says slowly, 'we do, don't we.'

* * *

Telephone call with Lloyd Preston, Network Rail
13 July 2018, 5.15 p.m.
On the call, DS Chris Gislingham

CG: Hello? This is Thames Valley Police, am I speaking with Lloyd Preston?

LP: Yeah, that's me. Thames Valley, did you say?

CG: Yes, sir – just a couple more routine questions about the incident at Walton Well –?

LP: I don't know what else I can tell you. I already told that other police bloke everything I saw. Sparrow, was it?

CG: DC Farrow.

LP: Yeah, that's the one. So are you his boss or what?

CG: Something like that. Like I said, it's just routine.

LP: So what do you want to know?

CG: Do you remember seeing anyone on the bridge that night? Either before or after you saw the body fall?

LP: No. Like I said to the other bloke. That's why I thought it was a suicide.

CG: What about a car, a van?

LP: You can't see the road from the tracks.

CG: Then maybe you heard something? That time of night, when there's no other noise, it must be much easier to hear a vehicle –

LP: I'm not sure –

CG: Take your time.

LP: Look, I can't be sure, OK? There may have been.

CG: When exactly? Before or after you saw the body?

LP: Before. As soon as we saw the girl we were just focused on getting through to the control room A-SAP so that's all we were thinking about. I wouldn't have noticed a car then.

CG: How long before, do you think? A minute? Five minutes?

LP: More than that, but I couldn't tell you exactly.

CG: So if the man driving that vehicle was the same one who threw the body on the track, he could have been there for some time before he did it? He could have been waiting for you to be in range?

LP: That's a hell of a lot of 'could ofs'.

CG: But it's possible?

LP: Yeah, OK, I suppose it's *possible*. Just don't ask me to stand up in court and swear to it.

* * *

She could have made an official appointment, but McHugh reckons Ruth Gallagher might be more amenable if she's caught off guard. She knows Gallagher has a young family and calculates (rightly) that she's not going to have much time for presenteeism, especially not on a Friday night. So she loiters for a while on a bench with her Kindle and a grandstand view of the St Aldate's entrance, and at just after six, she gets her reward. Gallagher emerges from the door into the evening sunshine and heads briskly to an old Volvo estate on the far side of the car park.

It's not the car McHugh had bet on – her money was on the shiny hybrid SUV on the other side. She'd dismissed the Volvo as far too earnest and disorganized for a senior DI. It was the junk in the back that did it. Plastic boxes of old clothes, discarded toys, dog-eared books – there's a whole squadron of middle-aged Oxford women driving round with crap like that in the back of their cars, but McHugh didn't have Gallagher down for one of them. Just shows – you never can tell.

'DI Gallagher?' she says, slightly out of breath after the dash across the road.

The Inspector turns. She doesn't look especially enthused at the sight of her.

'Sorry to ambush you, but could I have a quick word?'

You can almost see Gallagher's heart sink.

'I'm not sure this is quite the place –'

'I just had a couple of questions – just factual stuff. It won't take long.'

Gallagher weighs her car keys in her hand. 'I'm afraid I have to get back to my kids. My husband's out tonight and I'm on the pizza rota.'

'Oh,' says McHugh brightly, 'you live in Summertown, right? I'm in Kidlington. Why don't I come with you as far as the shops and I can get my bus from there?'

And it's true. McHugh does indeed live in Kidlington. She also has her own car parked in the Westgate multi-storey. But Gallagher doesn't need to know that.

The DI frowns and opens her mouth to say something, but it's too late. McHugh is already reaching for the car door, smiling broadly. 'Thanks *so* much. I really appreciate it.'

* * *

Somer is one of the last patients of the day. The only other people waiting were an elderly chap with trembling hands, bent double over his walking frame, and a harassed mother with two overactive toddlers long past their bedtime. After the shrieks and the tantrums and the tumbling plastic bricks, the silence of the consulting room is something of a relief. But not enough to quiet the anxiety slithering in her gut.

She finishes doing up her skirt and comes back out from behind the screen. Her doctor is at the desk, a page of notes open on her screen. Somer sits down, swallows.

'I'm pregnant, aren't I.' It's a statement, not a question. 'I mean, I know the test was negative, but those High Street things, they're not always accurate, are they –'

The doctor sits back and adjusts her glasses. 'Have you been trying for a baby, Erica?'

'No. I mean, I do want children eventually, but right now –' She throws up her hands. 'It's complicated, that's all.'

The doctor smiles. 'These things usually are.'

Somer takes a deep breath. 'Me and my partner – we haven't been seeing each other that long and we haven't even discussed having children. He has two already – teenage girls. I have no idea if he wants to start all over again. And, in any case, there's my career – it would be terrible timing –'

She stops, realizing there's a sob in the back of her throat.

The doctor is watching her. 'You're not pregnant.'

Somer stares at her. 'But – are you sure?'

'Absolutely.'

'But what about the other symptoms – the nausea –?'

The doctor shifts a little in her seat. 'There are other things that can cause that, but ovarian cysts are the usual culprit. And based on the internal examination I just did, I suspect that may well be the case here.'

She turns to her screen and starts tapping at her keyboard. 'I'm going to book you in for an ultrasound at the JR so we can be sure.'

Somer's struggling to keep up with her own feelings. She doesn't even know if she's relieved or regretful that there's no child, and now –

'I'm sorry – I wasn't expecting this. I don't know anything about ovarian cysts – are they serious? Should I be worried?'

The doctor is businesslike. 'Most are nothing to be concerned about. Where there are complications, it's usually because they cause an infection, which can sometimes lead to difficulty in conceiving at a later date. That's why I asked whether you've been trying for a baby.'

'But –' Somer takes a breath, realizes her fingernails are digging into her palms. 'You said "most" are nothing to worry about, so some of them are, right?'

'Those are very rare –'

'But even those, the rare ones – they're benign? We're not talking about –'

The doctor gives a quick professional smile. 'Let's not get ahead of ourselves. Like I said, the vast majority are not serious. Let's get that ultrasound done, shall we, and see where we go from there.'

* * *

Having been sandbagged into spending twenty minutes with McHugh in a confined space, Gallagher's evidently going to make the lawyer work for her scraps. She certainly isn't volunteering anything as they edge through the rush-hour traffic in Oxpens Road.

'It was the CCTV I was going to ask about,' says McHugh, turning to look out of the window as if the question isn't really that important. There's a queue outside the ice rink. She used to take her own kids there, but that was before they turned teenagers and skating wasn't cool any more. It'd be cool now though, on a hot night like this. The air sparkling with ice, the swoop of the skates –

'There isn't any,' says Gallagher, who clearly knows a thing or two about cool herself. 'CCTV, I mean.'

It was a long shot at best; McHugh tries another tack.

'Have you ascertained Gavin Parrie's movements on the night of July the 9th?'

Gallagher looks across at her and raises her eyebrows,

then turns her gaze back to the road. 'I take it you do realize quite how preposterous that sounds?'

McHugh shrugs. 'That's as may be. I still need to ask.'

The van in front shifts suddenly and Gallagher puts the car in gear. 'The answer is yes, we have. And no, he was nowhere near Oxford that night.'

'How near is nowhere near?'

Gallagher frowns a little, though whether it's the traffic that's irritating her or her passenger, it's hard to say.

'Leamington Spa,' she says after a moment. 'He's in a halfway house near there, and has been ever since he left Wandsworth. That information is, of course, confidential, but *in the circumstances*, it may help you to know.'

It may help put paid to this wild and implausible theory: the message is clear enough, even though her tone is studiously objective.

'Does he have access to a vehicle?'

Gallagher shoots her a glance, *Well, what do you think?*

'How is Adam?' she asks after a moment, her voice still neutral, her eyes still fixed on the road.

'Much like anyone in his situation, I imagine,' says McHugh. 'Stressed to the eyeballs. Angry. Worried about his wife. What do you expect?'

'He's always been a fine officer,' says Gallagher, 'and speaking personally, I like him very much —'

'But?' says McHugh, who's registered that initial past tense.

Gallagher looks at her and then away. 'But however hard we look — and believe me, we've tried — we cannot find a single piece of evidence to exonerate him. Or even cast a reasonable doubt —'

'Not even this man Cleland? He had a motive.'

'Possibly. But that's all. There is absolutely nothing else linking him to the crime. No witnesses, no forensics, no proof he went anywhere near there.' She glances across again. 'I'm sorry. I want it to be Cleland as much as you do, but it's a non-starter. Everything we have points to Adam, and you've given me nothing I can use to refute it. And as for this obsession of his about Gavin Parrie – it's – it's *insane*.'

McHugh's about to answer, but Gallagher's still talking. 'I have to confess I've become increasingly concerned about him – the way he's been reacting, it's so out of character. My whole team has noticed.'

Is she asking me if Fawley's losing it? thinks McHugh. Is that really where they're going with this?

Gallagher sighs now. 'And what with the baby, and coming so soon after losing Jake – even the strongest people can break under stress like that –'

She doesn't finish the sentence but the inference is up there now in neon lights: Are you sure your client is of entirely sound mind? Could he, in fact, be so unstable, under such intolerable pressure, that he actually *did* this?

* * *

'Giles? It's me. Look, I'm really sorry but I can't come down tomorrow after all. Something – something's come up.'

He doesn't reply straight away, but this is Giles: unlike most men, he thinks before he speaks.

'Is everything OK?' By which he really means 'Are you OK?' But he's trying not to crowd her, not to intrude.

'Yes, it's just,' she takes a breath, 'work stuff, you know.

306

This sexual assault case is a nightmare, and appraisals are coming up, and then there's Fawley being arrested –'

She stops herself, but not quickly enough. She's heard Fawley say it a hundred times – you can always tell a liar from the overkill. Three answers when one is plenty.

'OK,' he says, after a moment. She can hear the hurt in his voice. 'I'm really sorry I won't see you, but I understand.'

She nods, knowing it's pointless because he can't see her, but she can't trust herself to speak.

'Look – I'm not going to push it, but I think there's something worrying you, and if there is, and I can help, you only have to ask. I hope you know that. I just want you to be happy, OK? That's all.'

She puts the phone down and sits there in her empty flat. She's never felt so utterly alone.

* * *

Sent: Fri 13/07/2018, 20.35   **Importance: High**
From: Colin.Boddie@ouh.nhs.uk
To: DIRuthGallagher@ThamesValley.police.uk

Subject: Case no 75983/02 Smith, E

In re the request from Penelope McHugh for information relating to the post-mortem, I can confirm that only one earring was retrieved from the body (a silver hoop), but as this was merely hooked in, with no rear fixing, the second one probably came off either during a struggle with her assailant or when the body was dumped. Likewise a very small amount of the victim's hair does indeed seem to be missing at the rear of the scalp (see photo attached). But as you will see, the quantum is so small it is very unlikely to be significant and was, again, probably the result of a struggle.

For the avoidance of doubt, I am sceptical that either the earring or the missing hair form any deliberate part of the killer's MO. That, combined with the absence of ligature marks on either the wrists or ankles, leads me to caution against any comparison with the Gavin Parrie case.

Should further evidence emerge which leads me to reconsider this view, I will, of course, inform you.

CRB

* * *

Telephone interview with Sgt Vince Hall,
Warwickshire Police, Leamington Spa
14 July 2018, 8.15 a.m.
On the call, DI Ruth Gallagher

VH: Sorry it's taken me so long to get back to you, but I've checked the records you were asking about, and I've spoken to the probation officer as well.

RG: Excellent – thank you.

VH: The tag logs show Gavin Parrie never breached his licence conditions at any time on the night you're interested in. He was either at the hostel or at most a mile away from it, the entire night. There's no way he could have been anywhere near Oxford.

RG: And we're sure the tag is fully functional?

VH: Yup. Only got checked last month. Nothing
wrong with it.

RG: Good. I'm glad we've been able to clear that
up. And I take it he has no access to any sort
of car?

VH: Sorry?

RG: No, I'm sorry I even had to ask. I'm just
covering all the bases. Our suspect's lawyer
has a bee in her bonnet about it.

VH: Well, for the record, he doesn't. And for what
it's worth, the PO says Parrie's been a right
little goody-two-shoes since he got out.
Spends half his time with youth offender
programmes, giving them dire warnings about
the error of their ways.

RG: And she thinks it's genuine – this
transformation of his?

VH: She's not some rookie straight out of training –
she's been on the job fifteen years. And he was
a model prisoner too, Parrie. So yes, it's
always possible he could be faking it, but he's
kept it up a bloody long time if he is.

* * *

Everett's Friday evening wasn't exactly restful. Most of it
was eaten up by a week's worth of undone chores, and
she ended up so ragged with exhaustion she slept through
this morning's alarm. She drives down the Banbury
Road under a sultry grey-yellow sky, which does nothing

for her headache, and the low-level throb of guilt about her father and that call she still hasn't made to Elaine Baylis isn't helping much either. She keeps telling herself she's doing as much as anyone could expect; that her dad's being well looked after, he's eating and people are trying to involve him in group activities like whist and bingo, all of which he despises at the top of his voice whenever any of the staff are near enough to hear. His contempt ought to reassure her, it's so completely in character, but there's a vehemence to it now which leaves her uneasy.

The rest of the team are already at their desks when she gets in. Somer looks up briefly but doesn't meet her eye, and is then so intent on looking busy she might as well hang up a sign saying 'Leave me alone'. Ev unloads her phone and notebook from her bag, wondering how she should play it. She's pretty sure Somer had an appointment last night with her doctor, but she never actually said so, and Ev's attempts to WhatsApp her later got nothing more than one-word answers.

* * *

For an expert in body language, Bryan Gow isn't very good at masking his own. When he rounds the corner and sees Gislingham in the corridor outside CID his reaction is such a perfect picture of acute embarrassment he could use it as an example in his next PowerPoint presentation.

Gis frowns. 'I thought your assistant said we couldn't meet up because you were busy today?'

Gow flushes a little. 'We can't – that is, I am.' He hesitates. 'If you must know, Ruth Gallagher asked me to come in.' He makes a face. 'Hashtag *awkward*.'

Because he's helping her on the Emma Smith case. Because he's helping to convict Fawley.

Gis forces away the thought, and the resentment that comes with it. All this shit – none of it's Gow's fault.

'I was going to ask you to look at some footage for us. The Fisher case again.'

Gow nods slowly. 'OK, I can do that. I'll drop by later.' He looks round. 'And in the meantime, perhaps you could tell me what Gallagher has done with her team, because that office of theirs is doing a pretty good impersonation of the *Mary Celeste*.'

* * *

Gow wasn't the only one wrong-footed by that this morning. Major Crimes were just as confounded themselves. Overnight, without warning, their entire operation had been tea-crated and relocated upstairs. The first thing everyone noticed was that the new office is about as far away from CID as it's possible to get; the second was the secure-access keypad on the door.

And just in case anyone was being especially dense, Dave King makes a big show of getting the facilities manager to reset the code right in front of them.

'From now on, we're the only ones who'll have access to this room,' he says, staring round. 'Not even the bloody cleaners are getting in here without one of us present. So if there are any more leaks about this investigation – external *or internal* – I'll know it was someone here, not one of Fawley's arse-lickers gone rogue. Do I make myself clear?'

Evidently so.

He nods, makes as if to go, then has second thoughts. 'Oh, and if any of you happen to see DS Gislingham in the khazi, do make sure to pass that on.'

There's an exchange of glances now, the odd murmur.

'Right,' says King. 'Well, get on with it, then.'

The room kicks into action and King watches for a moment before making his way over to Simon Farrow's desk. He smiles at him; Farrow is immediately wary. 'I was going to ask,' says King, perilously jovial. 'It wasn't you by any chance, was it, slipped CID a look at our files? Because someone made a call to that railway engineer last night and it wasn't one of us.'

Farrow's eyes widen. 'Why are you asking me?'

The teeth are showing in King's grin. 'Yeah, well, it's not gone unnoticed that you've got a bad case of the hots for that Erica Somer. Can't say I blame you, though. I'd do her in a shot.'

Farrow drops his eyes. 'Always a bad idea,' he mumbles, 'getting involved with people at work.'

King gives a quick bark of laughter. 'Well, evidently *she* doesn't think so. She was banging Gareth Quinn a while back for a start –'

One of the other DCs looks up. 'And Fawley too, from what I hear.'

'Really?' says King sharply.

The man shrugs. 'It was all round the station a few months ago.'

312

'Interesting,' says King, his tone half thoughtful, half sneer. 'Not such a bleeding paragon of virtue after all, eh.'

'Was there anything else you wanted, Sarge?' says Farrow. 'Only –'

King turns to him. 'Yeah, sorry. Yeah, there was. Apparently Fawley's lawyer had a "little chat" with Gallagher last night.' He's dropped his voice now. 'She was crapping on again about CCTV at the bridge. I take it we've bloody confirmed that, have we? I don't want it coming back to bite me in the arse.'

Farrow reddens slightly, though he has no reason to: he's checked already. Twice. 'No, Sarge. No cameras in that area at all.'

'What about the clothes – the ones Fawley claims Smith was wearing – where are we on that?'

Farrow pulls up a file on his screen. 'Here's the inventory from the flat – no leggings or T-shirts matching that description.'

'So he's lying.'

Farrow hesitates. 'Well, I guess if it really was Gavin Parrie who killed her, he'd deffo have got rid of the gear –'

King gives an incredulous scoff. 'Don't tell me you actually *believe* that bollocks.'

Farrow reddens again. 'No, Sarge. Of course not. I'm just saying that the clothes not being there now doesn't prove they never were. Absence of evidence isn't evidence of –'

'Oh, for fuck's sake,' begins King, but then there's a tap at the glass panel in the door and they look up to see Ruth Gallagher outside. No one appears to have thought to give her the key code. King curses under his breath as one of the DCs rushes to open it. Gallagher thanks him, rather pointedly, takes a few steps into the room.

'Just wanted to let you all know I finally had a call back from Warwickshire. They've confirmed Gavin Parrie's electronic tag is fully functional and shows him as being within a mile of his designated accommodation the entire night of July 9th. Whoever killed Emma Smith, it certainly wasn't him.'

Dave King does a fist pump. 'Fucking nailed it,' he says.

'No,' says Gallagher calmly, 'we haven't "nailed" anything. Gavin Parrie has been eliminated from the inquiry; Hugh Cleland is likely to be. Adam Fawley remains by far the most likely suspect. But right now, that's all he is: a suspect.'

No title, no 'DI'. Just Adam Fawley. No one in the room underestimates the significance of that.

'But until I decide otherwise, you say nothing.' She glances round at them, one by one, taking her time about it. 'Am I clear? However tempted you may be, you are to say *nothing* – not to your mates, your family, even other Thames Valley officers. And if there's anyone who thinks they might find that a bit of a challenge after a couple in the Red Lion, I suggest you play it safe and go straight home. Do your career a favour, if not your liver.'

She gives King a long last look, turns and is gone.

* * *

Ev decides, for once, to pack it in at five. The CID office is half empty anyway. Gis has been AWOL for at least an hour and she has no idea where Somer's been all day.

Bugger it, she thinks; it is Saturday, after all. She clatters her stuff into her bag before she has time for a rush of conscience, but it seems the universe has a sense of humour: the phone goes.

She looks round, hoping someone else will do the decent, and eventually Asante picks it up.

'CID, DC Asante.'

She sees him nod then look over towards her. 'Line two. Asking for you.'

She sighs, slides her bag back on to her desk and picks up the phone. But she is not sitting back down, she is *not* sitting back down –

'Miss Everett? It's Elaine Baylis again.' There's just the slightest stress on that last word.

'Look, I'm sorry I haven't been back to you –'

'It's not that,' she says crisply. 'I'm afraid there's been another incident with your father.'

Ev grips the phone, turns away from Asante's discreetly quizzical glance. 'What sort of "incident"?'

'An altercation with another resident. Nothing to be worried about, but in a community like this, even small disagreements can be very disruptive. I'm sure you can appreciate that –'

'I do, I'm just not sure what I can do about –'

'Could you come in tomorrow? Two thirty?'

Ev's heart sinks. She had her Sunday all planned. A lie-in, brunch at Gail's, a walk round Christ Church meadow. Not a twenty-mile round trip in thirty-degree heat and another dressing-down by matron in an office that smells of pee.

'I appreciate you have a demanding job,' says Baylis in a tone that rings with *don't we all*, 'but this is about your

father's welfare and that of the other residents in our care.'
A heavy, self-righteous pause. 'It's *important*.'

'OK,' says Ev, gritting her teeth and reminding herself
that Baylis will be working on Sunday too. 'Two thirty. I'll
see you then.'

She puts down the phone and turns to see Asante still
looking at her.

'Line three,' he says.

'You're taking the piss.'

But Asante doesn't take the piss.

He shrugs. 'Sorry. I did try. But it's you he wants.'

'Someone down here to see you,' says one of the desk
officers when she picks up.

'Oh yes?'

'Won't give her name,' he says, slightly more loudly, as
if he wants the visitor, whoever they are, to hear quite
how hacked off he is.

Ev frowns. 'So why –?'

'Has to be someone on the Fisher case, she says. And it
has to be a *woman*.'

*   *   *

'Show it to me again?'

Gis rewinds the footage and presses play. 'See – where
we ask him about the tattoo? He seems to almost stop
breathing.'

Gow nods slowly. 'It's a textbook anxiety response. I
suspect that was a question he hadn't prepared for.' He
glances up at Gis, who has his arms folded, thoughtful.
'Does that help?'

316

Gis starts a little; he was miles away.

'Yeah,' he says. 'It does.'

Gow gets up and reaches for his briefcase. 'Well, if there's nothing else, I shall return to my weekend.'

Gis grins. 'Hot date with a steam locomotive?'

Gow winks at him. 'Well, let's just say you're *half* right.'

He edges round the table towards the door, but just as he gets there Gislingham calls him back.

'Did he do it?'

Gow turns, frowns. 'I just told you –'

Gis shakes his head. 'I'm not talking about Morgan. I'm talking about Fawley.'

Gow takes hold of the door handle. 'No,' he says after a moment. 'I don't think he did.'

* * *

The coffee shop the girl chooses isn't one students usually go to and Ev suspects she picked it for exactly that reason. An old-style caff down one of the narrow passages leading off the High Street, with a nail bar one side and a Chinese takeaway the other, lino on the floor and a fad-free menu board where the only sort of coffee started life in a jar.

Ev sends the girl to a table in the far corner – largely so she can't turn tail and scarper without her seeing – and queues up at the counter for two mugs of tea, shooting surreptitious glances at the girl all the while. She must be twenty-two or -three, with green eyes and soft auburn hair that's only just long enough for the tiny ponytail at the nape of her neck. She was picking at her nails at the station and she's fretting with the bowl of sugar now; Ev suspects it took a long time for her to make up her mind to come here at all.

Ev collects her order, goes over to the table and sits down. The red-and-white oilskin cloth is slightly sticky and the ketchup comes in a large plastic tomato. It's like being inside an Alan Bennett.

She's going to give the girl as much time as she needs to broach this her own way, but there's only so much fiddling with the milk sachet she can do. Eventually, just as she's about to give up –

'My name's Zoe. Zoe Longworth.'

Ev nods. 'OK.'

She flickers a look up at Ev, then stares doggedly back at her tea. 'I saw it online.'

'The story about Professor Fisher?'

The girl nods. 'I mean, it didn't actually name her but it was pretty bloody obvious who it was. At least to me.'

'You know her?' says Ev.

There's a pause.

'Did she teach you?'

A longer pause then another nod. 'She used to. I'm in London now. But I was here before, a couple of years ago. If I hadn't seen it on Twitter I'd never have realized – I had no idea she'd done this to someone else.'

Ev nods. Every time there's a controversy about identifying people charged with sexual offences the same rationale is trotted out: disclosing perpetrators' names means other victims come forward – victims who might otherwise have remained silent. Or ignorant. But this girl can't be a victim. Can she?

'So why did you want to talk to us, Zoe?'

She's stirring the tea now, almost obsessively. The clang of the spoon is setting Ev's teeth on edge.

'It was great to start with – having Marina as a supervisor. She was really supportive, got really involved. I couldn't believe my luck.'

Caleb Morgan, remembers Ev, said exactly the same thing.

'We both thought so.'

Ev frowns. '*We?*'

Longworth looks up briefly. 'My boyfriend, Seb. Seb Young.'

So that's it, thinks Ev. But she keeps it from her face. 'Go on.'

'One Friday night, out of the blue, she invited us for drinks at her house. We thought all her grad students were going but when we turned up it was only us.'

'I see.'

'Her little boy was there. Must have been ages after his bedtime but she didn't make him go upstairs. She kept saying how well he took to us – how he was really shy with most people, but he'd taken to us straight away. You could have fooled me – he barely opened his mouth, but she kept going on and on about it.'

'Let me guess – she started asking you to babysit?'

She bites her lip, nods. 'And to start with, it was fine. Better than fine. She'd leave out wine and tell us we could raid the fridge, watch her Sky. We had sod-all money so it was like a night out.'

There's a silence.

'So what changed?' says Ev eventually.

She sighs. 'I didn't realize it *had*, not at first. And then I started noticing that we seemed to be round there every Friday, and sometimes two or three other nights as well. It was all just a bit full-on. And when we did actually babysit, she wasn't paying. Like she didn't need to bother offering us money any more, and of course we were too embarrassed to ask. I felt like we were being used.' She hesitates, puts down the spoon, looks up. 'And then there was the thing with Tobin.'

'What thing, Zoe?'

'She had this huge vase in the sitting room – an ugly purple thing. I thought it looked like something out of some sleazy seventies cocktail bar, but apparently it was worth, like, a grand. Anyway, one afternoon we were there babysitting while she was at some event in London and Tobin had one of his meltdowns and it got broken.'

'So?'

'When she got back we told her what happened and she was actually quite nice about it – she said she knew Tobin could be a bit "lively" and it was OK, she was insured and they'd pay for it. Then she went upstairs to talk to him, and I just happened to go to the loo at the same time and I overheard them. He was telling her *we'd* done it. And he was *really* convincing. It completely freaked me out.'

Ev frowns. 'You didn't confront her – tell her the truth?'

'I was going to,' says the girl, 'but Seb said to forget it. That it would be embarrassing to admit I'd been eavesdropping and, in any case, I probably got the wrong end of the stick because kids his age just aren't that good at lying.' She makes a grim face. 'Yeah, right.'

* * *

'I'm glad I caught you before you left. Someone dropped this in for you earlier. I did call up at the time but you were engaged.' The woman on the front desk smiles at Asante, not unkindly. 'I think she was a bit upset to miss you.'

Asante registers the smile but doesn't return it. He slits open the envelope and drops the contents on to the counter. A comps slip from the adoption service, with a couple of lines from Beth Monroe to say that the enclosed arrived at the office for Emma, and she didn't know if it might be important. Asante picks it up. It's a postcard of Verona, with a short message on the back in a big confident hand.

Lovely here.
Enjoying the
Franciacorta
(no surprises there).
Turandot tomorrow.
Hope you're OK,

A

Emma Smith
c/o Council Adoption
and Fostering Service
Iffley Road
Oxford OX4

Asante's detective antennae flare for a moment, only to sag again when he sees from the postmark that it was sent the same day Emma died. All the same, he should probably pass it on to Gallagher's team. Just for completeness.

'Thanks,' he says absent-mindedly as he turns back towards the stairs. When he gets up to the Major Crimes office the only person there is Simon Farrow. Asante taps on the glass and Farrow looks up with a frown, then pushes back his chair and comes over.

'Yeah, what is it?' he says, wedging the door open with one foot.

Asante hands him the postcard. 'This arrived at the adoption service for Emma Smith. It's clearly personal, though given it was sent to her office, it doesn't suggest anyone particularly close. But I guess you never know.'

Farrow scans it, then looks up. 'Probably Amanda Haskell – she's the woman Smith was seeing.'

Asante raises an eyebrow. 'Woman? Sorry, I had no idea she was gay.'

Farrow glances up. 'No, we only just found out too. Haskell came forward – she didn't see the news before because she'd been away.' He holds up the card. 'Which this rather proves.'

'Sorry – I just thought, you know.'

'No, no, you were right. I'll pass it on to DC Carroway. It'll make a nice change from the assorted loonies, nosey parkers and nutters on the tip line.'

Asante grins. 'Or forty-eight hours of CCTV.'

Farrow grimaces. 'If only. If they'd put some sodding cameras on that bridge I wouldn't be spending my

Saturday going squared-eyed at traffic cams. There must be hundreds of bloody Mondeos in this town –' He stops, flushes a little, realizes he's said too much.

Asante frowns. 'You're looking for Fawley's car? You've ruled out everyone else?'

Farrow looks a little embarrassed. 'Pretty much. The boss ain't interested in Hugh Cleland any more, that's for sure.'

And the boss in question isn't Gallagher. That's pretty clear too.

Farrow lets the door go and it starts to close. 'Thanks for this, anyway.'

'No problem,' says Asante. But when the door clicks shut he's still standing there, his face thoughtful.

* * *

'So what happened, Zoe? Why did you come all the way from London to talk to us?'

The girl takes a deep breath. She's put the spoon down but the tea is still untouched.

'It was that summer. She messaged Seb one Saturday morning saying there was some light bulb or other that needed changing, and she didn't like going up stepladders, so could he pop round later and do it for her. I think she assumed he'd go on his own – she had a funny look on her face when she saw me on the doorstep and I hadn't been there five minutes when she turns round and asks me to take Tobin to the pictures.'

Ev sighs. 'She wanted you out of the house.'

She makes a bitter face. 'It was *Despicable Me*. Ironic,

huh? So anyway, off we go, leaving Seb there with her, and of course the light bulb is in her bedroom, isn't it. So he gets up the ladder to change it and when he comes back down she's standing there in the doorway behind him, all tarted up in stilettos and a red silk number that looked like Ann Summers, but knowing her was probably more like bloody Agent Provocateur.' She bites her lip, looks away. 'I mean, what a fucking cliché.'

'How did he react to that?'

'He laughed.'

'Ah,' says Ev. 'I don't imagine she took that very well, did she?'

'No, she bloody well didn't.' There's a harshness in her voice now. 'She told him he ought to think very carefully because he had precisely three minutes to make a decision and it had better be the right one. She was his supervisor – she could make him or break him. She could get him stuck in some shithole for the rest of his career.'

She picks up her spoon again, starts drawing circles in the droplets of water on the tablecloth.

'She was going on about how she could offer him so much more than I could. That I was just a stupid little girl who was not only an also-ran in the brains department but probably didn't have a bloody clue when it came to sex either. Whereas she –' She stops, takes a breath that buckles into a sob.

'It's OK,' says Ev gently. 'Take your time.'

She reaches for a napkin, wipes her eyes. 'Anyway, I'd taken Tobin to the bloody film but we'd only been there about ten minutes when he started screaming the place down and I had to take him home.'

Ev shakes her head. 'I think I know what's coming next.'

She gives a fierce nod. 'Right. I could tell what was going on the minute we came through the door. I mean, the bloody *noise* they were making.' She tosses the spoon back down on the table with a clatter. 'I told Tobin to go down to the kitchen and I went straight up there. And there she was. On top of him, naked, *screwing* him.'

Ev takes a breath. 'What did you do?'

Zoe gives a contemptuous snort. 'What do you think I did? I took a fucking picture, didn't I.'

* * *

Oxford Mail online

Saturday 14 July 2018 Last updated at 18:12

BREAKING: Man arrested in murder of Headington woman

By Richard Yates

The Oxford Mail has learned that a 46-year-old man has been arrested in connection with the murder and suspected sexual assault of local Headington resident Emma Smith, 44, whose body was discovered in the early hours of Tuesday morning.

This breaking news story is being updated and more details will be published shortly.

Do you have information about this story? Email me at richard. yates@ox-mailnews.co.uk

* * *

'And what happened then?'

'I just walked out. Went back to my flat. Seb came round about half an hour later. He was in a terrible state.'

'That's when he told you that she'd coerced him?'

She nods. 'He was crying – he knew what it must've looked like – he knew what I'd think.'

No shit, Sherlock, thinks Ev. I'd have had his balls for the barbecue.

'But you believed him.'

'Not to start with. But yeah. In the end.'

'And that was the end of it?'

Zoe shakes her head slowly. 'No, that was only the beginning. Later that week Seb has a supervision with her and she asks him when they're going to "meet up" again. So he tells her no way – that it should never have happened –'

Ev sighs. 'Let me guess.'

'Right. She tried to persuade him but he kept saying no, and in the end he thought she'd backed off.'

Ev waits.

She swallows. 'Two days after that I got a phone call. From *her.*'

'What did she say?'

The girl's gone very pale. 'That Tobin had been having nightmares, and when she talked to him about it he told her that I'd been grooming him. He didn't use that word but that's what she meant. *Grooming* him.' She's shaking her head. 'He was *six*, for fuck's sake. If it wasn't so horrific it'd be totally hilarious.'

But Ev isn't laughing. 'She must have had some evidence to make an accusation like that.'

'She had *nothing*,' she says, shrill now – so shrill that a couple of other customers turn and look at them. 'She claimed I'd been having an "inappropriate" relationship with him – that I'd been showing him "unsuitable material" on TV behind her back – it was David fucking *Attenborough*, for Christ's sake, when I was looking after her kid when she couldn't be fucking *bothered* –'

She must realize that people are staring, because she drops her voice. Her cheeks are flushed now and there's a red stain reaching up her neck like a rash. She takes a deep breath, and then another. 'I realized there was absolutely nothing I could do – it would just be her word against mine.'

Here we go again, thinks Ev. Only now it's *she said/she said*.

'She could say anything she liked, accuse me of the most vile and horrible things, because Tobin would say exactly what she told him to. He used to trail around after her like some sort of lovesick puppy. He'd do anything, just to please her.'

'I suspect,' says Ev, 'that she was getting her defence in first. A pre-emptive move – just in case Sebastian decided to make a complaint against her.'

Zoe nods. 'That's what he said too. So he went to see her, to try to sort it out. I wanted to go too but he said that would make things worse. And he was probably right. I'd have just ended up screaming the place down.'

And it was never about you anyway, thinks Everett. Not really. You're just collateral damage.

'He went round that Friday. Took a bottle of wine. He thought it would help keep things civilized but she obviously got the wrong end of the stick because she started saying she knew he'd see sense, and he wouldn't regret it –'

'Oh dear.'

The girl flicks a look at her. 'Right. It just made things ten times worse. When he finally managed to convince her that he wasn't there to screw her she just totally flipped out. She said she'd ruin me. She'd take Tobin to the police and he'd tell them what I'd been doing to him. She actually went and got Tobin and made him repeat the whole thing, then and there, in front of him. Seb said it was terrifying – anyone hearing that would have believed it.'

'So what did you do?'

Zoe throws up her hands. 'We caved. What else could we do? Marina agreed to drop the grooming accusation on condition that Seb and I signed an NDA agreeing never to talk about her or share any "material" about her –'

'Of course, the photo.'

She nods. 'Yeah, the photo. And we weren't to disclose anything *at all* about our relationship with her, either publicly or privately.'

'And I assume that included the university authorities?'

'*And* the police.' She sits back. 'She could sue me, just for being here, having this conversation.'

She reaches into her bag and pulls out a white envelope. 'Here, see for yourself.'

Ev opens it in silence and takes out the document inside.

'Now you know why I was scared to come,' says Zoe softly. 'I know what that woman is capable of.'

* * *

328

Ev gets her lie-in, but has to make do with yogurt and fruit at home rather than brunch at Gail's. As for the walk in Christ Church meadow, that's on permanent hold. When she turns up at Gislingham's door at just gone 11.00 it's his wife, Janet, who opens the door. She's obviously been in the garden a lot lately – her shoulders are pink and the skin on her nose is a bit raw. She wasn't expecting Ev but she smiles all the same, and Ev realizes suddenly that she'd been slightly apprehensive about her welcome. She knows how long the Gislinghams had to wait for their son, and how hard they had it in the months after his birth. There was a period when Gis was doing everything around the house and Janet was barely leaving it. So much so that Ev had been close to wondering out loud whether Janet might have postnatal depression. But then things seemed to get a little better, and then a little better still. Gis lost the grey look he had that first year; he became DS, first temporarily and then permanently, and he started talking about his wife the way he had before Billy was conceived. And now, when someone turns up on the doorstep unannounced, Janet just takes it in her stride.

'Hello, stranger,' she says gaily. 'I haven't seen you for *ages*! Come on in – Chris is out the back.'

Ev follows her down the hall to the kitchen and Janet gestures at the kettle. 'Fancy a coffee?'

'God, yes,' says Ev with a grin. 'I'm gasping.'

Janet smiles again. 'I'll bring it through.'

Janet must be watering her patio pots every day because the marguerites and geraniums are lush, but the rest of the garden looks tired and the borders are shrivelling. In the middle, on the brown grass, Gis is playing football with Billy, who's wearing a miniature Chelsea strip with 'Gis' and the number one on his back. He's nearly two now and even though he's small for his age he's sturdy, and more than capable of giving his dad the runaround – literally. Gis rolls the ball towards him and the little boy swings out a foot and bangs it against the fence.

'*GOAL!!!*'

Gis bends over, leaning on his knees, breathing heavily, then spots Ev and straightens up.

'Boy, am I glad to see you,' he says, coming slowly towards her. 'It's too bloody hot to be cavorting about like this.'

'*Da – ad*,' says Billy, in the beginning of a whine, but Gis gives him a firm look. 'Now, we don't do that, do we? No one likes a whinger.'

Billy's mouth puckers a little, but Gis tousles his hair and the smile eventually comes. 'Now, why don't you go and see if Mummy's got any more of that juice, while I have a quick chat with Auntie Ev?'

'Not sure about "Auntie Ev",' she says, giving him a firm look of her own.

'Godmother's privilege,' he says, grinning. 'Now, what dragged you all the way from Summertown on a Sunday morning?'

* * *

'I mean, you've got to have fish at The Perch, haven't you?' says Caroline Asante gaily. 'Stands to reason.'

They came early because they know how busy this place gets at the weekend, and in this weather, shady spots in the garden are at a premium. But once in possession of a prize position, they're taking their time. On the next table, there's another middle-aged couple with their daughter and what's clearly her fairly new boyfriend: he's smiling a lot and trying a little too hard. Further over, a gaggle of kids is trying to climb the huge old willow tree. There's jazz coming from the marquee and people are sitting about on the grass because for once it's dry enough to do that in an English summer. The whole thing is almost too perfect.

'I'm considering the mussels,' begins Asante's father carefully, 'or perhaps the Cumberland ring.'

His mother laughs, reaching for her glass of Pinot Grigio. 'Honestly, Kwame, you manage to sound like a diplomat even when you're ordering sausages and mash.'

He smiles at her; it's an old joke. He was a Ghanaian trade attaché for more than twenty years.

'I'll go in and order,' says Asante, making to get up, but his mother stops him.

'No need to rush. Let's have a chat.'

Parent code for 'you never tell us anything'. He stifles a sigh.

'How's the job going?' His father now. They always ask, as a point of honour, even though they've never really reconciled themselves to their only son going into the police. It simply baffled them, even when he was accepted on the fast-track graduate scheme. But they were, as always, too well bred, too 'diplomatic' to say so. Your children must be allowed to make their own choices, even if you'd much rather they opted for medicine or the law, even – if all else fails – the City.

'It's good,' says Asante. 'Better than Brixton.'

'In what way?' His mother, 'showing an interest'.

'The job's more varied. And the town. More interesting people.'

'Oh yes?' says Caroline in that alert-for-a-girlfriend tone all mothers seem to develop. But then again, as Asante reminds himself, he isn't just an only son but an only child.

'Don't get too excited, Mum,' he says. 'I don't get out much. Those people I mentioned – they're the ones I'm arresting.'

* * *

'Bloody hell,' says Gis, sitting back.

'I know,' replies Ev, finishing the last of her coffee. 'And for once in this bloody case, we don't have to just take her word for it. There's the NDA.'

'Yeah,' he says, frowning and pulling the sheet of paper back towards him, 'but it's not that explicit, is it? It just stops them talking about her. It doesn't say why. There's absolutely nothing about the grooming or the kid or anything.'

'True – but we know Fisher slept with Young. I saw the picture – and believe me, there is absolutely *no* mistaking what they're doing.'

'But all that proves is that they had sex. Not that Fisher forced him to do it. Don't get me wrong,' he says quickly, 'I'm with you. I'm just anticipating what the CPS will say. No one knows the full story but them.'

Ev points at the logo at the head of the paper. 'Niamh Kennedy must, surely? If she drafted this thing?'

Gis shrugs. 'Possibly, though perhaps not all the details. But I bet you any money you like she'll hide behind client confidentiality even if she does.'

Ev frowns. 'Well, *I* reckon she knows a *hell* of a sight more than she's saying. I remembered, after I spoke to Zoe – last time they were in she called Fisher "Marina". Like you would if you were friends, rather than just lawyer and client.'

Gis sits back again, staring up towards the house. Janet is at the kitchen window. She looks up and gives them a wave.

'I reckon you're right,' he says after a moment. 'For what it's worth, I reckon Caleb Morgan may well be just the last in a whole line of poor naive saps Fisher's done this to.'

'Only this time it's different,' says Ev. 'This time, the sap's fighting back.'

* * *

'We can easily drop you, Anthony,' says his mother, opening the car door. 'It's barely even out of our way –'

But he was prepared for this – he knew they'd offer, and he knew he'd need a good excuse.

'It's fine, Mum, really. It's a beautiful day and I can walk back across Port Meadow. It'll do me good to get some fresh air.'

He knows she'll struggle to argue back at that, but she still gives it a go.

'You don't exactly have the right shoes for a hike, darling.'

He smiles. 'OK, confession time. There's something I want to check. To do with a case.'

She purses her lips. 'If it's work-related it should be done on work time.'

'That's just it, Mum. It's not exactly "official".'

*   *   *

Ev checks her watch and reaches for her bag. 'I think that's everything, boss. Young's coming in this afternoon to give a statement, so I'll give you a call afterwards.'

'Good work,' he says. 'I'd see if Somer's free to sit in on that as well, if I were you.'

'Already done,' she says, smiling. 'And I've let Fisher's lawyer know we'll want to talk to her again tomorrow.'

She gets to her feet. 'I have to go.'

He makes a face. 'Your dad?'

'Yeah,' she says with a sigh. Only a small one, but even that feels disloyal. 'My dad.'

*   *   *

As for Quinn, he's spending his Sunday in Boars Hill. Maisie raised an eyebrow when he suggested it ('With my *parents*? Are you feeling OK?'), but he just laughed and said who wouldn't want a swim in this weather? And that genuinely was a good half of the motivation. As for the rest, well, that's a rather longer game.

Her parents have made themselves admirably and discreetly scarce, so it's been just the two of them by the pool most of the morning, Quinn on a lounger, within a languid stretch of an ice bucket stacked with beer, and Maisie a few feet away, floating gently on an inflatable blue-and-white-striped hammock (blow-up flamingos are evidently too Benidorm for Boars Hill). Maisie's wearing a floppy pink cotton sun hat and a pair of huge Jackie O sunglasses; she looks like she's walked straight out of the Profumo affair. Down below, in the valley, the city glitters like a mirage.

'Love the hat,' says Quinn.

She looks up from her book. 'This? It's completely ancient. I've had it since I was at school.'

Her hair has corkscrewed in the wet, and with no make-up she looks adorably fresh-faced.

'I bet your school was the sort that had straw boaters.' She sticks her tongue out and he starts laughing. 'It *did*, didn't it?'

She grabs an ice cube out of her drink and lobs it at him but it misses by miles and plops harmlessly into the water.

He grins. 'Have you still got it? I mean, you'd look *seriously* hot in school uniform –'

She looks at him witheringly over her sunglasses. 'Honestly, *blokes*. You're all the same. Perving over gymslips.'

'Blimey, have you got one of those too?'

She sighs loudly and returns, rather pointedly, to her book.

'What's it like?' he says, gesturing at it. 'Any good?'

'OK so far,' she says, without looking up. 'Though you know what it's like with crime – it's all about the ending.'

He gives a dry laugh. 'Tell me about it.'

'Though apparently this one's OK. The ending, I mean. That's what Mum said, anyway.'

'What's it about?'

She glances up now. 'A missing girl. Her parents are really horrible so you're supposed to think one of them must have done it, but it obviously won't be as simple as that. And the kid is *really* manipulative.' She laughs. 'Reminds me a bit of me. I used to tell the most *enormous* fibs at that age, but Dad swallowed it every time.'

'What about your mum?'

She smiles. 'She was far too shrewd. But Dad just couldn't believe sweet little eight-year-old girls could be such good liars.'

Quinn reaches for another beer; Maisie's definitely going to have to drive them home. Twice in two weeks – it's becoming a habit.

'Not just girls,' he says. 'The kid in that sexual assault case I'm working on? He's exactly the same age and he tells whoppers the size of Birmingham.'

Maisie pulls her sunglasses down her nose. 'Didn't you say he was probably on the spectrum or something?'

Quinn's can fizzes open. 'Yeah, he's definitely not all there. Bright – just, you know, a bit of a weirdo. And no, before you ask, I didn't actually *say* that.'

But her face is serious. 'What was he lying about?'

'That call I got on the way here? Looks like this isn't the first time the mother's got involved in something like this. Only last time she threatened to report the bloke's girlfriend for grooming the kid. But it was all a complete fabrication, just to stop them blabbing.'

She frowns. 'That makes the mother the liar, not him.'

Quinn shrugs. 'Whatever. All I know is that the kid had the whole thing off pat.'

Maisie puts her book down in her lap. 'That doesn't sound right to me. If he really is autistic he'd find that really, really difficult. Kids like that – they can't even do little white lies, never mind great big complicated ones. Why do you think they have so much trouble dealing with other people? There's such a thing as too *much* truth.'

Quinn wedges his can back into the ice. 'How come you know so much about it all of a sudden?'

She shrugs. 'I read a couple of articles about it after that Chris Packham programme.'

Up at the house, her mother is waving at them from the edge of the terrace.

Maisie checks her watch. 'God, is that the time? Lunch must be ready.' She slips off the hammock into the water, moves over to the side and pulls herself out.

'You coming?' she asks, picking up a towel; Quinn still hasn't moved.

'In a minute.' He's frowning, staring into the distance, tapping his fingers against the table.

'OK,' she says, slipping on her sundress. 'I'll see you up there.'

He nods, not looking up.

As soon as she's out of earshot he reaches for his phone.

* * *

Sebastian Young is already in reception when Somer gets there, looking for all the world like he's come for a job interview in his light cotton suit and button-down shirt. Ev was apologetic about dragging her in on a Sunday, but frankly it was a relief. Anything to stop her thinking about where she was supposed to be this weekend. And why she isn't. But she's careful not to arrive at the station too early, because she can't risk any small-talk time with Ev. She's incredibly fond of her, and she knows how much she cares, but right now, she isn't in the mood for confessions.

She isn't in the mood for Dave King, either. Her heart plummets when she spots him at the coffee machine right outside CID. And the fact that it's obvious what's dragged him into the office on a Sunday doesn't help. She's been trying not to think about Fawley; she can't believe he's guilty of something so unimaginable, but she can't square away the evidence either. It's all too much, on top of everything else – Giles, the baby that wasn't, the ultrasound –

King extracts a cup and presses the button, then looks at her with a nasty knowing smile.

'I don't suppose you'll be seeing much of the boyfriend now then, all things considered?'

She stares at him; how the hell does he even know about Giles? What business is it –

He takes his cup and straightens up. 'I mean, you could do a whole lot better than that. Even if he is a sodding *DI.*' She glares at him and he lifts his hands, all innocence. 'Just saying.'

'You don't know the *first thing* about him.'

He raises an eyebrow, evidently amused. 'Ah, now that's where you're wrong. We worked a case or two together, back in the day.' He takes a step closer. 'I know a *lot* about that bastard – much more than you think –'

He has his coffee black, which is unfortunate, because it means the liquid is scalding as it hits his face, his eyes, his chest – splattering over the floor, running down his neck –

'*What was that for?*' he gasps, staggering back. 'You fuck-ing *bitch* how fucking *dare* you – look at my fucking *shirt* –'

He's shouting now, because she's walking away. 'You *bitch* – I'll get you for this – you hear me? I'll fucking *get* you for this –'

* * *

Alex Fawley looks at her watch again. Ten to four. Some-where in her brain she registers Nell next door in the bathroom, sorting laundry, Gerry downstairs with the kids, one of the neighbour's dogs barking. She checks her tablet, refreshes the page. Her fingertip leaves a damp mark across the screen.

* * *

PODCASTS › DOCUMENTARIES › **TRUE CRIME**

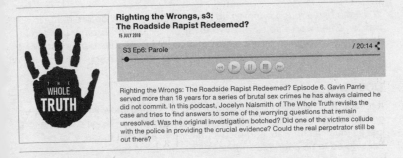

Righting the Wrongs, s3:
The Roadside Rapist Redeemed?
15 JULY 2018

S3 Ep6: Parole   / 20:14

Righting the Wrongs: The Roadside Rapist Redeemed? Episode 6. Gavin Parrie served more than 18 years for a series of brutal sex crimes he has always claimed he did not commit. In this podcast, Jocelyn Naismith of The Whole Truth revisits the case and tries to find answers to some of the worrying questions that remain unresolved. Was the original investigation botched? Did one of the victims collude with the police in providing the crucial evidence? Could the real perpetrator still be out there?

[ARCHIVE TAPE OF BBC JOURNALIST, OUTSIDE THE OLD BAILEY, 20 DECEMBER 1999]

'After a nine-week trial, Gavin Parrie, the so-called "Roadside Rapist", was today sentenced to life for the rape and attempted rape of seven young women in the Oxford area. Judge Peter Healey described Parrie as "evil,

unrepentant and depraved" and recommended he serve at least fifteen years. There was uproar in court as the sentence was announced, with Parrie's family abusing both the judge and jury from the public gallery. As Parrie was led away, he shouted threats at the officer who had been instrumental in his arrest, saying he would "get him" and he and his family would "spend the rest of their lives watching their backs". The officer in question, Detective Sergeant Adam Fawley, has received a commendation from the Thames Valley Chief Constable for the role he played in securing the conviction.'

[JOCELYN]

I wasn't in court that day. I was still at college. But I do remember the case, and I remember thinking what sort of man could not only commit such terrible crimes against women, but then threaten the family of the man who'd helped convict him.

Now, of course, I know a lot more than I did then. I've also talked at length to Gavin myself, and I know he sincerely regrets any distress he caused that day. He has also been deeply affected by the terrible toll the trial took on his own family, especially his children. Even though the Parries were divorced by the time he was convicted, his family were hounded – by the press, by vigilantes, by their own neighbours. They became pariahs, and Sandra was eventually forced to move to Scotland and revert to using her maiden name, purely in order to protect her kids.

[SANDRA]

'It'd been bad enough bringing up three kids on my own before that – it was ten times worse so far away from my family. Gavin's brother used to send me cash whenever he could, but most of the time we barely got by. As for traipsing five hundred sodding miles to visit Gav, forget it.'

[JOCELYN]

It meant Gavin scarcely saw them, of course, but he knew what they were going through – he knew his family were the Roadside Rapist's victims too, just as much as he was, and the women were. And that made what he considered to be a terrible injustice all the harder to bear.

Because his position has never changed: he did not assault those women, and the man who did is still out there. He still believes the Thames Valley investigation was fundamentally flawed, though these days he doesn't use words like 'framed' or 'fitted up'. He's older and wiser and more measured (eighteen years in prison will do that to you). But regardless of whether it was a cock-up or a conspiracy, the end result is the same. He's spent the best years of his life in jail for crimes he did not commit.

I'm Jocelyn Naismith, and I'm the co-founder of The Whole Truth, a not-for-profit organization that campaigns to overturn miscarriages of justice. This is Righting the Wrongs, series 3: The Roadside Rapist Redeemed?

Chapter six: Parole

[THEME SONG – AARON NEVILLE COVER VERSION OF 'I SHALL BE RELEASED']

[JOCELYN]

I'm going to start this episode with a confession. The first time Gavin and his lawyers approached The Whole Truth to take on his case, we turned them down. And the second. But then the case hit the headlines again, and everything changed.

Earlier this year, when Gavin was still in Wandsworth prison, there were two horrific assaults on young women in Oxford – assaults that bore an uncanny and terrifying resemblance to the attacks Gavin was accused of. Was it a copycat or were these attacks the work of the *real* Roadside Rapist?

That's when Gavin's lawyer, Jeremy Peters, contacted us again, and it didn't take us long to realize that this was a case that deserved our attention.

[JEREMY PETERS]

'Gavin's conviction was reviewed by the Criminal Cases Review Commission in 2002, but they declined to send it back to the Court of Appeal. And even though he'd been a model prisoner, he'd always refused to admit guilt, and that hampered his ability to get parole, even though he'd have been eligible for it after fifteen years. So by early 2018, we were running out of options.'

[JOCELYN]

The fact that Gavin had never wavered in his insistence on his innocence, even though that was working against him, was probably the single most important factor in our decision to take on his case. And having made that decision, we did what we always do: we went right back to the very start and looked at the whole investigation. The statements, the forensics, the witnesses. How the police carried out their enquiries, the evidence the jury were presented with in court.

And – crucially – the evidence the jury *never saw at all*. Because there's an element in this case that makes it unique in our experience: the fact that one of the leading detectives subsequently had a relationship with – indeed actually married – one of the victims. And not only *a* victim: *the* victim. The woman whose intervention led the police directly to the one and only piece of forensic evidence that definitively linked Gavin Parrie to the crimes: a strand of her hair, recovered in his lock-up. Hair Gavin Parrie has always believed was planted. Possibly with Adam Fawley's knowledge; even – perhaps – at his instigation.

[JEREMY]

'The Fawleys' subsequent marriage should have been grounds for appeal on its own, but they both gave sworn affidavits to the CCRC that their relationship didn't start until after the trial was over, and this was supported by other witnesses, including several of his superior officers and partners from her law firm. The CCRC had no choice but to accept that.'

[JOCELYN]

So however uneasy we were about the possibility that the Fawleys might have colluded in planting the evidence against Gavin, we knew it would be impossible to prove it. So we turned our attention elsewhere – to what had happened in the earlier stages of the investigation.

And when we did that, it quickly became clear that Thames Valley's case against Gavin Parrie was what we call a 'Frankenstein file'. Sadly, we encounter this all too often in prosecutions that turn out to be miscarriages of justice: cases that have been stitched together from bits and pieces of circumstantial evidence, which appear to add up to something monstrous, but are, fundamentally, 'made-up'.

The police claimed that Gavin Parrie was angry, volatile and resentful. That he felt let down by life and let down by women, after he was rejected first by his wife and then by Julie, his girlfriend in Cowley. In fact, they went so far as to suggest that it was this second rejection, by Julie, that triggered the first attack on Erin Pope (they even claimed that Erin had a physical resemblance to Julie, and put up pictures in court to prove it).

They also cited the extreme nature of the porn found in Gavin's lock-up, which he has never denied was his. But using porn – even hardcore porn – doesn't make you a rapist.

They emphasized Gavin's lack of a steady job, which would have given him the time and flexibility to stalk his victims, and stake out the locations prior to the attacks.

And they pointed out that he had his own van, and access to his brother Bobby's. Bobby who was a plasterer and always had calcium sulphate residue inside his vehicle.

As far as they were concerned, it all fitted.

But that doesn't mean it was true.

We worked closely with Gavin's lawyers on a detailed analysis of the case, which was submitted to the Parole Board as part of their review. And I'm glad to say that we were successful. Gavin was released from Wandsworth prison on May 23rd 2018. But that's not the same as being exonerated. His conviction still stands. He has to wear an electronic tag and observe strict licence conditions, which effectively prevent him leading anything like a normal life. And that includes having the sort of ordinary social contact that other people take for granted. He had a girlfriend when he left prison, but the relationship wasn't strong enough to withstand the difficult process of adjustment post-release, and now, once again, he's on his own.

But with luck and perseverance this won't be the end of Gavin's story. We're still supporting Gavin and his lawyers, with a view to making a second application to the Criminal Cases Review Commission early next year.

In the meantime, Gavin's determined to make the years he still has left count for something. He's spending a lot of time with young offenders and rebuilding his relationship with his children. And, of course, they're not kids any more. Ryan is working in the leisure and wellness sector, and Dawn now has a family of her own, as does her sister, Stacey, who's living and working in Glasgow.

Gavin didn't want to be interviewed on this podcast, but he's been closely involved in producing it. He wants his story told, if only to help ensure other people don't suffer the way he has.

I'll give the last word to his ex-wife, Sandra.

[SANDRA]
'The Gavin I've seen since he was released is the Gavin I first fell in love with. Things could have turned out so differently for him. If he'd got some

qualifications for a start, or if he'd been a bit savvier about dealing with people. A bit less mouthy. Trouble with Gav is that every time he's got himself into a situation it's gone the wrong way. But that wasn't always his fault – he always did have shit luck. But who knows, perhaps that's changing now. Perhaps he's finally going to get what he deserves.'

[UNDER BED OF 'I SHALL BE RELEASED']

I'm Jocelyn Naismith and this is Righting the Wrongs. You can listen to this and other podcasts from The Whole Truth on Spotify, or wherever you get your podcasts.

[FADE OUT]

* * *

Alex puts her tablet down, then slowly reaches her hand to her mouth.

There's a look on her face that's hard to read.

But it's not fear.

Not this time.

* * *

Not for the first time, Dave King is glad he keeps a spare shirt in the office. Though he's made bloody sure to stick the wrecked one in an evidence bag. And take some majorly incriminating selfies to go with it. He's going to cook that bitch's goose good and proper. But first he's going to deal with the Fawley fuck-up. *Really* deal with it this time.

He pushes open the door to the side office. They could have done this somewhere else, but he likes the idea of making it feel official, of upping the discomfort factor. And judging by the look he gets as he sits down, it's working.

344

'Sorry about the delay,' says King breezily. 'Managed to get coffee all down my fucking shirt.' He puts his tablet on the table in front of him and leans forward. 'So, you said on the phone you've got something to show me?'

'Look,' says Anthony Asante. 'This is really difficult – what I found, it isn't what I expected –'

King snorts. 'Thought you'd be able to get the boss off the hook, did you? Play the hero and bank some major brownie points? Well, tough titties. You're a copper. That's how it is. Now give.'

Asante isn't happy, that much is obvious, but he has no choice, and he knows it. 'It's CCTV,' he says. 'From the night Emma Smith died.'

* * *

'Standing room only, I see,' says Bryan Gow drily as he edges round the furniture to the only empty chair. Gislingham is already installed in front of the two video screens and the CPS rape prosecutor is taking a yellow counsel's notepad out of her briefcase. Gis is tempted to ask if she has a couple of spares; she's going to need them.

Gow takes his seat and glances across at Gis. 'I sent Quinn some background info last night and talked him through it, so he should be fully briefed.'

'I've read it too,' says the CPS lawyer. 'And I've read the NDA as well.' She takes a print-out from her bag and tosses it on to the table with as much contempt as she can muster.

'He's played a bit of a blinder on this, by the way,' says

Gow. 'Quinn, I mean. That was a pretty sharp insight of his about the boy.'

Gis nods. 'I know. And I'll make sure Harrison knows too, if it gets us a result. Though I suspect Quinn will probably beat me to it.'

They exchange a smile; Quinn is as predictable as he is ambitious.

'And the rest of your team are prepped, are they?' says the lawyer as the video monitors ping into life. 'They know the score?'

'Oh yes,' says Gis softly. 'They know the score.'

On the left-hand screen, Somer and Asante are showing Caleb Morgan and his lawyers into an interview room. As they take their seats and start going through the preliminaries, Morgan looks straight up into the camera, holding his gaze there long enough for the message to be clear: he knows they're there.

But there's one thing he doesn't know.

He's not the only one they're watching.

* * *

Interview with Marina Fisher, conducted at St Aldate's police station, Oxford

16 July 2018, 9.15 a.m.

In attendance, DC G. Quinn, DC V. Everett, Ms N. Kennedy (solicitor)

GQ: This is the fourth interview with Professor
     Marina Fisher in connection with an allegation

of sexual assault made by Caleb Morgan, alleged to have taken place on July 6th 2018. Professor Fisher, I need to remind you once again that you are still under caution –

NK: What on earth is going on here? I thought we'd established that it was *Marina* who was assaulted, not Morgan. It's him you should be interrogating, not her.

GQ: We're still working to establish exactly what happened that night, and we need the Professor's help to do that. And as I'm sure you can appreciate, any case where the principal witness is a very young child is especially complicated –

NK: But –

GQ: – and as Professor Fisher remains, for the time being, under arrest, we don't have any choice but to conduct any interview with her under caution. As I'm sure you're aware.

NK: [*pause*]
OK. Fair enough. What do you want to know?

* * *

'So, Mr Morgan,' says Asante. 'I'd like to start by asking you again about what Tobin Fisher saw on the night of July 6th –'

Meredith Melia rolls her eyes. 'Not *again*.'

Patrick Dunn clears his throat. 'I have to say, I agree. We've already discussed this, repeatedly and at length. Whatever that child saw or thinks he saw, he's a child. A young, impressionable and therefore – by definition – unreliable *child*.'

Morgan turns to him. 'No, it's not just that – he's a lying little toerag. He lies *all the time* – if he told me the sky was blue, I'd go and fucking check.'

Asante glances at Somer. Her turn.

'You told us before you thought he had "problems".'

Morgan nods. 'Right. Exactly.'

'A child like that, he'd probably find any sexual act alarming, wouldn't you agree?'

He frowns, unsure, suddenly, where this is going.

'You see,' says Somer, sitting forward now, 'we think we know what happened that night. There never was an assault, was there, Caleb?'

His head drops, but he says nothing.

'What Tobin saw was his mother having sex. He'd never seen it before, he had no idea what it meant and he was understandably frightened. But he had no need to be: his mother wasn't in any danger. Like I said, she was just having sex. But if that's what happened – if that's *all it was* – you've got a lot of questions to answer. Starting with why the hell you've been lying to us all this time.'

* * *

GQ: As I said, it's much harder to bring a
    successful prosecution where the case relies
    on a child as the only eyewitness. Juries
    worry that they might have been coached or
    told what to say.

MF: I would never do *anything* like that.

GQ: All the same, you can appreciate that before we
      go any further we need to establish whether
      Tobin's testimony can be relied upon.

MF: I'm not sure I understand –

VE: Morgan's lawyers are also questioning his
      reliability. Which is not unreasonable, given
      his age.

GQ: So, Professor Fisher, is your son a truthful
      child, would you say?

* * *

The room is silent. Morgan's head is in his hands. He's
shaking his head slowly, again and again. The time on the
recording machine moves steadily on; a minute, a minute
and a half, two.

'Was she threatening you, Caleb?' says Somer eventually. 'Is that why you lied?'

Meredith Melia leans over and puts a hand on Morgan's shoulder. 'Caleb,' she says quietly. 'Are you OK?'

There's no response. Melia turns to the officers. 'Perhaps you could give us an explanation for this sudden
interrogatory volte-face?'

Somer and Asante exchange a glance.

'The leak of Professor Fisher's identity,' says Asante.
'It's prompted someone to come forward. Someone who
went through a similar experience.'

'Halle-bloody-lujah,' says Dunn, under his breath.

* * *

MF: What are you suggesting? Of course he's truthful –

GQ: In one of our earlier interviews you told us he lied to you about the dress.

MF: That was different.

GQ: Different? How, exactly?

MF: [*silence*]

GQ: So he has, in fact, lied, on one occasion, at least. Does he make things up as well? Tell stories about things that turn out not to have happened?

MF: No, of course he doesn't.

GQ: Ah, you see, that's the problem. I spoke to Tobin's teacher, yesterday afternoon. And before you ask, Ms Kennedy, the conversation was authorized by an Inspector under Section 29 of the Data Protection Act 1998, which allows for the disclosure of personal information without parental consent for the purposes of detecting or preventing crime.

NK: Even so –

GQ: And given that the enquiry we were making might potentially *exonerate* Professor Fisher, it would be very odd if she were to object to it now.
[*pause*]
Wouldn't you agree?

* * *

'Did you know?' says Somer. 'That this had happened before? That she'd done the same thing to someone else?'

Morgan shakes his head. He looks like he's struggling to take this on.

'The young man in question transferred to King's London eighteen months ago,' Somer continues. 'Before you came to Oxford. He couldn't face staying here after what happened to him. That's why we need you to tell us the truth. And *all* of it, this time.'

Morgan sits back. His face is pale and he's having difficulty making eye contact.

'OK, I admit it – I slept with Marina. Once. *Once*. It was when me and Freya were on a break. Freya never knew.' He glances up at them. 'And I don't want you telling her now, either.'

'So when you told us you'd never had sex with Professor Fisher, that was a lie?'

He hesitates, then nods. He'd dropped his gaze again and his face is flushed now. 'I thought if I admitted it, you wouldn't believe me about that night.'

Somer nods slowly. How many women have thought the same thing, over the years? How many rape victims decided not to come forward for exactly the same reason?

'Go on,' says Asante.

Morgan's still not looking at them. 'I told her it was over. That I was back with Freya, and her and me were finished. That we never even *started*.'

'When did you tell her that?'

He flickers a look at them. 'That night. After the dinner. I just wanted to get it over with and get out of there – but like I told you before, she was buzzing. She said she wanted a drink and she wanted sex – you know, right there and then, on the bloody kitchen table.'

Ev nods. 'And what did you say to that?'

'I said no – that I wished I hadn't done it the first time and I wasn't going to make the same mistake again. But she refused to accept it.'

'What happened next?'

The flush deepens. 'Like I said, she just wasn't taking no for an answer.' He stops, starts rubbing the back of his head. 'So, well, you know –'

'You had sex.'

He nods. 'I said, OK, for old times' sake and all that. But *just once*. She seemed OK with it at the time.'

'But afterwards, she changed her mind?'

He glances up, looks away again. 'Yeah. I said to her, after we'd – you know – done it, that it was over now. *Really* over. That was when she turned nasty.'

* * *

GQ: You know what the school told us, don't you, Professor Fisher?

MF: [*silence*]

VE: According to his teacher, Tobin's been caught out lying several times in the last few months.

MF: [*silence*]

GQ: On one occasion he lied to get another child into trouble. A child he disliked.

MF: He didn't realize – it was just a silly mistake – he was confused –

NK: Oh come *on* – you're actually taking this
    playground stuff seriously?

MF: It's the other children – they make things up
    to make him look bad –

NK: [*quietly*]
    I don't think we need to discuss this any
    further, Marina.

GQ: Was that why you kept telling us you couldn't
    remember what happened to the dress? We never
    could figure that out. But it makes sense now.
    You were embarrassed to admit just how good a
    liar your eight-year-old son is.

MF: [*silence*]

GQ: Though, of course, some kids really do
    struggle telling lies – they find it hard to
    concoct stuff because their brains just aren't
    wired that way.

MF: [*silence*]

GQ: Kids with autism, say, or Asperger's. They
    have difficulty making things up, just as they
    have difficulty interacting with other people.
    If something like that applied to Tobin then,
    of course, it would be much easier to believe
    that all those incidents with the other kids
    really were just 'misunderstandings'.

MF: [*silence*]

GQ: You thought that might be the explanation,
    didn't you, back then? In fact, you went so
    far as to have him tested.

* * *

Morgan takes a deep breath. 'She told me that if I wanted her help – if I wanted a decent reference – then I should do what she wanted. It was entirely up to me, but if I didn't, well –'

'What did you say to that?'

He rubs his hand through his hair again. 'I don't know – I was all over the place – my career, my research – all that work – I just bottled it – said I'd think it over. I just wanted to buy myself some time.'

'And after that you went home?' says Asante.

He nods. 'Right. And I just sat there for a while, churning it all up. And eventually I went round to see Freya. I felt trapped – I didn't know what the hell to do.'

'She must have been angry,' says Somer. 'When you told her you'd slept with Fisher. Especially after you refusing to let her into the house. If you had, none of this would ever have happened.'

He makes a face. 'Don't think that hasn't occurred to me. And yeah, she was pretty pissed off with me. But she was absolutely fucking *furious* with Marina.'

He sits back and looks at them, finally, square in the face. 'The assault allegation – reporting it to college, to you. The whole thing. It was all Freya's idea.'

* * *

GQ: According to the teacher, Tobin went through a full developmental assessment earlier this year, at your request.

NK: [*to her client*]
    You never told me that.

354

GQ: Only it didn't come up with anything, did it, Professor Fisher? The child psychologist concluded that he does indeed have difficulties socializing with other kids, but it's not because he has any sort of 'developmental issue'. It's far *more* likely to be a reflection of his home environment, and in particular, his relationship with *you* –

MF: I absolutely do *not* accept that. I'm getting another opinion – I'm not about to take the word of some local authority second-rater –

GQ: According to the professionals, Tobin is highly intelligent, but extremely anxious, especially when separated from you. He has problems interacting with strangers, and coping with negative emotions, even to the point of aggression.

NK: I haven't got a clue what you're on about –

GQ: Oh, I think you'll find Professor Fisher does. She knows exactly what I'm talking about.

* * *

In the adjoining room, Gislingham is staring at the screen. 'She was so bloody convincing,' he says, half to himself. 'I bought the whole thing.'

'Don't beat yourself up too much,' says Gow, making a note. 'I've come across subjects like her before.'

'No wonder the kid is so messed up,' says the CPS lawyer darkly. 'Poor little sod.'

''Fraid so,' says Gow with a sigh. 'Motherhood's one thing even those machines of hers can't fake.'

* * *

GQ: [*picks up a sheet of paper*]
     'Anxious attachment is usually the result of
     inconsistent, erratic or absent parenting.
     Such children become highly insecure and
     over-focused on the parent in question, which
     manifests itself in clinging and suspicious
     responses, and a willingness to do almost
     anything to please that parent and secure
     their attention.'
     'Almost anything', Professor Fisher. Including,
     I suggest, a willingness to lie. If Mummy
     asked him to.
MF: [*angrily*]
     Tobin was *never* diagnosed with that.
GQ: No, he wasn't. Not officially. But only because
     you withdrew him from the assessment before
     that could happen. But it would certainly
     tally with everything our team has seen of
     him over the last week or so. As well as
     everything we've learnt of his behaviour in
     the past. Because this has happened before,
     hasn't it? He's lied for you before.
MF: What the hell are you talking about?
VE: Does the name Sebastian Young ring any bells?

* * *

'I thought it was crazy – that we'd never pull it off – but Freya said we just had to be clever. She said Marina always assumed she was the smartest person in the room, but we could play her at her own game.'

Asante and Somer exchange a glance.

'So what did that involve, exactly?'

'Freya said that even if we reported an assault straight away it would be hours before the police got to question Marina. That there was no way she wouldn't have showered by then, and I'd used a condom anyway, so there'd be no proof we'd actually had sex.'

'And Freya helped you?' says Somer. 'To fabricate the evidence – preserve DNA in the right places and get rid of the rest?'

He nods. He looks uncomfortable.

'It was a big risk, though, wasn't it?' says Asante. 'How did you know Marina wouldn't just tell us straight out that the two of you had been having an affair?'

But Somer's shaking her head. 'No. They knew what they were doing. They knew she'd never do that – she'd risk losing her job.'

Morgan looks at her and then away. His cheeks are flushed.

'That's right, isn't it, Caleb?'

* * *

GQ: You know who we're talking about, right?
      Sebastian Young? He's the one who signed that
      fancy NDA Ms Kennedy here drew up for you.
      But just in case you need reminding –

357

       [*pushes a photograph across the table and
       points at it*]
       Keeping on top of your work, eh?
NK: Oh, *please* –
GQ: Marina Imogen Fisher, I am arresting you on
       suspicion of sexual assault against Sebastian
       James Young, on or about 20th November 2016.
       You do not have to say anything, but it may
       harm your defence if you do not mention when
       questioned something which you later rely on
       in court. Anything you do say may be given in
       evidence.

* * *

'Look,' says Morgan, 'I'm sorry, OK? We shouldn't have done it.'

'No,' says Somer heavily. 'You absolutely shouldn't have.'

He slumps back in his chair, throws up his hands. 'I just didn't know what else to *do*. She was using me – abusing her position –'

'That's not the point. It's perverting the course of justice.'

'And now you're telling me she's done this *before*?'

Somer sits forward. 'You say she was abusing her power – why didn't you just report her for that? Tell the college what was going on?'

He makes a sardonic face. 'And say what, precisely?'

'That she was blackmailing you into having sex with her, for a start.'

He scoffs. 'Yeah, right. They were *definitely* going to believe that.'

* * *

MF: This is crazy – I didn't *assault* Sebastian, any more than I assaulted Caleb. And you *know* I didn't do that – you said yourselves –

GQ: [*points at the photograph*]
Perhaps. But we do 'know' you did this.

MF: [*takes a breath*]
Look – it was just that once and it was a *huge* mistake. It should never have happened.

GQ: I think we can all agree on that.

MF: You don't understand. I was really struggling at the time. The relationship I was in had just broken up. I was lonely, vulnerable. And then there was the divorce, I'd just hit forty, it was all just – overwhelming. But I know that's no excuse – I should never have let myself get drawn in.

VE: You're saying *he* seduced *you*?

MF: [*irritated*]
Yes, of course *he* seduced *me*. What sort of person do you think I am? And then that horrible girlfriend of his marches in and takes that wretched picture and it all turned into a complete bloody nightmare. That's why I needed an NDA – that girl was *blackmailing* me – threatening to release the picture to the department, the University –

GQ: So you gave her a dose of her own medicine?
Said you'd go to the police and tell them some
cock-and-bull story about Zoe grooming Tobin?

MF: [*flushes*]
It wasn't like that.
[*looking from one officer to the other*]
Don't look at me like that – I'm *telling the truth* –

GQ: But you got Tobin to lie, didn't you? That
story he told Sebastian Young about being
groomed – none of that was true.

MF: But –

GQ: You coached him.

MF: Yes, I suppose, if you put it like that. But
just to get them to back off. I'd never have
taken it any further. Look, can't you
understand? I didn't have any *choice* – I was
going to lose my job – my position –
everything I'd worked for –

NK: And might I remind you that whatever might
have happened *then*, it doesn't mean Tobin
isn't telling the truth *now*.

VE: [*silence*]
Shall I tell you what *I* think is the truth?

MF: [*looks away*]

VE: I think you and Caleb Morgan had sex that
night. Straightforward, consensual sex. And it
wasn't the first time, either. So when Morgan
came forward and accused you of assault, you
were completely thrown – what on earth was he
playing at? You couldn't tell us what really
happened because you couldn't admit you were

360

sleeping with a student, so the only option was to hope it would all just go away. And you're clever, you worked out pretty quickly that it would only ever be *he said/she said*. All you had to do was tough it out. Tell us you couldn't remember. Because there's no way we could prove it one way or the other, right?

MF: No – that's not what happened. I *never* slept with him, *never* –

VE: But then you were outed on Twitter and everything changed. Your career was on the line now. It wasn't just the Morgan relationship, either – it could all come out about Sebastian Young as well. You had to *do* something. So you did exactly what you did the first time round, with Sebastian. You turned the tables. Played Caleb Morgan at his own game.

MF: No – I *didn't* –

VE: You made *yourself* into the victim. But you had to be clever about how you did it. You couldn't just turn round and start making accusations against Morgan – it had to be a lot subtler than that. You needed us to think *we'd* worked it out – that us 'second-rate' minds had actually managed to crack the case.

MF: [*shaking her head*]
This is madness.

VE: All that time you'd been claiming you couldn't remember, hoping it would all go away – it's only now you realized what a fabulous get-out-of-jail card that could be.

MF: It's not a *claim* – it's the truth.

VE: A date-rape drug. What could be simpler?

MF: No – *no* –

VE: You're a scientist – you knew how quickly those things metabolize, so forensics wouldn't be a problem. But you couldn't plant the idea yourself. To be really credible, it had to come from somewhere else. And who better than an innocent eight-year-old boy? You used *your own son*. After all, you knew he'd be convincing. He'd lied for you before.

MF: [*becoming distressed*]

VE: You told him what to say – what story to tell. You told him about the red dragon –

MF: [*looking from one officer to the other*] Dragon? What *dragon*?

VE: You told him to say Morgan was 'hurting' you – that your dress was up over your waist, that you were all 'floppy' and 'sleepy'. You planted those ideas in your son's mind, you made him see those pictures in his head –

MF: [*extremely distressed now*] No – I never said anything about any of that – I was raped – he *raped* me –

NK: That's enough, Constable.

* * *

Morgan's lawyers are on their feet now, collecting papers, surreptitiously checking their phones.

'So you understand, Mr Morgan?' says Somer, forcing

his attention. 'We'll need to talk to the CPS, but I doubt they'll decide to take any further action against you. If so, you'll be issued with a formal caution.'

'Don't worry, Caleb,' says Melia. 'We'll talk you through all that.'

'It's not a get-out-of-jail card,' continues Somer, making him look at her. 'It's serious. And it has consequences – you do understand that?'

Morgan hesitates a moment then nods. 'Yeah, I understand.'

* * *

In the adjoining room, Gislingham turns to the CPS prosecutor. 'What do you think – should we interview Tobin again – see if we can get him to admit that his mother told him what to say?'

The lawyer sighs. 'I doubt it's worth the effort – no jury is going to believe that child now.'

She starts to pack her notebooks into her bag. 'And the physical evidence is all over the place – the whole case is a complete morass.'

Gow glances up, raises his eyebrows. Evidently he agrees.

'Let her sweat a bit,' says the lawyer, 'then let her go.'

Gis frowns. 'He gets a caution and a criminal record, but she goes scot-free?'

'He *admitted* what he did. She's denying it, and we can't prove it. It's all circumstantial.'

'We could contact her other students – say we're investigating sexual assault allegations and ask anyone with information to contact us?'

The lawyer nods. 'I don't have any problem with you doing that. It may help keep the press off your backs, if nothing else. But unless someone else comes forward with a case that will actually stand up in court, I'm afraid this is a non-starter.'

'So she just gets away with it.'

The prosecutor gives him a heavy look. 'You think having her name dragged through the dirt and wrecking her career is "getting away with it"?'

Gis considers. 'Well, I guess if you put it that way . . .'

* * *

Dave King presses pause on his tablet screen and turns to Ruth Gallagher.

'It's enough, right?' he says. 'Enough to nail him?'

She frowns. 'Play it again.'

She's already seen the CCTV footage three times, and she's rarely seen evidence so incontrovertible. That's not what's holding her back. It's the look on the face of the man who's showing it to her. There's been a zeal, almost a fanaticism, about King these last few days that's made her increasingly uneasy. No police officer should be that elated about bringing down one of their own – whatever he's supposed to have done.

King starts the footage again. She can see how hard he's working not to betray his impatience. There's a little vein pulsing in the side of his neck.

The camera is from one of the flats on the corner of William Lucy Way, looking straight at Walton Well Road. The bridge is out of range to the left, but you can see anything – and anyone – heading towards it. Including the car that passes at speed at 01.09 on Tuesday 10 July, fifteen minutes before a team of Network Rail engineers will spot a body falling on to the northbound line.

'That stretch of road is a dead end,' says King, as if Gallagher didn't already know. 'And with all the parked cars it's too narrow for a three-point. He had to go down to the car park by Port Meadow to turn round.' His eyes narrow. 'Just a pity the tosser who put up the camera didn't stick it somewhere where we could see the sodding reg number.'

On the screen, the road is now deserted. No passers-by, no other vehicles. No signs of life at all until 01.31, when the car reappears going in the opposite direction, heading back fast towards town. Gallagher swallows. She knows what this man just did. And what he had in that car.

King freezes the image. It's impossible to see who's driving, but the car itself is clear enough.

It's a dark-blue Ford Mondeo.

* * *

The day is still stifling but the sky has clouded. The air is thickening with approaching thunder and despite the high ceilings and long windows, the sitting room at St Luke Street feels grey, oppressive. On the sofa, Marina clutches her sobbing son on her lap, like some ghastly perversion of a Madonna and Child.

'It's not *fair*!' he wails. 'They said I was lying but I *wasn't*!'

'I know you weren't, darling,' she whispers, rocking him against her. 'I know you weren't.'

'I saw him, Mummy! I *saw* him! I *saw* him!'

'I know, sweetheart, I know.'

His sobs stutter, turn to gasps. He sits back and looks at her. 'Then why –?'

She strokes his hair, her own eyes filling with tears now. 'It's like that sometimes, darling – it's not fair and it can break your heart, but people don't always believe you. Even if you are telling the truth.'

* * *

'So you're going to charge him?' says Harrison. He has his jacket off and his shirt sleeves rolled up. Safe to say he's feeling the heat, whichever way you look at it.

'Yes, sir,' says Gallagher. 'We need to put the new evidence to him in interview first, but the CPS are confident that the case against DI Fawley is now very sound.'

'I gather we have DS King to thank for that.'

She frowns slightly; even if that were true, King had no business talking to Harrison behind her back. 'Actually, sir, it was DC Asante who tracked the footage down. He knows the area around the bridge and thought it likely some of the residents would have their own security systems. And he was right.'

Harrison looks up. 'Really? Asante? Getting off his backside and using his initiative, eh? We could do with a bit more of that round here, frankly.'

'Yes, sir. Though I suspect he isn't feeling much like celebrating. He clearly thought it would be Hugh Cleland's car we found on that footage.'

'Ah – tricky.'

'But I'll speak to him – pass on your comments.'

'Yes, do that.' He sits back, frowns again. 'Meanwhile –'

'Meanwhile, Adam Fawley will be charged this afternoon – the press office would rather we didn't do it any earlier as they'd prefer he didn't go before the magistrate until tomorrow morning. Give them as much time as possible to man the barricades.'

'Yes, well, I can't imagine they're exactly thrilled by the prospect.'

Gallagher grimaces. 'They can't say they didn't know it was a possibility.'

He gives her a knowing look. 'Believe me, Ruth, you can never do too much prep for a shitstorm like this.'

Above their heads, there's a rumble of thunder. The symbolism is painful.

Harrison sits back. 'And as if having one of our own DIs up for rape and murder wasn't enough, there's now this other little matter.'

'The timing is certainly unfortunate. But if you're happy with how I propose to deal with it –'

'Yes, yes,' he says curtly. 'Whatever it takes as long as it's out of my in tray. *And* off the front page of the bloody *Oxford Mail.*'

* * *

Gislingham clears his throat. 'So you understand that by accepting a caution you are admitting to attempting to pervert the course of justice?'

Morgan nods.

'And that this information could be revealed as part of

a criminal record check and might affect your ability to travel to certain jurisdictions?'

Another nod. He's starting to look impatient.

'And you're happy you've received appropriate legal advice and understand the full implications –'

'Yeah, yeah,' he says tetchily, 'let's just get it over with.'

Sergeant Woods exchanges a dry look with Gislingham and passes Morgan the form.

'Sign here, please.'

* * *

The atmosphere in the CID office is as changed as the weather. After the adrenaline high of the last hour they're all going a bit cold turkey. Except Quinn, of course, who's nowhere to be seen. Probably wandering the corridors, thinks Ev, hoping he'll 'accidentally' run into Harrison and be able to bask in the warmth of his appreciation. Though she has to admit Quinn deserves his pat on the back this time. His intuition about Tobin was what unlogged the jam. But when they're handing out the plaudits she hopes Gis gets a look-in too: he's handled this minefield of a case really well, and almost entirely without benefit of DI.

So when she looks up a few minutes later and sees the DS standing in the doorway she's momentarily thrown. Because he's frowning. Really frowning, in a way he hardly ever does.

'I thought that went pretty well,' she begins, only to falter because he's shaking his head.

'It's not that. It's Gallagher. She wants to see you. Now.'
But it's not Ev he's looking at. It's Somer.

* * *

'Ah, DC Somer, come in. And close the door, please.'

Gallagher sits back in her chair. It's hard to read her face. She has a track record of supporting junior female officers, as Ev and Somer well know, but right now there's a thin grim line between her brows. A line that says unease, as much as it says displeasure.

'DS King says you threw coffee in his face. Scalding-hot coffee. What the hell were you thinking? He'd have every right to pursue you for ABH – I assume you do know that?'

'Yes, ma'am,' says Somer. She's staring at the floor, her body rigid.

Gallagher frowns. 'DC Somer – *Erica* – I know you. Or at least I thought I did. You're astute, thoughtful, the very opposite of impulsive. I can quite easily see DC Quinn flipping a latte at someone in a fit of pique, but *you*?'

Somer bites her lip. She can feel tears prickling the back of her throat, but she will not cry, she *will not cry* –

Gallagher's still staring at her. 'Help me out here, will you, because I just don't get it.'

Somer takes a breath. 'DS King made a derogatory remark. I just – reacted.'

Gallagher's frown deepens. 'A remark about you?'

Somer shakes her head. 'No. About my boyfriend. About when they worked together.'

Gallagher is taken aback. 'Worked together? When was this?'

Somer can feel her cheeks going hot. Sweat is seeping down her back. 'I don't know.'

Gallagher just looks baffled now. 'But surely you've checked with – Giles, isn't it? What does he say?'

Somer's cheeks are burning. 'I haven't spoken to him about it.'

Gallagher sighs. There's clearly more to this than she feels comfortable prising out. 'Well, for what it's worth, I know for a fact that DS King has never worked either with or for Hants Police. In any case, there must be some sort of misunderstanding at the root of this, because DS King says you were discussing the Emma Smith case at the time –'

She stops; Somer suddenly has her hand to her mouth, swallowing, as if she's trying not to be sick.

'I think, ma'am,' she says quietly, 'I think I may have got it wrong. What DS King said, I think it must have been about DI Fawley.'

'DI Fawley? But why? He's not your boyfriend –' Gallagher stops, counts to ten, then takes a deep breath. 'Unless you're trying to tell me there's been something going on between you two?'

Somer is shaking her head vigorously and looking her, finally, in the eye. 'No. There isn't and there never has been. But, a few months back, there were rumours – some people thought –' She makes a sad, despairing gesture. 'He'd supported me – brought me into CID – so they thought we were – you know.'

Gallagher nods slowly; she knows, all right. Not about

this specifically, but how common 'this' still is. The casual assumption – even by people who'd never think of themselves as sexist – that an attractive and ambitious woman must be using the one to further the other. She's faced it enough times in her own career, but she'd been hoping dinosaur attitudes like that were finally dying out.

'What *exactly* did DS King say?'

Somer looks up at her again, then drops her gaze. 'He said he assumed I'd be finishing with him and I could do a lot better. That even if he was a "sodding DI" he was still a bastard.'

Gallagher sighs. Needless to say, King's story is rather different, though given the way he's been gunning for Fawley she suspects Somer's version of events is likely to be closer to the truth. But even if she could prove it, that's still no excuse for what Somer did.

'OK,' she says. 'This is what's going to happen. I've already spoken to DS King and he's not minded to resolve this informally, which is regrettable, but unless he has a change of heart, a formal misconduct investigation will have to be instigated.'

Somer drops her head, nods.

'There's nothing I can do about that, even if I wanted to. And in any case, Superintendent Harrison has already decided to refer the case to Professional Standards. So what *you* need to do now is talk to a Police Federation rep as soon as you can – today, if possible. Take them through exactly what happened. All of it, mind – the precise words he used, the assumptions he made – the whole thing. You understand what I'm telling you?'

Somer nods again.

'I'm not going to recommend suspension –'

Somer gasps – but surely she must have realized it was a possibility?

'– but I am going to suggest you transfer temporarily to other duties. But right now, this minute, I want you to go home and contact your rep. You look completely bloody exhausted.'

Somer says nothing. There's something about her demeanour – the deadness of it – that makes Gallagher suddenly wonder –

'Are you OK, Erica? Is there something I should know – something that might affect your case?'

Somer shakes her head. 'No, ma'am,' she says. 'Nothing at all.'

* * *

Fair to say it's been a slow news day for Richard Yates at the *Oxford Mail*. There are only so many ways you can say 'Phew, what a scorcher' without actually saying 'Phew, what a scorcher', and what with the usual silly season crap, the pickings right now are particularly parched. He sifts idly through the latest crop of press releases but nothing's popping; another round of *Endeavour* filming really isn't cutting it as 'news' these days, and as for the Martin Scorsese honorary degree, he's already squeezed two bylines out of that and his suggestion for a vox pop at the station cab rank was well and truly spiked ('That's enough *Taxi Driver* references, Ed', as his editor took great delight in scrawling on Yates's message pad).

He sits back in his desk chair and swings it idly from

side to side. His mobile starts to ring, but he doesn't exactly jump to it. The way today's going, it's probably his mum.

'Dick, old mate, how are you?'

There's only one person who calls him that. It fucks him off every time, but he bites his tongue because of who this bloke is.

'You got something for me?'

'Off the record, right? *Really* off. Because if it gets out you got this from me, they'll have my arse.'

Yates sits forward, scoop feelers on full alert. 'Yeah, yeah,' he says as casually as he can muster. 'When have I ever dumped on you?'

There's a sigh at the other end. 'OK. Just needed to say it, right?'

Yates pulls his notebook towards him. 'So what've you got?'

'Emma Smith. We've charged someone.'

'That forty-six-year-old bloke you arrested?'

'Right. We won't be making an announcement but he'll be up before the beak first thing tomorrow, so make sure you're down there waiting, OK? And take a bloody photographer.'

Yates is writing furiously. 'You think he's definitely your man?'

No mistaking the self-satisfaction at the other end. 'Oh yeah, he's our man, all right. But it's not that. It's *who he is*. Seriously, mate, this is hold-the-fucking-front-page territory.'

Yates grasps the phone a bit tighter. 'You going to give me a heads-up or just be a bloody prick-tease?'

'If I do, you can't break it early, right? You'll have to wait for the court list. Security on this one is as tight as a duck's backside.'

'Yeah, yeah –'

A low laugh. 'Let's just say you could do worse than mugging up on the life and career of one Adam John Fawley.'

Yates frowns; he knows that name. Every reporter in this city knows that name. 'Hang on, are you seriously telling me –'

'Too right, mate. That's *exactly* what I'm telling you. The bastard who raped and murdered Emma Smith? It was *Detective Inspector* Adam Fawley.'

* * *

'I wanted Cheerios,' says Ben, standing by the open cupboard. He's just back from his bike ride, sweaty, dusty and in quest of quick carbs. 'But we've run out.'

Nell Heneghan glances across from the sink. 'I'm sure we haven't, darling. I only got another packet a couple of days ago.'

Ben is standing his ground. 'We've run out,' he says in martyred tones, 'because Auntie Alex keeps eating them. They're supposed to be for *me*.'

Nell smiles. 'I told you, didn't I – pregnant ladies sometimes have weird cravings. I stuffed myself with pickled onions when I was carrying you – I've never been able to eat a single one since. Auntie Alex just happens to fancy Cheerios right now, OK? It's not a problem – there's plenty to go round.'

'No,' says Ben stolidly. 'There *isn't*.'

Nell's slightly nettled now. 'You're probably just not looking properly.'

Like his father, like *her* father. It's one of those bloke things.

Ben's still not moving, so she puts down the potato peeler with an audible sigh and goes over to the larder. But three frustrated minutes later she has to concede defeat.

'Can't you have something else? I can make toast – there's Nutella –'

Ben's the one frowning now. 'But what about tomorrow? What about *breakfast*?'

Nell checks her watch. She could nip out now and be back in time to get the food on, and then go and collect Nicky from judo. And Gerry should be back in twenty minutes.

'OK,' she says, 'I'll pop down to Tesco to get some. Can you keep an eye on Auntie Alex while I'm gone?'

He shrugs. 'I can't. She's got the door closed.'

'Don't be so literal, darling. You know what I mean. I'll just pop up and tell her before I go. And in the meantime, the toaster's over there if you're on the brink of death.'

She tousles his hair, gets an annoyed shrug for her pains, then turns and goes upstairs.

There's no sound from the spare room and Nell hesitates at the door. Because what Ben said has rekindled her own concern. Alex has been acting oddly all day – in fact, she's been acting oddly ever since last night. She hardly ate anything, just kept fiddling with her tablet, which really got on Gerry's nerves, because they don't let the boys bring devices to the table. And she didn't appear for breakfast at all. Nell's been up twice with cups of tea, but Alex just called out that she was fine and would be down soon. Nell knows her sister is a private person – that she's acutely embarrassed about taking up space in the house and getting in the way – but this is getting ridiculous.

'Alex?' she says, knocking firmly this time. 'I'm just nipping out to the shops. Do you need anything?'

Silence.

Nell's heart quickens – privacy is one thing but her sister is pregnant, *very* pregnant –

She hesitates one second more, then grips the handle and opens the door.

*   *   *

The pub is busy. It may be Monday but it's hot, and it's the holidays, and the place is heaving, though the first fat drops of rain dropping on to the scorching tarmac have scuttled people back to the gloom inside, where the loud drinks in primary colours with straws and umbrellas now look ludicrously, endearingly out of place.

Despite the rain, the door's wedged open to get what passes for fresh air on the Banbury Road, and there's a slight blonde woman standing at the threshold. And she's not just looking for a way to stay dry – she's intent, scanning the crowd. The light is behind her and the room dark, so it'll probably take a few moments for your eyes to adjust. But you'll recognize her soon enough.

She starts to move now, through the crowd towards a

376

table near the back. There are two young people sitting there already, a young man and woman talking in low voices, their heads and bodies close together. He has a white T-shirt and an angular hawk-like tattoo on his left forearm that you've seen somewhere before. As for the girl, she has her auburn hair in a tiny ponytail . . .

There's a bottle of wine on the table and three glasses. When they look up, you can see the expectation in their eyes.

The blonde girl dumps her bag and sits down.

'It's done,' she says, the words coming in a rush of breath. 'He just called from the police station. They're giving him a caution, and he says I'll probably get one too, but that's it – nothing more. It's over. Pour me a bloody drink, will you, Sebastian – I fucking need one.'

The other two are looking at each other; triumph on her face, relief on his.

'You aced it, Freya,' says the girl, holding out her glass for wine. 'We seriously owe you one.'

'It's Caleb you should be thanking, not me.'

'Thank God he's only getting a caution– I mean, after they arrested him and everything –'

Freya nods. 'I know – I was really worried for a moment back there. I thought the whole thing might be going to shit.'

'And you're sure the cops didn't suspect anything?' begins the man tentatively. 'Because if they worked out me and Caleb knew each other from rugby, they'd work it all out –'

Zoe frowns. 'Oh, stop being such a girl, Seb. Why would they even think that? And we scrubbed our phones – there won't be anything there even if they go looking. *Which they won't.*'

He makes a face. 'OK, OK, sorry. I just feel a bit of a shit, that's all. I mean, yes, Marina did make up that crap about the grooming, but only because of that picture – because she was scared. And as for the sex, I mean, you know how much I wish it had never happened, but it just *did* – she never *forced* me – she was just upset –'

'Well, she forced Caleb,' says Freya quickly, glaring at him. 'Remember?'

She stares at him, holding his gaze. After a moment he drops his eyes. 'I still don't know why you needed to drag me in.'

'*Because no one would have believed us otherwise,*' she insists. 'It would just have been her word against Caleb's. There had to be another victim to make them take us seriously. Especially after she got that bloody kid to lie for her.'

Zoe shakes her head. 'Jesus, Freya, I'm so sorry – I *never* thought she'd dare do that again.'

'And we *agreed*, remember,' says Freya, still staring at Sebastian, 'that night, after it happened? All *four* of us: you, me, Zo, Caleb. We had to *do* something, right? Once was bad enough – but twice? You can't *do* that – you can't just go around screwing other people's *boyfriends* and expect there to be no comeback. She had to be *stopped.*'

Zoe reaches out and touches Sebastian on the arm. 'She was a class-one bitch over that NDA, babe. She practically drove us out of Oxford. Why should she get away with that?'

'And what if it was the other way round?' says Freya

quickly. 'What if it'd been Zo and a male tutor – what would you say then – would you think *that* was OK?'

Sebastian is still staring down at his wine.

'Because it's no bloody different,' says Freya. 'She's in a position of power and that means that what she did was *abuse*. Abuse of Caleb and abuse of you – whether you think she "forced" you or not. The only person who's done anything wrong here is *her* and she's finally going to get what she deserves.'

She raises her glass and the other girl follows, and then, after a moment, Sebastian does too.

'To revenge,' says Zoe.

'To *justice*,' says Freya.

* * *

It's obvious why Alex didn't answer Nell's knock. She's sitting cross-legged on the bed in her pyjamas, earphones in, staring at her laptop, making notes on a counsel's pad. Her hair is straggly and she clearly hasn't showered.

'Alex,' cries Nell, 'for God's sake, you're not *working*? This is *crazy* – after everything the doctor said –'

Alex looks up. Her cheeks are flushed, but she doesn't look unwell – she looks excited, wired.

'Nell,' she says, pulling out one earphone. But only one. 'Sorry. I didn't hear you.'

Her sister takes a step forward, her face grave. 'What are you *doing*?' She gestures at the laptop, the paper. 'You're *on leave* – you shouldn't even be *thinking* about this stuff, never mind –'

Alex cuts across her. 'I'm fine, Nell, really. And it's not work. I promise.'

Nell frowns. 'You should be taking it easy – *resting*. Remember what the doctor said?'

Alex smiles, placatory. 'I know – and I'm fine. Really.' Her hand is already poised to put her earphone back.

'OK,' says Nell with a sigh. She knows better than to argue with Alex when she gets in this mood. And at least there's some colour in her cheeks now. 'I'm popping out to the shops. I'll only be half an hour. Ben's downstairs if you need anything. And Gerry won't be long.'

But Alex has already gone back to her programme.

Nell stands there for a few more moments, but her sister doesn't even seem to register her presence. She's paused the audio and is making another note, underlining something.

Nell reaches for the door and pulls it quietly closed.

* * *

9 July 2018, 9.25 p.m.
62a Shrivenham Close, Headington, Oxford

Despite the heat, she has the doors and windows closed, but it's not making her feel safe, just even more paranoid. She's scared all the time now. At home, in the street, on her own, near other people. All the time.

No wonder Amanda dumped her – it must have been like dating a double agent. If they'd known each other better, perhaps she could have told her, but she was too afraid of the look in her eyes, of what she'd say – what everyone would say

380

if they knew. Her friends, her parents, Beth at work. They'd want to be sympathetic, they'd want to believe – of course they would – but the more she said, the more they'd wonder. The more she'd see the doubt in their eyes. Because, yes, something like this happened once before, and she was wrong about it then, and the guy she accused got no end of shit he didn't deserve. And no, she can't be *totally* sure this time either. She's never seen his face, never really seen him, not properly. Just an impression, a quick movement, a silhouette, always just out of sight, always just out of reach. It's all shadows and glimpses and bad vibes. Just like last time.

Only this time it's different. Because this time it's true.

If only she could believe it was Hugh Cleland. At least that would be logical, something she could explain. But she knows she would be kidding herself. This man – whoever he is – is thinner, slighter, nimbler. And in any case, he's been stalking her for weeks. Long before it all blew up with the Clelands.

The ring on the doorbell makes her jump. She holds a hand to her chest for a moment, feeling the beat against the bone. *For God's sake, pull yourself together. Just see who it is, OK? You don't have to open the door. Not unless you want to. Not unless you know them.*

She takes a deep breath and goes down the hall, telling herself to walk with purpose, to get a grip. There's a peephole in the panelling and she puts her hand to the wood, squinting into the glass. Then she straightens up and smiles a little *see-you're-just-overreacting-again* smile.

She takes off the chain and opens the door.

* * *

It's more like forty-five minutes in the end. The storm broke like Niagara while Nell was in the store and the months-dry roads are awash. Even at twenty miles an hour she can barely see where she's going – the windscreen wipers just can't work fast enough and the car's steaming up inside. The sheer effort of driving in a straight line is making her eyes ache. When she finally turns into their road there's a blur of red and blue lights up ahead. Up ahead, *where they live*. She frowns. Don't be stupid, she tells herself sternly. It's not us, of course it's not us –

But it is. The ambulance is outside *their* house, it's *their* front door that's open.

There's iron in her chest now – *not one of the boys – please don't let it be one of the boys –*

She puts her foot down, loses control for a moment, slides sideways, and the car crunches metal.

Shit

Shit shit shit

She stops the car, throws open the door. Two paramedics are manoeuvring a stretcher down the path.

Not one of the boys. Not Gerry –

Alex.

She splashes down the pavement, soaked in seconds, rain running down her face.

The paramedics are lifting the stretcher now, sliding it into position. Alex's face is white against the pillow, her eyes closed, an oxygen mask pushed over her nose and mouth.

One of the medics turns and sees her, frowns a little. 'Are you the sister? She was asking for you.'

'What happened?' gasps Nell. 'Is she OK?'

'Her waters broke. All happened very suddenly apparently. Your son called us. Just as well he did. Bit of a responsibility though, for such a young kid.'

The frown explains itself now. Nell swallows. *Oh my God, this is all my fault. What sort of mother leaves a heavily pregnant woman alone with an eleven-year-old child?*

'My husband was on his way,' she stammers. 'Isn't he here?'

The man shrugs. 'Got held up. So your son said.'

The other paramedic steps down and nods to her colleague. Nell darts forward and peers up into the back through the rain.

'Alex? It's me – everything's going to be fine, OK? I'll follow as soon as I can.'

Alex opens her eyes and tries to sit up, reaching out desperate hands, trying to say something, but the second medic is already closing the doors.

'We need to get moving,' says the woman. 'I'm worried about her heart rate – the baby could be in distress.' And then, to Nell, 'She asked you to get a message to her husband.'

'Yes, yes,' Nell says as they walk back round to the cab. 'Tell her I will –'

The engine starts up and she takes a step back, blinking away tears. This baby, this longed-for baby, is finally coming and her sister is going to the hospital alone. It wasn't supposed to be like this.

* * *

He smiles at her. She has no interest in men, but she can see why other women might go for him. The dark hair, the hazel eyes. She finds herself thinking – irrelevantly – that he'd probably look pretty good in a suit; he doesn't look that bad even in an old trackie top and joggers.

'Hi,' he says.

* * *

Ben is standing white-faced on the doorstep, watching as the ambulance pulls away.

'Is she going to be OK?' he asks in a small voice.

Nell reaches out and puts an arm around his shoulders, faking a confidence she doesn't feel.

'Of course she is. And apparently I have a hero for a son – phoning for the ambulance like that. Well done, you.'

His lip is trembling a little. 'She just asked me to phone 999. I didn't really do anything.'

She squeezes his shoulder. '*Yes, you did.* And she'll be really grateful. Just you wait.'

He hangs his head. 'It was horrible, Mum. She was breathing funny, and it really hurt, I could tell, and the bed was all wet –'

She grasps him to her, stroking his back. 'It's OK, darling,' she whispers. 'I know it looks frightening if you haven't seen it before, but that's just what happens when a baby is coming.'

He's trying not to cry. She kisses the top of his head.

'You were very brave and I am *very* proud of you. And I'm so so sorry I wasn't here.'

He sniffs, pulls away. 'It's OK.' He smiles, a little wobbly. 'It was my fault, wanting the Cheerios.'

She puts her hand to her mouth. 'Oh Lord, I left the car running.' She glances down the street – the car's door is open and the lights on, but at least someone hasn't nicked it. Gerry's going to be pissed off enough about the prang. It would have to be the Wilders' SUV, now wouldn't it.

'I'm just going to get the shopping –'

She's turning to go when Ben grabs her sleeve. 'She wanted you to phone someone called Gislingham. She wrote down his number.'

'Don't worry, darling,' she says, turning her collar up against the rain. 'I'll do it as soon as I've sorted the car.'

'No,' he says, surprisingly insistent. 'She said it was *urgent* – it's about Uncle Adam being arrested.'

She starts; the children weren't supposed to know about that. Not yet, anyway. Not while there's still some hope it's all just some ghastly misunderstanding.

'She made me promise,' Ben's saying. 'She said she's found something out.'

She stares at him. 'What are you talking about? Found out? Found out what?'

He looks down, shrugs. 'I don't know. She said it was too difficult to explain. But it was all on her notepad. That you should look at that. And tell this person Gislingham. She said he'd know what to do.'

She frowns. 'OK. So you really do think it's important?'

He looks up at her, his brown eyes serious. 'Yeah. I think it is.'

9 July 2018, 9.27p.m.

'I'm collecting for UNICEF,' he says, holding out the card he'd held up at the peephole for her to see. 'The Children of Syria Appeal. Would you consider making –'

'But I know you, right?' she says, interrupting him. 'You run at Shotover, Saturday mornings?'

He starts, then recognition dawns. 'You helped me out a couple of weeks ago – when that little kid fell over on the path and started screaming the place down? Poor little beggar, heaven only knows where his mum had got to.'

She smiles. 'I remember – you were really good with him.'

He grins. 'Had a lot of practice. Not with my own,' he says quickly. 'But I've had to take care of my brother's kids. You know, when he couldn't be around.'

His face had become serious, but he smiles again now. 'How about that? Coincidence, eh?'

She holds out her hand for the charity envelope. 'If you wait here a minute, I'll go and get my purse.'

* * *

When Gislingham's phone goes, he's standing at the coffee machine, trying to work out the least-worst option. Needs must: it's definitely not a day to be going outside. He stares at the screen, frowns. He doesn't recognize the number.

'DS Gislingham – hello?'

He can't make out what she's saying at first – it's all in a rush, and breathless, and half panicked – but when he gets her to slow down, the first word that registers is a name.

Adam.

* * *

9 July 2018, 9.45 p.m.

RAGE

Rage and fear and frustration at her idiocy, her absolute and total stupidity

How could she have been so bloody *naive*?

She shouldn't have had that wine

She shouldn't have opened the door

He knew she wouldn't let him in – not unless she recognized him, not unless she knew his face

He made her think he was harmless – he made her think he was like her – a runner – someone who cares about kids

The UNICEF envelope, Shotover, that charade with the boy – all of it – it was all *deliberate*

He wasn't running there by accident all those weeks – he was there *because she was*

How long has he been planning this?

She struggles again, trying to dislodge the gag, loosen her wrists, her ankles. Whatever he's tied her with is soft against her skin but wire underneath. It will not move.

She can hear him now, in the bathroom, in the bedroom. The jangle of hangers, the slide of drawers. Fingering her things with those horrible latex gloves. He was in here earlier, laughing to himself

Reading her diary – laughing at his own cleverness – seeing just how pathetic she is, how stupid, how *scared*

She has no idea who this man is, but he's been three steps ahead of her right from the start

And now –

Now it's too late

* * *

'Ma'am, can I have a word?'

Ruth Gallagher looks up. Gislingham, at her office door. He looks agitated.

She waves him in. 'What is it, Chris?'

She gestures at the chair but he doesn't take it. He has a piece of paper in his hand.

'I need to get a message to Fawley – they said you'd *charged* him?'

She sighs. 'Yes, I'm sorry, I should have told you. We've had new evidence – CCTV from Walton Well.'

He frowns. 'I didn't think there were cameras on the bridge?'

'There aren't. But there are some on the flats on William Lucy Way. It was Asante who worked it out –'

He gapes. '*Asante?* You got the evidence to charge Fawley from *Asante?*'

She looks a little embarrassed. 'Yes, it's rather awkward – I don't think that was what he hoped –'

But he's moved on. 'Forget it – this isn't about that. I just had a call from Nell Heneghan – she's Fawley's sister-in-law. His wife has gone into labour.'

Gallagher looks concerned. 'That's a bit early, isn't it?'

He makes a face. 'Yeah, *way* too early.'

She sits forward and reaches for her phone. 'Newbury custody suite, please. Hello – is that the Custody Sergeant? It's DI Gallagher, Major Crimes. Can you arrange for a squad car to take DI Fawley to the John Radcliffe hospital in Oxford. As soon as possible, please. Yes, the maternity suite. Tell him his wife is in labour, but that's all the information I have at present.'

She puts the phone down.

'Thank you, ma'am,' says Gislingham. But he isn't moving.

'Was there something else, Sergeant?'

'Alex – Mrs Fawley – you probably know – she's a lawyer.'

She nods. 'Yes, I did know that.'

He looks half embarrassed now. 'Well, according to her

sister, Mrs Fawley thinks she found something. About the Parrie case.'

Gallagher frowns. 'What, exactly?'

'That's just it. I'm not sure. And neither is Nell. Alex didn't get a chance to tell her. Just left a message to look on her notepad.'

He puts the sheet of paper down on her desk.

'Nell took a photo and WhatsApped it to me.'

The image is slightly off centre, as if taken in a hurry. Words and phrases, single letters, underlinings, circlings, arrows, question marks. Ruth looks up at Gislingham.

'How on earth are we supposed to make head or tail of this? It's just a load of random jottings.'

Gislingham pulls out a chair and sits down, pulling the paper round so they can both see.

'Not all of it,' he says. 'See this here, *Ep*? That must mean "episode". I think Alex has been listening to that podcast about Parrie. The Whole Truth one.' He points, '*TWT*, see?'

'Ye gods, I can't imagine anything I'd want to avoid more. Especially if I was one of his victims.'

Gislingham nods. 'Me too. But if that's what she's been doing, perhaps there's something in it – something new? She wouldn't have been in court for the whole trial – perhaps she's found out something she didn't know before? Maybe even something *we* didn't know before?'

EMMA

Why her — because she knew Adam
How did he know?
Saw her here
Watching house

If it was Parrie, how did he do it?

Wd have needed transport — get body to bridge
Not easy under licence but not impossible
To frame Adam it wd need to look like be same as his car
CCTV etc

Must be in halfway house
Where? Do the timings
add up there and back?

People hiring
Ford Mondeos?

of N Ireland
cases 2017 -
14 in a batch
proved 'faulty'

Tag
Malfunction? check
Collusion with PO - Too much of a stretch
Accomplice? But who?

HOWEVER of Operation
Glen Falls 2017 re collusion
between offenders and tag
monitoring staff

FAMILY

Adam's DNA how? where from?

Poss sources
The house No one had access / no break ins
Office TVP personnel only
Car? Garage? last time serviced? check
clothes — dry cleaners — not since March? unlikely
                    changing rooms
            St Aldate's? showers there but colleagues only But check
            gym — wd have to be a member?

No motive

TWT

Ryan — in 'leisure and wellness sector' end of Ep6
Using Powell? of Sandra Ep 1

HH!?
check website

RP

Gallagher looks up at Gislingham. 'She may have been listening to the podcast, but it's not the Roadside Rapes she's interested in. This is the Smith case.'

Alex Fawley is looking for a way to get her husband off. Gallagher sighs; not all that again. Just when she thought everybody had moved on. Though judging from the look on Gislingham's face, that's everybody minus at least one.

'I'm not sure what she thought she could achieve,' she

says heavily. 'I'm sure she's a very good lawyer, but she can't possibly know the case in enough detail to draw any conclusions.'

Gis shrugs. 'I don't know, it looks to me like she's going about it pretty much the same way we've done.' He points. 'Transport, tag, DNA – the logic's there.'

'As far as it goes,' says Gallagher drily. 'Though she doesn't appear to be aware that we found one of her husband's pubic hairs in the victim's vagina.'

'Yeah, well,' mutters Gislingham, staring at the floor, 'she wouldn't, would she.'

But Gallagher doesn't seem to have heard him. When he lifts his head she's looking at the paper, her forehead puckering into a frown. She glances up at him, a question in her eyes. 'Ryan? Who's Ryan?'

'Parrie's son. Must be twenty-odd now.'

The frown deepens. 'Looks like there's something relating to him at the end of episode six?'

They exchange a glance, then Gis gets out his phone. He finds the right page, swipes forward to the last five minutes and puts it on speaker.

'Gavin was released from Wandsworth prison on May 23rd 2018. But that's not the same as being exonerated. His conviction still stands. He has to wear an electronic tag and observe strict licence conditions, which effectively prevent him leading anything like a normal life. And that includes having the sort of ordinary social contact that other people take for granted. He had a girlfriend when he left prison, but the relationship wasn't strong enough to withstand the difficult process of adjustment post-release, and now, once again, he's on his own.

But with luck and perseverance this won't be the end of Gavin's story. We're still supporting Gavin and his lawyers, with a view to making a second application to the Criminal Cases Review Commission early next year.

In the meantime, Gavin's determined to make the years he still has left count for something. He's spending a lot of time with young offenders and rebuilding his relationship with his children. And, of course, they're not kids any more. Ryan is working in the leisure and wellness sector, and Dawn now has a family of her own . . .'

'A gym,' says Gislingham. 'Ryan Powell is working at a bloody *gym*. Jesus, why didn't I think of that? How much DNA do you think gets left behind on a bloody gym towel? You just dump the damn things in those bins and don't give it a second thought. *That's* how they framed Fawley –'

'Hang on, hang on,' says Gallagher. Though she seems to have gone very pale. 'You're jumping to vast conclusions –'

Gislingham's stabbing at his phone, breathing heavily now. 'Look,' he says after a moment, holding it towards her, his hand trembling with purpose. '*Look* – Headington Health and Leisure – *HHL* – it's the *boss's gym* –'

A line of PT instructors smile out of the screen, neat and tidy in branded polo shirts, by a row of gleaming exercise machines. Rhona Hammond, Daryl Jones, Polly Lewis, Jad Muhammad, Ryan Powell.

A bright, open face, fair hair. He looks clean-cut, honest, genuine. But Gallagher is not fooled.

Gislingham is watching her. 'That pubic hair you mentioned? The one thing the boss has never been able to explain?'

She looks up. 'Yes?'

'If you were trying to filch one of those from someone without them knowing, I can't think of many better sources than a used gym towel. Can you?'

She opens her mouth, closes it again. *Shit*, she thinks. *Shit*.

* * *

Alex watches the doctor standing over the foetal heart monitor. Even with the oxygen, her own pulse is beating so fast she feels light-headed. The midwife has her by the hand, trying to calm her, telling her it's all going to be fine, but they wouldn't have called the obstetrician if there wasn't a problem – they wouldn't have brought in that machine if they weren't concerned –

The doctor looks up. 'The heart rate's tachycardic,' she says crisply. 'Prep for caesarean, please, and notify Theatre Two. We need to get this baby out.'

* * *

'But even if you're right about the hair,' says Gallagher, 'we still need to check if you can actually transfer viable DNA from a towel –'

Gislingham cuts across her. 'But it fits, doesn't it? It all fits.' He points at the 'RP' ringed at the bottom of the page. 'And it looks like Alex thinks so too.'

'Do we know if Ryan's been in contact with his father?'

Gis shakes his head. 'I don't, no, but we can easily check. Though from what I know of Parrie, he'll have found a way to do it that doesn't leave a trace. Snail mail would be my bet.'

Gallagher looks back at the paper. 'This point she makes here, about him watching their house –'

Gislingham makes a face. 'According to Nell, Alex's been convinced there was someone watching the house for weeks, but everyone kept telling her she was imagining it — that Parrie had a tag so there was no way it could be him.'

Gallagher nods slowly. 'And they were right. He wasn't.'

'No, he wasn't. But we were all reckoning without his son, weren't we? He was completely under the radar. Especially if he's been calling himself Ryan Powell. And if he's been watching the Fawleys, he'd know a shitload about *both* of them — where they shop, who their friends are, the fact that the boss goes to Headington Health and Leisure —'

Gallagher takes a deep breath. 'So he gets himself hired at the same gym — is that what you're thinking?'

Gis shrugs. 'Why not? Places like that are always looking for staff. And Alex is right about the car too. It'd be easy enough to rent a Ford Mondeo — there must be hundreds of the bloody things.'

'And poor Emma Smith just happened to do the wrong thing at the wrong time.'

Gislingham is nodding. 'Going round to see the Fawleys when Ryan was sat outside, right.' He sits back again; he looks troubled now. 'He must have worked out pretty smartish that she was just what they were looking for: a single woman who lived alone and had hardly any friends. The ideal victim.'

Gallagher sighs. That poor woman, she thinks. She was sure someone was stalking her, she just didn't know why.

Or who.

Gislingham is watching her face. 'Smith never saw

enough to ID him, but Ryan made bloody sure she knew he was there – he *wanted* her to know.'

Gallagher stares. 'But why –?'

'Think about it, ma'am – if you're scared you're being stalked and you know a DI, who are you going to ask for advice?'

'She could have just spoken to him on the phone. There was no guarantee he'd actually go round there.' She's saying the words, but it's just the devil's advocate kicking in. She knows he's right.

'Parrie's had nigh on twenty years to plan this. He'd have found a way to get Fawley round to that flat sooner or later. Staged a break-in – something.' He shrugs. 'And the minute he did turn up – *bingo* – game on.'

'So it was Ryan who killed her – is that what you're saying?'

He shakes his head. 'Nah. After all those years inside, Parrie's not going to pass up the chance to do another girl, is he? What was done to Emma, that has him written all over it. Even down to that tiny bit of hair he just couldn't stop himself taking.'

She gives him a dry look. 'There's still the not-so-small matter of the electronic tag. Despite what Alex Fawley says, they really don't malfunction that often. And as for some sort of conspiracy with his PO, that's just absurd –'

But Gis is shaking his head. 'There's nothing wrong with the bloody tag. Parrie didn't come to Oxford to kill Emma Smith, because he didn't need to. He had his evil little shit of a son deliver her straight to his door.'

* * *

'Put the bloody siren on, can't you?'

It's thirty miles from Newbury nick to the JR – forty minutes on a good day, but it's not a good day. Rain coming down like iron rods, lorries, vans, tourist buses, bloody *people* everywhere.

We've been stuck at this set of lights for over five minutes now, inching forward, staring an HGV up the arse.

I lean forward. 'My wife is in *labour* –'

The two PCs exchange a look and the one in the driving seat reaches for the switch.

The blue light's blaring now and people are trying to get out of the way, but it's still too slow, too fucking *slow* –

I throw myself back in the seat, helpless with anxiety and fear and guilt – because this is all my fault – if Alex loses the baby – if my child dies – it will be all my fault –

The traffic parts suddenly and we jolt forward –

*   *   *

Gallagher reaches for her keyboard and pulls up the Police National Computer, her heart hammering, trying to stifle the panic, the consequences, cursing King for his fixation with Fawley.

'Ryan Sean Powell,' she begins, 'born 8/10/95 –' Then her voice trails off. 'There's nothing here. He's clean.'

Gislingham frowns. 'Nothing *at all*?'

She shakes her head. 'Not even a bloody speeding fine.'

'But it *has* to be him – it all fits –'

She looks up. 'On paper, yes — but we have absolutely no *evidence*.'

'Not enough for an arrest, but enough to at least *talk* to him, surely? That's if he hasn't bolted — he could be half-way to Florida by now.'

'Yes,' she says, the panic surging back, only worse now, because he's right: it may already be too late. 'Yes, we can do that — get up to that gym — even if he's not there, they'll have an address. And I'll call Warwickshire — get them over to that hostel.'

Gislingham is almost at the door when she calls him back. 'Chris?'

He stops and turns.

'Take someone with you — Asante —'

He looks her straight in the eye. 'No, ma'am. I'm sorry, but no. I'm taking Quinn.'

* * *

9 July 2018, 10.50 p.m.

She can smell petrol and sweat and her own urine, and underneath it, a thick chemical waft of cleaning fluid. He blindfolded her but she knew where she was, even before the boot thudded shut and the engine started. Her knees bent double against her face, the hot plastic under her sticking to her skin. No room to straighten, to brace against the sides when the car rounds a bend. And he's driving fast — that much she knows, though she's lost sense now of how long they've been moving. She can't see, can't loosen her hands, but she's trying to feel around behind her — for a tyre iron, a jack, anything she could use. But there's nothing, nothing at all. The boot is empty. As if the car isn't even his — as if he hired it — *as if he hired it just for this —*

Oh God — oh God —

They stop.
The door.
Footsteps.
The boot opens.
A rush of air, of sound. Wind. Trees?
More footsteps.
And a voice.

But it's not his.

* * *

Gallagher sits back in her chair. She's still breathing far too fast. It can't be good for you, this sort of stress. And now she's stuck here, powerless, waiting for news. If that doesn't sum up the female dilemma since the dawn of time, she doesn't know what does. She reaches for the paper Gislingham left behind; anything to deflect some of this useless energy.

Alex's writing is more familiar now, so it's easier to detect the clear, methodical thinking under all the apparently haphazard annotations. Gallagher remembers all at once that sudden, almost euphoric release of energy she felt just before her own children were born. The body preparing for labour. Perhaps she's looking at the fruits of that here.

She's about to put it down again when something catches her eye. She holds the page a little closer, frowns and changes the angle. Hand-scrawl to photo to printout makes it third-hand imperfect at best, and she could be making something out of nothing. But all the same –

She reaches for her phone.

* * *

Gislingham is stuck in traffic too, crawling yard by yard through the centre of town. Quinn's drumming his fingers against the windowsill; he hates being driven, even at the best of times. And this is not the best of times.

'Should have gone the other way,' he mutters. 'Rush hour – fucking monsoon – every sodding car in Oxford is on the road.'

Thanks for that, thinks Gislingham, I'd never have worked it out if you hadn't told me.

His mobile goes and he puts it on speaker.

'DS Gislingham.'

'Chris – it's DI Gallagher –'

'I'm afraid we're stuck in traffic, ma'am –'

'It's not that. I was just looking at these notes again. Did you print out the whole thing? There's no chance part of the page could have got missed off?'

Gis glances across at the phone. 'Don't think so. Why?'

'Is there any way I can check?'

Gislingham frowns; Quinn's taking an interest now too.

'You could phone Nell Heneghan?' says Gislingham. 'I'll text you her mobile number. And if that's off they're probably in the book. His initial's G and they live in Abingdon.'

He can hear her writing it down. A bus goes past on the other side of the road, arcing water over the front of the car. Quinn swears as the water deluges down the windscreen and Gislingham stands on his brakes.

'Anything I should know about, ma'am?' he says, raising his voice slightly.

'No, no,' she replies quickly. 'It may be nothing. But if it isn't, I'll let you know.'

The line goes dead.

* * *

'Alex Fawley – she came in earlier – I'm her sister.'

Nell's lungs are ragged with running across the waterlogged car park and up two sets of stairs. She leans heavily against the reception desk, her heart racing, her hair hanging in rat-tails.

The nurse looks at her kindly. 'Just catch your breath a minute, love – we don't want you admitted as well, do we?'

She scans down her screen then looks up. 'She's in Room 216 – down the corridor on the left.'

Nell shoots her a thank-you smile and rounds the corner, muttering frenzied prayers to a God she's never believed in that *it will be OK, it will be OK*, but Alex is already on a stretcher, being wheeled away, a drip and a mask and machines – too many machines –

'Oh my God – Alex – Alex!'

She races to catch up with the orderlies.

'Alex – are you OK?'

Her sister grabs at her hand, her eyes frantic, her voice muffled through the mask. 'Did you speak to Gislingham?'

'Yes, yes, I told him – I sent him a picture –'

Alex drops her head back on the pillow and closes her eyes. 'Gis – thank God –'

'Are you coming to the delivery room?' says the orderly. 'Only we need to keep moving here.'

'Yes, yes,' says Nell quickly. 'I'm coming with her.'

* * *

'Hello?'

It's a man who answers. Gallagher can hear other voices in the background. It sounds like the radio. BBC news.

'Hello – Mr Heneghan? You don't know me – my name's Ruth Gallagher – I'm an Inspector at Thames Valley.'

'Oh yes? What's this about?'

'Is your wife there?'

'Afraid not. She's at the JR with her sister.'

Of course she is, thinks Gallagher. Of course she is. That's why her mobile is off.

'Well, you may be able to help me. Your wife sent a photo to one of our sergeants earlier – Chris Gislingham –'

'Ah, right, yes, she said something about that. But it was all a bit rushed – I'm afraid she left as soon as I got here so I don't really know much about it.'

'The picture was of one of the pages in Mrs Fawley's notebook. I was hoping to get another shot of it.'

'Hold on a minute,' he says. 'Ben may know more than I do.'

There are scuffling noises the other end, the sound of Gerry calling Ben's name, and then, eventually, another voice. Younger, softer.

'Hello?'

'Hello – Ben, is it? My name's Ruth. I'm hoping you can help me with something. Your mum took a picture earlier –'

'Auntie Alex's notebook.'

'Yes – exactly. That's *exactly* what I mean. I think your mum may have been in a bit of a hurry when she did it and there may be something missing on the photo. At the bottom of the page?'

'She was worried about Auntie Alex. The ambulance men took her away. They had the lights on.'

You can tell how much that frightened him and Gallagher bites her lip – not the least of her many looming guilts is the effect all this has had on Fawley's already stressed and vulnerable wife. And if something happens to that baby –

She forces the thought down, tries to sound reassuring.

'I'm sure everything will be OK. It's a really good hospital. But it's important I have another look at that notepad.'

'Is it about Uncle Adam? I like Uncle Adam.'

And from nowhere there are tears in her eyes. 'I do too. I like him a lot. That's why I'm trying to help him.'

'OK,' says Ben. Nonchalant now, in one of those on-a-sixpence mood changes children always wrong-foot you with. 'What do you want me to do?'

'Can you get your dad to help you take another picture of the same page? And make sure it includes the whole thing? And then could you please text it to this number?'

She repeats it twice and he writes it down, and she tells

him how grateful she is, and how Uncle Adam and Auntie Alex will be too, and by the time she puts the phone down she's crying for real.

*   *   *

Headington Health and Leisure is behind the parade of shops on the London Road, not far from the ring road. A tired thirties building obviously chosen solely for the size of its car park. They've done their best to drag the exterior into the new millennium but it was always going to be a challenge. Inside, though, it's a different story. The whole ground floor has been gutted, knocked through and fully sleeked-out with state-of-the-art lighting, funky graphics and a health-food café offering chai lattes and vegan quiche.

Gislingham strides up to the reception desk ('*Ask us how we can help you achieve your personal goals*') and flashes his warrant card. 'Detective Sergeant Chris Gislingham, Thames Valley Police; this is DC Quinn. I believe you have a member of staff here called Ryan Powell?'

The girl at the desk looks completely terrified. She opens her mouth to say something but no sound comes.

Quinn leans on the counter and puts on his affable face. 'According to your website, Powell has an abs class starting in fifteen minutes. So I reckon he's probably around here somewhere, don't you?'

She swallows, shakes her head. 'No.'

Gislingham's eyes narrow. 'What do you mean "no"?'

'He's on holiday.' She's flushed red now. 'Malaga. He's been there two weeks.'

The men exchange a glance, a glance that quickly turns into a frown as they do the math.

'Two *weeks*?' says Gislingham.

She nods.

'OK,' says Quinn slowly. 'So when *exactly* did he leave?'

*   *   *

The text pings in and Gallagher almost sends her mobile skittering on to the floor as she grabs at it. She's just opening up the image when the phone starts to ring. She sticks it on speaker so she can still see the text.

'Ma'am, it's Gislingham.'

She's too distracted to register his tone. His defeat.

She scrolls down, zooms in – it's there – she's *right* – it wasn't just a random line, it was an *arrow* –

Gis is still speaking. 'I'm sorry, ma'am. Ryan Powell didn't abduct Emma. He had nothing to do with it – he's been in Spain since July 3rd. We'll double-check he definitely boarded the flight but he's sent photos to some of his mates at the gym, so I reckon the alibi's legit.'

A sigh so loud she can hear it, even over the traffic noise.

'Back to square one.'

'No,' she says, finally listening to him properly. 'No – we're not. I think you were right about Ryan. I reckon he may well have been the source of the DNA, but he didn't take Emma to Leamington and he didn't dispose of her body. Those initials in Alex's notes? RP isn't Ryan Powell. RP is *someone else*.'

*   *   *

'Did anyone see you?'

The new voice is different. Rougher. Crueller.

'No. I was careful. I've got pretty good at this, you know.'

'And you know what you have to do when you get back?'

'Yeah. It's all set up, just like you said. And I checked – they're still doing the works on the line. It was going on all night last night.'

'Nice one.'

There are hands on Emma now, pulling her roughly up and out, scraping her skin against the metal.

She's upright but she can't stand straight, she can't breathe. The urine runs down her legs and she feels herself go hot with shame.

The second man sneers, 'Oh bless, I think she's scared. You were right, she's fucking *perfect*. I'm going to enjoy this.'

'Yeah, well, I owed you one, didn't I. For not letting on I was with you for that Donnelly bird.'

'Well, it wasn't your fault I got framed. And no bloody use both of us getting banged up, either. At least that way you could keep an eye on the kids.'

The click of a lighter, an intake of breath. 'Talking of which, I got a text from your Ryan. He says Malaga's even hotter than here.'

'Blimey, he must be roasting his arse. But it was good timing, him being out of the way. Even Thames fucking Valley can't fit him up for this if he's in sodding Spain.'

A long exhalation. 'You're overreacting, mate – they'll never make the connection. No way.'

'All the same, you don't think Ryan cottoned on, do you? About the gym? I mean, I wouldn't want him to think –'

A quick laugh. 'Nah, no risk of that, bless him. Right little goody-two-shoes, that one. It was as much as I could do to get him to sign me into that place on the QT. He was crapping himself just doing that.' A laugh now. 'Shitting hell, Gav, that Fawley is a tedious fucker. Takeaway Friday, shopping Saturday, gym four times a week, same time, same days, even the same fucking *machines*. Jesus.'

'Don't knock it – made it easier to get hold of the stuff, didn't it?'

Another laugh. 'Like shooting fish in a fucking barrel.'

'Right,' says the second man. Emma feels his grip tightening on her shoulder. 'So, fancy joining the party? Once more for old times' sake?'

'Nah, mate, this one's all yours. I'll go for a fag – keep an eye out.'

'Fair enough. But don't hurry back. I'm planning to take my time. Reckon I deserve it, don't you?'

The sound of footsteps now, and then he's shoving her forward and pushing her face into the hot, dry grass.

* * *

gym — wd have to be a member?

TWT

Ryan — in 'leisure and wellness sector' end of Ep6 → HHI?
Using Powell? of Sandra Ep 1 / check website

RP

Ep 4 6 AD van * First time — why?
7 LH van * Coincidence?
change of MO Also two rapes — vaginal then anal
'Different' — violent second time but not first

VAN * Alibi? Were there TWO assailants?
Questioned? Did they both attack her?

* * *

'There were *two* of them?'

Gislingham's at Gallagher's desk, staring at the screen on her phone, his sodden suit soaking the seat; behind him, Quinn's obsessively smoothing his hair, rain still running down the back of his neck.

Gallagher sits forward. 'I listened to episode four of that podcast — the one Alex highlights. It was an interview with Alison Donnelly. She was very articulate, very clear. She said she was raped once, then her attacker came back a few minutes later and raped her again. She says he was different that time. More violent. More brutal.' She sighs. 'She had a plastic bag over her head. She couldn't see anything, couldn't hear properly. And in any case, he never spoke. She had no way of knowing that the second time it was a completely different man.'

'Jesus,' breathes Gislingham. 'Why the hell wasn't this picked up in '98?'

Gallagher shrugs. 'There was no DNA, nothing to

408

suggest Parrie had an accomplice. And as far as I can tell, he didn't – apart, that is, from that one time. And those questions Alex is asking? She's bang on. I've had a look at the file. He *was* questioned, but they were more interested in establishing if he could provide Parrie with an alibi than whether he had one himself. Which, as it turned out, he did. At least for the last victim. He'd gone up to see his mum in Coventry, so there was CCTV at the railway station *and* a time-stamped ticket. There was no way he could have attacked that last girl, so he just got scrubbed from the list. No one even thought to ask where he was the night Alison Donnelly was raped. No one, that is, till now.'

'Sorry,' says Quinn, stopping mid-gesture. 'Am I missing something? If RP isn't Ryan Powell, who the hell are we talking about?'

She looks up at him. 'Robert Parrie. Known to his family as Bobby. Gavin Parrie's little brother.'

* * *

'I don't know what you think you're going to find. I don't do drugs and I've got no booze.'

He's leaning against the doorway, arms folded, elaborately casual, but there's an edge to his energy and a wariness in his eyes.

A uniformed officer is in the tiny bathroom, going through the pedestal cupboard, and a female sergeant is in the bedroom checking the chest of drawers. The bedding has been stripped and piled anyhow on the floor, along with the entire contents of the wardrobe. Which isn't much. A couple of pairs of jeans, some T-shirts, a hoodie. There's a shelving unit on the other wall, but it's empty; no books, no photos, no personal items. The room barely looks lived in.

'Look at that bloody mess. Fucking invasion of privacy, that's what this is.'

The woman glances up. 'You're on licence, Parrie,' she says briskly. 'Random searches are part of the deal. And we don't need to ask your permission. You *know* that.'

She whisks the drawer shut and goes over to the bed-side table. In the bathroom, the officer is on his hands and knees, squinting up into the pipework under the basin.

Parrie's eyes narrow.

*   *   *

They know there's someone in because the windows are open and there's music coming from inside. The Rolling Stones. Loud. Like so many other houses in this part of Cowley, the front garden is concreted over, thick now with the mud and litter washed in by the day's floods. There's a wheelie bin with the lid open, a crate of empty lager cans, a white van parked out front.

RP Plastering – No Job Too Small

*   *   *

'Sarge? Think we may have something here.'

The officer is gesturing up at the inside of the cup-board. The sergeant shoots Parrie a look, then goes over to the bathroom and crouches down to see for herself.

'Well, well, well,' she says. 'What do we have here, then?'

It's so small, so watchfully hidden, that no casual observer would even see it. The small ziplock bag taped carefully to the back of the U-bend. But these are not casual observers. And they knew exactly what they were looking for.

Parrie takes a step back towards the door but there's an officer barring the way.

An officer who wasn't there five minutes before.

The sergeant peels the bag away from the pipe and gets back to her feet. You can see now what's inside. The piece of white tissue carefully folded, as if what it contains is precious and needs to be kept safe.

She unzips the bag and slowly opens the paper out, hearing the gasp from her colleague when he realizes what it is.

A silver hoop earring, the metal spotted here and there with dark stains.

And coiled beside it, a single strand of long blonde hair.

* * *

'It took a while because he went all the way to Banbury to cover his tracks, but we've got it now, in black and white. Bobby Parrie picked up a dark-blue Ford Mondeo on Saturday 7th July and returned it, *already valeted*, three days later. Uniform are on their way to pick it up.'

'So we're good to go, ma'am?'

There's some crackling on the line now, but Gallagher's voice is loud and clear. 'You're good to go.'

The two men exchange a look and then, in silence, get out of the car and walk up the path.

The man who answers the door has a beer bottle in one hand and a tea towel chucked over his shoulder. Dark hair, hazel eyes, a ready smile. A smile that quickly hardens.

'Robert Craig Parrie?' says the man on the step, holding out his warrant card. 'DC Tony Asante, Thames Valley; this is DC Farrow. We're here to arrest you.'

* * *

Adam Fawley
16 July 2018
19.09

I don't know how I got my legs to move – that poor bloody PC was half carrying me by the end. The people we passed in the wards must have thought I was the one in danger – I was the one who needed medical attention. And perhaps I do, because by the time we get to the delivery room it feels like my chest is breaking open – all I can see is a blur of people in gowns and hairnets – all I can hear is the beating in my skull –

Someone's coming towards me now, getting hold of my arms.

'Adam –' says a voice. Low. Kind. Familiar.

I know who this is – Nell – *Nell* –

'She's OK, Adam,' she's saying, shaking me, trying to make me listen. *'Alex is OK –'*

And suddenly the green wall parts and I can see her. On the bed, her hair spread over the pillow, her skin grey with exhaustion.

'Adam,' she breathes, reaching out for me, her face wrung with concern, 'my God – you look terrible –'

Someone pushes me forward and I'm holding her hand,

412

touching her cheek. 'Alex, my darling, I'm so sorry – this is all my fault –'

'No, it isn't,' she whispers. 'None of it. I know what happened – I know you didn't do it.' She reaches for my hand, squeezes my fingers. 'I've told Gis everything – it's going to be all right. *It's going to be all right.*'

I stare at her. 'Gis? But how –?'

I feel Nell's hand on my shoulder. 'That can wait,' she whispers. 'There's something else much more important right now.'

She pulls me gently round. There's a nurse smiling into my dazzled face.

'Mr Fawley,' she says. 'You missed all the excitement, I'm afraid. It seems this little one couldn't wait to be born.'

And as I take my baby in my arms for the first time, I feel the warmth and the weight of my real, breathing child, the little fists paddling the big new air, the soft mouth opening and closing like a tiny bird, and after all these last terrible days when I barricaded my emotions, put my heart in lockdown, the tears spill finally down my cheeks because she is here and she is perfect.

My daughter.

Perfect, and alive, and as beautiful as her name.

Epilogue

He's down in the kitchen when he hears the front door slam and the sound of footsteps on the wooden stairs.

A moment later she swings into the room in a crackle of sequins and high heels. The scent she's wearing is so dense in the hot night air he can taste it in his throat.

She drops her evening bag on to the table, and tosses back her hair. Her face radiates into a smile. 'I did it, Caleb,' she says. '*I did it*. Two hundred bloody million. And all because of me – not that bunch of self-important old farts – *me*.'

He gets up, moving towards her with a smile. 'You are just fucking amazing – I bet they were eating out of your hand.'

The smile falters for a moment and she seems about to say something but obviously changes her mind. 'Christ,' she says, looking at her watch. 'Is it really that late? I'm exhausted.'

She makes to move past him but he grasps her, holding her upper arms. 'Come on – *tell me the details* – what did they say?'

His lips are inches from hers now and he can feel the heat coming off her body. The sheer excitement – the exhilaration of her success. She's been giving him 'Fuck Me' signals for weeks, and as far as he's concerned that's a game you've no business playing unless you're prepared to follow through. And in any case, what's Seb got that he hasn't? Because she screwed *him* – it's supposed to be some big secret but of course Seb couldn't resist rubbing his nose in it, the smug bastard.

She frowns again now, pulls back.

'No, Caleb – you know what I said –'

He smiles. 'Oh, come on, Marina – you know you want to – you know *I* want to – there's no one like you – *no one* – the way you look, the way you smell, everything about you – you're driving me fucking *crazy* –'

She's shaking her head, pushing him away. 'How many more times – I told you. I *like* you, you know I do, but it would just make things too bloody complicated.'

'If it's Freya you're worried about –'

'No – it's not that –'

'– then honestly, it's not an issue – I mean, she's OK and I like her but it's not *serious*. And look at you – Jesus, there isn't a bloke in the world who'd choose her over you, given the choice.' He smiles now, turning up the charm. 'I mean, why have prosecco when you can have the real thing? And I mean the *Real* Thing.'

But she's shaking her head. 'No, Caleb, I'm sorry, but no. You're just not listening. You and me – it's never going to happen.'

A darkness crosses his face and he turns away and leans heavily against the worktop. She feels a tiny pang of remorse. He's very young, and he probably wouldn't be that bad in bed. With a bit of coaching, he might even be quite passable. But she's not the one who's going to do it. Absolutely not. She made that mistake once before. She's not risking all *that* again.

She reaches across and touches him gently on the shoulder. 'Friends?'

He looks at her, then gives a rueful smile. 'Course.' He straightens up. 'Right, I think we have something to celebrate.' He goes over to the fridge. 'Champagne?'

She smiles. 'Not for me. I've already had *far* too much and Tobin could wake up at any moment.'

'He won't,' he says with a quick glance back at her. 'I just went up to check. He won't disturb us.'

'Honestly, I really don't want any more –'

But it's too late – the cork pops and the wine gushes down into the glasses, up over the rim, down on to the counter. She bridles a little, behind his back. For heaven's sake, that's Bollinger Grande Année.

He's fiddling with the champagne flutes now, wiping up the spill. She thinks he's just being good-mannered – he's well brought up, probably a bit embarrassed at his faux pas.

But she's wrong. He's buying himself time. A few crucial seconds for the effervescence to do its job – for that little sachet of white powder to completely disappear. Because he knew there was always a risk she really was just a colossal prick-tease, and he came prepared. And he's not stupid, either. No way Fisher's going to fuck him around like she did to Seb. No fucking way. This is going to be on *his* terms, and with no blowback.

He turns to her at last and hands over the glass.

'To you,' he says with a dazzling smile. 'To your triumph. And to getting everything – and I mean *everything* – you deserve.'

Acknowledgements

This was the book that got finished during lockdown, in that strange period of half-life that should have made concentrating easier but somehow didn't. It's been a year of upheavals for everyone, including the publishing industry, but 'Team Fawley' has kept going throughout, adapting to circumstances, experimenting with new approaches, and basically just getting on with it and refusing to be defeated. So even though I thank them with every book, they deserve it more than ever this time. My fabulous editor Katy Loftus, and the whole Penguin Viking team – Jane Gentle, Olivia Mead, Ellie Hudson, Georgia Taylor and Vikki Moynes. My exceptional agent Anna Power, and Hélène Butler, also at Johnson & Alcock, who's now taken the number of overseas editions to twenty-five. My copyeditor Karen Whitlock, and the whole production team at Penguin, led by Emma Brown. Jessica Barnfield and the team at Penguin audiobooks, as well – of course – as Lee Ingleby and Emma Cunniffe for doing such a fabulous job as narrators. Julia Connolly, who developed the new cover design, which has really taken the look of the books to the next level. And, last but not least, the dedicated crime-lovers at Dead Good for their support.

My 'pro team' have again been superb – DI Andy Thompson, Joey Giddings, Nicholas Syfret QC, and a new member of the team, Dr Paul Zollinger-Read. None of the books would have been the same without their professional know-how, and their tireless willingness to share it. Any inaccuracies that remain are mine alone.

Thank you also to my 'early readers', whose insights and suggestions made a huge difference in the final stages – probably more so this time than in previous books: my husband Simon, Sarah Wall, Stephen Gill, Richard Croker, Deborah Woudhuysen, Andrew Weltch, Peter Croxford, Elizabeth Price, Neera Gajjar, Stuart Fletcher and Trish Fletcher.

One of the many things I've missed this year has been meeting up with both readers and other authors at festivals and bookshop events. Here's to a more sociable 2021, and in the meantime I'd like to thank some of my fellow writers for their support and encouragement, especially online: Ian Rankin, Shari Lapena, John Marrs, JP Delaney and Simon Lelic.

One more special thank-you for this book in particular. I listened to a lot of true-crime podcasts as I was doing the research; partly for fun, of course, but also to get the right tone and style for The Whole Truth episodes in the book. One of the best was *Shreds*, made by the BBC's Ceri Jackson. She was kind enough to do an interview with me for my newsletter, and also to share the layout typically used in podcast scripts (and you all know what a nerd I am about that sort of thing!).

And finally, you may have picked up in the news that we have now sold the TV rights to the series to Castlefield TV, part of the Fremantle group. They're a fabulous production company and it's been a genuine dream-come-true moment. I can't wait to see what they make of the books. And, of course, who they cast . . .

Sign up to
CARA HUNTER's
Newsletter

Get **exclusive offers**, Cara's
recommendations for the
best crime books around and
insider information on her **new novels**
before anyone else.

**Use the following link to receive
regular emails from Cara:**

https://www.penguin.co.uk/newsletters/carahunter/

THE NEXT BOOK IN
THE DI FAWLEY SERIES

COME
TO
HARM

DI Adam Fawley Thriller 6

COMING 2022
PRE-ORDER NOW

CARA HUNTER

Have you read them all yet?

CARA HUNTER

All the Rage

DI Adam Fawley Thriller 4

THE FIRST GIRL CAME BACK.
THE NEXT MIGHT NOT BE SO LUCKY.

A girl is taken from the streets of Oxford.
But it's unlike any abduction DI Fawley's seen before . . .

Faith Appleford was attacked, a plastic bag tied over
her head, taken to an isolated location . . . and then,
by some miracle, she escaped.

What's more, when DC Erica Somer interviews Faith,
she quickly becomes convinced that Faith knows
the identity of her abductor.

Yet Faith refuses to press charges.

Without more evidence, it's looking like the police may
have to drop the case.

But what happens if Faith's attacker strikes again?